More praise for the international bestseller that has become "Europe's oddball literary sensation of the decade" (New York Newsday) . . .

Sophie's World

"A page-turner."   —*Entertainment Weekly*

"First, think of a beginner's guide to philosophy, written by a schoolteacher . . . Next, imagine a fantasy novel— something like a modern-day version of *Through the Looking Glass*. Meld these disparate genres, and what do you get? Well, what you get is an improbable international bestseller . . . a runaway hit . . . [a] tour de force."

—*Time*

"Compelling."   —*Los Angeles Times*

"Its depth of learning, its intelligence and its totally original conception give it enormous magnetic appeal . . . To be fully human, and to feel our continuity with 3,000 years of philosophical inquiry, we need to put ourselves in Sophie's world."   —*Boston Sunday Globe*

"Involving and often humorous."   —*USA Today*

"In the adroit hands of Jostein Gaarder, the whole sweep of three millennia of Western philosophy is rendered as lively as a gossip column . . . Literary sorcery of the first rank."   —*Fort Worth Star-Telegram*

(*continued on next page*)

Sophie's World

A Novel About the
History of Philosophy

JOSTEIN GAARDER

Translated by Paulette Møller

BERKLEY BOOKS, NEW YORK

SOPHIE'S WORLD

A Berkley Book / published by arrangement with
Farrar, Straus and Giroux, Inc.

PRINTING HISTORY
Farrar, Straus and Giroux, Inc., edition published 1994
Berkley edition / March 1996

The Putnam Berkley World Wide Web site address is
http://www.berkley.com

ISBN: 0-425-15225-1

BERKLEY®
Berkley Books are published by The Berkley Publishing Group,
200 Madison Avenue, New York, New York 10016.
BERKLEY and the "B" design
are trademarks belonging to Berkley Publishing Corporation.

PRINTED IN THE UNITED STATES OF AMERICA

10 9 8 7 6 5 4 3 2 1

Acknowledgments

This book would not have been possible without the support and encouragement of Siri Dannevig. Thanks are also due to Maiken Ims for reading the manuscript and making useful comments, and to Trond Berg Eriksen for his trenchant observations and knowledgeable support through the years.

J.G.

Contents

CONTENTS

CONTENTS

THE BIG BANG

He who cannot draw on three thousand years

is living from hand to mouth.

GOETHE

Sophie's World

Jostein Gaarder.

The Garden of Eden

*. . . at some point something must have come from
nothing . . .*

Sophie Amundsen was on her way home from school.
She had walked the first part of the way with Joanna.
They had been discussing robots. Joanna thought the human brain was like an advanced computer. Sophie was
not certain she agreed. Surely a person was more than
a piece of hardware?

When they got to the supermarket they went their separate ways. Sophie lived on the outskirts of a sprawling
suburb and had almost twice as far to school as Joanna.
There were no other houses beyond her garden, which
made it seem as if her house lay at the end of the world.
This was where the woods began.

She turned the corner into Clover Close. At the end
of the road there was a sharp bend, known as Captain's
Bend. People seldom went that way except on the weekend.

It was early May. In some of the gardens the fruit
trees were encircled with dense clusters of daffodils. The
birches were already in pale green leaf.

It was extraordinary how everything burst forth at this
time of year! What made this great mass of green veg-
etation come welling up from the dead earth as soon as
it got warm and the last traces of snow disappeared?

As Sophie opened her garden gate, she looked in the
mailbox. There was usually a lot of junk mail and a few

big envelopes for her mother, a pile to dump on the
kitchen table before she went up to her room to start her
homework.

From time to time there would be a few letters from
the bank for her father, but then he was not a normal
father. Sophie's father was the captain of a big oil
tanker, and was away for most of the year. During the
few weeks at a time when he was at home, he would
shuffle around the house making it nice and cozy for
Sophie and her mother. But when he was at sea he could
seem very distant.

There was only one letter in the mailbox—and it was
for Sophie. The white envelope read: ''Sophie Amundsen, 3 Clover Close.'' That was all; it did not say who
it was from. There was no stamp on it either.

As soon as Sophie had closed the gate behind her she
opened the envelope. It contained only a slip of paper
no bigger than the envelope. It read: *Who are you?*

Nothing else, only the three words, written by hand,
and followed by a large question mark.

She looked at the envelope again. The letter was definitely for her. Who could have dropped it in the mailbox?

Sophie let herself quickly into the red house. As always, her cat Sherekan managed to slink out of the
bushes, jump onto the front step, and slip in through the
door before she closed it behind her.

Whenever Sophie's mother was in a bad mood, she
would call the house they lived in a menagerie. A menagerie was a collection of animals. Sophie certainly had
one and was quite happy with it. It had begun with the
three goldfish, Goldtop, Red Ridinghood, and Black
Jack. Next she got two budgerigars called Smitt and
Smule, then Govinda the tortoise, and finally the mar-
malade cat Sherekan. They had all been given to her to
make up for the fact that her mother never got home
from work until late in the afternoon and her father was
away so much, sailing all over the world.

Sophie slung her schoolbag on the floor and put a
bowl of cat food out for Sherekan. Then she sat down

on a kitchen stool with the mysterious letter in her hand.

Who are you?

She had no idea. She was Sophie Amundsen, of course, but who was that? She had not really figured that out—yet.

What if she had been given a different name? Anne Knutsen, for instance. Would she then have *been* someone else?

She suddenly remembered that Dad had originally wanted her to be called Lillemor. Sophie tried to imagine herself shaking hands and introducing herself as Lillemor Amundsen, but it seemed all wrong. It was someone else who kept introducing herself.

She jumped up and went into the bathroom with the strange letter in her hand. She stood in front of the mirror and stared into her own eyes.

"I am Sophie Amundsen," she said.

The girl in the mirror did not react with as much as a twitch. Whatever Sophie did, she did exactly the same. Sophie tried to beat her reflection to it with a lightning movement but the other girl was just as fast.

"Who are you?" Sophie asked.

She received no response to this either, but felt a momentary confusion as to whether it was she or her reflection who had asked the question.

Sophie pressed her index finger to the nose in the mirror and said, "You are me."

As she got no answer to this, she turned the sentence around and said, "I am you."

Sophie Amundsen was often dissatisfied with her appearance. She was frequently told that she had beautiful almond-shaped eyes, but that was probably just something people said because her nose was too small and her mouth was a bit too big. And her ears were much too close to her eyes. Worst of all was her straight hair, which it was impossible to do anything with. Sometimes her father would stroke her hair and call her "the girl with the flaxen hair," after a piece of music by Claude Debussy. It was all right for him, he was not condemned to living with this straight dark hair. Neither mousse nor styling gel had the slightest effect on So-

phie's hair. Sometimes she thought she was so ugly that
she wondered if she was malformed at birth. Her mother
always went on about her difficult labor. But was that
really what determined how you looked?

Wasn't it odd that she didn't know who she was? And
wasn't it unreasonable that she hadn't been allowed to
have any say in what she would look like? Her looks
had just been dumped on her. She could choose her own
friends, but she certainly hadn't chosen herself. She had
not even chosen to be a human being.

What was a human being?

Sophie looked up at the girl in the mirror again.

"I think I'll go upstairs and do my biology homework," she said, almost apologetically. Once she was
out in the hall, she thought, No, I'd rather go out in the
garden.

"Kitty, kitty, kitty!"

Sophie chased the cat out onto the doorstep and closed
the front door behind her.

As she stood outside on the gravel path with the mysterious letter in her hand, the strangest feeling came over
her. She felt like a doll that had suddenly been brought
to life by the wave of a magic wand.

Wasn't it extraordinary to be in the world right now,
wandering around in a wonderful adventure!

Sherekan sprang lightly across the gravel and slid into
a dense clump of red-currant bushes. A live cat, vibrant
with energy from its white whiskers to the twitching tail
at the end of its sleek body. It was here in the garden
too, but hardly aware of it in the same way as Sophie.

As Sophie started to think about being alive, she began to realize that she would not be alive forever. I am
in the world now, she thought, but one day I shall be
gone.

Was there a life after death? This was another question the cat was blissfully unaware of.

It was not long since Sophie's grandmother had died.
For more than six months Sophie had missed her every
single day. How unfair that life had to end!

Sophie stood on the gravel path, thinking. She tried

to think extra hard about being alive so as to forget that she would not be alive forever. But it was impossible. As soon as she concentrated on being alive now, the thought of dying also came into her mind. The same thing happened the other way around: only by conjuring up an intense feeling of one day being dead could she appreciate how terribly good it was to be alive. It was like two sides of a coin that she kept turning over and over. And the bigger and clearer one side of the coin became, the bigger and clearer the other side became too.

You can't experience being alive without realizing that you have to die, she thought. But it's just as impossible to realize you have to die without thinking how incredibly amazing it is to be alive.

Sophie remembered Granny saying something like that the day the doctor told her she was ill. "I never realized how rich life was until now," she said.

How tragic that most people had to get ill before they understood what a gift it was to be alive. Or else they had to find a mysterious letter in the mailbox!

Perhaps she should go and see if any more letters had arrived. Sophie hurried to the gate and looked inside the green mailbox. She was startled to find that it contained another white envelope, exactly like the first. But the mailbox had definitely been empty when she took the first envelope! This envelope had her name on it as well. She tore it open and fished out a note the same size as the first one.

Where does the world come from? it said.

I don't know, Sophie thought. Surely nobody really *knows*. And yet—Sophie thought it was a fair question. For the first time in her life she felt it wasn't right to live in the world without at least *inquiring* where it came from.

The mysterious letters had made Sophie's head spin. She decided to go and sit in the den.

The den was Sophie's top secret hiding place. It was where she went when she was terribly angry, terribly miserable, or terribly happy. Today she was simply confused.

*   *   *

The red house was surrounded by a large garden with
lots of flowerbeds, fruit bushes, fruit trees of different
kinds, a spacious lawn with a glider and a little gazebo
that Granddad had built for Granny when she lost their
first child a few weeks after it was born. The child's
name was Marie. On her gravestone were the words:
"Little Marie to us came, greeted us, and left again."

Down in a corner of the garden behind all the rasp-
berry bushes was a dense thicket where neither flowers
nor berries would grow. Actually, it was an old hedge
that had once marked the boundary to the woods, but
because nobody had trimmed it for the last twenty years
it had grown into a tangled and impenetrable mass.
Granny used to say the hedge made it harder for the
foxes to take the chickens during the war, when the
chickens had free range of the garden.

To everyone but Sophie, the old hedge was just as
useless as the rabbit hutches at the other end of the garden. But that was only because they hadn't discovered
Sophie's secret.

Sophie had known about the little hole in the hedge
for as long as she could remember. When she crawled
through it she came into a large cavity between the
bushes. It was like a little house. She knew nobody
would find her there.

Clutching the two envelopes in her hand, Sophie ran
through the garden, crouched down on all fours, and
wormed her way through the hedge. The den was almost
high enough for her to stand upright, but today she sat
down on a clump of gnarled roots. From there she could
look out through tiny peepholes between the twigs and
leaves. Although none of the holes was bigger than a
small coin, she had a good view of the whole garden.
When she was little she used to think it was fun to watch
her mother and father searching for her among the trees.

Sophie had always thought the garden was a world of
its own. Each time she heard about the Garden of Eden
in the Bible it reminded her of sitting here in the den,
surveying her own little paradise.

Where does the world come from?

She hadn't the faintest idea. Sophie knew that the world was only a small planet in space. But where did space come from?

It was possible that space had always existed, in which case she would not also need to figure out where it came from. But *could* anything have always existed? Something deep down inside her protested at the idea. Surely everything that exists must have had a beginning? So space must sometime have been created out of something else.

But if space had come from something else, then that something else must also have come from something. Sophie felt she was only deferring the problem. At some point, something must have come from nothing. But was that possible? Wasn't that just as impossible as the idea that the world had always existed?

They had learned at school that God created the world. Sophie tried to console herself with the thought that this was probably the best solution to the whole problem. But then she started to think again. She could accept that God had created space, but what about God himself? Had he created himself out of nothing? Again there was something deep down inside her that protested. Even though God could create all kinds of things, he could hardly create himself *before* he had a "self" to create with. So there was only one possibility left: God had always existed. But she had already rejected that possibility! Everything that existed had to have a beginning.

Oh, drat!

She opened the two envelopes again.

Who are you?

Where does the world come from?

What annoying questions! And anyway where did the letters come from? That was just as mysterious, almost.

Who had jolted Sophie out of her everyday existence and suddenly brought her face to face with the great riddles of the universe?

For the third time Sophie went to the mailbox. The mailman had just delivered the day's mail. Sophie fished out a bulky pile of junk mail, periodicals, and a couple of letters for her mother. There was also a postcard of a tropical beach. She turned the card over. It had a Norwegian stamp on it and was postmarked "UN Battalion." Could it be from Dad? But wasn't he in a completely different place? It wasn't his handwriting either.

Sophie felt her pulse quicken a little as she saw who the postcard was addressed to: "Hilde Møller Knag, c/o Sophie Amundsen, 3 Clover Close . . ." The rest of the address was correct. The card read:

> Dear Hilde, Happy 15th birthday! As I'm sure you'll understand, I want to give you a present that will help you grow. Forgive me for sending the card c/o Sophie. It was the easiest way. Love from Dad.

Sophie raced back to the house and into the kitchen. Her mind was in a turmoil. Who was this "Hilde," whose fifteenth birthday was just a month before her own?

Sophie got out the telephone book. There were a lot of people called Møller, and quite a few called Knag. But there was nobody in the entire directory called Møller Knag.

She examined the mysterious card again. It certainly seemed genuine enough; it had a stamp and a postmark.

Why would a father send a birthday card to Sophie's address when it was quite obviously intended to go somewhere else? What kind of father would cheat his own daughter of a birthday card by purposely sending it astray? How could it be "the easiest way"? And above all, how was she supposed to trace this Hilde person?

So now Sophie had another problem to worry about. She tried to get her thoughts in order:

This afternoon, in the space of two short hours, she had been presented with three problems. The first problem was who had put the two white envelopes in her mailbox. The second was the difficult questions these letters contained. The third problem was who Hilde

Møller Knag could be, and why Sophie had been sent her birthday card. She was sure that the three problems were interconnected in some way. They had to be, because until today she had lived a perfectly ordinary life.

The Top Hat

∞

*. . . the only thing we require to be good
philosophers is the
faculty of wonder . . .*

Sophie was sure she would hear from the anonymous
letter writer again. She decided not to tell anyone about
the letters for the time being.

At school she had trouble concentrating on what the
teachers said. They seemed to talk only about unimportant things. Why couldn't they talk about what a human
being is—or about what the world is and how it came
into being?

For the first time she began to feel that at school as
well as everywhere else people were only concerned
with trivialities. There were major problems that needed
to be solved.

Did anybody have answers to these questions? Sophie
felt that thinking about them was more important than
memorizing irregular verbs.

When the bell rang after the last class, she left the
school so fast that Joanna had to run to catch up with
her.

After a while Joanna said, "Do you want to play cards
this evening?"

Sophie shrugged her shoulders.

"I'm not that interested in card games any more."

Joanna looked surprised.

"You're not? Let's play badminton then."

Sophie stared down at the pavement—then up at her friend.

"I don't think I'm that interested in badminton either."

"You're kidding!"

Sophie noticed the touch of bitterness in Joanna's tone.

"Do you mind telling me what's suddenly so important?"

Sophie just shook her head. "It's . . . it's a secret."

"Yuck! You're probably in love!"

The two girls walked on for a while without saying anything. When they got to the soccer field Joanna said, "I'm going across the field."

Across the field! It was the quickest way for Joanna, but she only went that way when she had to hurry home in time for visitors or a dental appointment.

Sophie regretted having been mean to her. But what else could she have said? That she had suddenly become so engrossed in who she was and where the world came from that she had no time to play badminton? Would Joanna have understood?

Why was it so difficult to be absorbed in the most vital and, in a way, the most natural of all questions?

She felt her heart beating faster as she opened the mailbox. At first she found only a letter from the bank and some big brown envelopes for her mother. Darn! Sophie had been looking forward to getting another letter from the unknown sender.

As she closed the gate behind her she noticed her own name on one of the big envelopes. Turning it over, she saw written on the back: "Course in Philosophy. Handle with care."

Sophie ran up the gravel path and flung her schoolbag onto the step. Stuffing the other letters under the doormat, she ran around into the back garden and sought refuge in the den. This was the only place to open the big letter.

Sherekan came jumping after her but Sophie had to put up with that. She knew the cat would not give her away.

Inside the envelope there were three typewritten pages held together with a paper clip. Sophie began to read.

WHAT IS PHILOSOPHY?

Dear Sophie,

Lots of people have hobbies. Some people collect old coins or foreign stamps, some do needlework, others spend most of their spare time on a particular sport.

A lot of people enjoy reading. But reading tastes differ widely. Some people only read newspapers or comics, some like reading novels, while others prefer books on astronomy, wildlife, or technological discoveries.

If I happen to be interested in horses or precious stones, I cannot expect everyone else to share my enthusiasm. If I watch all the sports programs on TV with great pleasure, I must put up with the fact that other people find sports boring.

Is there nothing that interests us all? Is there nothing that concerns everyone—no matter who they are or where they live in the world? Yes, dear Sophie, there are questions that certainly should interest everyone. They are precisely the questions this course is about.

What is the most important thing in life? If we ask someone living on the edge of starvation, the answer is food. If we ask someone dying of cold, the answer is warmth. If we put the same question to someone who feels lonely and isolated, the answer will probably be the company of other people.

But when these basic needs have been satisfied—will there still be something that everybody needs? Philosophers think so. They believe that man cannot live by bread alone. Of course everyone needs food. And everyone needs love and care. But there is something else—apart from that—which everyone needs, and that is to figure out who we are and why we are here.

Being interested in why we are here is not a "casual" interest like collecting stamps. People who ask such questions are taking part in a debate that has gone on as long as man has lived on this planet. How the universe, the earth, and life came into being is a bigger and more important question than who won the most gold medals in the last Olympics.

*   *   *

The best way of approaching philosophy is to ask a few philosophical questions:

How was the world created? Is there any will or meaning behind what happens? Is there a life after death? How can we answer these questions? And most important, how ought we to live? People have been asking these questions throughout the ages. We know of no culture which has not concerned itself with what man is and where the world came from.

Basically there are not many philosophical questions to ask. We have already asked some of the most important ones. But history presents us with many different answers to each question. So it is easier to ask philosophical questions than to answer them.

Today as well each individual has to discover his own answer to these same questions. You cannot find out whether there is a God or whether there is life after death by looking in an encyclopedia. Nor does the encyclopedia tell us how we ought to live. However, reading what other people have believed can help us formulate our own view of life.

Philosophers' search for the truth resembles a detective story. Some think Andersen was the murderer, others think it was Nielsen or Jensen. The police are sometimes able to solve a real crime. But it is equally possible that they never get to the bottom of it, although there is a solution somewhere. So even if it is difficult to answer a question, there may be one—and only one—right answer. Either there is a kind of existence after death—or there is not.

A lot of age-old enigmas have now been explained by science. What the dark side of the moon looks like was once shrouded in mystery. It was not the kind of thing that could be solved by discussion, it was left to the imagination of the individual. But today we know exactly what the dark side of the moon looks like, and no one can "believe" any longer in the Man in the Moon, or that the moon is made of green cheese.

A Greek philosopher who lived more than two thousand years ago believed that philosophy had its origin in man's sense of wonder. Man thought it was so astonishing to be alive that philosophical questions arose of their own accord.

It is like watching a magic trick. We cannot understand how it is done. So we ask: how can the magician change a couple of white silk scarves into a live rabbit?

A lot of people experience the world with the same incredulity as when a magician suddenly pulls a rabbit out of a hat which has just been shown to them empty.

In the case of the rabbit, we know the magician has tricked us. What we would like to know is just how he did it. But when it comes to the world it's somewhat different. We know that the world is not all sleight of hand and deception because here we are in it, we are part of it. Actually, we *are* the white rabbit being pulled out of the hat. The only difference between us and the white rabbit is that the rabbit does not realize it is taking part in a magic trick. Unlike us. We feel we are part of something mysterious and we would like to know how it all works.

P.S. As far as the white rabbit is concerned, it might be better to compare it with the whole universe. We who live here are microscopic insects existing deep down in the rabbit's fur. But philosophers are always trying to climb up the fine hairs of the fur in order to stare right into the magician's eyes.

Are you still there, Sophie? To be continued . . .

Sophie was completely exhausted. Still there? She could not even remember if she had taken the time to breathe while she read.

Who had brought this letter? It couldn't be the same person who had sent the birthday card to Hilde Møller Knag because that card had both a stamp and a postmark. The brown envelope had been delivered by hand to the mailbox exactly like the two white ones.

Sophie looked at her watch. It was a quarter to three. Her mother would not be home from work for over two hours.

Sophie crawled out into the garden again and ran to the mailbox. Perhaps there was another letter.

She found one more brown envelope with her name on it. This time she looked all around but there was nobody in sight. Sophie ran to the edge of the woods and looked down the path.

No one was there. Suddenly she thought she heard a twig snap deep in the woods. But she was not completely sure, and anyway it would be pointless to chase after someone who was determined to get away.

Sophie let herself into the house. She ran upstairs to her room and took out a big cookie tin full of pretty stones. She emptied the stones onto the floor and put both large envelopes into the tin. Then she hurried out into the garden again, holding the tin securely with both hands. Before she went she put some food out for Sherekan.

"Kitty, kitty, kitty!"

Once back in the den she opened the second brown envelope and drew out the new typewritten pages. She began to read.

A STRANGE CREATURE

Hello again! As you see, this short course in philosophy will come in handy-sized portions. Here are a few more introductory remarks:

Did I say that the only thing we require to be good philosophers is the faculty of wonder? If I did not, I say it now: THE ONLY THING WE REQUIRE TO BE GOOD PHILOSOPHERS IS THE FACULTY OF WONDER.

Babies have this faculty. That is not surprising. After a few short months in the womb they slip out into a brand-new reality. But as they grow up the faculty of wonder seems to diminish. Why is this? Do you know?

If a newborn baby could talk, it would probably say something about what an extraordinary world it had come into. We see how it looks around and reaches out in curiosity to everything it sees.

As words are gradually acquired, the child looks up and says "Bow-wow" every time it sees a dog. It jumps up and down in its stroller, waving its arms: "Bow-wow! Bow-wow!" We who are older and wiser may feel somewhat exhausted by the child's enthusiasm. "All right, all right, it's a bow-wow," we say, unimpressed. "Please sit still." We are not enthralled. We have seen a dog before.

This rapturous performance may repeat itself hundreds of times before the child learns to pass a dog without going crazy. Or an elephant, or a hippopotamus. But long before the child learns to talk properly—and long before it learns to think philosophically—the world will have become a habit.

A pity, if you ask me.

My concern is that you do not grow up to be one of those people who take the world for granted, Sophie dear. So just to make sure, we are going to do a couple of experiments in thought before we begin on the course itself.

Imagine that one day you are out for a walk in the woods. Suddenly you see a small spaceship on the path in front of you. A tiny Martian climbs out of the spaceship and stands on the ground looking up at you . . .

What would you think? Never mind, it's not important. But have you ever given any thought to the fact that you are a Martian yourself?

It is obviously unlikely that you will ever stumble upon a creature from another planet. We do not even know that there is life on other planets. But you might stumble upon yourself one day. You might suddenly stop short and see yourself in a completely new light. On just such a walk in the woods.

I am an extraordinary being, you think. I am a mysterious creature.

You feel as if you are waking from an enchanted slumber. Who am I? you ask. You know that you are stumbling around on a planet in the universe. But what is the universe?

If you discover yourself in this manner you will have discovered something as mysterious as the Martian we just mentioned. You will not only have seen a being from outer space. You will feel deep down that you are yourself an extraordinary being.

Do you follow me, Sophie? Let's do another experiment in thought:

One morning, Mom, Dad, and little Thomas, aged two or three, are having breakfast in the kitchen. After a while Mom gets up and goes over to the kitchen sink, and Dad—yes, Dad—flies up and floats around under the ceiling while Thomas sits watching. What do you think Thomas says? Perhaps he points up at his father and says: "Daddy's flying!" Thomas will certainly be astonished, but then he very often is. Dad does so many strange things that this business of a little flight over the breakfast table makes no difference to him. Every day Dad shaves with a funny machine, sometimes he climbs onto the roof and turns the TV aerial—or else he sticks his head under the hood of the car and comes up black in the face.

Now it's Mom's turn. She hears what Thomas says and turns around abruptly. How do you think she reacts to the sight of Dad floating nonchalantly over the kitchen table?

She drops the jam jar on the floor and screams with fright. She may even need medical attention once Dad has returned respectably to his chair. (He should have learned better table manners by now!) Why do you think Thomas and his mother react so differently?

It all has to do with *habit.* (Note this!) Mom has learned that people cannot fly. Thomas has not. He still isn't certain what you can and cannot do in this world.

But what about the world itself, Sophie? Do you think *it* can do what it does? The world is also floating in space.

Sadly it is not only the force of gravity we get used to as we grow up. The world itself becomes a habit in no time at all. It seems as if in the process of growing up we lose the ability to wonder about the world. And in doing so, we lose something central—something philosophers try to restore. For somewhere inside ourselves, something tells us that life is a huge mystery. This is something we once experienced, long before we learned to think the thought.

To be more precise: Although philosophical questions concern us all, we do not all become philosophers. For various reasons most people get so caught up in everyday affairs that their astonishment at the world gets pushed into the background. (They crawl deep into the rabbit's fur, snuggle down comfortably, and stay there for the rest of their lives.)

To children, the world and everything in it is *new*, something that gives rise to astonishment. It is not like that for adults. Most adults accept the world as a matter of course.

This is precisely where philosophers are a notable exception. A philosopher never gets quite used to the world. To him or her, the world continues to seem a bit unreasonable—bewildering, even enigmatic. Philosophers and small children thus have an important faculty in common. You might say that throughout his life a philosopher remains as thin-skinned as a child.

So now you must choose, Sophie. Are you a child who has not yet become world-weary? Or are you a philosopher who will vow never to become so?

If you just shake your head, not recognizing yourself as either a child or a philosopher, then you have gotten so used to the world that it no longer astonishes you. Watch out! You are on thin ice. And this is why you are receiving this course in philosophy, just in case. I will not allow you, of all people, to join the ranks of the apathetic and the indifferent. I want you to have an inquiring mind.

The whole course is free of charge, so you get no money back if you do not complete it. If you choose to break off the course you are free to do so. In that case you must leave a message for me in the mailbox. A live frog would be eminently suitable. Something green, at least, otherwise the mailman might get scared.

To summarize briefly: A white rabbit is pulled out of a top hat. Because it is an extremely large rabbit, the trick takes many billions of years. All mortals are born at the very tip of the rabbit's fine hairs, where they are in a position to wonder at the impossibility of the trick. But as they grow older they work themselves ever deeper into the fur. And there they stay. They become so comfortable they never risk crawling back up the fragile hairs again. Only philosophers embark on this perilous expedition to the outermost reaches of language and existence. Some of them fall off, but others cling on desperately and yell at the people nestling deep in the snug softness, stuffing themselves with delicious food and drink.

"Ladies and gentlemen," they yell, "we are floating in space!" But none of the people down there care.

"What a bunch of troublemakers!" they say. And they keep on chatting: Would you pass the butter, please? How much have our stocks risen today? What is the price of tomatoes? Have you heard that Princess Di is expecting again?

When Sophie's mother got home later that afternoon, Sophie was practically in shock. The tin containing the letters from the mysterious philosopher was safely hidden in the den. Sophie had tried to start her homework but could only sit thinking about what she had read.

She had never thought so hard before! She was no longer a child—but she wasn't really grown up either. Sophie realized that she had already begun to crawl down into the cozy rabbit's fur, the very same rabbit that had been pulled from the top hat of the universe. But the philosopher had stopped her. He—or was it a she?—had grabbed her by the back of the neck and pulled her up again to the tip of the fur where she had played as a child. And there, on the outermost tips of the fine hairs, she was once again seeing the world as if for the very first time.

The philosopher had rescued her. No doubt about it. The unknown letter writer had saved her from the triviality of everyday existence.

When Mom got home at five o'clock, Sophie dragged her into the living room and pushed her into an armchair.

"Mom—don't you think it's astonishing to be alive?" she began.

Her mother was so surprised that she didn't answer at first. Sophie was usually doing her homework when she got home.

"I suppose I do—sometimes," she said.

"Sometimes? Yes, but—don't you think it's astonishing that the world *exists* at all?"

"Now look, Sophie. Stop talking like that."

"Why? Perhaps you think the world is quite normal?"

"Well, isn't it? More or less, anyway."

Sophie saw that the philosopher was right. Grownups took the world for granted. They had let themselves be lulled into the enchanted sleep of their humdrum existence once and for all.

"You've just grown so used to the world that nothing surprises you any more."

"What on earth are you talking about?"

"I'm talking about you getting so used to everything. Totally dim, in other words."

"I will not be spoken to like that, Sophie!"

"All right, I'll put it another way. You've made yourself comfortable deep down in the fur of a white rabbit that is being pulled out of the universe's top hat right now. And in a minute you'll put the potatoes on. Then you'll read the paper and after half an hour's nap you'll watch the news on TV!"

An anxious expression came over her mother's face. She did indeed go into the kitchen and put the potatoes on. After a while she came back into the living room, and this time it was she who pushed Sophie into an armchair.

"There's something I must talk to you about," she began. Sophie could tell by her voice that it was something serious.

"You haven't gotten yourself mixed up with drugs, have you, dear?"

Sophie was just about to laugh, but she understood why the question was being brought up now.

"Are you nuts?" she said. "That only makes you *duller*!"

No more was said that evening about either drugs or white rabbits.

The Myths

∞

*. . . a precarious balance between the forces of
good and evil . . .*

There was no letter for Sophie the next morning. All
through the interminable day at school she was bored
stiff. She took care to be extra nice to Joanna during the
breaks. On the way home they talked about going camping as soon as the woods were dry enough.

After what seemed an eternity she was once again at
the mailbox. First she opened a letter postmarked in
Mexico. It was from her father. He wrote about how
much he was longing for home and how for the first
time he had managed to beat the Chief Officer at chess.
Apart from that he had almost finished the pile of books
he had brought aboard with him after his winter leave.

And then, there it was—a brown envelope with her
name on it! Leaving her schoolbag and the rest of the
mail in the house, Sophie ran to the den. She pulled out
the new typewritten pages and began to read:

THE MYTHOLOGICAL WORLD PICTURE

Hello there, Sophie! We have a lot to do, so we'll get
started without delay.

By philosophy we mean the completely new way of
thinking that evolved in Greece about six hundred years
before the birth of Christ. Until that time people had found

answers to all their questions in various religions. These religious explanations were handed down from generation to generation in the form of *myths*. A myth is a story about the gods which sets out to explain why life is as it is.

Over the millennia a wild profusion of mythological explanations of philosophical questions spread across the world. The Greek philosophers attempted to prove that these explanations were not to be trusted.

In order to understand how the early philosophers thought, we have to understand what it was like to have a mythological picture of the world. We can take some Nordic myths as examples. (There is no need to carry coals to Newcastle.)

You have probably heard of Thor and his hammer. Before Christianity came to Norway, people believed that Thor rode across the sky in a chariot drawn by two goats. When he swung his hammer it made thunder and lightning. The word "thunder" in Norwegian—"Thordøn"—means Thor's roar. In Swedish, the word for thunder is "åska," originally "ås-aka," which means "god's journey" over the heavens.

When there is thunder and lightning there is also rain, which was vital to the Viking farmers. So Thor was worshipped as the god of fertility.

The mythological explanation for rain was therefore that Thor was swinging his hammer. And when it rained the corn germinated and thrived in the fields.

How the plants of the field could grow and yield crops was not understood. But it was clearly somehow connected with the rain. And since everybody believed that the rain had something to do with Thor, he was one of the most important of the Norse gods.

There was another reason why Thor was important, a reason related to the entire world order.

The Vikings believed that the inhabited world was an island under constant threat from outside dangers. They called this part of the world Midgard, which means the kingdom in the middle. Within Midgard lay Asgard, the domain of the gods.

Outside Midgard was the kingdom of Utgard, the domain of the treacherous giants, who resorted to all kinds of cunning tricks to try and destroy the world. Evil monsters like these are often referred to as the "forces of chaos." Not only in Norse mythology but in almost all other cultures, people found that there was a precarious balance between the forces of good and evil.

One of the ways in which the giants could destroy Midgard was by abducting Freyja, the goddess of fertility. If they could do this, nothing would grow in the fields and the women would no longer have children. So it was vital to hold these giants in check.

Thor was a central figure in this battle with the giants. His hammer could do more than make rain; it was a key weapon in the struggle against the dangerous forces of chaos. It gave him almost unlimited power. For example, he could hurl it at the giants and slay them. And he never had to worry about losing it because it always came back to him, just like a boomerang.

This was the *mythological explanation* for how the balance of nature was maintained and why there was a constant struggle between good and evil. And this was precisely the kind of explanation that the philosophers rejected.

But it was not a question of explanations alone.

Mortals could not just sit idly by and wait for the gods to intervene while catastrophes such as drought or plague loomed. They had to act for themselves in the struggle against evil. This they did by performing various religious ceremonies, or *rites*.

The most significant religious ceremony in Norse times was the *offering*. Making an offering to a god had the effect of increasing that god's power. For example, mortals had to make offerings to the gods to give them the strength to conquer the forces of chaos. They could do this by sacrificing an animal to the god. The offering to Thor was usually a goat. Offerings to Odin sometimes took the form of human sacrifices.

The myth that is best known in the Nordic countries comes from the Eddic poem "The Lay of Thrym." It tells how Thor, rising from sleep, finds that his hammer is gone. This makes him so angry that his hands tremble and his beard shakes. Accompanied by his henchman Loki he goes to Freyja to ask if Loki may borrow her wings so that he can fly to Jotunheim, the land of the giants, and find out if they are the ones who have stolen Thor's hammer.

At Jotunheim Loki meets Thrym, the king of the giants, who sure enough begins to boast that he has hidden the hammer seven leagues under the earth. And he adds that the gods will not get the hammer back until Thrym is given Freyja as his bride.

Can you picture it, Sophie? Suddenly the good gods find themselves in the midst of a full-blown hostage incident. The giants have seized the gods' most vital defensive weapon. This is an utterly unacceptable situation. As long as the giants have Thor's hammer, they have total control over the world of gods and mortals. In exchange for the hammer they are demanding Freyja. But this is equally unacceptable. If the gods have to give up their goddess of fertility—she who protects all life—the grass will disappear from the fields and all gods and mortals will die. The situation is deadlocked.

Loki returns to Asgard, so the myth goes, and tells Freyja to put on her wedding attire for she is (alas!) to wed the king of the giants. Freyja is furious, and says people will think she is absolutely man-crazy if she agrees to marry a giant.

Then the god Heimdall has an idea. He suggests that Thor dress up as a bride. With his hair up and two stones under his tunic he will look like a woman. Understandably, Thor is not wildly enthusiastic about the idea, but he finally accepts that this is the only way he will ever get his hammer back.

So Thor allows himself to be attired in bridal costume, with Loki as his bridesmaid.

To put it in present-day terms, Thor and Loki are the gods' "anti-terrorist squad." Disguised as women, their mission is to breach the giants' stronghold and recapture Thor's hammer.

When the gods arrive at Jotunheim, the giants begin to prepare the wedding feast. But during the feast, the bride—Thor, that is—devours an entire ox and eight salmon. He also drinks three barrels of beer. This astonishes Thrym. The true identity of the "commandos" is very nearly revealed. But Loki manages to avert the danger by explaining that Freyja has been looking forward to coming to Jotunheim so much that she has not eaten for a week.

When Thrym lifts the bridal veil to kiss the bride, he is startled to find himself looking into Thor's burning eyes. Once again Loki saves the situation by explaining that the bride has not slept for a week because she is so excited about the wedding. At this, Thrym commands that the hammer be brought forth and laid in the bride's lap during the wedding ceremony.

Thor roars with laughter when he is given the hammer. First he kills Thrym with it, and then he wipes out the giants and all their kin. And thus the gruesome hostage affair has a happy ending. Thor—the Batman or James Bond of the gods—has once again conquered the forces of evil.

So much for the myth itself, Sophie. But what is the real meaning behind it? It wasn't made up just for entertainment. The myth also tries to *explain* something. Here is one possible interpretation:

When a drought occurred, people sought an explanation of why there was no rain. Could it be that the giants had stolen Thor's hammer?

Perhaps the myth was an attempt to explain the changing seasons of the year: in the winter Nature dies because Thor's hammer is in Jotunheim. But in the spring he succeeds in winning it back. So the myth tried to give people an explanation for something they could not understand.

But a myth was not only an explanation. People also carried out religious ceremonies related to the myths. We can imagine how people's response to drought or crop failure would be to enact a drama about the events in the myth. Perhaps a man from the village would dress up as a bride—with stones for breasts—in order to steal the hammer back from the giants. By doing this, people were taking some action to make it rain so the crops would grow in their fields.

There are a great many examples from other parts of the world of the way people dramatized their myths of the seasons in order to speed up the processes of nature.

So far we have only taken a brief glimpse at the world of Norse mythology. But there were countless myths about Thor and Odin, Freyr and Freyja, Hoder and Balder and many other gods. Mythological notions of this kind flourished all over the world until philosophers began to tamper with them.

A mythological world picture also existed in Greece when the first philosophy was evolving. The stories of the Greek gods had been handed down from generation to generation for centuries. In Greece the gods were called Zeus and Apollo, Hera and Athene, Dionysos and Asclepios, Heracles and Hephaestos, to mention only a few of them.

Around 700 B.C., much of the Greek mythology was written down by Homer and Hesiod. This created a whole new situation. Now that the myths existed in written form, it was possible to discuss them.

The earliest Greek philosophers criticized Homer's mythology because the gods resembled mortals too much and were just as egoistic and treacherous. For the first time it was said that the myths were nothing but human notions.

One exponent of this view was the philosopher Xenophanes, who lived from about 570 B.C. Men have created the gods in their own image, he said. They believe the gods were born and have bodies and clothes and language just as we have. Ethiopians believe that the gods are black and flat-nosed, Thracians imagine them to be blue-eyed and fair-haired. If oxen, horses, and lions could draw, they would depict gods that looked like oxen, horses, and lions!

During that period the Greeks founded many city-states, both in Greece itself and in the Greek colonies in Southern Italy and Asia Minor, where all manual work was done by slaves, leaving the citizens free to devote all their time to politics and culture.

In these city environments people began to think in a completely new way. Purely on his own behalf, any citizen could question the way society ought to be organized. Individuals could thus also ask philosophical questions without recourse to ancient myths.

We call this the development from a mythological mode of thought to one based on experience and reason. The aim of the early Greek philosophers was to find *natural*, rather than supernatural, explanations for natural processes.

Sophie left the den and wandered about in the large garden. She tried to forget what she had learned at school, especially in science classes.

If she had grown up in this garden without knowing anything at all about nature, how would she feel about the spring?

Would she try to invent some kind of explanation for why it suddenly started to rain one day? Would she work out some fantasy to explain where the snow went and why the sun rose in the morning?

Yes, she definitely would. She began to make up a story:

Winter held the land in its icy grip because the evil Muriat had imprisoned the beautiful Princess Sikita in a cold prison. But one morning the brave Prince Bravato came and rescued her. Sikita was so happy that she began to dance over the meadows, singing a song she had composed inside the dank prison. The earth and the trees were so moved that all the snow turned into tears. But then the sun came out and dried all the tears away. The birds imitated Sikita's song, and when the beautiful princess let down her golden tresses, a few locks of her hair fell onto the earth and turned into the lilies of the field . . .

Sophie liked her beautiful story. If she had not known any other explanation for the changing seasons, she felt sure she would have come to believe her own story in the end.

She understood that people had always felt a need to explain the processes of nature. Perhaps they could not live without such explanations. And that they made up all those myths in the time before there was anything called science.

The Natural
Philosophers

∽

... nothing can come from nothing ...

When her mother got home from work that afternoon
Sophie was sitting in the glider, pondering the possible
connection between the philosophy course and Hilde
Møller Knag, who would not be getting a birthday card
from her father.

Her mother called from the other end of the garden,
"Sophie! There's a letter for you!"

She caught her breath. She had already emptied the
mailbox, so the letter had to be from the philosopher.
What on earth would she say to her mother?

"There's no stamp on it. It's probably a love letter!"

Sophie took the letter.

"Aren't you going to open it?"

She had to find an excuse.

"Have you ever heard of anyone opening a love letter
with her mother looking over her shoulder?"

Let her mother think it was a love letter. Although it
was embarrassing enough, it would be even worse if her
mother found out that she was doing a correspondence
course with a complete stranger, a philosopher who was
playing hide-and-seek with her.

It was one of the little white envelopes. When Sophie
got upstairs to her room, she found three new questions:

*Is there a basic substance that everything else is
    made of?*
Can water turn into wine?
How can earth and water produce a live frog?

Sophie found the questions pretty stupid, but nevertheless they kept buzzing around in her head all evening.
She was still thinking about them at school the next day,
examining them one by one.

Could there be a "basic substance" that everything
was made of? If there was some such substance, how
could it suddenly turn into a flower or an elephant?

The same objection applied to the question of whether
water could turn into wine. Sophie knew the parable of
how Jesus turned water into wine, but she had never
taken it literally. And if Jesus really had turned water
into wine, it was because it was a miracle, something
that could not be done normally. Sophie knew there was
a lot of water, not only in wine but in all other growing
things. But even if a cucumber was 95 percent water,
there must be something else in it as well, because a
cucumber was a cucumber, not water.

And then there was the question about the frog. Her philosophy teacher had this really weird thing about frogs.

Sophie could possibly accept that a frog consisted of
earth and water, in which case the earth must consist of
more than one kind of substance. If the earth consisted
of a lot of different substances, it was obviously possible
that earth and water together could produce a frog. That
is, if the earth and the water went via frog spawn and
tadpoles. Because a frog could not just grow out of a
cabbage patch, however much you watered it.

When she got home from school that day there was a
fat envelope waiting for her in the mailbox. Sophie hid
in the den just as she had done the other days.

THE PHILOSOPHERS' PROJECT

Here we are again! We'll go directly to today's lesson
without detours around white rabbits and the like.

I'll outline very broadly the way people have thought

about philosophy, from the ancient Greeks right up to our own day. But we'll take things in their correct order.

Since some philosophers lived in a different age—and perhaps in a completely different culture from ours—it is a good idea to try and see what each philosopher's *project* is. By this I mean that we must try to grasp precisely what it is that each particular philosopher is especially concerned with finding out. One philosopher might want to know how plants and animals came into being. Another might want to know whether there is a God or whether man has an immortal soul.

Once we have determined what a particular philosopher's project is, it is easier to follow his line of thought, since no one philosopher concerns himself with the whole of philosophy.

I said *his* line of thought—referring to the philosopher, because this is also a story of men. Women of the past were subjugated both as females and as thinking beings, which is sad because a great deal of very important experience was lost as a result. It was not until this century that women really made their mark on the history of philosophy.

I do not intend to give you any homework—no difficult math questions, or anything like that, and conjugating English verbs is outside my sphere of interest. However, from time to time I'll give you a short assignment.

If you accept these conditions, we'll begin.

THE NATURAL PHILOSOPHERS

The earliest Greek philosophers are sometimes called *natural philosophers* because they were mainly concerned with the natural world and its processes.

We have already asked ourselves where everything comes from. Nowadays a lot of people imagine that at some time something must have come from nothing. This idea was not so widespread among the Greeks. For one reason or another, they assumed that "something" had always existed.

How everything could come from nothing was therefore

not the all-important question. On the other hand the Greeks marveled at how live fish could come from water, and huge trees and brilliantly colored flowers could come from the dead earth. Not to mention how a baby could come from its mother's womb!

The philosophers observed with their own eyes that nature was in a constant state of transformation. But how could such transformations occur?

How could something change from being substance to being a living thing, for example?

All the earliest philosophers shared the belief that there had to be a certain basic substance at the root of all change. How they arrived at this idea is hard to say. We only know that the notion gradually evolved that there must be a basic substance that was the hidden cause of all changes in nature. There had to be "something" that all things came from and returned to.

For us, the most interesting part is actually not what solutions these earliest philosophers arrived at, but which questions they asked and what type of answer they were looking for. We are more interested in how they thought than in exactly what they thought.

We know that they posed questions relating to the transformations they could observe in the physical world. They were looking for the underlying laws of nature. They wanted to understand what was happening around them without having to turn to the ancient myths. And most important, they wanted to understand the actual processes by studying nature itself. This was quite different from explaining thunder and lightning or winter and spring by telling stories about the gods.

So philosophy gradually liberated itself from religion. We could say that the natural philosophers took the first step in the direction of scientific reasoning, thereby becoming the precursors of what was to become science.

Only fragments have survived of what the natural philosophers said and wrote. What little we know is found in the writings of Aristotle, who lived two centuries later. He refers only to the conclusions the philosophers reached. So we do not always know by what paths they reached these conclusions. But what we do know enables us to establish that the earliest Greek philosophers' project concerned the question of a basic constituent substance and the changes in nature.

THREE PHILOSOPHERS FROM MILETUS

The first philosopher we know of is *Thales,* who came from Miletus, a Greek colony in Asia Minor. He traveled in many countries, including Egypt, where he is said to have calculated the height of a pyramid by measuring its shadow at the precise moment when the length of his own shadow was equal to his height. He is also said to have accurately predicted a solar eclipse in the year 585 B.C.

Thales thought that the source of all things was water. We do not know exactly what he meant by that, he may have believed that all life originated from water—and that all life returns to water again when it dissolves.

During his travels in Egypt he must have observed how the crops began to grow as soon as the floods of the Nile receded from the land areas in the Nile Delta. Perhaps he also noticed that frogs and worms appeared wherever it had just been raining.

It is likely that Thales thought about the way water turns to ice or vapor—and then turns back into water again.

Thales is also supposed to have said that "all things are full of gods." What he meant by that we can only surmise. Perhaps, seeing how the black earth was the source of everything from flowers and crops to insects and cockroaches, he imagined that the earth was filled with tiny invisible "life-germs." One thing is certain—he was not talking about Homer's gods.

The next philosopher we hear of is *Anaximander,* who also lived in Miletus at about the same time as Thales. He thought that our world was only one of a myriad of worlds that evolve and dissolve in something he called the boundless. It is not so easy to explain what he meant by the boundless, but it seems clear that he was not thinking of a known substance in the way that Thales had envisaged. Perhaps he meant that the substance which is the source of all things had to be something other than the things created. Because all created things are limited, that which comes before and after them must be "boundless." It is clear that this basic stuff could not be anything as ordinary as water.

A third philosopher from Miletus was *Anaximenes* (c. 570–526 B.C.). He thought that the source of all things must be "air" or "vapor." Anaximenes was of course familiar with Thales' theory of water. But where does water come from? Anaximenes thought that water was condensed air. We observe that when it rains, water is pressed from the air. When water is pressed even more, it becomes earth, he thought. He may have seen how earth and sand were pressed out of melting ice. He also thought that fire was rarefied air. According to Anaximenes, air was therefore the origin of earth, water, and fire.

It is not a far cry from water to the fruit of the earth. Perhaps Anaximenes thought that earth, air, and fire were all necessary to the creation of life, but that the source of all things was air or vapor. So, like Thales, he thought that there must be an underlying substance that is the source of all natural change.

Nothing Can Come from Nothing

These three Milesian philosophers all believed in the existence of a single basic substance as the source of all things. But how could one substance suddenly change into something else? We can call this the *problem of change*.

From about 500 B.C., there was a group of philosophers in the Greek colony of Elea in Southern Italy. These "Eleatics" were interested in this question.

The most important of these philosophers was *Parmenides* (c. 540–480 B.C.). Parmenides thought that everything that exists had always existed. This idea was not alien to the Greeks. They took it more or less for granted that everything that existed in the world was everlasting. Nothing can come out of nothing, thought Parmenides. And nothing that exists can become nothing.

But Parmenides took the idea further. He thought that

there was no such thing as actual change. Nothing could become anything other than it was.

Parmenides realized, of course, that nature is in a constant state of flux. He perceived with his senses that things changed. But he could not equate this with what his reason told him. When forced to choose between relying either on his senses or his reason, he chose reason.

You know the expression "I'll believe it when I see it." But Parmenides didn't even believe things when he saw them. He believed that our senses give us an incorrect picture of the world, a picture that does not tally with our reason. As a philosopher, he saw it as his task to expose all forms of perceptual illusion.

This unshakable faith in human reason is called *rationalism*. A rationalist is someone who believes that human reason is the primary source of our knowledge of the world.

All Things Flow

A contemporary of Parmenides was *Heraclitus* (c. 540–480 B.C.), who was from Ephesus in Asia Minor. He thought that constant change, or flow, was in fact the most basic characteristic of nature. We could perhaps say that Heraclitus had more faith in what he could perceive than Parmenides did.

"Everything flows," said Heraclitus. Everything is in constant flux and movement, nothing is abiding. Therefore we "cannot step twice into the same river." When I step into the river for the second time, neither I nor the river are the same.

Heraclitus pointed out that the world is characterized by opposites. If we were never ill, we would not know what it was to be well. If we never knew hunger, we would take no pleasure in being full. If there were never any war, we would not appreciate peace. And if there were no winter, we would never see the spring.

Both good and bad have their inevitable place in the order of things, Heraclitus believed. Without this constant interplay of opposites the world would cease to exist.

"God is day and night, winter and summer, war and peace, hunger and satiety," he said. He used the term "God," but he was clearly not referring to the gods of the mythology. To Heraclitus, God—or the Deity—was something that embraced the whole world. Indeed, God can be seen most clearly in the constant transformations and contrasts of nature.

Instead of the term "God," Heraclitus often used the Greek word *logos*, meaning reason. Although we humans do not always think alike or have the same degree of reason, Heraclitus believed that there must be a kind of "universal reason" guiding everything that happens in nature.

This "universal reason" or "universal law" is something common to us all, and something that everybody is guided by. And yet most people live by their individual reason, thought Heraclitus. In general, he despised his fellow beings. "The opinions of most people," he said, "are like the playthings of infants."

So in the midst of all nature's constant flux and opposites, Heraclitus saw an Entity or one-ness. This "something," which was the source of everything, he called God or *logos*.

Four Basic Elements

In one way, Parmenides and Heraclitus were the direct opposite of each other. Parmenides' *reason* made it clear that nothing could change. Heraclitus' *sense perceptions* made it equally clear that nature was in a constant state of change. Which of them was right? Should we let reason dictate or should we rely on our senses?

Parmenides and Heraclitus both say two things:

Parmenides says:

    a) that nothing can change, and

    b) that our sensory perceptions must therefore be unreliable.

Heraclitus, on the other hand, says:

    a) that everything changes ("all things flow"), and

    b) that our sensory perceptions are reliable.

*   *   *

Philosophers could hardly disagree more than that! But
who was right? It fell to *Empedocles* (c. 490–430 B.C.)
from Sicily to lead the way out of the tangle they had
gotten themselves into.

He thought they were both right in one of their asser-
tions but wrong in the other.

Empedocles found that the cause of their basic dis-
agreement was that both philosophers had assumed the
presence of only *one* element. If this were true, the gap
between what reason dictates and what "we can see with
our own eyes" would be unbridgeable.

Water obviously cannot turn into a fish or a butterfly.
In fact, water cannot change. Pure water will continue to
be pure water. So Parmenides was right in holding that
"nothing changes."

But at the same time Empedocles agreed with Heraclitus
that we must trust the evidence of our senses. We must
believe what we see, and what we see is precisely that
nature changes.

Empedocles concluded that it was the idea of a single
basic substance that had to be rejected. Neither water nor
air *alone* can change into a rosebush or a butterfly. The
source of nature cannot possibly be one single "element."

Empedocles believed that all in all, nature consisted of
four elements, or "roots" as he termed them. These four
roots were *earth, air, fire,* and *water.*

All natural processes were due to the coming together
and separating of these four elements. For all things were
a mixture of earth, air, fire, and water, but in varying
proportions. When a flower or an animal dies, he said,
the four elements separate again. We can register these
changes with the naked eye. But earth and air, fire and
water remain everlasting, "untouched" by all the compounds of which they are part. So it is not correct to say
that "everything" changes. Basically, nothing changes.
What happens is that the four elements are combined and
separated—only to be combined again.

We can make a comparison to painting. If a painter
only has one color—red, for instance—he cannot paint
green trees. But if he has yellow, red, blue, and black, he

can paint in hundreds of different colors because he can mix them in varying proportions.

An example from the kitchen illustrates the same thing. If I only have flour, I have to be a wizard to bake a cake. But if I have eggs, flour, milk, and sugar, then I can make any number of different cakes.

It was not purely by chance that Empedocles chose earth, air, fire, and water as nature's "roots." Other philosophers before him had tried to show that the primordial substance had to be either water, air, or fire. Thales and Anaximenes had pointed out that both water and air were essential elements in the physical world. The Greeks believed that fire was also essential. They observed, for example, the importance of the sun to all living things, and they also knew that both animals and humans have body heat.

Empedocles might have watched a piece of wood burning. Something disintegrates. We hear it crackle and splutter. That is "water." Something goes up in smoke. That is "air." The "fire" we can see. Something also remains when the fire is extinguished. That is the ashes—or "earth."

After Empedocles' clarification of nature's transformations as the combination and dissolution of the four "roots," something still remained to be explained. What makes these elements combine so that new life can occur? And what makes the "mixture" of, say, a flower dissolve again?

Empedocles believed that there were two different *forces* at work in nature. He called them *love* and *strife*. Love binds things together, and strife separates them.

He distinguishes between "substance" and "force." This is worth noting. Even today, scientists distinguish between *elements* and *natural forces*. Modern science holds that all natural processes can be explained as the interaction between different elements and various natural forces.

Empedocles also raised the question of what happens when we perceive something. How can I "see" a flower, for example? What is it that happens? Have you ever thought about it, Sophie?

Empedocles believed that the eyes consist of earth, air, fire, and water, just like everything else in nature. So the "earth" in my eye perceives what is of the earth in my surroundings, the "air" perceives what is of the air, the "fire" perceives what is of fire, and the "water" what is of water. Had my eyes lacked any of the four substances, I would not have seen all of nature.

Something of Everything in Everything

Anaxagoras (500–428 B.C.) was another philosopher who could not agree that one particular basic substance—water, for instance—might be transformed into everything we see in the natural world. Nor could he accept that earth, air, fire, and water can be transformed into blood and bone.

Anaxagoras held that nature is built up of an infinite number of minute particles invisible to the eye. Moreover, everything can be divided into even smaller parts, but even in the minutest parts there are fragments of all other things. If skin and bone are not a transformation of something else, there must also be skin and bone, he thought, in the milk we drink and the food we eat.

A couple of present-day examples can perhaps illustrate Anaxagoras' line of thinking. Modern laser technology can produce so-called holograms. If one of these holograms depicts a car, for example, and the hologram is fragmented, we will see a picture of the whole car even though we only have the part of the hologram that showed the bumper. This is because the whole subject is present in every tiny part.

In a sense, our bodies are built up in the same way. If I loosen a skin cell from my finger, the nucleus will contain not only the characteristics of my skin: the same cell will also reveal what kind of eyes I have, the color of my hair, the number and type of my fingers, and so on. Every cell of the human body carries a blueprint of the way all the other cells are constructed. So there is "something of everything" in every single cell. The whole exists in each tiny part.

Anaxagoras called these minuscule particles which have something of everything in them *seeds*.

Remember that Empedocles thought that it was "love" that joined the elements together in whole bodies. Anaxagoras also imagined "order" as a kind of force, creating animals and humans, flowers and trees. He called this force mind or intelligence (nous).

Anaxagoras is also interesting because he was the first philosopher we hear of in Athens. He was from Asia Minor but he moved to Athens at the age of forty. He was later accused of atheism and was ultimately forced to leave the city. Among other things, he said that the sun was not a god but a red-hot stone, bigger than the entire Peloponnesian peninsula.

Anaxagoras was generally very interested in astronomy. He believed that all heavenly bodies were made of the same substance as Earth. He reached this conclusion after studying a meteorite. This gave him the idea that there could be human life on other planets. He also pointed out that the Moon has no light of its own—its light comes from Earth, he said. He thought up an explanation for solar eclipses as well.

P.S. Thank you for your attention, Sophie. It is not unlikely that you will need to read this chapter two or three times before you understand it all. But understanding will always require some effort. You probably wouldn't admire a friend who was good at everything if it cost her no effort.

The best solution to the question of basic substance and the transformations in nature must wait until tomorrow, when you will meet Democritus. I'll say no more!

Sophie sat in the den looking out into the garden through a little hole in the dense thicket. She had to try and sort out her thoughts after all she had read.

It was as clear as daylight that plain water could never turn into anything other than ice or steam. Water couldn't even turn into a watermelon, because even watermelons consisted of more than just water. But she was only sure of that because that's what she had learned. Would she be absolutely certain, for example, that ice was only water if that wasn't what she had learned? At least, she would have to have studied very closely how water froze to ice and melted again.

Sophie tried once again to use her own common sense, and not to think about what she had learned from others.

Parmenides had refused to accept the idea of change in any form. And the more she thought about it, the more she was convinced that, in a way, he had been right. His intelligence could not accept that "something" could suddenly transform itself into "something completely different." It must have taken quite a bit of courage to come right out and say it, because it meant denying all the natural changes that people could see for themselves. Lots of people must have laughed at him.

And Empedocles must have been pretty smart too, when he proved that the world had to consist of more than one single substance. That made all the transformations of nature possible without anything actually changing.

The old Greek philosopher had found that out just by reasoning. Of course he had studied nature, but he didn't have the equipment to do chemical analysis the way scientists do nowadays.

Sophie was not sure whether she really believed that the source of everything actually was earth, air, fire, and water. But after all, what did that matter? In principle, Empedocles was right. The only way we can accept the transformations we can see with our own eyes—without losing our reason—is to admit the existence of more than one single basic substance.

Sophie found philosophy doubly exciting because she was able to follow all the ideas by using her own common sense—without having to remember everything she had learned at school. She decided that philosophy was not something you can learn; but perhaps you can learn to *think* philosophically.

Democritus

...the most ingenious toy in the world...

Sophie put all the typed pages from the unknown philosopher back into the cookie tin and put the lid on it. She crawled out of the den and stood for a while looking across the garden. She thought about what happened yesterday. Her mother had teased her about the "love letter" again at breakfast this morning. She walked quickly over to the mailbox to prevent the same thing from happening today. Getting a love letter two days in a row would be doubly embarrassing.

There was another little white envelope! Sophie began to discern a pattern in the deliveries: every afternoon she would find a big brown envelope. While she read the contents, the philosopher would sneak up to the mailbox with another little white envelope.

So now Sophie would be able to find out who he was. If it was a he! She had a good view of the mailbox from her room. If she stood at the window she would see the mysterious philosopher. White envelopes don't just appear out of thin air!

Sophie decided to keep a careful watch the following day. Tomorrow was Friday and she would have the whole weekend ahead of her.

She went up to her room and opened the envelope. There was only one question today, but it was even dumber than the previous three:

Why is Lego the most ingenious toy in the world?

For a start, Sophie was not at all sure she agreed that it was. It was years since she had played with the little plastic blocks. Moreover she could not for the life of her see what Lego could possibly have to do with philosophy.

But she was a dutiful student. Rummaging on the top shelf of her closet, she found a bag full of Lego blocks of all shapes and sizes.

For the first time in ages she began to build with them. As she worked, some ideas began to occur to her about the blocks.

They are easy to assemble, she thought. Even though they are all different, they all fit together. They are also unbreakable. She couldn't ever remember having seen a broken Lego block. All her blocks looked as bright and new as the day they were bought, many years ago. The best thing about them was that with Lego she could construct any kind of object. And then she could separate the blocks and construct something new.

What more could one ask of a toy? Sophie decided that Lego really could be called the most ingenious toy in the world. But what it had to do with philosophy was beyond her.

She had nearly finished constructing a big doll's house. Much as she hated to admit it, she hadn't had as much fun in ages.

Why did people quit playing when they grew up?

When her mother got home and saw what Sophie had been doing, she blurted out, "What fun! I'm so glad you're not too grown up to play!"

"I'm not playing!" Sophie retorted indignantly, "I'm doing a very complicated philosophical experiment!"

Her mother sighed deeply. She was probably thinking about the white rabbit and the top hat.

When Sophie got home from school the following day, there were several more pages for her in a big brown envelope. She took them upstairs to her room. She could not wait to read them, but she had to keep her eye on the mailbox at the same time.

THE ATOM THEORY

Here I am again, Sophie. Today you are going to hear about the last of the great natural philosophers. His name is *Democritus* (c. 460–370 B.C.) and he was from the little town of Abdera on the northern Aegean coast.

If you were able to answer the question about Lego blocks without difficulty, you should have no problem understanding what this philosopher's project was.

Democritus agreed with his predecessors that transformations in nature could not be due to the fact that anything actually "changed." He therefore assumed that everything was built up of tiny invisible blocks, each of which was eternal and immutable. Democritus called these smallest units *atoms*.

The word "a-tom" means "un-cuttable." For Democritus it was all-important to establish that the constituent parts that everything else was composed of could not be divided indefinitely into smaller parts. If this were possible, they could not be used as blocks. If atoms could eternally be broken down into ever smaller parts, nature would begin to dissolve like constantly diluted soup.

Moreover, nature's blocks had to be eternal—because nothing can come from nothing. In this, he agreed with Parmenides and the Eleatics. Also, he believed that all atoms were firm and solid. But they could not all be the same. If all atoms were identical, there would still be no satisfactory explanation of how they could combine to form everything from poppies and olive trees to goatskin and human hair.

Democritus believed that nature consisted of an unlimited number and variety of atoms. Some were round and smooth, others were irregular and jagged. And precisely because they were so different they could join together into all kinds of different bodies. But however infinite they might be in number and shape, they were all eternal, immutable, and indivisible.

When a body—a tree or an animal, for instance—died and disintegrated, the atoms dispersed and could be used again in new bodies. Atoms moved around in space, but because they had "hooks" and "barbs," they could join together to form all the things we see around us.

So now you see what I meant about Lego blocks. They have more or less the same properties as those which Democritus ascribed to atoms. And that is what makes them so much fun to build with. They are first and foremost indivisible. Then they have different shapes and sizes. They are solid and impermeable. They also have "hooks" and "barbs" so that they can be connected to form every conceivable figure. These connections can later be broken again so that new figures can be constructed from the same blocks.

The fact that they can be used over and over is what has made Lego so popular. Each single Lego block can be part of a truck one day and part of a castle the day after. We could also say that Lego blocks are "eternal." Children of today can play with the same blocks their parents played with when they were little.

We can form things out of clay too, but clay cannot be used over and over, because it can be broken up into smaller and smaller pieces. These tiny pieces can never be joined together again to make something else.

Today we can establish that Democritus' atom theory was more or less correct. Nature really is built up of different "atoms" that join and separate again. A hydrogen atom in a cell at the end of my nose was once part of an elephant's trunk. A carbon atom in my cardiac muscle was once in the tail of a dinosaur.

In our own time, however, scientists have discovered that atoms can be broken into smaller "elemental particles." We call these elemental particles protons, neutrons, and electrons. These will possibly some day be broken into even lesser particles. But physicists agree that somewhere along the line there has to be a limit. There has to be a "minimal part" of which nature consists.

Democritus did not have access to modern electronic apparatus. His only proper equipment was his mind. But reason left him no real choice. Once it is accepted that nothing can change, that nothing can come out of nothing, and that nothing is ever lost, then nature *must* consist of infinitesimal blocks that can join and separate again.

Democritus did not believe in any "force" or "soul"

that could intervene in natural processes. The only things that existed, he believed, were atoms and the void. Since he believed in nothing but material things, we call him a *materialist*.

According to Democritus, there is no conscious "design" in the movement of atoms. In nature, everything happens quite mechanically. This does not mean that everything happens randomly, for everything obeys the inevitable laws of necessity. Everything that happens has a natural cause, a cause that is inherent in the thing itself. Democritus once said that he would rather discover a new cause of nature than be the King of Persia.

The atom theory also explains our *sense perception*, thought Democritus. When we sense something, it is due to the movement of atoms in space. When I see the moon, it is because "moon atoms" penetrate my eye.

But what about the "soul," then? Surely that could not consist of atoms, of material things? Indeed it could. Democritus believed that the soul was made up of special round, smooth "soul atoms." When a human being died, the soul atoms flew in all directions, and could then become part of a new soul formation.

This meant that human beings had no immortal soul, another belief that many people share today. They believe, like Democritus, that "soul" is connected with brain, and that we cannot have any form of consciousness once the brain disintegrates.

Democritus's atom theory marked the end of Greek natural philosophy for the time being. He agreed with Heraclitus that everything in nature "flowed," since forms come and go. But behind everything that flowed there were some eternal and immutable things that did not flow. Democritus called them atoms.

During her reading Sophie glanced out of the window several times to see whether her mysterious correspondent had turned up at the mailbox. Now she just sat staring down the road, thinking about what she had read.

She felt that Democritus's ideas had been so simple and yet so ingenious. He had discovered the real solution to the problem of "basic substance" and "transformation.'' This problem had been so complicated that philosophers had gone around puzzling over it for generations. And in the end Democritus had solved it on his own by using his common sense.

Sophie could hardly help smiling. It *had* to be true that nature was built up of small parts that never changed. At the same time Heraclitus was obviously right in thinking that all forms in nature ''flow.'' Because everybody dies, animals die, even a mountain range slowly disintegrates. The point was that the mountain range is made up of tiny indivisible parts that never break up.

At the same time Democritus had raised some new questions. For example, he had said that everything happened mechanically. He did not accept that there was any spiritual force in life—unlike Empedocles and Anaxagoras. Democritus also believed that man had no immortal soul.

Could she be sure of that?

She didn't know. But then she had only just begun the philosophy course.

Fate

∞

*... the "fortune-teller" is trying to foresee
something that is
really quite unforeseeable ...*

Sophie had been keeping her eye on the mailbox while
she read about Democritus. But just in case, she decided
nevertheless to take a stroll down to the garden gate.

When she opened the front door she saw a small envelope on the front step. And sure enough—it was addressed to Sophie Amundsen.

So he had tricked her! Today of all days, when she
had kept such careful watch on the mailbox, the mystery
man had sneaked up to the house from a different angle
and just laid the letter on the step before making off into
the woods again. Drat!

How did he know that Sophie was watching the mailbox today? Had he seen her at the window? Anyway,
she was glad to find the letter before her mother arrived.

Sophie went back to her room and opened the letter.
The white envelope was a bit wet around the edges, and
had two little holes in it. Why was that? It had not rained
for several days.

The little note inside read:

*Do you believe in Fate?
Is sickness the punishment of the gods?
What forces govern the course of history?*

Did she believe in Fate? She was not at all sure. But she knew a lot of people who did. There was a girl in her class who read horoscopes in magazines. But if they believed in astrology, they probably believed in Fate as well, because astrologers claimed that the position of the stars influenced people's lives on Earth.

If you believed that a black cat crossing your path meant bad luck—well, then you believed in Fate, didn't you? As she thought about it, several more examples of fatalism occurred to her. Why do so many people knock on wood, for example? And why was Friday the thirteenth an unlucky day? Sophie had heard that lots of hotels had no room number 13. It had to be because so many people were superstitious.

"Superstitious." What a strange word. If you believed in Christianity or Islam, it was called "faith." But if you believed in astrology or Friday the thirteenth it was superstition! Who had the right to call other people's belief superstition?

Sophie was sure of one thing, though. Democritus had *not* believed in fate. He was a materialist. He had only believed in atoms and empty space.

Sophie tried to think about the other questions on the note.

"Is sickness the punishment of the gods?" Surely nobody believed that nowadays? But it occurred to her that many people thought it helped to pray for recovery, so at any rate they must believe that God had some power over people's health.

The last question was harder to answer. Sophie had never given much thought to what governed the course of history. It had to be people, surely? If it was God or Fate, people had no free will.

The idea of free will made Sophie think of something else. Why should she put up with this mysterious philosopher playing cat and mouse with her? Why couldn't she write a letter to *him*? He (or she) would quite probably put another big envelope in the mailbox during the night or sometime tomorrow morning. She would see to it that there was a letter ready for this person.

Sophie began right away. It was difficult to write to

someone she had never seen. She didn't even know if it
was a man or a woman. Or if he or she was old or
young. For that matter, the mysterious philosopher could
even be someone she already knew.

She wrote:

Most respected philosopher, Your generous correspondence course in philosophy is greatly appreci-
ated by us here. But it bothers us not to know who
you are. We therefore request you to use your full
name. In return we would like to extend our hos-
pitality should you care to come and have coffee
with us, but preferably when my mother is at home.
She is at work from 7:30 a.m. to 5 p.m. every day
from Monday to Friday. I am at school during these
days, but I am always home by 2:15 p.m., except
on Thursdays. I am also very good at making coffee.

   Thanking you in advance, I remain
   Your attentive student,
   Sophie Amundsen (aged 14)

At the bottom of the page she wrote *RSVP*.

Sophie felt that the letter had turned out much too
formal. But it was hard to know which words to choose
when writing to a person without a face. She put the
letter in a pink envelope and addressed it "To the philosopher."

The problem was where to put it so her mother didn't
find it. She would have to wait for her to get home
before putting it in the mailbox. And she would also
have to remember to look in the mailbox early the next
morning before the newspaper arrived. If no new letter
came for her this evening or during the night, she would
have to take the pink envelope in again.

Why did it all have to be so complicated?

That evening Sophie went up to her room early, even
though it was Friday. Her mother tried to tempt her with
pizza and a thriller on TV, but Sophie said she was tired
and wanted to go to bed and read. While her mother sat

watching TV, she sneaked out to the mailbox with her letter.

Her mother was clearly worried. She had started speaking to Sophie in a different tone since the business with the white rabbit and the top hat. Sophie hated to be a worry to her mother, but she just had to go upstairs and keep an eye on the mailbox.

When her mother came up at about eleven o'clock, Sophie was sitting at the window staring down the road.

"You're not still sitting there staring at the mailbox!" she said.

"I can look at whatever I like."

"I really think you must be in love, Sophie. But if he is going to bring you another letter, he certainly won't come in the middle of the night."

Yuck! Sophie loathed all that soppy talk about love. But she had to let her mother go on believing it was true.

"Is he the one who told you about the rabbit and the top hat?" her mother asked.

Sophie nodded.

"He—he doesn't do drugs, does he?"

Now Sophie felt really sorry for her mother. She couldn't go on letting her worry this way, although it was completely nutty of her to think that just because someone had a slightly bizarre idea he must be on something. Grownups really were idiotic sometimes.

She said, "Mom, I promise you once and for all I'll never do any of that stuff . . . and he doesn't either. But he is very interested in philosophy."

"Is he older than you?"

Sophie shook her head.

"The same age?"

Sophie nodded.

"Well, I'm sure he's very sweet, darling. Now I think you should try and get some sleep."

But Sophie stayed sitting by the window for what seemed like hours. At last she could hardly keep her eyes open. It was one o'clock.

She was just about to go to bed when she suddenly caught sight of a shadow emerging from the woods.

Although it was almost dark outside, she could make out the shape of a human figure. It was a man, and Sophie thought he looked quite old. He was certainly not her age! He was wearing a beret of some kind.

She could have sworn he glanced up at the house, but Sophie's light was not on. The man went straight up to the mailbox and dropped a big envelope into it. As he let go of it, he caught sight of Sophie's letter. He reached down into the mailbox and fished it up. The next minute he was walking swiftly back toward the woods. He hurried down the woodland path and was gone.

Sophie felt her heart pounding. Her first instinct was to run after him in her pajamas but she didn't dare run after a stranger in the middle of the night. But she did have to go out and fetch the envelope.

After a minute or two she crept down the stairs, opened the front door quietly, and ran to the mailbox. In a flash she was back in her room with the envelope in her hand. She sat on her bed, holding her breath. After a few minutes had passed and all was still quiet in the house, she opened the letter and began to read.

She knew this would not be an answer to her own letter. That could not arrive until tomorrow.

FATE

Good morning once again, my dear Sophie. In case you should get any ideas, let me make it quite clear that you must never attempt to check up on me. One day we will meet, but I shall be the one to decide when and where. And that's final. You are not going to disobey me, are you?

But to return to the philosophers. We have seen how they tried to find natural explanations for the transformations in Nature. Previously these things had been explained through myths.

Old superstitions had to be cleared away in other areas as well. We see them at work in matters of sickness and health as well as in political events. In both these areas the Greeks were great believers in *fatalism*.

Fatalism is the belief that whatever happens is predestined. We find this belief all over the world, not only throughout history but in our own day as well. Here in the Nordic countries we find a strong belief in "lagnadan," or fate, in the old Icelandic sagas of the *Edda*.

We also find the belief, both in Ancient Greece and in other parts of the world, that people could learn their fate from some form of *oracle*. In other words, that the fate of a person or a country could be foreseen in various ways.

There are still a lot of people who believe that they can tell your fortune in the cards, read your palm, or predict your future in the stars.

A special Norwegian version of this is telling your fortune in coffee cups. When a coffee cup is empty there are usually some traces of coffee grounds left. These might form a certain image or pattern—at least, if we give our imagination free rein. If the grounds resemble a car, it might mean that the person who drank from the cup is going for a long drive.

Thus the "fortune-teller" is trying to foresee something that is really quite unforeseeable. This is characteristic of all forms of foreseeing. And precisely because what they "see" is so vague, it is hard to repudiate fortune-tellers' claims.

When we gaze up at the stars, we see a veritable chaos of twinkling dots. Nevertheless, throughout the ages there have always been people who believed that the stars could tell us something about our life on Earth. Even today there are political leaders who seek the advice of astrologers before they make any important decisions.

The Oracle at Delphi

The ancient Greeks believed that they could consult the famous oracle at Delphi about their fate. Apollo, the god of the oracle, spoke through his priestess Pythia, who sat on a stool over a fissure in the earth, from which arose hypnotic vapors that put Pythia in a trance. This enabled her to be Apollo's mouthpiece.

When people came to Delphi they had to present their

question to the priests of the oracle, who passed it on to Pythia. Her answer would be so obscure or ambiguous that the priests would have to interpret it. In that way, the people got the benefit of Apollo's wisdom, believing that he knew everything, even about the future.

There were many heads of state who dared not go to war or take other decisive steps until they had consulted the oracle at Delphi. The priests of Apollo thus functioned more or less as diplomats, or advisers. They were experts with an intimate knowledge of the people and the country.

Over the entrance to the temple at Delphi was a famous inscription: KNOW THYSELF! It reminded visitors that man must never believe himself to be more than mortal—and that no man can escape his destiny.

The Greeks had many stories of people whose destiny catches up with them. As time went by, a number of plays—tragedies—were written about these "tragic" people. The most famous one is the tragedy of King Oedipus.

History and Medicine

But Fate did not just govern the lives of individuals. The Greeks believed that even world history was governed by Fate, and that the fortunes of war could be swayed by the intervention of the gods. Today there are still many people who believe that God or some other mysterious power is steering the course of history.

But at the same time as Greek philosophers were trying to find natural explanations for the processes of nature, the first historians were beginning to search for natural explanations for the course of history. When a country lost a war, the vengeance of the gods was no longer an acceptable explanation to them. The best known Greek historians were *Herodotus* (484–424 B.C.) and *Thucydides* (460–400 B.C.).

The Greeks also believed that sickness could be ascribed to divine intervention. On the other hand, the gods could make people well again if they made the appropriate sacrifices.

This idea was in no way unique to the Greeks. Before

the development of modern medicine, the most widely accepted view was that sickness was due to supernatural causes. The word "influenza" actually means a malign influence from the stars.

Even today, there are a lot of people who believe that some diseases—AIDS, for example—are God's punishment. Many also believe that sick people can be cured with the help of the supernatural.

Concurrently with the new directions in Greek philosophy, a Greek medical science arose which tried to find natural explanations for sickness and health. The founder of Greek medicine is said to have been *Hippocrates,* who was born on the island of Cos around 460 B.C.

The most essential safeguards against sickness, according to the Hippocratic medical tradition, were moderation and a healthy lifestyle. Health is the natural condition. When sickness occurs, it is a sign that Nature has gone off course because of physical or mental imbalance. The road to health for everyone is through moderation, harmony, and a "sound mind in a sound body."

There is a lot of talk today about "medical ethics," which is another way of saying that a doctor must practice medicine according to certain ethical rules. For instance, a doctor may not give healthy people a prescription for narcotics. A doctor must also maintain professional secrecy, which means that he is not allowed to reveal anything a patient has told him about his illness. These ideas go back to Hippocrates. He required his pupils to take the following oath:

> I will follow that system or regimen which, according to my ability and judgment, I consider to be for the benefit of my patients, and abstain from whatever is deleterious and mischievous. I will give no deadly medicine to anyone if asked nor suggest any such counsel, and in like manner I will not give to a woman the means to produce an abortion. Whenever I go into a house, I will go for the benefit of the sick and will abstain from every voluntary act of mischief and corruption, and further, from the seduction of females or males, whether freemen or slaves.

Whatever, in connection with my professional practice, I see or hear which ought not to be spoken abroad, I will keep secret. So long as I continue to carry out this oath unviolated, may it be granted to me to enjoy life and the practice of the art, respected by all men in all times, but should I violate this oath, may the reverse be my lot.

Sophie awoke with a start on Saturday morning. Was it a dream or had she really seen the philosopher?

She felt under the bed with one hand. Yes—there lay the letter that had come during the night. It wasn't only a dream.

She had definitely seen the philosopher! And what's more, with her own eyes she had seen him take her letter!

She crouched down on the floor and pulled out all the typewritten pages from under the bed. But what was that? Right by the wall there was something red. A scarf, perhaps?

Sophie edged herself in under the bed and pulled out a red silk scarf. It wasn't hers, that was for sure!

She examined it more closely and gasped when she saw HILDE written in ink along the seam.

Hilde! But who *was* Hilde? How could their paths keep crossing like this?

Socrates

∽

. . . wisest is she who knows she does not know . . .

Sophie put on a summer dress and hurried down to the kitchen. Her mother was standing by the kitchen table. Sophie decided not to say anything about the silk scarf.

"Did you bring in the newspaper?" she asked.

Her mother turned.

"Would you get it for me?"

Sophie was out of the door in a flash, down the gravel path to the mailbox.

Only the newspaper. She couldn't expect an answer so soon, she supposed. On the front page of the paper she read something about the Norwegian UN battalion in Lebanon.

The UN battalion . . . wasn't that the postmark on the card from Hilde's father? But the postage stamp had been Norwegian. Maybe the Norwegian UN soldiers had their own post office with them.

"You've become very interested in the newspaper," said her mother drily when Sophie returned to the kitchen.

Luckily her mother said no more about mailboxes and stuff, either during breakfast or later on that day. When she went shopping, Sophie took her letter about Fate down to the den.

She was surprised to see a little white envelope beside the cookie tin with the other letters from the philosopher. Sophie was quite sure she had not put it there.

This envelope was also wet around the edges. And it had a couple of deep holes in it, just like the one she had received yesterday.

Had the philosopher been here? Did he know about her secret hiding place? Why was the envelope wet?

All these questions made her head spin. She opened the letter and read the note:

Dear Sophie, I read your letter with great interest— and not without some regret. I must unfortunately disappoint you with regard to the invitation. We shall meet one day, but it will probably be quite a while before I can come in person to Captain's Bend.

I must add that from now on I will no longer be able to deliver the letters personally. It would be much too risky in the long run. In the future, letters will be delivered by my little messenger. On the other hand, they will be brought directly to the secret place in the garden.

You may continue to contact me whenever you feel the need. When you do, put a pink envelope out with a cookie or a lump of sugar in it. When the messenger finds it, he will bring it straight to me.

P.S. It is not pleasant to decline a young lady's invitation to coffee, but sometimes it is a matter of necessity.

P.P.S. If you should come across a red silk scarf anywhere, please take care of it. Sometimes personal property gets mixed up. Especially at school and places like that, and this is a philosophy school.

Yours, Alberto Knox

Sophie had lived for almost fifteen years, and had received quite a lot of letters in her young life, at least at Christmas and on birthdays. But this letter was the strangest one she had ever received.

It had no postage stamp. It hadn't even been put in the mailbox. It had been brought straight to Sophie's top-secret hideout in the old hedge. The fact that it was wet in the dry spring weather was also most mystifying.

The strangest thing of all was the silk scarf, of course. The philosopher must have another pupil. That was it. And this other pupil had lost a red silk scarf. Right. But how had she managed to lose it under Sophie's bed?

And Alberto Knox. . . . what kind of a name was that?

One thing was confirmed—the connection between the philosopher and Hilde Møller Knag. But that Hilde's own father was now confusing their addresses—that was completely incomprehensible.

Sophie sat for a long time thinking about what connection there could possibly be between Hilde and herself. Finally she gave up. The philosopher had written that she would meet him one day. Perhaps she would meet Hilde too.

She turned the letter over. She now saw that there were some sentences written on the back as well:

> Is there such a thing as natural modesty?
> Wisest is she who knows she does not know . . .
> True insight comes from within.
> He who knows what is right will do right.

Sophie knew that the short sentences that came in the white envelopes were intended to prepare her for the next big envelope, which would arrive shortly thereafter. She suddenly had an idea. If the "messenger" came to the den to deliver a brown envelope, Sophie could simply sit and wait for him. Or was it a her? She would definitely hang on to whoever it was until he or she told her more about the philosopher! The letter said that the "messenger" was little. Could it be a child?

"Is there such a thing as natural modesty?"

Sophie knew that "modesty" was an old-fashioned word for shyness—for example, about being seen naked. But was it really natural to be embarrassed about that? If something was natural, she supposed, it was the same for everybody. In many parts of the world it was completely natural to be naked. So it must be *society* that decides what you can and can't do. When Grandma was young you certainly couldn't sunbathe topless. But today, most people think it is "natural," even though it is still strictly forbidden in lots of countries. Was this philosophy? Sophie wondered.

The next sentence was: "Wisest is she who knows she does not know."

Wiser than who? If the philosopher meant that someone who realized that she didn't know everything under the sun was wiser than someone who knew just a little, but who thought she knew a whole lot—well, that wasn't so difficult to agree with. Sophie had never thought about it before. But the more she did, the more clearly she saw that knowing what you don't know is also a kind of knowledge. The stupidest thing she knew was for people to act like they knew all about things they knew absolutely nothing about.

The next sentence was about true insight coming from within. But didn't all knowledge come into people's heads from the outside? On the other hand, Sophie could remember situations when her mother or the teachers at school had tried to teach her something that she hadn't been receptive to. And whenever she had really *learned* something, it was when she had somehow contributed to it herself. Now and then, even, she would suddenly understand a thing she'd drawn a total blank on before. That was probably what people meant by "insight."

So far, so good. Sophie thought she had done reasonably well on the first three questions. But the next statement was so odd she couldn't help smiling: "He who knows what is right will do right."

Did that mean that when a bank robber robbed a bank it was because he didn't know any better? Sophie didn't think so.

On the contrary, she thought that both children and adults did stupid things that they probably regretted afterwards, precisely because they had done them against their better judgment.

While she sat thinking, she heard something rustling in the dry undergrowth on the other side of the hedge nearest the woods. Could it be the messenger? Her heart started beating faster. It sounded like a panting animal was coming.

The next moment a big Labrador pushed its way into the den.

In its mouth it held a big brown envelope which it dropped at Sophie's feet. It all happened so quickly that Sophie had no time to react. A second later she was sitting with the big envelope in her hands—and the golden Labrador had scampered off into the woods again.

Once it was all over she reacted. She started to cry.

She sat like that for a while, losing all sense of time.

Then she looked up suddenly.

So that was his famous messenger! Sophie breathed a sigh of relief. Of course that was why the white envelopes were wet around the edges and had holes in them. Why hadn't she thought of it? Now it made sense to put a cookie or a lump of sugar in the envelope when she wrote to the philosopher.

She may not always have been as smart as she would like, but who could have guessed that the messenger was a trained dog! It was a bit out of the ordinary, to put it mildly! She could certainly forget all about forcing the messenger to reveal Alberto Knox's whereabouts.

Sophie opened the big envelope and began to read.

THE PHILOSOPHY OF ATHENS

Dear Sophie, When you read this you may already have met Hermes. In case you haven't, I'll add that he is a dog. But don't worry. He is very good-tempered—and moreover, a good deal more intelligent than a lot of people. In any event he never tries to give the impression of being cleverer than he is.

You may also note that his name is not without significance.

In Greek mythology, *Hermes* was the messenger of the gods. He was also the god of seafarers, but we shall not bother about that, at least not for the moment. It is more important that Hermes also gave his name to the word "hermetic," which means hidden or inaccessible—not inappropriate for the way Hermes takes care to keep the two of us hidden from each other.

So the messenger has herewith been introduced. Naturally he answers to his name and is altogether very well behaved.

But to return to philosophy. We have already completed the first part of the course. I refer to the natural philosophers and their decisive break with the mythological world picture. Now we are going to meet the three great classical philosophers, Socrates, Plato, and Aristotle. Each in his own way, these philosophers influenced the whole of European civilization.

The natural philosophers are also called the pre-Socratics, because they lived before Socrates. Although Democritus died some years after Socrates, all his ideas belong to pre-Socratic natural philosophy. Socrates represents a new era, geographically as well as temporally. He was the first of the great philosophers to be born in Athens, and both he and his two successors lived and worked there. You may recall that Anaxagoras also lived in Athens for a while but was hounded out because he said the sun was a red-hot stone. (Socrates fared no better!)

From the time of Socrates, Athens was the center of Greek culture. It is also important to note the change of character in the philosophical project itself as it progresses from natural philosophy to Socrates. But before we meet Socrates, let us hear a little about the so-called Sophists, who dominated the Athenian scene at the time of Socrates.

Curtain up, Sophie! The history of ideas is like a drama in many acts.

Man at the Center

After about 450 B.C., Athens was the cultural center of the Greek world. From this time on, philosophy took a new direction.

The natural philosophers had been mainly concerned

with the nature of the physical world. This gives them a central position in the history of science. In Athens, interest was now focused on the individual and the individual's place in society. Gradually a democracy evolved, with popular assemblies and courts of law.

In order for democracy to work, people had to be educated enough to take part in the democratic process. We have seen in our own time how a young democracy needs popular enlightenment. For the Athenians, it was first and foremost essential to master the art of rhetoric, which means saying things in a convincing manner.

A group of itinerant teachers and philosophers from the Greek colonies flocked to Athens. They called themselves *Sophists*. The word "sophist" means a wise and informed person. In Athens, the Sophists made a living out of teaching the citizens for money.

The Sophists had one characteristic in common with the natural philosophers: they were critical of the traditional mythology. But at the same time the Sophists rejected what they regarded as fruitless philosophical speculation. Their opinion was that although answers to philosophical questions may exist, man cannot know the truth about the riddles of nature and of the universe. In philosophy a view like this is called *skepticism*.

But even if we cannot know the answers to all of nature's riddles, we know that people have to learn to live together. The Sophists chose to concern themselves with man and his place in society.

"Man is the measure of all things," said the Sophist *Protagoras* (c. 485–410 B.C.). By that he meant that the question of whether a thing is right or wrong, good or bad, must always be considered in relation to a person's needs. On being asked whether he believed in the Greek gods, he answered, "The question is complex and life is short." A person who is unable to say categorically whether or not the gods or God exists is called an *agnostic*.

The Sophists were as a rule men who had traveled widely and seen different forms of government. Both conventions and local laws in the city-states could vary widely. This led the Sophists to raise the question of what was *natural* and what was *socially induced*. By doing this, they paved the way for social criticism in the city-state of Athens.

They could for example point out that the use of an expression like "natural modesty" is not always defensible, for if it is "natural" to be modest, it must be something you are born with, something innate. But is it really innate, Sophie—or is it socially induced? To someone who has traveled the world, the answer should be simple: It is not "natural"—or innate—to be afraid to show yourself naked. Modesty—or the lack of it—is first and foremost a matter of social convention.

As you can imagine, the wandering Sophists created bitter wrangling in Athens by pointing out that there were no *absolute norms* for what was right or wrong.

Socrates, on the other hand, tried to show that some such norms *are* in fact absolute and universally valid.

Who Was Socrates?

Socrates (470–399 B.C.) is possibly the most enigmatic figure in the entire history of philosophy. He never wrote a single line. Yet he is one of the philosophers who has had the greatest influence on European thought, not least because of the dramatic manner of his death.

We know he was born in Athens, and that he spent most of his life in the city squares and marketplaces talking with the people he met there. "The trees in the countryside can teach me nothing," he said. He could also stand lost in thought for hours on end.

Even during his lifetime he was considered somewhat enigmatic, and fairly soon after his death he was held to be the founder of any number of different philosophical schools of thought. The very fact that he was so enigmatic and ambiguous made it possible for widely differing schools of thought to claim him as their own.

We know for a certainty that he was extremely ugly. He was potbellied, and had bulging eyes and a snub nose. But inside he was said to be "perfectly delightful." It was also said of him that "You can seek him in the present, you can seek him in the past, but you will never find his equal." Nevertheless he was sentenced to death for his philosophical activities.

The life of Socrates is mainly known to us through the writings of Plato, who was one of his pupils and who became one of the greatest philosophers of all time. Plato wrote a number of *Dialogues*, or dramatized discussions on philosophy, in which he uses Socrates as his principal character and mouthpiece.

Since Plato is putting his own philosophy in Socrates' mouth, we cannot be sure that the words he speaks in the dialogues were ever actually uttered by him. So it is no easy matter to distinguish between the teachings of Socrates and the philosophy of Plato. Exactly the same problem applies to many other historical persons who left no written accounts. The classic example, of course, is Jesus. We cannot be certain that the "historical" Jesus actually spoke the words that Matthew or Luke ascribed to him. Similarly, what the "historical" Socrates actually said will always be shrouded in mystery.

But who Socrates "really" was is relatively unimportant. It is Plato's portrait of Socrates that has inspired thinkers in the Western world for nearly 2,500 years.

The Art of Discourse

The essential nature of Socrates' art lay in the fact that he did not appear to want to instruct people. On the contrary he gave the impression of one desiring to learn from those he spoke with. So instead of lecturing like a traditional schoolmaster, he *discussed*.

Obviously he would not have become a famous philosopher had he confined himself purely to listening to others. Nor would he have been sentenced to death. But he just asked questions, especially to begin a conversation, as if he knew nothing. In the course of the discussion he would generally get his opponents to recognize the weakness of their arguments, and, forced into a corner, they would finally be obliged to realize what was right and what was wrong.

Socrates, whose mother was a midwife, used to say that his art was like the art of the midwife. She does not herself give birth to the child, but she is there to help during its delivery. Similarly, Socrates saw his task as helping people to "give birth" to the correct insight, since real understanding must come from within. It cannot be imparted by someone else. And only the understanding that comes from within can lead to true insight.

Let me put it more precisely: The ability to give birth is a natural characteristic. In the same way, everybody can grasp philosophical truths if they just use their innate reason. Using your innate reason means reaching down inside yourself and using what is there.

By playing ignorant, Socrates forced the people he met to use their common sense. Socrates could feign ignorance—or pretend to be dumber than he was. We call this Socratic irony. This enabled him to continually expose the weaknesses in people's thinking. He was not averse to doing this in the middle of the city square. If you met Socrates, you thus might end up being made a fool of publicly.

So it is not surprising that, as time went by, people found him increasingly exasperating, especially people who had status in the community. "Athens is like a sluggish horse," he is reputed to have said, "and I am the gadfly trying to sting it into life."

(What do we do with gadflies, Sophie?)

A Divine Voice

It was not in order to torment his fellow beings that Socrates kept on stinging them. Something within him left him no choice. He always said that he had a "divine voice" inside him. Socrates protested, for example, against having any part in condemning people to death. He moreover refused to inform on his political enemies. This was eventually to cost him his life.

In the year 399 B.C. he was accused of "introducing new gods and corrupting the youth," as well as not believing in the accepted gods. With a slender majority, a jury of five hundred found him guilty.

He could very likely have appealed for leniency. At least he could have saved his life by agreeing to leave Athens. But had he done this he would not have been Socrates. He valued his conscience—and the truth— higher than life. He assured the jury that he had only acted in the best interests of the state. He was nevertheless condemned to drink hemlock. Shortly thereafter, he drank the poison in the presence of his friends, and died.

Why, Sophie? Why did Socrates have to die? People have been asking this question for 2,400 years. However, he was not the only person in history to have seen things through to the bitter end and suffered death for the sake of their convictions.

I have mentioned Jesus already, and in fact there are several striking parallels between them.

Both Jesus and Socrates were enigmatic personalities, also to their contemporaries. Neither of them wrote down their teachings, so we are forced to rely on the picture we have of them from their disciples. But we do know that they were both masters of the art of discourse. They both spoke with a characteristic self-assuredness that could fascinate as well as exasperate. And not least, they both believed that they spoke on behalf of something greater than themselves. They challenged the power of the community by criticizing all forms of injustice and corruption. And finally—their activities cost them their lives.

The trials of Jesus and Socrates also exhibit clear parallels.

They could certainly both have saved themselves by appealing for mercy, but they both felt they had a mission that would have been betrayed unless they kept faith to the bitter end. And by meeting their death so bravely they commanded an enormous following, also after they had died.

I do not mean to suggest that Jesus and Socrates were alike. I am merely drawing attention to the fact that they both had a message that was inseparably linked to their personal courage.

A Joker in Athens

Socrates, Sophie! We aren't done with him yet. We have talked about his method. But what was his philosophical project?

Socrates lived at the same time as the Sophists. Like them, he was more concerned with man and his place in society than with the forces of nature. As a Roman philosopher, Cicero, said of him a few hundred years later, Socrates "called philosophy down from the sky and established her in the towns and introduced her into homes and forced her to investigate life, ethics, good and evil."

But Socrates differed from the Sophists in one significant way. He did not consider himself to be a "sophist"—that is, a learned or wise person. Unlike the Sophists, he did not teach for money. No, Socrates called himself a philosopher in the true sense of the word. A "philo-sopher" really means "one who loves wisdom."

Are you sitting comfortably, Sophie? Because it is central to the rest of this course that you fully understand the difference between a sophist and a philosopher. The Sophists took money for their more or less hairsplitting expoundings, and sophists of this kind have come and gone from time immemorial. I am referring to all the schoolmasters and self-opinionated know-it-alls who are satisfied with what little they know, or who boast of knowing a whole lot about subjects they haven't the faintest notion of. You have probably come across a few of these sophists in your young life. A real *philosopher*, Sophie, is a completely different kettle of fish—the direct opposite, in fact. A philosopher knows that in reality he knows very little. That is why he constantly strives to achieve true insight. Socrates was one of these rare people. He *knew* that he knew nothing about life and about the world. And now comes the important part: it troubled him that he knew so little.

A philosopher is therefore someone who recognizes that there is a lot he does not understand, and is troubled by it. In that sense, he is still wiser than all those who brag about their knowledge of things they know nothing about. "Wisest is she who knows she does not know," I said previously. Socrates himself said, "One thing only I know, and that is that I know nothing."

Remember this statement, because it is an admission that is rare, even among philosophers. Moreover, it can be so dangerous to say it in public that it can cost you your life. The most subversive people are those who ask questions. Giving answers is not nearly as threatening. Any one question can be more explosive than a thousand answers.

You remember the story of the emperor's new clothes? The emperor was actually stark naked but none of his subjects dared say so. Suddenly a child burst out, "But he's got nothing on!" That was a *courageous* child, Sophie. Like Socrates, who dared tell people how little we humans know. The similarity between children and philosophers is something we have already talked about.

To be precise: Mankind is faced with a number of difficult questions that we have no satisfactory answers to. So now two possibilities present themselves: We can either fool ourselves and the rest of the world by pretending that we know all there is to know, or we can shut our eyes to the central issues once and for all and abandon all progress. In this sense, humanity is divided. People are, generally speaking, either dead certain or totally indifferent. (Both types are crawling around deep down in the rabbit's fur!)

It is like dividing a deck of cards into two piles, Sophie. You lay the black cards in one pile and the red in the other. But from time to time a joker turns up that is neither heart nor club, neither diamond nor spade. Socrates was this joker in Athens. He was neither certain nor indifferent. All he knew was that he knew nothing—and it troubled him. So he became a philosopher—someone who does not give up but tirelessly pursues his quest for truth.

An Athenian is said to have asked the oracle at Delphi who the wisest man in Athens was. The oracle answered that Socrates of all mortals was the wisest. When Socrates heard this he was astounded, to put it mildly. (He must have laughed, Sophie!) He went straight to the person in the city whom he, and everyone else, thought was excessively wise. But when it turned out that this person was unable to give Socrates satisfactory answers to his questions, Socrates realized that the oracle had been right.

Socrates felt that it was necessary to establish a solid foundation for our knowledge. He believed that this foundation lay in man's reason. With his unshakable faith in human reason he was decidedly a *rationalist*.

The Right Insight Leads to the Right Action

As I have mentioned earlier, Socrates claimed that he was guided by a divine inner voice, and that this "conscience" told him what was right. "He who knows what good is will do good," he said.

By this he meant that the right insight leads to the right action. And only he who does right can be a "virtuous man." When we do wrong it is because we don't know any better. That is why it is so important to go on learning. Socrates was concerned with finding clear and universally valid definitions of right and wrong. Unlike the Sophists, he believed that the ability to distinguish between right and wrong lies in people's reason and not in society.

You may perhaps think this last part is a bit too obscure, Sophie. Let me put it like this: Socrates thought that no one could possibly be happy if they acted against their better judgment. And he who knows how to achieve happiness will do so. Therefore, he who knows what is right will do right. Because why would anybody choose to be unhappy?

What do you think, Sophie? Can you live a happy life if you continually do things you know deep down are wrong? There are lots of people who lie and cheat and speak ill of others. Are they aware that these things are not right—or fair, if you prefer? Do you think these people are happy?

Socrates didn't.

When Sophie had read the letter, she quickly put it in the cookie tin and crawled out into the garden. She wanted to go indoors before her mother got back with the shopping in order to avoid any questions about where she had been. And she had promised to do the dishes.

She had just filled the sink with water when her mother came staggering in with two huge shopping bags. Perhaps that was why her mother said, "You are rather preoccupied these days, Sophie."

Sophie didn't know why she said it; the words just tumbled out of her mouth: "So was Socrates."

"Socrates?"

Her mother stared at her, wide-eyed.

"It was just so sad that he had to die as a result," Sophie went on thoughtfully.

"My goodness! Sophie! I don't know what I'm to do!"

"Neither did Socrates. All he knew was that he knew nothing. And yet he was the cleverest person in Athens."

Her mother was speechless.

Finally she said, "Is this something you've learned at school?"

Sophie shook her head energetically.

"We don't learn anything there. The difference between schoolteachers and philosophers is that schoolteachers think they know a lot of stuff that they try to force down our throats. Philosophers try to figure things out together with the pupils."

"Now we're back to white rabbits again! You know something? I demand to know who your boyfriend really is. Otherwise I'll begin to think he is a bit disturbed."

Sophie turned her back on the dishes and pointed at her mother with the dish mop.

"It's not him who's disturbed. But he likes to disturb others—to shake them out of their rut."

"That's enough of that! I think he sounds a bit too impertinent." Sophie turned back to the dishes.

"He is neither impertinent nor pertinent," said Sophie. "But he is trying to reach real wisdom. That's the great difference between a real joker and all the other cards in the deck."

"Did you say joker?"

Sophie nodded. "Have you ever thought about the

fact that there are a lot of hearts and diamonds in a pack of cards? And a lot of spades and clubs. But there's only one joker.''

''Good grief, how you talk back, Sophie!''

''And how you ask!''

Her mother had put all the groceries away. Now she took the newspaper and went into the living room. Sophie thought she closed the door more loudly than usual.

Sophie finished doing the dishes and went upstairs to her room. She had put the red silk scarf on the top shelf of the closet with the Lego blocks. She took it down and examined it carefully.

Hilde . . .

Athens

∽

. . . several tall buildings had risen from the ruins . . .

Early that evening Sophie's mother went to visit a friend. As soon as she was out of the house Sophie went down the garden to the den. There she found a thick package beside the big cookie tin. Sophie tore it open. It was a video cassette.

She ran back to the house. A video tape! How on earth did the philosopher know they had a VCR? And what was on the cassette?

Sophie put the cassette into the recorder. A sprawling city appeared on the TV screen. As the camera zoomed in on the Acropolis Sophie realized that the city must be Athens. She had often seen pictures of the ancient ruins there.

It was a live shot. Summer-clad tourists with cameras slung about them were swarming among the ruins. One of them looked as if he was carrying a notice board. There it was again. Didn't it say "Hilde"?

After a minute or two there was a close-up of a middle-aged man. He was rather short, with a black, well-trimmed beard, and he was wearing a blue beret. He looked into the camera and said: "Welcome to Athens, Sophie. As you have probably guessed, I am Alberto Knox. If not, I will just reiterate that the big rabbit is still being pulled from the top hat of the universe.

"We are standing at the Acropolis. The word means

'citadel'—or more precisely, 'the city on the hill.' People have lived up here since the Stone Age. The reason, naturally, was its unique location. The elevated plateau was easy to defend against marauders. From the Acropolis there was also an excellent view down to one of the best harbors in the Mediterranean. As the early Athens began to develop on the plain below the plateau, the Acropolis was used as a fortress and sacred shrine . . . During the first half of the fifth century B.C., a bitter war was waged against the Persians, and in 480 the Persian king Xerxes plundered Athens and burned all the old wooden buildings of the Acropolis. A year later the Persians were defeated, and that was the beginning of the Golden Age of Athens. The Acropolis was rebuilt—prouder and more magnificent than ever—and now purely as a sacred shrine.

"This was the period when Socrates walked through the streets and squares talking with the Athenians. He could thus have witnessed the rebirth of the Acropolis and watched the construction of all the proud buildings we see around us. And what a building site it was! Behind me you can see the biggest temple, the Parthenon, which means 'the Virgin's Place.' It was built in honor of Athene, the patron goddess of Athens. The huge marble structure does not have a single straight line; all four sides are slightly curved to make the building appear less heavy. In spite of its colossal dimensions, it gives the impression of lightness. In other words, it presents an optical illusion. The columns lean slightly inwards, and would form a pyramid 1,500 meters high if they were continued to a point above the temple. The temple contained nothing but a twelve-meter-high statue of Athene. The white marble, which in those days was painted in vivid colors, was transported here from a mountain sixteen kilometers away."

Sophie sat with her heart in her mouth. Was this really the philosopher talking to her? She had only seen his profile that one time in the darkness. Could he be the same man who was now standing at the Acropolis in Athens?

He began to walk along the length of the temple and

the camera followed him. He walked right to the edge of the terrace and pointed out over the landscape. The camera focused on an old theater which lay just below the plateau of the Acropolis.

"There you can see the old Dionysos Theater," continued the man in the beret. "It is probably the very oldest theater in Europe. This is where the great tragedies of Aeschylus, Sophocles, and Euripides were performed during the time of Socrates. I referred earlier to the ill-fated King Oedipus. The tragedy about him, by Sophocles, was first performed here. But they also played comedies. The best known writer of comedies was Aristophanes, who also wrote a spiteful comedy about Socrates as the buffoon of Athens. Right at the back you can see the stone wall which the actors used as a backdrop. It was called *skēnē*, and is the origin of our word 'scene.' Incidentally, the word 'theater' comes from an old Greek word meaning 'to see.' But we must get back to the philosophers, Sophie. We are going around the Parthenon and down through the gateway . . ."

The little man walked around the huge temple and passed some smaller temples on his right. Then he began to walk down some steps between several tall columns. When he reached the foot of the Acropolis, he went up a small hill and pointed out toward Athens: "The hill we are standing on is called Areopagos. It was here that the Athenian high court of justice passed judgment in murder trials. Many hundreds of years later, St. Paul the Apostle stood here and preached about Jesus and Christianity to the Athenians. We shall return to what he said on a later occasion. Down to the left you can see the remains of the old city square in Athens, the agora. With the exception of the large temple to Hephaestos, the god of smiths and metalworkers, only some blocks of marble are preserved. Let us go down . . ."

The next moment he appeared among the ancient ruins. High up beneath the sky—at the top of Sophie's screen—towered the monumental Athene temple on the Acropolis. Her philosophy teacher had seated himself on one of the blocks of marble. He looked into the camera and said: "We are sitting in the old agora in Athens. A sorry sight, don't you think? Today, I mean. But once it was surrounded by splendid temples, courts of justice and other public offices, shops, a concert hall, and even a large gymnastics building. All situated around the square, which was a large open space . . . The whole of European civilization was founded in this modest area.

"Words such as politics and democracy, economy and history, biology and physics, mathematics and logic, theology and philosophy, ethics and psychology, theory and method, idea and system date back to the tiny populace whose everyday life centered around this square. This is where Socrates spent so much of his time talking to the people he met. He might have buttonholed a slave bearing a jar of olive oil, and asked the unfortunate man a question on philosophy, for Socrates held that a slave had the same common sense as a man of rank. Perhaps he stood in an animated wrangle with one of the citizens—or held a subdued conversation with his young pupil Plato. It is extraordinary to think about. We still speak of Socratic or Platonic philosophy, but actually *being* Plato or Socrates is quite another matter."

Sophie certainly did think it was extraordinary to think about. But she thought it was just as extraordinary the way her philosopher was suddenly talking to her on a video that had been brought to her own secret hideout in the garden by a mysterious dog.

The philosopher rose from the block of marble he was sitting on and said quietly: "It was actually my intention to leave it at that, Sophie. I wanted you to see the Acropolis and the remains of the old agora in Athens. But I am not yet sure that you have grasped just how splendid these surroundings once were . . . so I am very tempted to go a bit further. It is quite irregular of course . . . but I am sure I can count on it remaining just between the two of us. Oh well, a tiny glimpse will suffice anyway . . ."

He said no more, but remained standing there for a long time, staring into the camera. While he stood there, several tall buildings had risen from the ruins. As if by magic, all the old buildings were once again standing.

Above the skyline Sophie could still see the Acropolis, but now both that and all the buildings down on the square were brand-new. They were covered with gold and painted in garish colors. Gaily dressed people were strolling about the square. Some wore swords, others carried jars on their heads, and one of them had a roll of papyrus under his arm.

Then Sophie recognized her philosophy teacher. He was still wearing the blue beret, but now he was dressed in a yellow tunic in the same style as everyone else. He came toward Sophie, looked into the camera, and said:

"That's better! Now we are in the Athens of antiquity, Sophie. I wanted you to come here in person, you see. We are in the year 402 B.C., only three years before Socrates dies. I hope you appreciate this exclusive visit because it was very difficult to hire a video camera . . ."

Sophie felt dizzy. How could this weird man suddenly be in Athens 2,400 years ago? How could she be seeing a video film of a totally different age? There were no videos in antiquity . . . so could this be a movie?

But all the marble buildings looked real. If they had recreated all of the old square in Athens as well as the Acropolis just for the sake of a film—the sets would have cost a fortune. At any rate it would be a colossal price to pay just to teach Sophie about Athens.

The man in the beret looked up at her again.

"Do you see those two men over there under the colonnade?"

Sophie noticed an elderly man in a crumpled tunic. He had a long unkempt beard, a snub nose, eyes like gimlets, and chubby cheeks. Beside him stood a handsome young man.

"That is Socrates and his young pupil, Plato. You are going to meet them personally."

The philosopher went over to the two men, took off his beret, and said something which Sophie did not understand. It must have been in Greek. Then he looked into the camera and said, "I told them you were a Norwegian girl who would very much like to meet them. So now Plato will give you some questions to think about. But we must do it quickly before the guards discover us.''

Sophie felt the blood pounding in her temples as the young man stepped forward and looked into the camera.

''Welcome to Athens, Sophie,'' he said in a gentle voice. He spoke with an accent. ''My name is Plato and I am going to give you four tasks. First you must think over how a baker can bake fifty absolutely identical cookies. Then you can ask yourself why all horses are the same. Next you must decide whether you think that man has an immortal soul. And finally you must say whether men and women are equally sensible. Good luck!''

Then the picture on the TV screen disappeared. Sophie wound and rewound the tape but she had seen all there was.

Sophie tried to think things through clearly. But as soon as she thought one thought, another one crowded in before she had thought the first one to its end.

She had known from the start that her philosophy teacher was eccentric. But when he started to use teaching methods that defied all the laws of nature, Sophie thought he was going too far.

Had she really seen Socrates and Plato on TV? Of course not, that was impossible. But it definitely wasn't a cartoon.

Sophie took the cassette out of the video recorder and ran up to her room with it. She put it on the top shelf with all the Lego blocks. Then she sank onto the bed, exhausted, and fell asleep.

Some hours later her mother came into the room. She shook Sophie gently and said:

''What's the matter, Sophie?''

''Mmmm?''

''You've gone to sleep with all your clothes on!''

Sophie blinked her eyes sleepily.

''I've been to Athens,'' she mumbled. That was all she could manage to say as she turned over and went back to sleep.

Plato

❧

. . . a longing to return to the realm of the soul . . .

Sophie woke with a start early the next morning. She glanced at the clock. It was only a little after five but she was so wide awake that she sat up in bed. Why was she wearing a dress? Then she remembered everything.

She climbed onto a stool and looked on the top shelf of the closet. Yes—there, at the back, was the video cassette. It hadn't been a dream after all; at least, not all of it.

But she couldn't really have *seen* Plato and Socrates . . . oh, never mind! She didn't have the energy to think about it any more. Perhaps her mother was right, perhaps she was acting a bit nuts these days.

Anyway, she couldn't go back to sleep. Perhaps she ought to go down to the den and see if the dog had left another letter. Sophie crept downstairs, put on a pair of jogging shoes, and went out.

In the garden everything was wonderfully clear and still. The birds were chirping so energetically that Sophie could hardly keep from laughing. The morning dew twinkled in the grass like drops of crystal. Once again she was struck by the incredible wonder of the world.

Inside the old hedge it was also very damp. Sophie saw no new letter from the philosopher, but nevertheless she wiped off one of the thick roots and sat down.

She recalled that the video-Plato had given her some questions to answer. The first was something about how a baker could bake fifty identical cookies.

Sophie had to think very carefully about that, because it definitely wouldn't be easy. When her mother occasionally baked a batch of cookies, they were never all exactly the same. But then she was not an expert pastry cook; sometimes the kitchen looked as if a bomb had hit it. Even the cookies they bought at the baker's were never exactly the same. Every single cookie was shaped separately in the baker's hands.

Then a satisfied smile spread over Sophie's face. She remembered how once she and her father went shopping while her mother was busy baking Christmas cookies. When they got back there were a lot of gingerbread men spread out on the kitchen table. Even though they weren't all perfect, in a way they were all the same. And why was that? Obviously because her mother had used the same *mold* for all of them.

Sophie felt so pleased with herself for having remembered the incident that she pronounced herself done with the first question. If a baker makes fifty absolutely identical cookies, he must be using the same pastry mold for all of them. And that's that!

Then the video-Plato had looked into the camera and asked why all horses were the same. But they weren't at all! On the contrary, Sophie thought no two horses were the same, just as no two people were the same.

She was ready to give up on that one when she remembered what she had thought about the cookies. No one of them was exactly like any of the others. Some were a bit thicker than the others, and some were broken. But still, everyone could see that they were—in a way— "exactly the same."

What Plato was really asking was perhaps why a horse was always a horse, and not, for example, a cross between a horse and a pig. Because even though some horses were as brown as bears and others were as white as lambs, all horses had something in common. Sophie had yet to meet a horse with six or eight legs, for example.

But surely Plato couldn't believe that what made all

horses alike was that they were made with the same mold?

Then Plato had asked her a really difficult question. Does man have an immortal soul? *That* was something Sophie felt quite unqualified to answer. All she knew was that dead bodies were either cremated or buried, so there was no future for them. If man had an immortal soul, one would have to believe that a person consisted of two separate parts: a body that gets worn out after many years—and a soul that operates more or less independently of what happens to the body. Her grandmother had said once that she felt it was only her body that was old. Inside she had always been the same young girl.

The thought of the "young girl" led Sophie to the last question: Are women and men equally sensible? She was not so sure about that. It depended on what Plato meant by sensible.

Something the philosopher had said about Socrates came into her mind. Socrates had pointed out that everyone could understand philosophical truths if they just used their common sense. He had also said that a slave had the same common sense as a nobleman. Sophie was sure that he would also have said that women had the same common sense as men.

While she sat thinking, there was a sudden rustling in the hedge, and the sound of something puffing and blowing like a steam engine. The next second, the golden Labrador slipped into the den. It had a large envelope in its mouth.

"Hermes!" cried Sophie. "Drop it! Drop it!"

The dog dropped the envelope in Sophie's lap, and Sophie stretched out her hand to pat the dog's head.

"Good boy, Hermes!" she said.

The dog lay down and allowed itself to be patted. But after a couple of minutes it got up and began to push its way back through the hedge the same way it had come in. Sophie followed with the brown envelope in her hand. She crawled through the dense thicket and was soon outside the garden.

Hermes had already started to run toward the edge of

the woods, and Sophie followed a few yards behind. Twice the dog turned around and growled, but Sophie was not to be deterred.

This time she was determined to find the philosopher—even if it meant running all the way to Athens.

The dog ran faster and suddenly turned off down a narrow path. Sophie chased him, but after a few minutes he turned and faced her, barking like a watchdog. Sophie still refused to give up, taking the opportunity to lessen the distance between them.

Hermes turned and raced down the path. Sophie realized that she would never catch up with him. She stood quite still for what seemed like an eternity, listening to him running farther and farther away. Then all was silent.

She sat down on a tree stump by a little clearing in the woods. She still had the brown envelope in her hand. She opened it, drew out several typewritten pages, and began to read:

PLATO'S ACADEMY

Thank you for the pleasant time we spent together, Sophie. In Athens, I mean. So now I have at least introduced myself. And since I have also introduced Plato, we might as well begin without further ado.

Plato (428–347 B.C.) was twenty-nine years old when Socrates drank the hemlock. He had been a pupil of Socrates for some time and had followed his trial very closely. The fact that Athens could condemn its noblest citizen to death did more than make a profound impression on him. It was to shape the course of his entire philosophic endeavor.

To Plato, the death of Socrates was a striking example of the conflict that can exist between society as it really is and the *true* or *ideal* society. Plato's first deed as a philosopher was to publish Socrates' *Apology*, an account of his plea to the large jury.

As you will no doubt recall, Socrates never wrote anything down, although many of the pre-Socratics did. The problem is that hardly any of their written material remains. But in the case of Plato, we believe that all his principal works have been preserved. (In addition to Socrates' *Apology*, Plato wrote a collection of *Epistles* and about twenty-five philosophical *Dialogues*.) That we have these works today is due not least to the fact that Plato set up his own school of philosophy in a grove not far from Athens, named after the legendary Greek hero Academus. The school was therefore known as the Academy. (Since then, many thousands of "academies" have been established all over the world. We still speak of "academics" and "academic subjects.")

The subjects taught at Plato's Academy were philosophy, mathematics, and gymnastics—although perhaps "taught" is hardly the right word. Lively discourse was considered most important at Plato's Academy. So it was not purely by chance that Plato's writings took the form of dialogues.

The Eternally True, Eternally Beautiful, and Eternally Good

In the introduction to this course I mentioned that it could often be a good idea to ask what a particular philosopher's project was. So now I ask: what were the problems Plato was concerned with?

Briefly, we can establish that Plato was concerned with the relationship between what is eternal and immutable, on the one hand, and what "flows," on the other. (Just like the pre-Socratics, in fact.) We've seen how the Sophists and Socrates turned their attention from questions of natural philosophy to problems related to man and society. And yet in one sense, even Socrates and the Sophists were preoccupied with the relationship between the eternal and immutable, and the "flowing." They were interested in the problem as it related to human *morals* and society's ideals or virtues. Very briefly, the Sophists thought that perceptions of what was right or wrong varied from one city-state to another, and from one generation to the next. So right and wrong was something that "flowed." This was totally unacceptable to Socrates. He believed in the existence of eternal and absolute rules for what was right or wrong. By using our common sense we can all arrive at these immutable *norms*, since human reason is in fact eternal and immutable.

Do you follow, Sophie? Then along comes Plato. He is concerned with *both* what is eternal and immutable in nature *and* what is eternal and immutable as regards morals and society. To Plato, these two problems were one and the same. He tried to grasp a "reality" that was eternal and immutable.

And to be quite frank, that is precisely what we need philosophers for. We do not need them to choose a beauty queen or the day's bargain in tomatoes. (This is why they are often unpopular!) Philosophers will try to ignore highly topical affairs and instead try to draw people's attention to what is eternally "true," eternally "beautiful," and eternally "good."

We can thus begin to glimpse at least the outline of Plato's philosophical project. But let's take one thing at a time. We are attempting to understand an extraordinary mind, a mind that was to have a profound influence on all subsequent European philosophy.

The World of Ideas

Both Empedocles and Democritus had drawn attention to the fact that although in the natural world everything "flows," there must nevertheless be "something" that never changes (the "four roots," or the "atoms"). Plato agreed with the proposition as such—but in quite a different way.

Plato believed that *everything* tangible in nature "flows." So there are no "substances" that do not dissolve. Absolutely everything that belongs to the "material world" is made of a material that time can erode, but everything is made after a timeless "mold" or "form" that is eternal and immutable.

You see? No, you don't.

Why are horses the same, Sophie? You probably don't

think they are at all. But there is something that all horses have in common, something that enables us to identify them as horses. A particular horse "flows," naturally. It might be old and lame, and in time it will die. But the "form" of the horse is eternal and immutable.

That which is eternal and immutable, to Plato, is therefore not a physical "basic substance," as it was for Empedocles and Democritus. Plato's conception was of eternal and immutable patterns, spiritual and abstract in their nature, that all things are fashioned after.

Let me put it like this: The pre-Socratics had given a reasonably good explanation of natural change without having to presuppose that anything actually "changed." In the midst of nature's cycle there were some eternal and immutable smallest elements that did not dissolve, they thought. Fair enough, Sophie! But they had no reasonable explanation for *how* these "smallest elements" that were once building blocks in a horse could suddenly whirl together four or five hundred years later and fashion themselves into a completely new horse. Or an elephant or a crocodile, for that matter. Plato's point was that Democritus' atoms never fashioned themselves into an "eledile" or a "crocophant." This was what set his philosophical reflections going.

If you already understand what I am getting at, you may skip this next paragraph. But just in case, I will clarify: You have a box of Lego and you build a Lego horse. You then take it apart and put the blocks back in the box. You cannot expect to make a new horse just by shaking the box. How could Lego blocks of their own accord find each other and become a new horse again? No, *you* have to rebuild the horse, Sophie. And the reason you can do it is that you have a picture in your mind of what the horse looked like. The Lego horse is made from a model which remains unchanged from horse to horse.

How did you do with the fifty identical cookies? Let us assume that you have dropped in from outer space and have never seen a baker before. You stumble into a tempting bakery—and there you catch sight of fifty identical gingerbread men on a shelf. I imagine you would wonder how they could be exactly alike. It might well be that one of them has an arm missing, another has lost a bit of its head, and a third has a funny bump on its stomach. But after careful thought, you would nevertheless conclude that all gingerbread men have something *in common*. Although none of them is perfect, you would suspect that they had a common origin. You would realize that all the cookies were formed in the same mold. And what is more, Sophie, you are now seized by the irresistible desire to see this mold. Because clearly, the mold itself must be utter perfection—and in a sense, more beautiful—in comparison with these crude copies.

If you solved this problem all by yourself, you arrived at the philosophical solution in exactly the same way that Plato did.

Like most philosophers, he "dropped in from outer space." (He stood up on the very tip of one of the fine hairs of the rabbit's fur.) He was astonished at the way all natural phenomena could be so alike, and he concluded that it had to be because there are a limited number of *forms* "behind" everything we see around us. Plato called these forms *ideas*. Behind every horse, pig, or human being, there is the "idea horse," "idea pig," and "idea human being." (In the same way, the bakery we spoke of can have gingerbread men, gingerbread horses, and gingerbread pigs. Because every self-respecting bakery has more than one mold. But one mold is enough for each *type* of gingerbread cookie.)

Plato came to the conclusion that there must be a reality behind the "material world." He called this reality *the world of ideas*; it contained the eternal and immutable "patterns" behind the various phenomena we come across in nature. This remarkable view is known as Plato's *theory of ideas*.

True Knowledge

I'm sure you've been following me, Sophie dear. But you may be wondering whether Plato was being serious. Did he really believe that forms like these actually existed in a completely different reality?

He probably didn't believe it literally in the same way for all his life, but in some of his dialogues that is certainly how he means to be understood. Let us try to follow his train of thought.

A philosopher, as we have seen, tries to grasp something that is eternal and immutable. It would serve no purpose, for instance, to write a philosophic treatise on the existence of a particular soap bubble. Partly because one would hardly have time to study it in depth before it burst, and partly because it would probably be rather difficult to find a market for a philosophic treatise on something nobody has ever seen, and which only existed for five seconds.

Plato believed that everything we see around us in nature, everything tangible, can be likened to a soap bubble, since nothing that exists in the world of the senses is lasting. We know, of course, that sooner or later every human being and every animal will die and decompose. Even a block of marble changes and gradually disintegrates. (The Acropolis is falling into ruin, Sophie! It is a scandal, but that's the way it is.) Plato's point is that we can never have true knowledge of anything that is in a constant state of change. We can only have *opinions* about things that belong to the world of the senses, tangible things. We can only have true *knowledge* of things that can be understood with our reason.

All right, Sophie, I'll explain it more clearly: a gingerbread man can be so lopsided after all that baking that it can be quite hard to see what it is meant to be. But having seen dozens of gingerbread men that were more or less successful, I can be pretty sure what the cookie mold was like. I can guess, even though I have never seen it. It might not even be an advantage to see the actual mold with my own eyes because we cannot always trust the evidence of our senses. The faculty of vision can vary from person to person. On the other hand, we can rely on what our reason tells us because that is the same for everyone.

If you are sitting in a classroom with thirty other pupils, and the teacher asks the class which color of the rainbow is the prettiest, he will probably get a lot of different answers. But if he asks what 8 times 3 is, the whole class will—we hope—give the same answer. Because now reason is speaking and reason is, in a way, the direct opposite of "thinking so" or "feeling." We could say that reason is eternal and universal precisely because it only expresses eternal and universal states.

Plato found mathematics very absorbing because mathematical states never change. They are therefore states we can have true knowledge of. But here we need an example.

Imagine you find a round pinecone out in the woods. Perhaps you say you "think" it looks completely round, whereas Joanna insists it is a bit flattened on one side. (Then you start arguing about it!) But you cannot have true knowledge of anything you can perceive with your eyes. On the other hand you can say with absolute certainty that the sum of the angles in a circle is 360 degrees. In this case you would be talking about an *ideal* circle which might not exist in the physical world but which you can clearly visualize. (You are dealing with the hidden gingerbread-man mold and not with the particular cookie on the kitchen table.)

In short, we can only have inexact conceptions of things we perceive with our senses. But we can have true knowledge of things we *understand* with our reason. The sum of the angles in a triangle will remain 180 degrees to the end of time. And similarly the "idea" horse will walk on four legs even if all the horses in the sensory world break a leg.

An Immortal Soul

As I explained, Plato believed that reality is divided into two regions.

One region is the *world of the senses*, about which we can only have approximate or incomplete knowledge by using our five (approximate or incomplete) senses. In this sensory world, "everything flows" and nothing is permanent. Nothing in the sensory world *is*, there are only things that come to be and pass away.

The other region is the *world of ideas*, about which we can have true knowledge by using our reason. This world of ideas cannot be perceived by the senses, but the ideas (or forms) are eternal and immutable.

According to Plato, man is a dual creature. We have a body that "flows," is inseparably bound to the world of the senses, and is subject to the same fate as everything else in this world—a soap bubble, for example. All our senses are based in the body and are consequently unreliable. But we also have an immortal *soul*—and this soul is the realm of reason. And not being physical, the soul can survey the world of ideas.

But that's not all, Sophie. IT'S NOT ALL!

Plato also believed that the soul existed *before* it inhabited the body. (It was lying on a shelf in the closet with all the cookie molds.) But as soon as the soul wakes up in a human body, it has forgotten all the perfect ideas. Then something starts to happen. In fact, a wondrous process begins. As the human being discovers the various forms in the natural world, a vague recollection stirs his soul. He sees a horse—but an imperfect horse. (A gingerbread horse!) The sight of it is sufficient to awaken in the soul a faint recollection of the perfect "horse," which the soul once saw in the world of ideas, and this stirs the soul with a yearning to return to its true realm. Plato calls this yearning *eros*—which means love. The soul, then, experiences a "longing to return to its true origin." From now on, the body and the whole sensory world is experienced as imperfect and insignificant. The soul yearns to fly home on the wings of love to the world of ideas. It longs to be freed from the chains of the body.

Let me quickly emphasize that Plato is describing an ideal course of life, since by no means all humans set the soul free to begin its journey back to the world of ideas. Most people cling to the sensory world's "reflections" of ideas. They see a horse—and another horse. But they never see that of which every horse is only a feeble imitation. (They rush into the kitchen and stuff themselves with gingerbread cookies without so much as a thought as to where they came from.) What Plato describes is the *philosophers'* way. His philosophy can be read as a description of philosophic practice.

When you see a shadow, Sophie, you will assume that there must be something casting the shadow. You see the shadow of an animal. You think it may be a horse, but you are not quite sure. So you turn around and see the horse itself—which of course is infinitely more beautiful and sharper in outline than the blurred "horse-shadow." *Plato believed similarly that all natural phenomena are merely shadows of the eternal forms or ideas.* But most people are content with a life among shadows. They give no thought to what is casting the shadows. They think shadows are all there are, never realizing even that they are, in fact, shadows. And thus they pay no heed to the immortality of their own soul.

Out of the Darkness of the Cave

Plato relates a myth which illustrates this. We call it the *Myth of the Cave.* I'll retell it in my own words.

Imagine some people living in an underground cave. They sit with their backs to the mouth of the cave with their hands and feet bound in such a way that they can only look at the back wall of the cave. Behind them is a high wall, and behind that wall pass human-like creatures, holding up various figures above the top of the wall. Because there is a fire behind these figures, they cast flickering shadows on the back wall of the cave. So the only thing the cave dwellers can see is this shadow play. They have been sitting in this position since they were born, so they think these shadows are all there are.

Imagine now that one of the cave dwellers manages to free himself from his bonds. The first thing he asks himself is where all these shadows on the cave wall come from. What do you think happens when he turns around and sees the figures being held up above the wall? To begin with he is dazzled by the sharp sunlight. He is also dazzled by the clarity of the figures because until now he has only seen their shadow. If he manages to climb over the wall and get past the fire into the world outside, he will be even more dazzled. But after rubbing his eyes he will be struck by the beauty of everything. For the first time he will see colors and clear shapes. He will see the real animals and flowers that the cave shadows were only poor reflections of. But even now he will ask himself where all the animals and flowers come from. Then he will see the sun in the sky, and realize that this is what gives life to these flowers and animals, just as the fire made the shadows visible.

The joyful cave dweller could now have gone skipping away into the countryside, delighting in his new-found freedom. But instead he thinks of all the others who are still down in the cave. He goes back. Once there, he tries to convince the cave dwellers that the shadows on the cave wall are but flickering reflections of "real" things. But they don't believe him. They point to the cave wall and say that what they see is all there is. Finally they kill him.

What Plato was illustrating in the Myth of the Cave is the philosopher's road from shadowy images to the true ideas behind all natural phenomena. He was probably also thinking of Socrates, whom the "cave dwellers" killed because he disturbed their conventional ideas and tried to light the way to true insight. The Myth of the Cave illustrates Socrates' courage and his sense of pedagogic responsibility.

Plato's point was that the relationship between the darkness of the cave and the world beyond corresponds to the relationship between the forms of the natural world and the world of ideas. Not that he meant that the natural world is dark and dreary, but that it is dark and dreary *in comparison with* the clarity of ideas. A picture of a beautiful landscape is not dark and dreary either. But it is only a picture.

The Philosophic State

The Myth of the Cave is found in Plato's dialogue the *Republic*. In this dialogue Plato also presents a picture of the "ideal state," that is to say an imaginary, ideal, or what we would call a Utopian, state. Briefly, we could say that Plato believed the state should be governed by philosophers. He bases his explanation of this on the construction of the human body.

According to Plato, the human body is composed of three parts: the head, the chest, and the abdomen. For each of these three parts there is a corresponding faculty of the soul. *Reason* belongs to the head, *will* belongs to the chest, and *appetite* belongs to the abdomen. Each of these soul faculties also has an ideal, or "virtue." Reason aspires to *wisdom*, Will aspires to *courage*, and Appetite must be curbed so that *temperance* can be exercised. Only when the three parts of the body function together as a unity do we get a harmonious or "virtuous" individual. At school, a child must first learn to curb its appetites, then it must develop courage, and finally reason leads to wisdom.

Plato now imagines a state built up exactly like the tripartite human body. Where the body has head, chest, and abdomen, the State has *rulers, auxiliaries,* and *laborers* (farmers, for example). Here Plato clearly uses Greek medical science as his model. Just as a healthy and harmonious man exercises balance and temperance, so a "virtuous" state is characterized by everyone knowing their place in the overall picture.

Like every aspect of Plato's philosophy, his political philosophy is characterized by *rationalism*. The creation of a good state depends on its being governed with *reason*. Just as the head governs the body, so philosophers must rule society.

Let us attempt a simple illustration of the relationship between the three parts of man and the state:

BODY	SOUL	VIRTUE	STATE
head	reason	wisdom	rulers
chest	will	courage	auxiliaries
abdomen	appetite	temperance	laborers

Plato's ideal state is not unlike the old Hindu caste system, in which each and every person has his or her particular function for the good of the whole. Even before Plato's time the Hindu caste system had the same tripartite division between the auxiliary caste (or priest caste), the warrior caste, and the laborer caste. Nowadays we would perhaps call Plato's state totalitarian. But it is worth noting that he believed women could govern just as effectively as men for the simple reason that the rulers govern by virtue of their *reason*. Women, he asserted, have exactly the same powers of reasoning as men, provided they get the same training and are exempt from child rearing and housekeeping. In Plato's ideal state, rulers and warriors are not allowed family life or private property. The rearing of children is considered too important to be left to the individual and should be the responsibility of the state. (Plato was the first philosopher to advocate state-organized nursery schools and full-time education.)

After a number of significant political setbacks, Plato wrote the *Laws*, in which he described the "constitutional state" as the next-best state. He now reintroduced both private property and family ties. Women's freedom thus became more restricted. However, he did say that a state that does not educate and train women is like a man who only trains his right arm.

All in all, we can say that Plato had a positive view of women—considering the time he lived in. In the dialogue *Symposium*, he gives a woman, the legendary priestess *Diotima*, the honor of having given Socrates his philosophic insight.

So that was Plato, Sophie. His astonishing theories have been discussed—and criticized—for more than two thousand years. The first man to do so was one of the pupils from his own Academy. His name was Aristotle, and he was the third great philosopher from Athens.

I'll say no more!

While Sophie had been reading about Plato, the sun had risen over the woods to the east. It was peeping over the horizon just as she was reading how one man clambered out of the cave and blinked in the dazzling light outside.

It was almost as if she had herself emerged from an underground cave. Sophie felt that she saw nature in a completely different way after reading about Plato. It was rather like having been color-blind. She had seen some shadows but had not seen the clear ideas.

She was not sure Plato was right in everything he had said about the eternal patterns, but it was a beautiful thought that all living things were imperfect copies of the eternal forms in the world of ideas. Because wasn't it true that all flowers, trees, human beings, and animals were "imperfect"?

Everything she saw around her was so beautiful and so alive that Sophie had to rub her eyes to really believe it. But nothing she was looking at now would *last*. And yet—in a hundred years the same flowers and the same animals would be here again. Even if every single flower and every single animal should fade away and be forgotten, there would be something that "recollected" how it all looked.

Sophie gazed out at the world. Suddenly a squirrel ran up the trunk of a pine tree. It circled the trunk a few times and disappeared into the branches.

"I've seen you before!" thought Sophie. She realized that maybe it was not the same squirrel that she had seen previously, but she had seen the same "form." For all she knew, Plato could have been right. Maybe she really had seen the eternal "squirrel" before—in the world of ideas, before her soul had taken residence in a human body.

Could it be true that she had lived before? Had her soul existed before it got a body to move around in? And was it really true that she carried a little golden nugget inside her—a jewel that cannot be corroded by time, a soul that would live on when her own body grew old and died?

The Major's Cabin

∞

... the girl in the mirror winked with both eyes ...

It was only a quarter past seven. There was no need to hurry home. Sophie's mother always took it easy on Sundays, so she would probably sleep for another two hours.

Should she go a bit farther into the woods and try to find Alberto Knox? And why had the dog snarled at her so viciously?

Sophie got up and began to walk down the path Hermes had taken. She had the brown envelope with the pages on Plato in her hand. Wherever the path diverged she took the wider one.

Birds were chirping everywhere—in the trees and in the air, in bush and thicket. They were busily occupied with their morning pursuits. They knew no difference between weekdays and Sundays. Who had taught them to do all that? Was there a tiny computer inside each one of them, programming them to do certain things?

The path led up over a little hill, then steeply down between tall pine trees. The woods were so dense now that she could only see a few yards between the trees.

Suddenly she caught sight of something glittering between the pine trunks. It must be a little lake. The path went the other way but Sophie picked her way among the trees. Without really knowing why, she let her feet lead her.

The lake was no bigger than a soccer field. Over on

the other side she could see a red-painted cabin in a small clearing surrounded by silver birches. A faint wisp of smoke was rising from the chimney.

Sophie went down to the water's edge. It was very muddy in many places, but then she noticed a rowboat. It was drawn halfway out of the water. There was a pair of oars in it.

Sophie looked around. Whatever she did, it would be impossible to get around the lake to the red cabin without getting her shoes soaked. She went resolutely over to the boat and pushed it into the water. Then she climbed aboard, set the oars in the rowlocks, and rowed across the lake. The boat soon touched the opposite bank. Sophie went ashore and tried to pull the boat up after her. The bank was much steeper here than the opposite bank had been.

She glanced over her shoulder only once before walking up toward the cabin.

She was quite startled at her own boldness. How did she dare do this? She had no idea. It was as if "something" impelled her.

Sophie went up to the door and knocked. She waited a while but nobody answered. She tried the handle cautiously, and the door opened.

"Hallo!" she called. "Is anyone at home?"

She went in and found herself in a living room. She dared not shut the door behind her.

Somebody was obviously living here. Sophie could hear wood crackling in the old stove. Someone had been here very recently.

On a big dining table stood a typewriter, some books, a couple of pencils, and a pile of paper. A smaller table and two chairs stood by the window that overlooked the lake. Apart from that there was very little furniture, although the whole of one wall was lined with bookshelves filled with books. Above a white chest of drawers hung a large round mirror in a heavy brass frame. It looked very old.

On one of the walls hung two pictures. One was an oil painting of a white house which lay a stone's throw from a little bay with a red boathouse. Between the house and the boathouse was a sloping garden with an apple tree, a few thick bushes, and some rocks. A dense fringe of birch trees framed the garden like a garland. The title of the painting was "Bjerkely."

Beside that painting hung an old portrait of a man sitting in a chair by a window. He had a book in his lap. This picture also had a little bay with trees and rocks in the background. It looked as though it had been painted several hundred years ago. The title of the picture was "Berkeley." The painter's name was Smibert.

Berkeley and Bjerkely. How strange!

Sophie continued her investigation. A door led from the living room to a small kitchen. Someone had just done the dishes. Plates and glasses were piled on a tea towel, some of them still glistening with drops of soapy water. There was a tin bowl on the floor with some left-over scraps of food in it. Whoever lived here had a pet, a dog or a cat.

Sophie went back to the living room. Another door led to a tiny bedroom. On the floor next to the bed there were a couple of blankets in a thick bundle. Sophie discovered some golden hairs on the blankets. Here was the evidence! Now Sophie knew that the occupants of the cabin were Alberto Knox and Hermes.

Back in the living room, Sophie stood in front of the mirror. The glass was matte and scratched, and her reflection correspondingly blurred. Sophie began to make faces at herself like she did at home in the bathroom. Her reflection did exactly the same, which was only to be expected.

But all of a sudden something scary happened. Just once—in the space of a split second—Sophie saw quite clearly that the girl in the mirror winked with both eyes. Sophie started back in fright. If she herself had winked—how could she have *seen* the other girl wink? And not only that, it seemed as though the other girl had winked at Sophie as if to say: I can see you, Sophie. I am in here, on the other side.

Sophie felt her heart beating, and at the same time she heard a dog barking in the distance. Hermes! She had to get out of here at once. Then she noticed a green wallet on the chest of drawers under the mirror. It contained a hundred-crown note, a fifty, and a school I.D. card. It showed a picture of a girl with fair hair. Under the picture was the girl's name: Hilde Møller Knag . . .

Sophie shivered. Again she heard the dog bark. She had to get out, at once!

As she hurried past the table she noticed a white envelope between all the books and the pile of paper. It had one word written on it: SOPHIE.

Before she had time to realize what she was doing, she grabbed the envelope and stuffed it into the brown envelope with the Plato pages. Then she rushed out of the door and slammed it behind her.

The barking was getting closer. But worst of all was that the boat was gone. After a second or two she saw it, adrift halfway across the lake. One of the oars was floating beside it. All because she hadn't been able to pull it completely up on land. She heard the dog barking quite nearby now and saw movements between the trees on the other side of the lake.

Sophie didn't hesitate any longer. With the big envelope in her hand, she plunged into the bushes behind the cabin. Soon she was having to wade through marshy ground, sinking in several times to well above her ankles. But she had to keep going. She had to get home.

Presently she stumbled onto a path. Was it the path she had taken earlier? She stopped to wring out her dress. And then she began to cry.

How could she have been so stupid? The worst of all was the boat. She couldn't forget the sight of the rowboat with the one oar drifting helplessly on the lake. It was all so embarrassing, so shameful . . .

The philosophy teacher had probably reached the lake by now. He would need the boat to get home. Sophie felt almost like a criminal. But she hadn't done it on purpose.

The envelope! That was probably even worse. Why had she taken it? Because her name was on it, of course, so in a way it was hers. But even so, she felt like a thief. And what's more, she had provided the evidence that it was *she* who had been there.

Sophie drew the note out of the envelope. It said:

What came first—the chicken or the "idea"
    chicken?
Are we born with innate "ideas"?
What is the difference between a plant, an
    animal, and a human?
Why does it rain?
What does it take to live a good life?

Sophie couldn't possibly think about these questions right now, but she assumed they had something to do with the next philosopher. Wasn't he called Aristotle?

When she finally saw the hedge after running so far through the woods it was like swimming ashore after a shipwreck. The hedge looked funny from the other side.

She didn't look at her watch until she had crawled into the den. It was ten-thirty. She put the big envelope into the biscuit tin with the other papers and stuffed the note with the new questions down her tights.

Her mother was on the telephone when she came in. When she saw Sophie she hung up quickly.

"Where on earth have you been?"

"I . . . went for a walk . . . in the woods," she stammered.

"So I see."

Sophie stood silently, watching the water dripping from her dress.

"I called Joanna . . ."

"Joanna?"

Her mother brought her some dry clothes. Sophie only just managed to hide the philosopher's note. Then they sat together in the kitchen, and her mother made some hot chocolate.

"Were you with him?" she asked after a while.

"Him?"

Sophie could only think about her philosophy teacher.

"With *him*, yes. Him. . . . your rabbit!"

Sophie shook her head.

"What do you do when you're together, Sophie? Why are you so wet?"

Sophie sat staring gravely at the table. But deep down

inside she was laughing. Poor Mom, now she had *that* to worry about.

She shook her head again. Then more questions came raining down on her.

"Now I want the truth. Were you out all night? Why did you go to bed with your clothes on? Did you sneak out as soon as I had gone to bed? You're only fourteen, Sophie. I demand to know who you are seeing!"

Sophie started to cry. Then she talked. She was still frightened, and when you are frightened you usually talk.

She explained that she had woken up very early and had gone for a walk in the woods. She told her mother about the cabin and the boat, and about the mysterious mirror. But she mentioned nothing about the secret correspondence course. Neither did she mention the green wallet. She didn't quite know why, but she *had* to keep Hilde for herself.

Her mother put her arms around Sophie, and Sophie knew that her mother believed her now.

"I don't have a boyfriend," Sophie sniffed. "It was just something I said because you were so upset about the white rabbit."

"And you really went all the way to the major's cabin . . ." said her mother thoughtfully.

"The major's cabin?" Sophie stared at her mother.

"The little woodland cabin is called the major's cabin because some years ago an army major lived there for a time. He was rather eccentric, a little crazy, I think. But never mind that. Since then the cabin has been unoccupied."

"But it isn't! There's a philosopher living there now."

"Oh stop, don't start fantasizing again!"

Sophie stayed in her room, thinking about what had happened. Her head felt like a roaring circus full of lumbering elephants, silly clowns, daring trapeze flyers, and trained monkeys. But one image recurred unceasingly— a small rowboat with one oar drifting in a lake deep in the woods—and someone needing the boat to get home.

She felt sure that the philosophy teacher didn't wish

her any harm, and would certainly forgive her if he knew she had been to his cabin. But she had broken an agreement. That was all the thanks he got for taking on her philosophic education. How could she make up for it?

Sophie took out her pink notepaper and began to write:

Dear Philosopher, It was me who was in your cabin early Sunday morning. I wanted so much to meet you and discuss some of the philosophic problems. For the moment I am a Plato fan, but I am not so sure he was right about ideas or pattern pictures existing in another reality. Of course they exist in our souls, but I think—for the moment anyway— that this is a different thing. I have to admit too that I am not altogether convinced of the immortality of the soul. Personally, I have no recollections from my former lives. If you could convince me that my deceased grandmother's soul is happy in the world of ideas, I would be most grateful.

Actually, it was not for philosophic reasons that I started to write this letter (which I shall put in a pink envelope with a lump of sugar). I just wanted to say I was sorry for being disobedient. I tried to pull the boat completely up on shore but I was obviously not strong enough. Or perhaps a big wave dragged the boat out again.

I hope you managed to get home without getting your feet wet. If not, it might comfort you to know that I got soaked and will probably have a terrible cold. But that'll be my own fault.

I didn't touch anything in the cabin, but I am sorry to say that I couldn't resist the temptation to take the envelope that was on the table. It wasn't because I wanted to steal anything, but as my name was on it, I thought in my confusion that it belonged to me. I am really and truly sorry, and I promise never to disappoint you again.

P.S. I will think all the new questions through very carefully, starting now.

P.P.S. Is the mirror with the brass frame above

the white chest of drawers an ordinary mirror or a magic mirror? I'm only asking because I am not used to seeing my own reflection wink with both eyes.

    With regards from your sincerely interested pupil, SOPHIE

Sophie read the letter through twice before she put it in the envelope. She thought it was less formal than the previous letter she had written. Before she went downstairs to the kitchen to get a lump of sugar she looked at the note with the day's questions:

    "What came first—the chicken or the "idea" chicken?

This question was just as tricky as the old riddle of the chicken and the egg. There would be no chicken without the egg, and no egg without the chicken. Was it really just as complicated to figure out whether the chicken or the "idea" chicken came first? Sophie understood what Plato meant. He meant that the "idea" chicken had existed in the world of ideas long before chickens existed in the sensory world. According to Plato, the soul had "seen" the "idea" chicken before it took up residence in a body. But wasn't this just where Sophie thought Plato must be mistaken? How could a person who had never seen a live chicken or a picture of a chicken ever have any "idea" of a chicken? Which brought her to the next question:

    Are we born with innate "ideas"? Most unlikely, thought Sophie. She could hardly imagine a newborn baby being especially well equipped with ideas. One could obviously never be sure, because the fact that the baby had no language did not necessarily mean that it had no ideas in its head. But surely we have to see things in the world before we can know anything about them.

    "What is the difference between a plant, an animal, and a human?" Sophie could immediately see very clear differences.

    For instance, she did not think a plant had a very complicated emotional life. Who had ever heard of a bluebell with a broken heart? A plant grows, takes nourishment, and produces seeds so that it can reproduce itself. That's about all one could say about plants. Sophie concluded that everything that applied to plants also applied to animals and humans. But animals had other attributes as well. They could move, for example. (When did a rose ever run a marathon?) It was a bit harder to point to any differences between animals and humans. Humans could think, but couldn't animals do so as well? Sophie was convinced that her cat Sherekan could think. At least, it could be very calculating. But could it reflect on philosophical questions? Could a cat speculate about the difference between a plant, an animal, and a human? Hardly! A cat could probably be either contented or unhappy, but did it ever ask itself if there was a God or whether it had an immortal soul? Sophie thought that was extremely doubtful. But the same problem was raised here as with the baby and the innate ideas. It was just as difficult to talk to a cat about such questions as it would be to discuss them with a baby.

"Why does it rain?" Sophie shrugged her shoulders. It probably rains because seawater evaporates and the clouds condense into raindrops. Hadn't she learnt that in the third grade? Of course, one could always say that it rains so that plants and animals can grow. But was that true? Had a shower any actual purpose?

The last question definitely had something to do with purpose: "What does it take to live a good life?"

The philosopher had written something about this quite early on in the course. Everybody needs food, warmth, love, and care. Such basics were the primary condition for a good life, at any rate. Then he had pointed out that people also needed to find answers to certain philosophical questions. It was probably also quite important to have a job you liked. If you hated traffic, for instance, you would not be very happy as a taxi driver. And if you hated doing homework it would probably be a bad idea to become a teacher. Sophie loved animals and wanted to be a vet. But in any case she didn't think it was necessary to win a million in the lottery to live a good life.

Quite the opposite, more likely. There was a saying:

The devil finds work for idle hands.

Sophie stayed in her room until her mother called her down to a big midday meal. She had prepared sirloin steak and baked potatoes. There were cloudberries and cream for dessert.

They talked about all kinds of things. Sophie's mother asked her how she wanted to celebrate her fifteenth birthday. It was only a few weeks away.

Sophie shrugged.

"Aren't you going to invite anyone? I mean, don't you want to have a party?"

"Maybe."

"We could ask Martha and Anne Marie . . . and Helen. And Joanna, of course. And Jeremy, perhaps. But that's for you to decide. I remember my own fifteenth birthday so clearly, you know. It doesn't seem all that long ago. I felt I was already quite grown up. Isn't it odd, Sophie! I don't feel I have changed at all since then."

"You haven't. Nothing changes. You have just developed, gotten older . . ."

"Mm . . . that was a very grownup thing to say. I just think it's all happened so very quickly."

Aristotle

∞

*. . . a meticulous organizer who wanted to clarify
our concepts . . .*

While her mother was taking her afternoon nap, Sophie
went down to the den. She had put a lump of sugar in
the pink envelope and written "To Alberto" on the outside.

There was no new letter, but after a few minutes Sophie heard the dog approaching.

"Hermes!" she called, and the next moment he had
pushed his way into the den with a big brown envelope
in his mouth.

"Good boy!" Sophie put her arm around the dog,
which was snorting and snuffling like a walrus. She took
the pink envelope with the lump of sugar and put it in
the dog's mouth. He crawled through the hedge and
made off into the woods again.

Sophie opened the big envelope apprehensively, wondering whether it would contain anything about the cabin
and the boat.

It contained the usual typed pages held together with
a paperclip. But there was also a loose page inside. On
it was written:

Dear Miss Sleuth, or, to be more exact, Miss Bur-
glar. The case has already been handed over to the
police.

Not really. No, I'm not angry. If you are just as

curious when it comes to discovering answers to
the riddles of philosophy, I'd say your adventure
was very promising. It's just a little annoying that
I'll have to move now. Still, I have no one to blame
but myself, I suppose. I might have known you
were a person who would always want to get to the
bottom of things.

Greetings, Alberto

Sophie was relieved. So he was not angry after all.
But why would he have to move?

She took the papers and ran up to her room. It would
be prudent to be in the house when her mother woke up.
Lying comfortably on her bed, she began to read about
Aristotle.

PHILOSOPHER AND SCIENTIST

Dear Sophie: You were probably astonished by Plato's
theory of ideas. You are not the only one! I do not know
whether you swallowed the whole thing—hook, line, and
sinker—or whether you had any critical comments. But if
you did have, you can be sure that the self-same criticism
was raised by *Aristotle* (384–322 B.C.), who was a pupil
at Plato's Academy for almost twenty years.

Aristotle was not a native of Athens. He was born in
Macedonia and came to Plato's Academy when Plato
was 61. Aristotle's father was a respected physician—
and therefore a scientist. This background already tells us
something about Aristotle's philosophic project. What he
was most interested in was nature study. He was not only
the last of the great Greek philosophers, he was Europe's
first great biologist.

Taking it to extremes, we could say that Plato was so
engrossed in his eternal forms, or "ideas," that he took
very little notice of the changes in nature. Aristotle, on the
other hand, was preoccupied with just these changes—or
with what we nowadays describe as natural processes.

To exaggerate even more, we could say that Plato
turned his back on the sensory world and shut his eyes to

everything we see around us. (He wanted to escape from the cave and look out over the eternal world of ideas!) Aristotle did the opposite: he got down on all fours and studied frogs and fish, anemones and poppies.

While Plato used his reason, Aristotle used his senses as well.

We find decisive differences between the two, not least in their writing. Plato was a poet and mythologist; Aristotle's writings were as dry and precise as an encyclopedia. On the other hand, much of what he wrote was based on up-to-the-minute field studies.

Records from antiquity refer to 170 titles supposedly written by Aristotle. Of these, 47 are preserved. These are not complete books; they consist largely of lecture notes. In his time, philosophy was still mainly an oral activity.

The significance of Aristotle in European culture is due not least to the fact that he created the terminology that scientists use today. He was the great organizer who founded and classified the various sciences.

Since Aristotle wrote on all the sciences, I will limit myself to some of the most important areas. Now that I have told you such a lot about Plato, you must start by hearing how Aristotle refuted Plato's theory of ideas. Later we will look at the way he formulated his own natural philosophy, since it was Aristotle who summed up what the natural philosophers before him had said. We'll see how he categorizes our concepts and founds the discipline of Logic as a science. And finally I'll tell you a little about Aristotle's view of man and society.

No Innate Ideas

Like the philosophers before him, Plato wanted to find the eternal and immutable in the midst of all change. So he found the perfect ideas that were superior to the sensory world. Plato furthermore held that ideas were more real than all the phenomena of nature. First came the idea "horse," then came all the sensory world's horses trotting along like shadows on a cave wall. The idea "chicken" came before both the chicken and the egg.

Aristotle thought Plato had turned the whole thing upside down. He agreed with his teacher that the particular horse "flows" and that no horse lives forever. He also agreed that the actual form of the horse is eternal and immutable. But the "idea" horse was simply a concept that we humans had formed *after* seeing a certain number of horses. The "idea" or "form" horse thus had no existence of its own. To Aristotle, the "idea" or the "form" horse was made up of the horse's characteristics—which define what we today call the horse *species*.

To be more precise: by "form" horse, Aristotle meant that which is common to all horses. And here the metaphor of the gingerbread mold does not hold up because the mold exists independently of the particular gingerbread cookies. Aristotle did not believe in the existence of any such molds or forms that, as it were, lay on their own shelf beyond the natural world. On the contrary, to Aristotle the "forms" were *in the things*, because they were the particular characteristics of these things.

So Aristotle disagreed with Plato that the "idea" chicken came before the chicken. What Aristotle called the "form" chicken is present in every single chicken as the chicken's particular set characteristics—for one, that it lays eggs. The real chicken and the "form" chicken are thus just as inseparable as body and soul.

And that is really the essence of Aristotle's criticism of Plato's theory of ideas. But you should not ignore the fact that this was a dramatic turn of thought. The highest degree of reality, in Plato's theory, was that which we *think* with our reason. It was equally apparent to Aristotle that the highest degree of reality is that which we *perceive* with our senses. Plato thought that all the things we see in the natural world were purely reflections of things that existed in the higher reality of the world of ideas—and thereby in the human soul. Aristotle thought the opposite: things that are in the human soul were purely reflections of natural objects. So nature is the real world. According to Aristotle, Plato was trapped in a mythical world picture in which the human imagination was confused with the real world.

Aristotle pointed out that nothing exists in consciousness

that has not first been experienced by the senses. Plato would have said that there is nothing in the natural world that has not first existed in the world of ideas. Aristotle held that Plato was thus "doubling the number of things." He explained a horse by referring to the "idea" horse. But what kind of an explanation is that, Sophie? Where does the "idea" horse come from, is my question. Might there not even be a third horse, which the "idea" horse is just an imitation of?

Aristotle held that all our thoughts and ideas have come into our consciousness through what we have heard and seen. But we also have an innate power of reason. We have no innate ideas, as Plato held, but we have the innate faculty of organizing all sensory impressions into categories and classes. This is how concepts such as "stone," "plant," "animal," and "human" arise. Similarly there arise concepts like "horse," "lobster," and "canary."

Aristotle did not deny that humans have innate reason. On the contrary, it is precisely *reason*, according to Aristotle, that is man's most distinguishing characteristic. But our reason is completely empty until we have sensed something. So man has no innate "ideas."

The Form of a Thing Is Its Specific Characteristics

Having come to terms with Plato's theory of ideas, Aristotle decided that reality consisted of various separate things that constitute a unity of *form* and *substance*. The "substance" is what things are made of, while the "form" is each thing's specific characteristics.

A chicken is fluttering about in front of you, Sophie. The chicken's "form" is precisely that it flutters—and that it cackles and lays eggs. So by the "form" of a chicken, we mean the specific characteristics of its species—or in other words, what it *does*. When the chicken dies—and cackles no more—its "form" ceases to exist. The only thing that remains is the chicken's "substance" (sadly enough, Sophie), but then it is no longer a chicken.

As I said earlier, Aristotle was concerned with the changes in nature. "Substance" always contains the potentiality to realize a specific "form." We could say that "substance" always strives toward achieving an innate potentiality. Every change in nature, according to Aristotle, is a transformation of substance from the "potential" to the "actual."

Yes, I'll explain what I mean, Sophie. See if this funny story helps you. A sculptor is working on a large block of granite. He hacks away at the formless block every day. One day a little boy comes by and says, "What are you looking for?" "Wait and see," answers the sculptor. After a few days the little boy comes back, and now the sculptor has carved a beautiful horse out of the granite. The boy stares at it in amazement, then he turns to the sculptor and says, "How did you know it was in there?"

How indeed! In a sense, the sculptor had seen the horse's form in the block of granite, because that particular block of granite had the potentiality to be formed into the shape of a horse. Similarly Aristotle believed that everything in nature has the potentiality of realizing, or achieving, a specific "form."

Let us return to the chicken and the egg. A chicken's egg has the potentiality to become a chicken. This does not mean that all chicken's eggs become chickens—many of them end up on the breakfast table as fried eggs, omelettes, or scrambled eggs, without ever having realized their potentiality. But it is equally obvious that a chicken's egg cannot become a goose. *That* potentiality is not within a chicken's egg. The "form" of a thing, then, says something about its limitation as well as its potentiality.

When Aristotle talks about the "substance" and "form" of things, he does not only refer to living organisms. Just as it is the chicken's "form" to cackle, flutter its wings, and lay eggs, it is the form of the stone to fall to the ground. Just as the chicken cannot help cackling, the stone cannot help falling to the ground. You can, of course, lift a stone and hurl it high into the air, but because it is the stone's nature to fall to the ground, you cannot hurl it to the moon. (Take care when you perform this experiment, because the stone might take revenge and find the shortest route back to the earth!)

The Final Cause

Before we leave the subject of all living and dead things having a "form" that says something about their potential "action," I must add that Aristotle had a remarkable view of causality in nature.

Today when we talk about the "cause" of anything, we mean *how* it came to happen. The windowpane was smashed because Peter hurled a stone through it; a shoe is made because the shoemaker sews pieces of leather together. But Aristotle held that there were different types of cause in nature. Altogether he named four different causes. It is important to understand what he meant by what he called the "final cause."

In the case of window smashing, it is quite reasonable to ask *why* Peter threw the stone. We are thus asking what his purpose was. There can be no doubt that purpose played a role, also, in the matter of the shoe being made. But Aristotle also took into account a similar "purpose" when considering the purely lifeless processes in nature. Here's an example:

Why does it rain, Sophie? You have probably learned at school that it rains because the moisture in the clouds cools and condenses into raindrops that are drawn to the earth by the force of gravity. Aristotle would have nodded in agreement. But he would have added that so far you have only mentioned three of the causes. The "material cause" is that the moisture (the clouds) was there at the precise moment when the air cooled. The "efficient cause" is that the moisture cools, and the "formal cause" is that the "form," or nature of the water, is to fall to the earth. But if you stopped there, Aristotle would add that it rains *because* plants and animals need rainwater in order to grow. This he called the "final cause." Aristotle assigns the raindrops a life-task, or "purpose."

We would probably turn the whole thing upside down and say that plants grow because they find moisture. You can see the difference, can't you, Sophie? Aristotle believed that there is a purpose behind everything in nature. It rains so that plants can grow; oranges and grapes grow so that people can eat them.

That is not the nature of scientific reasoning today. We say that food and water are necessary conditions of life for man and beast. Had we not had these conditions we would not have existed. But it is not the *purpose* of water or oranges to be food for us.

In the question of causality then, we are tempted to say that Aristotle was wrong. But let us not be too hasty. Many people believe that God created the world as it is so that all His creatures could live in it. Viewed in this way, it can naturally be claimed that there is water in the rivers because animals and humans need water to live. But now we are talking about *God's* purpose. The raindrops and the waters of the river have no interest in our welfare.

Logic

The distinction between "form" and "substance" plays an important part in Aristotle's explanation of the way we discern things in the world.

When we discern things, we classify them in various groups or categories. I see a horse, then I see another horse, and another. The horses are not exactly alike, but they have something in common, and this common something is the horse's "form." Whatever might be distinctive, or individual, belongs to the horse's "substance."

So we go around pigeonholing everything. We put cows in cowsheds, horses in stables, pigs in pigsties, and chickens in chicken coops. The same happens when Sophie Amundsen tidies up her room. She puts her books on the bookshelf, her schoolbooks in her schoolbag, and her magazines in the drawer. Then she folds her clothes neatly and puts them in the closet—underwear on one shelf, sweaters on another, and socks in a drawer on their own. Notice that we do the same thing in our minds. We distinguish between things made of stone, things made of wool, and things made of rubber. We distinguish between things that are alive or dead, and we distinguish between vegetable, animal, and human.

Do you see, Sophie? Aristotle wanted to do a thorough clearing up in nature's "room." He tried to show that everything in nature belongs to different categories and subcategories. (Hermes is a live creature, more specifically an animal, more specifically a vertebrate, more specifically a mammal, more specifically a dog, more specifically a Labrador, more specifically a male Labrador.)

Go into your room, Sophie. Pick up something, anything, from the floor. Whatever you take, you will find that what you are holding belongs to a higher category. The day you see something you are unable to classify you will get a shock. If, for example, you discover a small whatsit, and you can't really say whether it is animal, vegetable, or mineral—I don't think you would dare touch it.

Saying animal, vegetable, and mineral reminds me of that party game where the victim is sent outside the room, and when he comes in again he has to guess what everyone else is thinking of. Everyone has agreed to think of Fluffy, the cat, which at the moment is in the neighbor's garden. The victim comes in and begins to guess. The others must only answer "yes" or "no." If the victim is a good Aristotelian—and therefore no victim—the game could go pretty much as follows:

Is it concrete? (Yes!) Mineral? (No!) Is it alive? (Yes!) Vegetable? (No!) Animal? (Yes!) Is it a bird? (No!) Is it a mammal? (Yes!) Is it the whole animal? (Yes!) Is it a cat? (Yes!) Is it Fluffy? (Yeah! Laughter . . .)

So Aristotle invented that game. We ought to give Plato the credit for having invented hide-and-seek. Democritus has already been credited with having invented Lego.

Aristotle was a meticulous organizer who set out to clarify our concepts. In fact, he founded the science of *Logic*. He demonstrated a number of laws governing conclusions or proofs that were valid. One example will suffice. If I first establish that "all living creatures are mortal" (first premise), and then establish that "Hermes is a living creature" (second premise), I can then elegantly conclude that "Hermes is mortal."

The example demonstrates that Aristotle's logic was based on the correlation of terms, in this case "living creature" and "mortal." Even though one has to admit that the above conclusion is 100% valid, we may also add that it hardly tells us anything new. We already knew that Hermes was "mortal." (He is a "dog" and all dogs are "living creatures"—which are "mortal," unlike the rock of Mount Everest.) Certainly we knew that, Sophie. But the relationship between classes of things is not always so obvious. From time to time it can be necessary to clarify our concepts.

For example: Is it really possible that tiny little baby mice suckle just like lambs and piglets? Mice certainly do not lay eggs. (When did I last see a mouse's egg?) So they give birth to live young—just like pigs and sheep. But we call animals that bear live young mammals—and mammals are animals that feed on their mother's milk. So—we got there. We had the answer inside us but we had to think it through. We forgot for the moment that mice really do suckle from their mother. Perhaps it was because we have never seen a baby mouse being suckled, for the simple reason that mice are rather shy of humans when they suckle their young.

Nature's Scale

When Aristotle "clears up" in life, he first of all points out that everything in the natural world can be divided into two main categories. On the one hand there are *nonliving things*, such as stones, drops of water, or clumps of soil. These things have no potentiality for change. According to Aristotle, nonliving things can only change through external influence. Only *living things* have the potentiality for change.

Aristotle divides "living things" into two different categories. One comprises *plants*, and the other *creatures*. Finally, these "creatures" can also be divided into two subcategories, namely *animals* and *humans*.

You have to admit that Aristotle's categories are clear and simple. There is a decisive difference between a living and a nonliving thing, for example a rose and a stone, just as there is a decisive difference between a plant and an animal, for example a rose and a horse. I would also claim that there definitely is a difference between a horse and a man. But what exactly does this difference consist of? Can you tell me that?

Unfortunately I do not have time to wait while you write the answer down and put it in a pink envelope with a lump of sugar, so I'll answer myself. When Aristotle divides natural phenomena into various categories, his criterion is the object's characteristics, or more specifically what it *can do* or what it *does*.

All living things (plants, animals, humans) have the ability to absorb nourishment, to grow, and to propagate. All "living creatures" (animals and humans) have in addition the ability to perceive the world around them and to move about. Moreover, all humans have the ability to think—or otherwise to order their perceptions into various categories and classes.

So there are in reality no sharp boundaries in the natural world. We observe a gradual transition from simple growths to more complicated plants, from simple animals to more complicated animals. At the top of this "scale" is man—who according to Aristotle lives the whole life of nature. Man grows and absorbs nourishment like plants, he has feelings and the ability to move like animals, but he also has a specific characteristic peculiar to humans, and that is the ability to think rationally.

Therefore, man has a spark of divine reason, Sophie. Yes, I did say divine. From time to time Aristotle reminds us that there must be a God who started all movement in the natural world. Therefore God must be at the very top of nature's scale.

Aristotle imagined the movement of the stars and the planets guiding all movement on Earth. But there had to be something causing the heavenly bodies to move. Aristotle called this the "first mover," or "God." The "first mover" is itself at rest, but it is the "formal cause" of the movement of the heavenly bodies, and thus of all movement in nature.

Ethics

Let us go back to man, Sophie. According to Aristotle, man's "form" comprises a soul, which has a plant-like part, an animal part, and a rational part. And now he asks: How should we live? What does it require to live a good life? His answer: Man can only achieve happiness by using all his abilities and capabilities.

Aristotle held that there are three forms of happiness. The first form of happiness is a life of pleasure and enjoyment. The second form of happiness is a life as a free and responsible citizen. The third form of happiness is a life as thinker and philosopher.

Aristotle then emphasized that all three criteria must be present at the same time for man to find happiness and fulfillment. He rejected all forms of imbalance. Had he lived today he might have said that a person who only develops his body lives a life that is just as unbalanced as someone who only uses his head. Both extremes are an expression of a warped way of life.

The same applies in human relationships, where Aristotle advocated the "Golden Mean." We must be neither cowardly nor rash, but courageous (too little courage is cowardice, too much is rashness), neither miserly nor extravagant but liberal (not liberal enough is miserly, too liberal is extravagant). The same goes for eating. It is dangerous to eat too little, but also dangerous to eat too much. The ethics of both Plato and Aristotle contain echoes of Greek medicine: only by exercising balance and temperance will I achieve a happy or "harmonious" life.

Politics

The undesirability of cultivating extremes is also expressed in Aristotle's view of society. He says that man is by nature a "political animal." Without a society around us, we are not real people, he claimed. He pointed out that the family and the village satisfy our primary needs of food, warmth, marriage, and child rearing. But the highest form of human fellowship is only to be found in the state.

This leads to the question of how the state should be organized. (You remember Plato's "philosophic state"?) Aristotle describes three good forms of constitution.

One is *monarchy*, or kingship—which means there is only one head of state. For this type of constitution to be good, it must not degenerate into "tyranny"—that is, when one ruler governs the state to his own advantage. Another good form of constitution is *aristocracy*, in which there is a larger or smaller group of rulers. This constitutional form must beware of degenerating into an "oligarchy"—when the government is run by a few people. An example of that would be a junta. The third good constitutional form is what Aristotle called *polity*, which means democracy. But this form also has its negative aspect. A democracy can quickly develop into mob rule. (Even if the tyrannic Hitler had not become head of state in Germany, all the lesser Nazis could have formed a terrifying mob rule.)

Views on Women

Finally, let us look at Aristotle's views on women. His was unfortunately not as uplifting as Plato's. Aristotle was more inclined to believe that women were incomplete in some way. A woman was an "unfinished man." In reproduction, woman is passive and receptive whilst man is active and productive; for the child inherits only the male characteristics, claimed Aristotle. He believed that all the child's characteristics lay complete in the male sperm. The woman was the soil, receiving and bringing forth the seed, whilst the man was the "sower." Or, in Aristotelian language, the man provides the "form" and the woman contributes the "substance."

It is of course both astonishing and highly regrettable that an otherwise so intelligent man could be so wrong about the relationship of the sexes. But it demonstrates two things: first, that Aristotle could not have had much practical experience regarding the lives of women and children, and second, it shows how wrong things can go when men are allowed to reign supreme in the fields of philosophy and science.

Aristotle's erroneous view of the sexes was doubly harmful because it was his—rather than Plato's—view that held sway throughout the Middle Ages. The church thus inherited a view of women that is entirely without foundation in the Bible. Jesus was certainly no woman hater!

I'll say no more. But you will be hearing from me again.

When Sophie had read the chapter on Aristotle one and a half times, she returned it to the brown envelope and remained sitting, staring into space. She suddenly became aware of the mess surrounding her. Books and ring binders lay scattered on the floor. Socks and sweaters, tights and jeans hung half out of the closet. On the chair in front of the writing desk was a huge pile of dirty laundry.

Sophie had an irresistible desire to clear up. The first thing she did was to pull all the clothes out of the closet and onto the floor. It was necessary to start all over. Then she began folding her things very neatly and stacking them all tidily on the shelves. The closet had seven shelves. One was for underwear, one for socks and tights, and one for jeans. She gradually filled up each shelf. She never had any question about where to put anything. Dirty laundry went into a plastic bag she found on the bottom shelf. One thing she did have trouble with—a white knee-length stocking. The problem was that the other one of the pair was missing. What's more, it had never been Sophie's.

She examined it carefully. There was nothing to identify the owner, but Sophie had a strong suspicion about who the owner was. She threw it up onto the top shelf to join the Lego, the video cassette, and the red silk scarf.

Sophie turned her attention to the floor. She sorted books, ring binders, magazines, and posters—exactly as the philosophy teacher had described in the chapter on Aristotle. When she had done that, she made her bed and got started on her writing desk.

The last thing she did was to gather all the pages on

Aristotle into a neat pile. She fished out an empty ring binder and a hole punch, made holes in the pages, and clipped them into the ring binder. This also went onto the top shelf. Later on in the day she would have to bring in the cookie tin from the den.

From now on things would be kept neat. And she didn't only mean in her room. After reading Aristotle, she realized it was just as important to keep her ideas orderly. She had reserved the top shelf of the closet especially for that kind of thing. It was the only place in the room that she did not yet have complete control over.

There had been no sign of life from her mother for over two hours. Sophie went downstairs. Before she woke her mother up she decided to feed her pets.

She bent over the goldfish bowl in the kitchen. One of the fishes was black, one orange, and one red and white. This was why she called them Black Jack, Goldtop, and Red Ridinghood.

As she sprinkled fish food into the water she said:

"You belong to Nature's living creatures, you can absorb nourishment, you can grow and reproduce yourselves. More specifically, you belong to the animal kingdom. So you can move around and look out at the world. To be precise, you are fish, and you breathe through your gills and can swim back and forth in the waters of life."

Sophie put the lid back on the fish food jar. She was quite satisfied with the way she had placed the goldfish in Nature's scale, and she was especially pleased with the expression "the waters of life." So now it was the budgerigars' turn.

Sophie poured a little birdseed in their feeding cup and said:

"Dear Smit and Smule. You have become dear little budgerigars because you grew out of dear little budgerigar eggs, and because these eggs had the form of being budgerigars, luckily you didn't grow into squawking parrots."

Sophie then went into the large bathroom, where the sluggish tortoise lay in a big box. Every now and then when her mother showered, she yelled that she would kill it one day. But so far it had been an empty threat. Sophie took a lettuce leaf from a large jam jar and laid it in the box.

"Dear Govinda," she said. "You are not one of the speediest animals, but you certainly are able to sense a tiny fraction of the great big world we live in. You'll have to content yourself with the fact that you are not the only one who can't exceed your own limits."

Sherekan was probably out catching mice—that was a cat's nature, after all. Sophie crossed the living room toward her mother's bedroom. A vase of daffodils stood on the coffee table. It was as if the yellow blooms bowed respectfully as Sophie went by. She stopped for a moment and let her fingers gently brush their smooth heads. "You belong to the living part of nature too," she said. "Actually, you are quite privileged compared to the vase you are in. But unfortunately you are not able to appreciate it."

Then Sophie tiptoed into her mother's bedroom. Although her mother was in a deep sleep, Sophie laid a hand on her forehead.

"You are one of the luckiest ones," she said, "because you are not only alive like the lilies of the field. And you are not only a living creature like Sherekan or Govinda. You are a human, and therefore have the rare capacity of thought."

"What on earth are you talking about, Sophie?"

Her mother had woken up more quickly than usual.

"I was just saying that you look like a lazy tortoise. I can otherwise inform you that I have tidied up my room, with philosophic thoroughness."

Her mother lifted her head.

"I'll be right there," she said. "Will you put the coffee on?"

Sophie did as she was asked, and they were soon sitting in the kitchen over coffee, juice, and chocolate.

Suddenly Sophie said, "Have you ever wondered why we are alive, Mom?"

"Oh, not again!"

"Yes, because now I know the answer. People live

on this planet so that someone can go around giving names to everything.''

''Is that right? I never thought of that.''

''Then you have a big problem, because a human is a thinking animal. If you don't think, you're not really a human.''

''Sophie!''

''Imagine if there were only vegetables and animals. Then there wouldn't have been anybody to tell the difference between 'cat' and 'dog,' or 'lily' and 'gooseberry.' Vegetables and animals are living too, but we are the only creatures that can categorize nature into different groups and classes.''

''You really are the most peculiar girl I have ever had,'' said her mother.

''I should hope so,'' said Sophie. ''Everybody is more or less peculiar. I am a person, so I am more or less peculiar. You have only one girl, so I am the most peculiar.''

''What I meant was that you scare the living daylights out of me with all that new talk.''

''You are easily scared, then.''

Later that afternoon Sophie went back to the den. She managed to smuggle the big cookie tin up to her room without her mother noticing.

First she put all the pages in the right order. Then she punched holes in them and put them in the ring binder, before the chapter on Aristotle. Finally she numbered each page in the top right-hand corner. There were in all over fifty pages. Sophie was in the process of compiling her own book on philosophy. It was not by her, but written especially for her.

She had no time to do her homework for Monday. They were probably going to have a test in Religious Knowledge, but the teacher always said he valued personal commitment and value judgments. Sophie felt she was beginning to have a certain basis for both.

Hellenism

∞

. . . a spark from the fire . . .

Although the philosophy teacher had begun sending his letters directly to the old hedge, Sophie nevertheless looked in the mailbox on Monday morning, more out of habit than anything else.

It was empty, not surprisingly. She began to walk down Clover Close.

Suddenly she noticed a photograph lying on the sidewalk. It was a picture of a white jeep and a blue flag with the letters UN on it. Wasn't that the United Nations flag?

Sophie turned the picture over and saw that it was a regular postcard. To "Hilde Møller Knag, c/o Sophie Amundsen . . ." It had a Norwegian stamp and was postmarked "UN Battalion" Friday June 15, 1990.

June 15! That was Sofie's birthday!

The card read:

Dear Hilde, I assume you are still celebrating your 15th birthday. Or is this the morning after? Anyway, it makes no difference to your present. In a sense, that will last a lifetime. But I'd like to wish you a happy birthday one more time. Perhaps you understand now why I send the cards to Sophie. I am sure she will pass them on to you.

P.S. Mom said you had lost your wallet. I hereby promise to reimburse you the 150 crowns. You will probably be able to get another school I.D. before they close for the summer vacation. Love from Dad.

Sophie stood glued to the spot. When was the previous card postmarked? She seemed to recall that the postcard of the beach was also postmarked June—even though it was a whole month off. She simply hadn't looked properly.

She glanced at her watch and then ran back to the house. She would just have to be late for school today!

Sophie let herself in and leaped upstairs to her room. She found the first postcard to Hilde under the red silk scarf. Yes! It was also postmarked June 15! Sophie's birthday and the day before the summer vacation.

Her mind was racing as she ran over to the supermarket to meet Joanna.

Who was Hilde? How could her father as good as take it for granted that Sophie would find her? In any case, it was senseless of him to send Sophie the cards instead of sending them directly to his daughter. It could not possibly be because he didn't know his own daughter's address. Was it a practical joke? Was he trying to surprise his daughter on her birthday by getting a perfect stranger to play detective and mailman? Was that why she was being given a month's headstart? And was using her as the go-between a way of giving his daughter a new girlfriend as a birthday present? Could she be the present that would "last a lifetime"?

If this joker really was in Lebanon, how had he gotten hold of Sophie's address? Also, Sophie and Hilde had at least two things in common. If Hilde's birthday was June 15, they were both born on the same day. And they both had fathers who were on the other side of the globe.

Sophie felt she was being drawn into an unnatural world. Maybe it was not so dumb after all to believe in fate. Still—she shouldn't be jumping to conclusions; it could all have a perfectly natural explanation. But how had Alberto Knox found Hilde's wallet when Hilde lived in Lillesand? Lillesand was hundreds of miles away. And why had Sophie found this postcard on her side-

walk? Did it fall out of the mailman's bag just as he got
to Sophie's mailbox? If so, why should he drop this
particular card?

"Are you completely insane?" Joanna burst out when
Sophie finally made it to the supermarket.

"Sorry!"

Joanna frowned at her severely, like a schoolteacher.

"You'd better have a good explanation."

"It has to do with the UN," said Sophie. "I was
detained by hostile troops in Lebanon."

"Sure . . . You're just in love!"

They ran to school as fast as their legs could carry
them.

The Religious Knowledge test that Sophie had not had
time to prepare for was given out in the third period.
The sheet read:

PHILOSOPHY OF LIFE AND TOLERANCE

1. Make a list of things we can know. Then make
a list of things we can only believe.

2. Indicate some of the factors contributing to a
person's philosophy of life.

3. What is meant by conscience? Do you think
conscience is the same for everyone?

4. What is meant by priority of values?

Sophie sat thinking for a long time before she started
to write. Could she use any of the ideas she had learned
from Alberto Knox? She was going to have to, because
she had not opened her Religious Knowledge book for
days. Once she began to write, the words simply flowed
from her pen.

She wrote that we know the moon is not made of
green cheese and that there are also craters on the dark
side of the moon, that both Socrates and Jesus were sentenced to death, that everybody has to die sooner or later,
that the great temples on the Acropolis were built after
the Persian wars in the fifth century B.C. and that the
most important oracle in ancient Greece was the oracle

at Delphi. As examples of what we can only believe, Sophie mentioned the questions of whether or not there is life on other planets, whether God exists or not, whether there is life after death, and whether Jesus was the son of God or merely a wise man. "We can certainly not know where the world came from," she wrote, completing her list. "The universe can be compared to a large rabbit pulled out of a top hat. Philosophers try to climb up one of the fine hairs of the rabbit's fur and stare straight into the eyes of the Great Magician. Whether they will ever succeed is an open question. But if each philosopher climbed onto another one's back, they would get even higher up in the rabbit's fur, and then, in my opinion, there would be some chance they would make it some day. P.S. In the Bible there is something that could have been one of the fine hairs of the rabbit's fur. The hair was called the Tower of Babel, and it was destroyed because the Magician didn't want the tiny human insects to crawl up that high out of the white rabbit he had just created."

Then there was the next question: "Indicate some of the factors contributing to a person's philosophy of life." Upbringing and environment were important here. People living at the time of Plato had a different philosophy of life than many people have today because they lived in a different age and a different environment. Another factor was the kind of experience people chose to get themselves. Common sense was not determined by environment. Everybody had that. Maybe one could compare environment and social situation with the conditions that existed deep down in Plato's cave. By using their intelligence individuals can start to drag themselves up from the darkness. But a journey like that requires personal courage. Socrates is a good example of a person who managed to free himself from the prevailing views of his time by his own intelligence. Finally, she wrote: "Nowadays, people of many lands and cultures are being intermingled more and more. Christians, Muslims, and Buddhists may live in the same apartment building. In which case it is more important to accept each other's beliefs than to ask why everyone does not believe the same thing.''

Not bad, thought Sophie. She certainly felt she had covered some ground with what she had learned from her philosophy teacher. And she could always supplement it with a dash of her own common sense and what she might have read and heard elsewhere.

She applied herself to the third question: "What is meant by conscience? Do you think conscience is the same for everyone?" This was something they had discussed a lot in class. Sophie wrote: Conscience is people's ability to respond to right and wrong. My personal opinion is that everyone is endowed with this ability, so in other words, conscience is innate. Socrates would have said the same. But just what conscience dictates can vary a lot from one person to the next. One could say that the Sophists had a point here. They thought that right and wrong is something mainly determined by the environment the individual grows up in. Socrates, on the other hand, believed that conscience is the same for everyone. Perhaps both views were right. Even if everybody doesn't feel guilty about showing themselves naked, most people will have a bad conscience if they are really mean to someone. Still, it must be remembered that having a conscience is not the same as using it. Sometimes it looks as if people act quite unscrupulously, but I believe they also have a kind of conscience somewhere, deep down. Just as it seems as if some people have no sense at all, but that's only because they are not using it. P.S. Common sense and conscience can both be compared to a muscle. If you don't use a muscle, it gets weaker and weaker.''

Now there was only one question left: "What is meant by priority of values?" This was another thing they had discussed a lot lately. For example, it could be of value to drive a car and get quickly from one place to another. But if driving led to deforestation and polluting the natural environment, you were facing a choice of values. After careful consideration Sophie felt she had come to the conclusion that healthy forests and a pure environment were more valuable than getting to work quickly. She gave several more examples. Finally she wrote: "Personally, I think Philosophy is a more important subject than English Grammar. It would therefore be a sensible priority of values to have Philosophy on the timetable and cut down a bit on English lessons."

In the last break the teacher drew Sophie aside.

"I have already read your Religion test," he said. "It was near the top of the pile."

"I hope it gave you some food for thought."

"That was exactly what I wanted to talk to you about. It was in many ways very mature. Surprisingly so. And self-reliant. But had you done your homework, Sophie?"

Sophie fidgeted a little.

"Well, you did say it was important to have a personal point of view."

"Well, yes I did . . . but there are limits."

Sophie looked him straight in the eye. She felt she could permit herself this after all she had experienced lately.

"I have started studying philosophy," she said. "It gives one a good background for personal opinions."

"But it doesn't make it easy for me to grade your paper. It will either be a D or an A."

"Because I was either quite right or quite wrong? Is that what you're saying?"

"So let's say A," said the teacher. "But next time, do your homework!"

When Sophie got home from school that afternoon, she flung her schoolbag on the steps and ran down to the den. A brown envelope lay on top of the gnarled roots. It was quite dry around the edges, so it must have been a long time since Hermes had dropped it.

She took the envelope with her and let herself in the front door. She fed the animals and then went upstairs to her room. Lying on her bed, she opened Alberto's letter and read:

HELLENISM

Here we are again, Sophie! Having read about the natural philosophers and Socrates, Plato, and Aristotle, you are now familiar with the foundations of European philosophy. So from now on we will drop the introductory questions which you earlier received in white envelopes. I imagine you probably have plenty of other assignments and tests at school.

I shall now tell you about the long period from Aristotle near the end of the fourth century B.C. right up to the early Middle Ages around A.D. 400. Notice that we can now write both B.C. and A.D. because Christianity was in fact one of the most important, and the most mysterious, factors of the period.

Aristotle died in the year 322 B.C., at the time when Athens had lost its dominant role. This was not least due to the political upheavals resulting from the conquests of Alexander the Great (356–323 B.C.).

Alexander the Great was the King of Macedonia. Aristotle was also from Macedonia, and for a time he was even the young Alexander's tutor. It was Alexander who won the final, decisive victory over the Persians. And moreover, Sophie, with his many conquests he linked both Egypt and the Orient as far east as India to the Greek civilization.

This marked the beginning of a new epoch in the history of mankind. A civilization sprang up in which Greek culture and the Greek language played a leading role. This period, which lasted for about 300 years, is known as Hellenism. The term Hellenism refers to both the period of time and the Greek-dominated culture that prevailed in the three Hellenistic kingdoms of Macedonia, Syria, and Egypt.

However, from about the year 50 B.C., Rome secured the upper hand in military and political affairs. The new superpower gradually conquered all the Hellenistic kingdoms, and from then on Roman culture and the Latin language were predominant from Spain in the west to far into Asia. This was the beginning of the Roman period, which we often refer to as Late Antiquity. But remember one thing—before the Romans managed to conquer the Hellenistic world, Rome itself was a province of Greek culture. So Greek culture and Greek philosophy came to play an important role long after the political influence of the Greeks was a thing of the past.

Religion, Philosophy and Science

Hellenism was characterized by the fact that the borders between the various countries and cultures became erased. Previously the Greeks, the Romans, the Egyptians, the Babylonians, the Syrians, and the Persians had worshipped their own gods within what we generally call a "national religion." Now the different cultures merged into one great witch's caldron of religious, philosophical, and scientific ideas.

We could perhaps say that the town square was replaced by the world arena. The old town square had also buzzed with voices, bringing now different wares to market, now different thoughts and ideas. The new aspect was that town squares were being filled with wares and ideas from all over the world. The voices were buzzing in many different languages.

We have already mentioned that the Greek view of life was now much more widespread than it had been in the former Greek cultural areas. But as time went on, Oriental gods were also worshipped in all the Mediterranean countries. New religious formations arose that could draw on the gods and the beliefs of many of the old nations. This is called *syncretism* or the fusion of creeds.

Prior to this, people had felt a strong affinity with their own folk and their own city-state. But as the borders and boundaries became erased, many people began to experience doubt and uncertainty about their philosophy of life. Late Antiquity was generally characterized by religious doubts, cultural dissolution, and pessimism. It was said that "the world has grown old."

A common feature of the new religious formations during the Hellenistic period was that they frequently contained teachings about how mankind could attain salvation from death. These teachings were often secret. By accepting the teachings and performing certain rituals, a believer could hope for the immortality of the soul and eternal life. A certain *insight* into the true nature of the universe could be just as important for the salvation of the soul as religious rituals.

So much for the new religions, Sophie. But *philosophy* was also moving increasingly in the direction of "salvation" and serenity. Philosophic insight, it was now thought, did not only have its own reward; it should also free mankind from pessimism and the fear of death. Thus the boundaries between religion and philosophy were gradually eliminated.

In general, the philosophy of Hellenism was not startlingly original. No new Plato or Aristotle appeared on the scene. On the contrary, the three great Athenian philosophers were a source of inspiration to a number of philosophic trends which I shall briefly describe in a moment.

Hellenistic *science*, too, was influenced by a blend of knowledge from the various cultures. The town of Alexandria played a key role here as a meeting place between East and West. While Athens remained the center of philosophy with still functioning schools of philosophy after Plato and Aristotle, Alexandria became the center for science. With its extensive library, it became the center for mathematics, astronomy, biology, and medicine.

Hellenistic culture could well be compared to the world of today. The twentieth century has also been influenced by an increasingly open civilization. In our own time, too, this opening out has resulted in tremendous upheavals for religion and philosophy. And just as in Rome around the beginning of the Christian era one could come across Greek, Egyptian, and Oriental religions, today, as we approach the end of the twentieth century, we can find in all European cities of any size religions from all parts of the world.

We also see nowadays how a conglomeration of old and new religions, philosophies, and sciences can form the basis of new offers on the "view-of-life" market. Much of this "new knowledge" is actually the flotsam of old thought, some of whose roots go back to Hellenism.

As I have said, Hellenistic philosophy continued to work with the problems raised by Socrates, Plato, and Aristotle. Common to them all was their desire to discover how mankind should best live and die. They were concerned with *ethics*. In the new civilization, this became the central philosophical project. The main emphasis was on finding out what true happiness was and how it could be achieved. We are going to look at four of these philosophical trends.

The Cynics

The story goes that one day Socrates stood gazing at a stall that sold all kinds of wares. Finally he said, "What a lot of things I don't need!"

This statement could be the motto for the *Cynic* school of philosophy, founded by *Antisthenes* in Athens around 400 B.C.

Antisthenes had been a pupil of Socrates, and had become particularly interested in his frugality.

The Cynics emphasized that true happiness is not found in external advantages such as material luxury, political power, or good health. True happiness lies in not being dependent on such random and fleeting things. And because happiness does not consist in benefits of this kind, it is within everyone's reach. Moreover, having once been attained, it can never be lost.

The best known of the Cynics was *Diogenes*, a pupil of Antisthenes, who reputedly lived in a barrel and owned nothing but a cloak, a stick, and a bread bag. (So it wasn't easy to steal his happiness from him!) One day while he was sitting beside his barrel enjoying the sun, he was visited by Alexander the Great. The emperor stood before him and asked if there was anything he could do for him. Was there anything he desired? "Yes," Diogenes replied. "Stand to one side. You're blocking the sun." Thus Diogenes showed that he was no less happy and rich than the great man before him. He *had* everything he desired.

The Cynics believed that people did not need to be

concerned about their own health. Even suffering and death should not disturb them. Nor should they let themselves be tormented by concern for other people's woes.

Nowadays the terms "cynical" and "cynicism" have come to mean a sneering disbelief in human sincerity, and they imply insensitivity to other people's suffering.

The Stoics

The Cynics were instrumental in the development of the *Stoic* school of philosophy, which grew up in Athens around 300 B.C. Its founder was *Zeno*, who came originally from Cyprus and joined the Cynics in Athens after being shipwrecked. He used to gather his followers under a portico. The name "Stoic" comes from the Greek word for portico (*stoa*). Stoicism was later to have great significance for Roman culture.

Like Heraclitus, the Stoics believed that everyone was a part of the same common sense—or "logos." They thought that each person was like a world in miniature, or "microcosmos," which is a reflection of the "macrocosmos."

This led to the thought that there exists a universal rightness, the so-called natural law. And because this natural law was based on timeless human and universal reason, it did not alter with time and place. In this, then, the Stoics sided with Socrates against the Sophists.

Natural law governed all mankind, even slaves. The Stoics considered the legal statutes of the various states merely as incomplete imitations of the "law" embedded in nature itself.

In the same way that the Stoics erased the difference between the individual and the universe, they also denied any conflict between "spirit" and "matter." There is only one nature, they averred. This kind of idea is called *monism* (in contrast to Plato's clear *dualism* or two-fold reality).

As true children of their time, the Stoics were distinctly "cosmopolitan," in that they were more receptive to contemporary culture than the "barrel philosophers" (the Cynics). They drew attention to human fellowship, they were preoccupied with politics, and many of them, notably the Roman Emperor *Marcus Aurelius* (A.D. 121–180), were active statesmen. They encouraged Greek culture and philosophy in Rome, one of the most distinguished of them being the orator, philosopher, and statesman *Cicero* (106–43 B.C.). It was he who formed the very concept of "humanism"—that is, a view of life that has the individual as its central focus. Some years later, the Stoic *Seneca* (4 B.C.–A.D. 65) said that "to mankind, mankind is holy." This has remained a slogan for humanism ever since.

The Stoics, moreover, emphasized that all natural processes, such as sickness and death, follow the unbreakable laws of nature. Man must therefore learn to accept his destiny. Nothing happens accidentally. Everything happens through necessity, so it is of little use to complain when fate comes knocking at the door. One must also accept the happy events of life unperturbed, they thought. In this we see their kinship with the Cynics, who claimed that all external events were unimportant. Even today we use the term "stoic calm" about someone who does not let his feelings take over.

The Epicureans

As we have seen, Socrates was concerned with finding out how man could live a good life. Both the Cynics and the Stoics interpreted his philosophy as meaning that man had to free himself from material luxuries. But Socrates also had a pupil named *Aristippus*. He believed that the aim of life was to attain the highest possible sensory enjoyment. "The highest good is pleasure," he said, "the greatest evil is pain." So he wished to develop a way of life whose aim was to avoid pain in all forms. (The Cynics and the Stoics believed in *enduring* pain of all kinds, which is not the same as setting out to *avoid* pain.)

Around the year 300 B.C., *Epicurus* (341–270) founded a school of philosophy in Athens. His followers were called Epicureans. He developed the pleasure ethic of Aristippus and combined it with the atom theory of Democritus.

The story goes that the Epicureans lived in a garden. They were therefore known as the "garden philosophers." Above the entrance to this garden there is said to have hung a notice saying, "Stranger, here you will live well. Here pleasure is the highest good."

Epicurus emphasized that the pleasurable results of an action must always be weighed against its possible side effects. If you have ever binged on chocolate you know what I mean. If you haven't, try this exercise: Take all your saved-up pocket money and buy two hundred crowns' worth of chocolate. (We'll assume you like chocolate.) It is essential to this exercise that you eat it all at one time. About half an hour later, when all that delicious chocolate is eaten, you will understand what Epicurus meant by side effects.

Epicurus also believed that a pleasurable result in the short term must be weighed against the possibility of a greater, more lasting, or more intense pleasure in the long term. (Maybe you abstain from eating chocolate for a whole year because you prefer to save up all your pocket money and buy a new bike or go on an expensive vacation abroad.) Unlike animals, we are able to plan our lives. We have the ability to make a "pleasure calculation." Chocolate is good, but a new bike or a trip to England is better.

Epicurus emphasized, though, that "pleasure" does not necessarily mean sensual pleasure—like eating chocolate, for instance. Values such as friendship and the appreciation of art also count. Moreover, the enjoyment of life required the old Greek ideals of self-control, temperance, and serenity. Desire must be curbed, and serenity will help us to endure pain.

Fear of the gods brought many people to the garden of Epicurus. In this connection, the atom theory of Democritus was a useful cure for religious superstitions. In order to live a good life it is not unimportant to overcome the fear of death. To this end Epicurus made use of Democritus's theory of the "soul atoms." You may perhaps remember that Democritus believed there was no life after death because when we die, the "soul atoms" disperse in all directions.

"Death does not concern us," Epicurus said quite simply, "because as long as we exist, death is not here. And when it does come, we no longer exist." (When you think about it, no one has ever been bothered by being dead.)

Epicurus summed up his liberating philosophy with what he called the four medicinal herbs:

> The gods are not to be feared. Death is nothing to worry about. Good is easy to attain. The fearful is easy to endure.

From a Greek point of view, there was nothing new in comparing philosophical projects with those of medical science. The intention was simply that man should equip himself with a "philosophic medicine chest" containing the four ingredients I mentioned.

In contrast to the Stoics, the Epicureans showed little or no interest in politics and the community. "Live in seclusion!" was the advice of Epicurus. We could perhaps compare his "garden" with our present-day communes. There are many people in our own time who have sought a "safe harbor"—away from society.

After Epicurus, many Epicureans developed an over-emphasis on self-indulgence. Their motto was "Live for the moment!" The word "epicurean" is used in a negative sense nowadays to describe someone who lives only for pleasure.

Neoplatonism

As I showed you, Cynicism, Stoicism, and Epicureanism all had their roots in the teaching of Socrates. They also made use of certain of the pre-Socratics like Heraclitus and Democritus.

But the most remarkable philosophic trend in the late Hellenistic period was first and foremost inspired by Plato's philosophy. We therefore call it Neoplatonism.

The most important figure in Neoplatonism was *Plotinus*

(c. 205–270), who studied philosophy in Alexandria but later settled in Rome. It is interesting to note that he came from Alexandria, the city that had been the central meeting point for Greek philosophy and Oriental mysticism for several centuries. Plotinus brought with him to Rome a doctrine of salvation that was to compete seriously with Christianity when its time came. However, Neoplatonism also became a strong influence in mainstream Christian theology as well.

Remember Plato's doctrine of ideas, Sophie, and the way he distinguished between the world of ideas and the sensory world. This meant establishing a clear division between the soul and the body. Man thus became a dual creature: our body consisted of earth and dust like everything else in the sensory world, but we also had an immortal soul. This was widely believed by many Greeks long before Plato. Plotinus was also familiar with similar ideas from Asia.

Plotinus believed that the world is a span between two poles. At one end is the divine light which he calls the One. Sometimes he calls it God. At the other end is absolute darkness, which receives none of the light from the One. But Plotinus's point is that this darkness actually has no existence. It is simply the absence of light—in other words, it IS not. All that exists is God, or the One, but in the same way that a beam of light grows progressively dimmer and is gradually extinguished, there is somewhere a point that the divine glow cannot reach.

According to Plotinus, the soul is illuminated by the light from the One, while matter is the darkness that has no real existence. But the forms in nature have a faint glow of the One.

Imagine a great burning bonfire in the night from which sparks fly in all directions. A wide radius of light from the bonfire turns night into day in the immediate area; but the glow from the fire is visible even from a distance of several miles. If we went even further away, we would be able to see a tiny speck of light like a far-off lantern in the dark, and if we went on moving away, at some point the light would not reach us. Somewhere the rays of light disappear into the night, and when it is completely dark we see nothing. There are neither shapes nor shadows.

Imagine now that reality is a bonfire like this. That which is burning is God—and the darkness beyond is the cold matter that man and animals are made of. Closest to God are the eternal ideas which are the primal forms of all creatures. The human soul, above all, is a "spark from the fire." Yet everywhere in nature some of the divine light is shining. We can see it in all living creatures; even a rose or a bluebell has its divine glow. Furthest away from the living God are earth and water and stone.

I am saying that there is something of the divine mystery in everything that exists. We can see it sparkle in a sunflower or a poppy. We sense more of this unfathomable mystery in a butterfly that flutters from a twig—or in a goldfish swimming in a bowl. But we are closest to God in our own soul. Only there can we become one with the great mystery of life. In truth, at very rare moments we can experience that *we ourselves are that divine mystery.*

Plotinus's metaphor is rather like Plato's myth of the cave: the closer we get to the mouth of the cave, the closer we get to that which all existence springs from. But in contrast to Plato's clear two-fold reality, Plotinus's doctrine is characterized by an experience of wholeness. Everything is one—for everything is God. Even the shadows deep down in Plato's cave have a faint glow of the One.

On rare occasions in his life, Plotinus experienced a fusion of his soul with God. We usually call this a *mystical experience.* Plotinus is not alone in having had such experiences. People have told of them at all times and in all cultures. The details might be different, but the essential features are the same. Let us take a look at some of these features.

Mysticism

A mystical experience is an experience of merging with God or the "cosmic spirit." Many religions emphasize the gulf between God and Creation, but the mystic experiences no such gulf. He or she has experienced being "one with God" or "merging" with Him.

The idea is that what we usually call "I" is not the true "I." In short glimpses we can experience an identification with a greater "I." Some mystics call it God, others call it the cosmic spirit, Nature, or the Universe. When the fusion happens, the mystic feels that he is "losing himself"; he disappears into God or is lost in God in the same way that a drop of water loses itself when it merges with the sea. An Indian mystic once expressed it in this way: "When I was, God was not. When God is, I am no more." The Christian mystic Angelus Silesius (1624–1677) put it another way: Every drop becomes the sea when it flows oceanward, just as at last the soul ascends and thus becomes the Lord.

Now you might feel that it cannot be particularly pleasant to "lose oneself." I know what you mean. But the point is that what you lose is so very much less than what you gain. You lose yourself only in the form you have at the moment, but at the same time you realize that you are something much bigger. You are the universe. In fact, you are the cosmic spirit itself, Sophie. It is you who are God. If you have to lose yourself as Sophie Amundsen, you can take comfort in the knowledge that this "everyday I" is something you will lose one day anyway. Your real "I"—which you can only experience if you are able to lose yourself—is, according to the mystics, like a mysterious fire that goes on burning to all eternity.

But a mystical experience like this does not always come of itself. The mystic may have to seek the path of "purification and enlightenment" to his meeting with God. This path consists of the simple life and various meditation techniques. Then all at once the mystic achieves his goal, and can exclaim, "I am God" or "I am You."

Mystical trends are found in all the great world religions. And the descriptions of mystical experiences given by the mystics show a remarkable similarity across all cultural boundaries. It is in the mystic's attempt to provide a religious or philosophic interpretation of the mystical experience that his cultural background reveals itself.

In *Western mysticism*—that is, within Judaism, Christianity, and Islam—the mystic emphasizes that his meeting is with a personal God. Although God is present both in nature and in the human soul, he is also far above and beyond the world. In *Eastern mysticism*—that is, Hinduism, Buddhism, and Chinese religion—it is more usual to emphasize that the mystic experiences a total fusion with God or the "cosmic spirit."

"I am the cosmic spirit," the mystic can exclaim, or "I am God." For God is not only present in the world; he has nowhere else to be.

In India, especially, there have been strong mystical movements since long before the time of Plato. Swami Vivekenanda, an Indian who was instrumental in bringing Hinduism to the west, once said, "Just as certain world religions say that people who do not believe in a personal God outside themselves are atheists, we say that a person who does not believe in himself is an atheist. Not believing in the splendor of one's own soul is what we call atheism."

A mystical experience can also have ethical significance. A former president of India, Sarvepalli Radhakrishnan, said once, "Love thy neighbor as thyself because you *are* your neighbor. It is an illusion that makes you think that your neighbor is someone other than yourself."

People of our own time who do not adhere to a particular religion also tell of mystical experiences. They have suddenly experienced something they have called "cosmic consciousness" or an "oceanic feeling." They have felt themselves wrenched out of Time and have experienced the world "from the perspective of eternity."

Sophie sat up in bed. She had to feel whether she still had a body. As she read more and more about Plato and the mystics, she had begun to feel as though she were floating around in the room, out of the window and far off above the town. From there she had looked down on all the people in the square, and had floated on and on over the globe that was her home, over the North Sea and Europe, down over the Sahara and across the African savanna.

The whole world had become almost like a living person, and it felt as if that person were Sophie herself. The world is me, she thought. The great big universe that she had often felt to be unfathomable and terrifying—was her own "I." Now, too, the universe was enormous and majestic, but now it was herself who was so big.

The extraordinary feeling was fleeting, but Sophie was sure she would never forget it. It felt as if something inside her had burst through her forehead and become merged with everything else, the way a drop of color can tint a whole jug of water.

When it was all over, it was like waking up with a headache after a wonderful dream. Sophie registered with a touch of disillusionment that she had a body which was trying to sit up in bed. Lying on her stomach reading the pages from Alberto Knox had given her a backache. But she had experienced something unforgettable.

Eventually she pulled herself together and stood up. The first thing she did was to punch holes in the pages and file them in her ring binder together with the other lessons. Then she went into the garden.

The birds were singing as if the world had just been born. The pale green of the birches behind the old rabbit hutches was so intense that it seemed as though the Creator had not yet finished blending the color.

Could she really believe that everything was one divine "I"? Could she believe that she carried within her a soul that was a "spark from the fire"? If it was true, then she was truly a divine creature.

The Postcards

∞

. . . I'm imposing a severe censorship on myself . . .

Several days went by without any word from the philosophy teacher. Tomorrow was Thursday, May 17— Norway's national day. School would be closed on the 18th as well. As they walked home after school Joanna suddenly exclaimed, "Let's go camping!"

Sophie's immediate reaction was that she couldn't be away from the house for long. But then she said, "Sure, why not?"

A couple of hours later Joanna arrived at Sophie's door with a large backpack. Sophie had packed hers as well, and she also had the tent. They both had bedrolls and sweaters, groundsheets and flashlights, large-size thermos bottles and plenty of their favorite food.

When Sophie's mother got home around five o'clock, she gave them a sermon about what they must and must not do. She also insisted on knowing where they were going to set up camp.

They told her they intended to make for Grouse Top. They might be lucky enough to hear the mating call of the grouse next morning.

Sophie had an ulterior motive for choosing that particular spot. She thought that Grouse Top must be pretty close to the major's cabin. Something was urging her to return to it, but she didn't dare go alone.

The two girls walked down the path that led from the little cul-de-sac just beyond Sophie's garden gate. They chatted about this and that, and Sophie enjoyed taking a little time off from everything having to do with philosophy.

By eight o'clock they had pitched their tent in a clearing by Grouse Top. They had prepared themselves for the night and their bedrolls were unfolded. When they had eaten their sandwiches, Sophie asked, "Have you ever heard of the major's cabin?"

"The major's cabin?"

"There's a hut in the woods somewhere near here . . . by a little lake. A strange man lived there once, a major, that's why it's called the major's cabin."

"Does anyone live there now?"

"Do you want to go and see?"

"Where is it?"

Sophie pointed in among the trees.

Joanna was not particularly eager, but in the end they set out. The sun was low in the sky.

They walked in between the tall pine trees at first, but soon they were pushing their way through bush and thicket. Eventually they made their way down to a path. Could it be the path Sophie had followed that Sunday morning?

It must have been—almost at once she could point to something shining between the trees to the right of the path.

"It's in there," she said.

They were soon standing at the edge of the small lake. Sophie gazed at the cabin across the water. All the windows were now shuttered up. The red building was the most deserted place she had seen for ages.

Joanna turned toward her. "Do we have to walk on the water?"

"Of course not. We'll row."

Sophie pointed down into the reeds. There lay the rowboat, just as before.

"Have you been here before?"

Sophie shook her head. Trying to explain her previous visit would be far too complicated. And then she would have to tell her friend about Alberto Knox and the philosophy course as well.

They laughed and joked as they rowed across the water. When they reached the opposite bank, Sophie made sure they drew the boat well up on land.

They went to the front door. As there was obviously nobody in the cabin, Joanna tried the door handle.

"Locked . . . you didn't expect it to be open, did you?"

"Maybe we can find a key," said Sophie.

She began to search in the crevices of the stonework foundation.

"Oh, let's go back to the tent instead," said Joanna after a few minutes.

But just then Sophie exclaimed, "Here it is! I found it!"

She held up the key triumphantly. She put it in the lock and the door swung open.

The two friends sneaked inside as if they were up to something criminal. It was cold and dark in the cabin.

"We can't see a thing!" said Joanna.

But Sophie had thought of that. She took a box of matches out of her pocket and struck one. They only had time to see that the cabin was deserted before the match went out. Sophie struck another, and this time she noticed a stump of candle in a wrought-iron candlestick on top of the stove. She lit it with the third match and the little room became light enough for them to look around.

"Isn't it odd that such a small candle can light up so much darkness?" said Sophie.

Her friend nodded.

"But somewhere the light disappears into the dark," Sophie went on. "Actually, darkness has no existence of its own. It's only a lack of light."

Joanna shivered. "That's creepy! Come on, let's go . . ."

"Not before we've looked in the mirror."

Sophie pointed to the brass mirror hanging above the chest of drawers, just as before.

"That's really pretty!" said Joanna.

"But it's a magic mirror."

"Mirror, mirror on the wall, who is the fairest of them all?"

"I'm not kidding, Joanna. I am sure you can look in it and see something on the other side."

"Are you sure you've never been here before? And why is it so amusing to scare me all the time?"

Sophie could not answer that one.

"Sorry."

Now it was Joanna who suddenly discovered something lying on the floor in the corner. It was a small box. Joanna picked it up.

"Postcards," she said.

Sophie gasped.

"Don't touch them! Do you hear—don't you dare touch them!"

Joanna jumped. She threw the box down as if she had burnt herself. The postcards were strewn all over the floor. The next second she began to laugh.

"They're only postcards!"

Joanna sat down on the floor and started to pick them up. After a while Sophie sat down beside her.

"Lebanon . . . Lebanon . . . Lebanon . . . They are all postmarked in Lebanon," Joanna discovered.

"I know," said Sophie.

Joanna sat bolt upright and looked Sophie in the eye.

"So you *have* been here before!"

"Yes, I guess I have."

It suddenly struck her that it would have been a whole lot easier if she had just admitted she had been here before. It couldn't do any harm if she let her friend in on the mysterious things she had experienced during the last few days.

"I didn't want to tell you before we were here."

Joanna began to read the cards.

"They are all addressed to someone called Hilde Møller Knag."

Sophie had not touched the cards yet.

"What address?"

Joanna read: "Hilde Møller Knag, c/o Alberto Knox, Lillesand, Norway."

Sophie breathed a sigh of relief. She was afraid they

would say c/o Sophie Amundsen.

She began to inspect them more closely.

"April 28 . . . May 4 . . . May 6 . . . May 9 . . . They were stamped a few days ago."

"But there's something else. All the postmarks are Norwegian! Look at that . . . UN Battalion . . . the stamps are Norwegian too!"

"I think that's the way they do it. They have to be sort of neutral, so they have their own Norwegian post office down there."

"But how do they get the mail home?"

"The air force, probably."

Sophie put the candlestick on the floor, and the two friends began to read the cards. Joanna arranged them in chronological order and read the first card:

Dear Hilde, I can't wait to come home to Lillesand. I expect to land at Kjevik airport early evening on Midsummer Eve. I would much rather have arrived in time for your 15th birthday but I'm under military command of course. To make up for it, I promise to devote all my loving care to the huge present you are getting for your birthday.

With love from someone who is always thinking about his daughter's future.

P.S. I'm sending a copy of this card to our mutual friend. I know you understand, Hilde. At the moment I'm being very secretive, but you will understand.

Sophie picked up the next card:

Dear Hilde, Down here we take one day at a time. If there is one thing I'm going to remember from these months in Lebanon, it's all this waiting. But I'm doing what I can so you have as great a 15th birthday as possible. I can't say any more at the moment. I'm imposing a severe censorship on myself. Love, Dad.

The two friends sat breathless with excitement. Neither of them spoke, they just read what was written on the cards:

My dear child, What I would like best would be to send you my secret thoughts with a white dove. But they are all out of white doves in Lebanon. If there is anything this war-torn country needs, it is white doves. I pray the UN will truly manage to make peace in the world some day.

P.S. Maybe your birthday present can be shared with other people. Let's talk about that when I get home. But you still have no idea what I'm talking about, right? Love from someone who has plenty of time to think for the both of us.

When they had read six cards, there was only one left. It read:

Dear Hilde, I am now so bursting with all these secrets for your birthday that I have to stop myself several times a day from calling home and blowing the whole thing. It is something that simply grows and grows. And as you know, when a thing gets bigger and bigger it's more difficult to keep it to yourself. Love from Dad.

P.S. Some day you will meet a girl called Sophie. To give you both a chance to get to know more about each other before you meet, I have begun sending her copies of all the cards I send to you. I expect she will soon begin to catch on, Hilde. As yet she knows no more than you. She has a girlfriend called Joanna. Maybe she can be of help?

After reading the last card, Joanna and Sophie sat quite still staring wildly at each other. Joanna was holding Sophie's wrist in a tight grip.

"I'm scared," she said.

"So am I."

"When was the last card stamped?"

Sophie looked again at the card.

"May 16," she said. "That's today."

"It can't be!" cried Joanna, almost angrily.

They examined the postmark carefully, but there was no mistaking it . . . 05-16-90.

"It's impossible," insisted Joanna. "And I can't imagine who could have written it. It must be someone who knows us. But how could they know we would come here on this particular day?"

Joanna was by far the more scared of the two. The business with Hilde and her father was nothing new to Sophie.

"I think it has something to do with the brass mirror."

Joanna jumped again.

"You don't actually think the cards come fluttering out of the mirror the minute they are stamped in Lebanon?"

"Do you have a better explanation?"

"No."

Sophie got to her feet and held the candle up in front of the two portraits on the wall. Joanna came over and peered at the pictures.

"Berkeley and Bjerkely. What does that mean?"

"I have no idea."

The candle was almost burnt down.

"Let's go," said Joanna. "Come on!"

"We must just take the mirror with us."

Sophie reached up and unhooked the large brass mirror from the wall above the chest of drawers. Joanna tried to stop her but Sophie would not be deterred.

When they got outside it was as dark as a May night can get. There was enough light in the sky for the clear outlines of bushes and trees to be visible. The small lake lay like a reflection of the sky above it. The two girls rowed pensively across to the other side.

Neither of them spoke much on the way back to the tent, but each knew that the other was thinking intensely about what they had seen. Now and then a frightened bird would start up, and a couple of times they heard the hooting of an owl.

As soon as they reached the tent, they crawled into

their bedrolls. Joanna refused to have the mirror inside the tent. Before they fell asleep, they agreed that it was scary enough, knowing it was just outside the tent flap. Sophie had also taken the postcards and put them in one of the pockets of her backpack.

They woke early next morning. Sophie was up first. She put her boots on and went outside the tent. There lay the large mirror in the grass, covered with dew.

Sophie wiped the dew off with her sweater and gazed down at her own reflection. It was as if she was looking down and up at herself at the same time. Luckily she found no early morning postcard from Lebanon.

Above the broad clearing behind the tent a ragged morning mist was drifting slowly into little wads of cotton. Small birds were chirping energetically but Sophie could neither see nor hear any grouse.

The girls put on extra sweaters and ate their breakfast outside the tent. Their conversation soon turned to the major's cabin and the mysterious cards.

After breakfast they folded up the tent and set off for home. Sophie carried the large mirror under her arm. From time to time she had to rest—Joanna refused to touch it.

As they approached the outskirts of the town they heard a few sporadic shots. Sophie recalled what Hilde's father had written about war-torn Lebanon, and she realized how lucky she was to have been born in a peaceful country. The "shots" they heard came from innocent fireworks celebrating the national holiday.

Sophie invited Joanna in for a cup of hot chocolate. Her mother was very curious to know where they had found the mirror. Sophie told her they had found it outside the major's cabin, and her mother repeated the story about nobody having lived there for many years.

When Joanna had gone, Sophie put on a red dress. The rest of the Norwegian national day passed quite normally. In the evening, the TV news had a feature on how the Norwegian UN battalion had celebrated the day in Lebanon. Sophie's eyes were glued to the screen. One of the men she was seeing could be Hilde's father.

The last thing Sophie did on May 17 was to hang the large mirror on the wall in her room. The following morning there was a new brown envelope in the den. She tore it open at once and began to read.

Two Cultures

∞

. . . the only way to avoid floating in a vacuum . . .

It won't be long now before we meet, my dear Sophie. I thought you would return to the major's cabin—that's why I left all the cards from Hilde's father there. That was the only way they could be delivered to her. Don't worry about how she will get them. A lot can happen before June 15.

We have seen how the Hellenistic philosophers recycled the ideas of earlier philosophers. Some even attempted to turn their predecessors into religious prophets. Plotinus came close to acclaiming Plato as the savior of humanity.

But as we know, another savior was born during the period we have just been discussing—and that happened outside the Greco-Roman area. I refer to Jesus of Nazareth. In this chapter we will see how Christianity gradually began to permeate the Greco-Roman world—more or less the same way that Hilde's world has gradually begun to permeate ours.

Jesus was a Jew, and the Jews belong to Semitic culture. The Greeks and the Romans belong to Indo-European culture. European civilization has its roots in both cultures. But before we take a closer look at the way Christianity influenced Greco-Roman culture, we must examine these roots.

THE INDO-EUROPEANS

By Indo-European we mean all the nations and cultures that use Indo-European languages. This covers all European nations except those whose inhabitants speak one of the Finno-Ugrian languages (Lapp, Finnish, Estonian, and Hungarian) or Basque. In addition, most Indian and Iranian languages belong to the Indo-European family of languages.

About 4,000 years ago, the primitive Indo-Europeans lived in areas bordering on the Black Sea and the Caspian Sea. From there, waves of these Indo-European tribes began to wander southeast into Iran and India, southwest to Greece, Italy, and Spain, westward through Central Europe to France and Britain, northwestward to Scandinavia and northward to Eastern Europe and Russia. Wherever they went, the Indo-Europeans assimilated with the local culture, although Indo-European languages and Indo-European religion came to play a dominant role.

The ancient Indian Veda scriptures and Greek philosophy, and for that matter *Snorri Sturluson*'s mythology are all written in related languages. But it is not only the languages that are related. Related languages often lead to related ideas. This is why we usually speak of an Indo-European "culture."

The culture of the Indo-Europeans was influenced most of all by their belief in many gods. This is called *polytheism*. The names of these gods as well as much of the religious terminology recur throughout the whole Indo-European area. I'll give you a few examples:

The ancient Indians worshipped the celestial god *Dyaus*, which in Sanskrit means the sky, day, heaven/Heaven. In Greek this god is called *Zeus*, in Latin, *Jupiter* (actually *iov-pater*, or "Father Heaven"), and in Old Norse, *Tyr*. So the names Dyaus, Zeus, Iov, and Tyr are dialectal variants of the same word.

You probably learned that the old Vikings believed in gods which they called *Aser*. This is another word we find recurring all over the Indo-European area. In Sanskrit, the ancient classical language of India, the gods are called *asura* and in Persian *Ahura*. Another word for "god" is *deva* in Sanskrit, *daeva* in Persian, *deus* in Latin and *tivurr* in Old Norse.

In Viking times, people also believed in a special group of fertility gods (such as Niord, Freyr, and Freyja). These gods were referred to by a special collective name, *vaner*, a word that is related to the Latin name for the goddess of fertility, *Venus*. Sanskrit has the related word *vani*, which means "desire."

There is also a clear affinity to be observed in some of the Indo-European myths. In Snorri's stories of the Old Norse gods, some of the myths are similar to the myths of India that were handed down from two to three thousand years earlier. Although Snorri's myths reflect the Nordic environment and the Indian myths reflect the Indian, many of them retain traces of a common origin. We can see these traces most clearly in myths about immortal potions and the struggles of the gods against the monsters of chaos.

We can also see clear similarities in modes of thought across the Indo-European cultures. A typical likeness is the way the world is seen as being the subject of a drama in which the forces of Good and Evil confront each other in a relentless struggle. Indo-Europeans have therefore often tried to "predict" how the battles between Good and Evil will turn out.

One could say with some truth that it was no accident that Greek philosophy originated in the Indo-European sphere of culture. Indian, Greek, and Norse mythology all have obvious leanings toward a philosophic, or "speculative," view of the world.

The Indo-Europeans sought "insight" into the history of the world. We can even trace a particular word for "insight" or "knowledge" from one culture to another all over the Indo-European world. In Sanskrit it is *vidya*. The word is identical to the Greek word *idéa*, which was so important in Plato's philosophy. From Latin, we have the word *video*, but on Roman ground the word simply means *to see*. For us, "I see" can mean "I understand," and in the cartoons, a light bulb can flash on above Woody Woodpecker's head when he gets a bright idea. (Not until our own day did "seeing" become synonymous with staring at the TV screen.) In English we know the words *wise* and *wisdom*—in German, *wissen* (to know). Norwegian has the word *viten*, which has the same root as the Indian word *vidya*, the Greek *idéa*, and the Latin *video*.

All in all, we can establish that **sight** was the most important of the senses for Indo-Europeans. The literature of Indians, Greeks, Persians, and Teutons alike was characterized by great cosmic visions. (There is that word again: "vision" comes from the Latin verb "*video*.") It was also characteristic for Indo-European culture to make pictures and sculptures of the gods and of mythical events.

Lastly, the Indo-Europeans had a *cyclic* view of history. This is the belief that history goes in circles, just like the seasons of the year. There is thus no beginning and no end to history, but there are different civilizations that rise and fall in an eternal interplay between birth and death.

Both of the two great Oriental religions, Hinduism and Buddhism, are Indo-European in origin. So is Greek philosophy, and we can see a number of clear parallels between Hinduism and Buddhism on the one hand and Greek philosophy on the other. Even today, Hinduism and Buddhism are strongly imbued with philosophical reflection.

Not infrequently we find in Hinduism and Buddhism an emphasis on the fact that the deity is present in all things (pantheism) and that man can become one with God through religious insight. (Remember Plotinus, Sophie?) To achieve this requires the practice of deep self-communion or meditation. Therefore in the Orient, passivity and seclusion can be religious ideals. In ancient Greece, too, there were many people who believed in an ascetic, or religiously secluded, way of life for the salvation of the soul. Many aspects of medieval monastic life can be traced back to beliefs dating from the Greco-Roman civilization.

Similarly, the transmigration of the soul, or the cycle of rebirth, is a fundamental belief in many Indo-European cultures. For more than 2,500 years, the ultimate purpose of life for every Indian has been the release from the cycle of rebirth. Plato also believed in the transmigration of the soul.

The Semites

Let us now turn to the Semites, Sophie. They belong to a completely different culture with a completely different language. The Semites originated in the Arabian Peninsula, but they also migrated to different parts of the world. The Jews lived far from their home for more than 2,000 years. Semitic history and religion reached furthest away from its roots by way of Christendom, although Semitic culture also became widely spread via Islam.

All three Western religions—Judaism, Christianity, and Islam—share a Semitic background. The Muslims' holy scripture, the *Koran*, and the *Old Testament* were both written in the Semitic family of languages. One of the Old Testament words for "god" has the same semantic root as the Muslim *Allah*. (The word "allah" means, quite simply, "god.")

When we get to Christianity the picture becomes more complicated. Christianity also has a Semitic background, but the *New Testament* was written in Greek, and when the Christian theology or creed was formulated, it was influenced by Greek and Latin, and thus also by Hellenistic philosophy.

The Indo-Europeans believed in many different gods. It was just as characteristic for the Semites that from earliest times they were united in their belief in one God. This is called *monotheism*. Judaism, Christianity, and Islam all share the same fundamental idea that there is only one God.

The Semites also had in common a *linear* view of history. In other words, history was seen as an ongoing line. In the beginning God created the world and that was the beginning of history. But one day history will end and that will be Judgment Day, when God judges the living and the dead.

The role played by history is an important feature of these three Western religions. The belief is that God intervenes in the course of history—even that history exists in order that God may manifest his will in the world. Just as he once led Abraham to the "Promised Land," he leads mankind's steps through history to the Day of Judgment. When that day comes, all evil in the world will be destroyed.

With their strong emphasis on God's activity in the course of history, the Semites were preoccupied with the writing of history for many thousands of years. And these historical roots constitute the very core of their holy scriptures.

Even today the city of Jerusalem is a significant religious center for Jews, Christians, and Muslims alike. This indicates something of the common background of these three religions.

The city comprises prominent (Jewish) synagogues, (Christian) churches, and (Islamic) mosques. It is therefore deeply tragic that Jerusalem should have become a bone of contention—with people killing each other by the thousand because they cannot agree on who is to have ascendancy over this "Eternal City." May the UN one day succeed in making Jerusalem a holy shrine for all three religions! (We shall not go any further into this more practical part of our philosophy course for the moment. We will leave it entirely to Hilde's father. You must have gathered by now that he is a UN observer in Lebanon. To be more precise, I can reveal that he is serving as a major. If you are beginning to see some connection, that's quite as it should be. On the other hand, let's not anticipate events!)

We said that the most important of the senses for Indo-Europeans was sight. How important *hearing* was to the Semitic cultures is just as interesting. It is no accident that the Jewish creed begins with the words: "Hear, O Israel!" In the Old Testament we read how the people "heard" the word of the Lord, and the Jewish prophets usually began their sermons with the words: "Thus spake Jehovah (God)." "Hearing" the word of God is also emphasized in Christianity. The religious ceremonies of Christianity, Judaism, and Islam are all characterized by reading aloud or "reciting."

I also mentioned that the Indo-Europeans always made pictorial representations or sculptures of their gods. It was just as characteristic for the Semites that they never did. They were not supposed to create pictures or sculptures of God or the "deity." The Old Testament commands that the people shall not make any image of God. This is still law today both for Judaism and Islam. Within Islam there is moreover a general aversion to both photography and art, because people should not compete with God in "creating" anything.

But the Christian churches are full of pictures of Jesus and God, you are probably thinking. True enough, Sophie, but this is just one example of how Christendom was influenced by the Greco-Roman world. (In the Greek Orthodox Church—that is, in Greece and in Russia—"graven images," or sculptures and crucifixes, from Bible stories are still forbidden.)

In contrast to the great religions of the Orient, the three Western religions emphasize that there is a distance between God and his creation. The purpose is not to be released from the cycle of rebirth, but to be redeemed from sin and blame. Moreover, religious life is characterized more by prayer, sermons, and the study of the scriptures than by self-communion and meditation.

Israel

I have no intention of competing with your religion teacher, Sophie, but let us just make a quick summary of Christianity's Jewish background.

It all began when God created the world. You can read how that happened on the very first page of the Bible. Then mankind began to rebel against God. Their punishment was not only that Adam and Eve were driven from the Garden of Eden—Death also came into the world.

Man's disobedience to God is a theme that runs right through the Bible. If we go further on in the Book of Genesis we read about the Flood and Noah's Ark. Then we read that God made a covenant with *Abraham* and his seed. This covenant—or pact—was that Abraham and all his seed would keep the Lord's commandments. In exchange God promised to protect all the children of Abraham. This covenant was renewed when *Moses* was given the Ten Commandments on Mount Sinai around the

year 1200 B.C. At that time the Israelites had long been
held as slaves in Egypt, but with God's help they were
led back to the land of Israel.

About 1,000 years before Christ—and therefore long
before there was anything called Greek philosophy—we
hear of three great kings of Israel. The first was *Saul*, then
came *David*, and after him came *Solomon*. Now all the
Israelites were united in one kingdom, and under King
David, especially, they experienced a period of political,
military, and cultural glory.

When kings were chosen, they were anointed by the
people. They thus received the title *Messiah*, which means
"the anointed one." In a religious sense kings were
looked upon as a go-between between God and his people. The king could therefore also be called the "Son of
God" and the country could be called the "Kingdom of
God."

But before long Israel began to lose its power and the
kingdom was divided into a Northern kingdom (Israel)
and a Southern kingdom (Judea). In 722 B.C. the Northern
kingdom was conquered by the Assyrians and it lost all
political and religious significance. The Southern kingdom
fared no better, being conquered by the Babylonians in
586 B.C. Its temple was destroyed and most of its people
were carried off to slavery in Babylon. This "Babylonian
captivity" lasted until 539 B.C. when the people were permitted to return to Jerusalem, and the great temple was
restored. But for the rest of the period before the birth of
Christ the Jews continued to live under foreign domination.

The question Jews constantly asked themselves was *why*
the Kingdom of David was destroyed and why catastrophe after catastrophe rained down on them, for God had
promised to hold Israel in his hand. But the people had
also promised to keep God's commandments. It gradually
became widely accepted that God was punishing Israel
for her disobedience.

From around 750 B.C. various prophets began to come
forward preaching God's wrath over Israel for not keeping his commandments. One day God would hold a Day
of Judgment over Israel, they said. We call prophecies

like these Doomsday prophecies.

In the course of time there came other prophets who preached that God would redeem a chosen few of his people and send them a "Prince of Peace" or a king of the House of David. He would restore the old Kingdom of David and the people would have a future of prosperity.

"The people that walked in darkness will see a great light," said the prophet Isaiah, and "they that dwell in the land of the shadow of death, upon them hath the light shined." We call prophecies like these prophecies of redemption.

To sum up: The children of Israel lived happily under King David. But later on when their situation deteriorated, their prophets began to proclaim that there would one day come a new king of the House of David. This "Messiah," or "Son of God," would "redeem" the people, restore Israel to greatness, and found a "Kingdom of God."

Jesus

I assume you are still with me, Sophie? The key words are "Messiah," "Son of God," and "Kingdom of God." At first it was all taken politically. In the time of Jesus, there were a lot of people who imagined that there would come a new "Messiah" in the sense of a political, military, and religious leader of the caliber of King David. This "savior" was thus looked upon as a national deliverer who would put an end to the suffering of the Jews under Roman domination.

Well and good. But there were also many people who were more farsighted. For the past two hundred years there had been prophets who believed that the promised "Messiah" would be the savior of the whole world. He would not simply free the Israelites from a foreign yoke, he would save all mankind from sin and blame—and not least, from death. The longing for "salvation" in the sense of redemption was widespread all over the Hellenistic world.

So along comes *Jesus of Nazareth*. He was not the only man ever to have come forward as the promised "Messiah." Jesus also uses the words "Son of God," the "Kingdom of God," and "redemption." In doing this he maintains the link with the old prophets. He rides into Jerusalem and allows himself to be acclaimed by the crowds as the savior of the people, thus playing directly on the way the old kings were installed in a characteristic "throne accession ritual." He also allows himself to be anointed by the people. "The time is fulfilled," he says, and "the Kingdom of God is at hand."

But here is a very important point: Jesus distinguished himself from the other "messiahs" by stating clearly that he was not a military or political rebel. His mission was much greater. He preached salvation and God's forgiveness for everyone. To the people he met on his way he said "Your sins are forgiven you for his name's sake."

Handing out the "remission of sins" in this way was totally unheard of. And what was even worse, he addressed God as "Father" (Abba). This was absolutely unprecedented in the Jewish community at that time. It was therefore not long before there arose a wave of protest against him among the scribes.

So here was the situation: a great many people at the time of Jesus were waiting for a Messiah who would reestablish the Kingdom of God with a great flourish of trumpets (in other words, with fire and sword). The expression "Kingdom of God" was indeed a recurring theme in the preachings of Jesus—but in a much broader sense. Jesus said that the "Kingdom of God" is loving thy neighbor, compassion for the weak and the poor, and forgiveness of those who have erred.

This was a dramatic shift in the meaning of an age-old expression with warlike overtones. People were expecting a military leader who would soon proclaim the establishment of the Kingdom of God, and along comes Jesus in kirtle and sandals telling them that the Kingdom of God—or the "new covenant"—is that you must "love thy neighbor as thyself." But that was not all, Sophie, he also said that we must love our enemies. When they strike us, we must not retaliate; we must even turn the other cheek. And we must forgive—not seven times but seventy times seven.

Jesus himself demonstrated that he was not above

talking to harlots, corrupt usurers, and the politically subversive. But he went even further: he said that a good-for-nothing who has squandered all his father's inheritance—or a humble publican who has pocketed official funds—is righteous before God when he repents and prays for forgiveness, so great is God's mercy.

But hang on—he went a step further: Jesus said that such sinners were *more* righteous in the eyes of God and *more* deserving of God's forgiveness than the spotless Pharisees who went around flaunting their virtue.

Jesus pointed out that nobody can *earn* God's mercy. We cannot redeem ourselves (as many of the Greeks believed). The severe ethical demands made by Jesus in the Sermon on the Mount were not only to teach what the will of God meant, but also to show that no man is righteous in the eyes of God. God's mercy is boundless, but we have to turn to God and pray for his forgiveness.

I shall leave a more thorough study of Jesus and his teachings to your religion teacher. He will have quite a task. I hope he will succeed in showing what an exceptional man Jesus was. In an ingenious way he used the language of his time to give the old war cries a totally new and broader content. It's not surprising that he ended on the Cross. His radical tidings of redemption were at odds with so many interests and power factors that he had to be removed.

When we talked about Socrates, we saw how dangerous it could be to appeal to people's reason. With Jesus we see how dangerous it can be to demand unconditional brotherly love and unconditional forgiveness. Even in the world of today we can see how mighty powers can come apart at the seams when confronted with simple demands for peace, love, food for the poor, and amnesty for the enemies of the state.

You may recall how incensed Plato was that the most righteous man in Athens had to forfeit his life. According to Christian teachings, Jesus was the only righteous person who ever lived. Nevertheless he was condemned to death. Christians say he died for the sake of humanity. This is what Christians usually call the "Passion" of Christ.

Jesus was the "suffering servant" who bore the sins of humanity in order that we could be "atoned" and saved from God's wrath.

Paul

A few days after Jesus had been crucified and buried, rumors spread that he had risen from the grave. He thereby proved that he was no ordinary man. He truly was the "Son of God."

We could say that the Christian Church was founded on Easter Morning with the rumors of the resurrection of Jesus. This is already established by Paul: "And if Christ be not risen, then is our preaching vain and your faith is also vain."

Now all mankind could hope for the resurrection of the body, for it was to save us that Jesus was crucified. But, dear Sophie, remember that from a Jewish point of view there was no question of the "immortality of the soul" or any form of "transmigration"; that was a Greek—and therefore an Indo-European—thought. According to Christianity there is nothing in man—no "soul," for example—that is in itself immortal. Although the Christian Church believes in the "resurrection of the body and eternal life," it is by God's miracle that we are saved from death and "damnation." It is neither through our own merit nor through any natural—or innate—ability.

So the early Christians began to preach the "glad tidings" of salvation through faith in Jesus Christ. Through his mediation, the "Kingdom of God" was about to become a reality. Now the entire world could be won for Christ. (The word "christ" is a Greek translation of the Hebrew word "messiah," the anointed one.)

A few years after the death of Jesus, the Pharisee *Paul* converted to Christianity. Through his many missionary journeys across the whole of the Greco-Roman world he made Christianity a worldwide religion. We hear of this in the Acts of the Apostles. Paul's preaching and guidance for the Christians is known to us from the many epistles written by him to the early Christian congregations.

He then turns up in Athens. He wanders straight into the city square of the philosophic capital. And it is said that "his spirit was stirred in him, when he saw the city wholly given to idolatry." He visited the Jewish synagogue in Athens and conversed with Epicurean and Stoic philosophers. They took him up to the Areopagos hill and asked him: "May we know what this new doctrine, whereof thou speakest, is? For thou bringest certain strange things to our ears: we would know therefore what these things mean."

Can you imagine it, Sophie? A Jew suddenly appears in the Athenian marketplace and starts talking about a savior who was hung on a cross and later rose from the grave. Even from this visit of Paul in Athens we sense a coming collision between Greek philosophy and the doctrine of Christian redemption. But Paul clearly succeeds in getting the Athenians to listen to him. From the Areopagos—and beneath the proud temples of the Acropolis—he makes the following speech:

"Ye men of Athens, I perceive that in all things ye are too superstitious. For as I passed by, and beheld your devotions, I found an altar with this inscription, TO THE UNKNOWN GOD. Whom therefore ye ignorantly worship, him declare I unto you.

God that made the world and all things therein, seeing that he is Lord of heaven and earth, dwelleth not in temples made with hands; neither is worshipped with men's hands, as though he needed any thing, seeing he giveth to all life, and breath, and all things. And hath made of one blood all nations of men for to dwell on all the face of the earth, and hath determined the times before appointed, and the bounds of their habitation; that they should seek the Lord, if haply they might feel after him and find him, though he be not far from every one of us. For in him we live, and move, and have our being; as certain also of your own poets have said, For we are also his offspring. Forasmuch then as we are the offspring of God, we ought not to think that the Godhead is like unto gold, or silver, or stone, graven by art and

man's device. And the times of this ignorance God
winked at; but now commandeth all men everywhere
to repent:

Because he hath appointed a day, in the which he
will judge the world in righteousness by that man
whom he hath ordained; whereof he hath given as-
surance unto all men, in that he hath raised him from
the dead.''

Paul in Athens, Sophie! Christianity has begun to penetrate the Greco-Roman world as something else,
something completely different from Epicurean, Stoic,
or Neoplatonic philosophy. But Paul nevertheless finds
some common ground in this culture. He emphasizes
that the search for God is natural to all men. This was
not new to the Greeks. But what was new in Paul's
preaching is that God has also revealed himself to mankind and has in truth reached out to them. So he is no
longer a ''philosophic God'' that people can approach
with their understanding. Neither is he ''an image of
gold or silver or stone''—there were plenty of those
both on the Acropolis and down in the marketplace! He
is a God that ''dwelleth not in temples made with
hands.'' He is a personal God who intervenes in the
course of history and dies on the Cross for the sake of
mankind.

When Paul had made his speech on the Areopagos,
we read in the Acts of the Apostles, some mocked him
for what he said about the resurrection from the dead.
But others said: ''We will hear thee again of this matter.'' There were also some who followed Paul and began to believe in Christianity. One of them, it is worth
noting, was a woman named Damaris. Women were
amongst the most fervent converts to Christianity.

So Paul continued his missionary activities. A few
decades after the death of Jesus, Christian congregations
were already established in all the important Greek and
Roman cities—in Athens, in Rome, in Alexandria, in
Ephesos, and in Corinth. In the space of three to four
hundred years, the entire Hellenistic world had become
Christian.

The Creed

It was not only as a missionary that Paul came to have a fundamental significance for Christianity. He also had great influence within the Christian congregations. There was a widespread need for spiritual guidance.

One important question in the early years after Jesus was whether non-Jews could become Christians without first becoming Jews. Should a Greek, for instance, observe the dietary laws? Paul believed it to be unnecessary. Christianity was more than a Jewish sect. It addressed itself to everybody in a universal message of salvation. The "Old Covenant" between God and Israel had been replaced by the "New Covenant" which Jesus had established between God and mankind.

However, Christianity was not the only religion at that time. We have seen how Hellenism was influenced by a fusion of religions. It was thus vitally necessary for the church to step forward with a concise summary of the Christian doctrine, both in order to distance itself from other religions and to prevent schisms within the Christian Church. Therefore the first *Creed* was established, summing up the central Christian "dogmas" or tenets.

One such central tenet was that Jesus was both God and man. He was not the "Son of God" on the strength of his actions alone. He was God himself. But he was also a "true man" who had shared the misfortunes of mankind and actually suffered on the Cross.

This may sound like a contradiction. But the message of the church was precisely that *God became man*. Jesus was not a "demigod" (which was half man, half god). Belief in such "demigods" was quite widespread in Greek and Hellenistic religions. The church taught that Jesus was "perfect God, perfect man."

Postscript

Let me try to say a few words about how all this hangs together, my dear Sophie. As Christianity makes its entry into the Greco-Roman world we are witnessing a dramatic meeting of two cultures. We are also seeing one of history's great cultural revolutions.

We are about to step out of antiquity. Almost one thousand years have passed since the days of the early Greek philosophers. Ahead of us we have the Christian Middle Ages, which also lasted for about a thousand years.

The German poet Goethe once said that "he who cannot draw on three thousand years is living from hand to mouth." I don't want you to end up in such a sad state. I will do what I can to acquaint you with your historical roots. It is the only way to become a human being. It is the only way to become more than a naked ape. It is the only way to avoid floating in a vacuum.

"It is the only way to become a human being. It is the only way to become more than a naked ape . . ."

Sophie sat for a while staring into the garden through the little holes in the hedge. She was beginning to understand why it was so important to know about her historical roots. It had certainly been important to the Children of Israel.

She herself was just an ordinary person. But if she knew her historical roots, she would be a little less ordinary.

She would not be living on this planet for more than a few years. But if the history of mankind was her own history, in a way she was thousands of years old.

The Middle Ages

∞

*. . . going only part of the way is not the same
as going the wrong way . . .*

A week passed without Sophie hearing from Alberto
Knox. There were no more postcards from Lebanon either, although she and Joanna still talked about the cards
they found in the major's cabin. Joanna had had the
fright of her life, but as nothing further seemed to happen, the immediate terror faded and was submerged in
homework and badminton.

Sophie read Alberto's letters over and over, looking
for some clue that would throw light on the Hilde mystery. Doing so also gave her plenty of opportunity to
digest the classical philosophy. She no longer had difficulty in distinguishing Democritus and Socrates, or
Plato and Aristotle, from each other.

On Friday, May 25, she was in the kitchen fixing dinner before her mother got home. It was their regular
Friday agreement. Today she was making fish soup with
fish balls and carrots. Plain and simple.

Outside it was becoming windy. As Sophie stood stir-
ring the casserole she turned toward the window. The
birch trees were waving like cornstalks.

Suddenly something smacked against the windowpane. Sophie turned around again and discovered a card
sticking to the window.

It was a postcard. She could read it through the glass:
"Hilde Møller Knag, c/o Sophie Amundsen."

She thought as much! She opened the window and took the card. It could hardly have blown all the way from Lebanon!

This card was also dated June 15. Sophie removed the casserole from the stove and sat down at the kitchen table. The card read:

Dear Hilde, I don't know whether it will still be your birthday when you read this card. I hope so, in a way; or at least that not too many days have gone by. A week or two for Sophie does not have to mean just as long for us. I shall be coming home for Midsummer Eve, so we can sit together for hours in the glider, looking out over the sea, Hilde. We have so much to talk about. Love from Dad, who sometimes gets very depressed about the thousand-year-long strife between Jews, Christians, and Muslims. I have to keep reminding myself that all three religions stem from Abraham. So I suppose they all pray to the same God. Down here, Cain and Abel have not finished killing each other.

P.S. Please say hello to Sophie. Poor child, she still doesn't know how this whole thing hangs together. But perhaps you do?

Sophie put her head down on the table, exhausted. One thing was certain—she had no idea how this thing hung together. But Hilde did, presumably.

If Hilde's father asked her to say hello to Sophie, it had to mean that Hilde knew more about Sophie than Sophie did about Hilde. It was all so complicated that Sophie went back to fixing dinner.

A postcard that smacked against the kitchen window all by itself! You could call that airmail!

As soon as she had set the casserole on the stove again, the telephone rang.

Suppose it was Dad! She wished desperately that he would come home so she could tell him everything that had happened in these last weeks. But it was probably only Joanna or Mom. Sophie snatched up the phone.

"Sophie Amundsen," she said.

"It's me," said a voice.

Sophie was sure of three things: it was not her father. But it was a man's voice, and a voice she knew she had heard before.

"Who is this?"

"It's Alberto."

"Ohhh!"

Sophie was at a loss for words. It was the voice from the Acropolis video that she had recognized.

"Are you all right?"

"Sure."

"From now on there will be no more letters."

"But I didn't send you a frog!"

"We must meet in person. It's beginning to be urgent, you see."

"Why?"

"Hilde's father is closing in on us."

"Closing in how?"

"On all sides, Sophie. We have to work together now."

"How . . . ?"

"But you can't help much before I have told you about the Middle Ages. We ought to cover the Renaissance and the seventeenth century as well. Berkeley is a key figure . . ."

"Wasn't he the man in the picture at the major's cabin?"

"That very same. Maybe the actual struggle will be waged over his philosophy."

"You make it sound like a war."

"I would rather call it a battle of wills. We have to attract Hilde's attention and get her over on our side before her father comes home to Lillesand."

"I don't get it at all."

"Perhaps the philosophers can open your eyes. Meet me at St. Mary's Church at eight o'clock tomorrow morning. But come alone, my child."

"So early in the morning?"

The telephone clicked.

"Hello?"

He had hung up! Sophie rushed back to the stove just

before the fish soup boiled over.

St. Mary's Church? That was an old stone church from the Middle Ages. It was only used for concerts and very special ceremonies. And in the summer it was sometimes open to tourists. But surely it wasn't open in the middle of the night?

When her mother got home, Sophie had put the card from Lebanon with everything else from Alberto and Hilde. After dinner she went over to Joanna's place.

"We have to make a very special arrangement," she said as soon as her friend opened the door.

She said no more until Joanna had closed her bedroom door.

"It's rather problematic," Sophie went on.

"Spit it out!"

"I'm going to have to tell Mom that I'm staying the night here."

"Great!"

"But it's only something I'm saying, you see. I've got to go somewhere else."

"That's bad. Is it a guy?"

"No, it's to do with Hilde."

Joanna whistled softly, and Sophie looked her severely in the eye.

"I'm coming over this evening," she said, "but at seven o'clock I've got to sneak out again. You've got to cover for me until I get back."

"But where are you going? What is it you *have* to do?"

"Sorry. My lips are sealed."

Sleepovers were never a problem. On the contrary, almost. Sometimes Sophie got the impression that her mother enjoyed having the house to herself.

"You'll be home for breakfast, I suppose?" was her mother's only remark as Sophie left the house.

"If I'm not, you know where I am."

What on earth made her say that? It was the one weak spot.

Sophie's visit began like any other sleepover, with talk until late into the night. The only difference was that when they finally settled down to sleep at about two o'clock, Sophie set the alarm clock to a quarter to seven.

Five hours later, Joanna woke briefly as Sophie switched off the buzzer.

"Take care," she mumbled.

Then Sophie was on her way. St. Mary's Church lay on the outskirts of the old part of town. It was several miles walk away, but even though she had only slept for a few hours she felt wide awake.

It was almost eight o'clock when she stood at the entrance to the old stone church. Sophie tried the massive door. It was unlocked!

Inside the church it was as deserted and silent as the church was old. A bluish light filtered in through the stained-glass windows revealing a myriad of tiny particles of dust hovering in the air. The dust seemed to gather in thick beams this way and that inside the church. Sophie sat on one of the benches in the center of the nave, staring toward the altar at an old crucifix painted with muted colors.

Some minutes passed. Suddenly the organ began to play. Sophie dared not look around. It sounded like an ancient hymn, probably from the Middle Ages.

There was silence again. Then she heard footsteps approaching from behind her. Should she look around? She chose instead to fix her eyes on the Cross.

The footsteps passed her on their way up the aisle and she saw a figure dressed in a brown monk's habit. Sophie could have sworn it was a monk right out of the Middle Ages.

She was nervous, but not scared out of her wits. In front of the altar the monk turned in a half-circle and then climbed up into the pulpit. He leaned over the edge, looked down at Sophie, and addressed her in Latin:

"Gloria Patri, et Filio, et Spiritui Sancto. Sicut erat in principio, et nunc, et semper et in sæcula sæculorum. Amen."

"Talk sense, silly!" Sophie burst out.

Her voice resounded all around the old stone church.

Although she realized that the monk had to be Alberto Knox, she regretted her outburst in this venerable place of worship. But she had been nervous, and when you're nervous it's comforting to break all taboos.

"Ssh!" Alberto held up one hand as priests do when they want the congregation to be seated.

"The Middle Ages began at four," he said.

"The Middle Ages began at four?" asked Sophie, feeling stupid but no longer nervous.

"About four o'clock, yes. And then it was five and six and seven. But it was as if time stood still. And it got to be eight and nine and ten. But it was still the Middle Ages, you see. Time to get up to a new day, you may think. Yes, I see what you mean. But it is still Sunday, one long endless row of Sundays. And it got to be eleven and twelve and thirteen. This was the period we call the High Gothic, when the great cathedrals of Europe were built. And then, some time around fourteen hours, at two in the afternoon, a cock crowed—and the interminable Middle Ages began to ebb away."

"So the Middle Ages lasted for ten hours then," said Sophie. Alberto thrust his head forward out of the brown monk's cowl and surveyed his congregation, which consisted of a fourteen-year-old girl.

"If each hour was a hundred years, yes. We can pretend that Jesus was born at midnight. Paul began his missionary journeys just before half past one in the morning and died in Rome a quarter of an hour later. Around three in the morning the Christian church was more or less banned, but by A.D. 313 it was an accepted religion in the Roman Empire. That was in the reign of the Emperor Constantine. The holy emperor himself was first baptized on his deathbed many years later. From the year 380 Christianity was the official religion throughout the entire Roman Empire."

"Didn't the Roman Empire fall?"

"It was just beginning to crumble. We are standing before one of the greatest changes in the history of culture. Rome in the fourth century was being threatened both by barbarians pressing in from the north and by disintegration from within. In A.D. 330 Constantine the Great moved the capital of the Empire from Rome to Constantinople, the city he had founded at the approach to the Black Sea. Many people considered the new city the "second Rome." In 395 the Roman Empire was divided in two—a Western Empire with Rome as its center, and an Eastern Empire with the new city of Constantinople as its capital. Rome was plundered by barbarians in 410, and in 476 the whole of the Western Empire was destroyed. The Eastern Empire continued to exist as a state right up until 1453 when the Turks conquered Constantinople.''

"And its name got changed to Istanbul?''

"That's right! Istanbul is its latest name. Another date we should notice is 529. That was the year when the church closed Plato's Academy in Athens. In the same year, the Benedictine order, the first of the great monastic orders, was founded. The year 529 thus became a symbol of the way the Christian Church put the lid on Greek philosophy. From then on, monasteries had the monopoly of education, reflection, and meditation. The clock was ticking toward half past five . . .''

Sophie saw what Alberto meant by all these times. Midnight was 0, one o'clock was 100 years after Christ, six o'clock was 600 years after Christ, and 14 hours was 1,400 years after Christ . . .

Alberto continued: "The Middle Ages actually means the period between two other epochs. The expression arose during the Renaissance. The Dark Ages, as they were also called, were seen then as one interminable thousand-year-long night which had settled over Europe between antiquity and the Renaissance. The word 'medieval' is used negatively nowadays about anything that is overauthoritative and inflexible. But many historians now consider the Middle Ages to have been a thousand-year period of germination and growth. The school system, for instance, was developed in the Middle Ages. The first convent schools were opened quite early on in the period, and cathedral schools followed in the twelfth century. Around the year 1200 the first universities were founded, and the subjects to be studied were grouped into various 'faculties,' just as they are today.''

"A thousand years is a really long time.''

"Yes, but Christianity took time to reach the masses. Moreover, in the course of the Middle Ages the various nation-states established themselves, with cities and citizens, folk music and folktales. What would fairy tales and folk songs have been without the Middle Ages? What would Europe have been, even? A Roman province, perhaps. Yet the resonance in such names as England, France, or Germany is the very same boundless deep we call the Middle Ages. There are many shining fish swimming around in those depths, although we do not always catch sight of them. Snorri lived in the Middle Ages. So did Saint Olaf and Charlemagne, to say nothing of Romeo and Juliet, Joan of Arc, Ivanhoe, the Pied Piper of Hamelin, and many mighty princes and majestic kings, chivalrous knights and fair damsels, anonymous stained-glass window makers and ingenious organ builders. And I haven't even mentioned friars, crusaders, or witches.''

"You haven't mentioned the clergy, either."

"Correct. Christianity didn't come to Norway, by the way, until the eleventh century. It would be an exaggeration to say that the Nordic countries converted to Christianity at one fell swoop. Ancient heathen beliefs persisted under the surface of Christianity, and many of these pre-Christian elements became integrated with Christianity. In Scandinavian Christmas celebrations, for example, Christian and Old Norse customs are wedded even to this day. And here the old saying applies, that married folk grow to resemble each other. Yuletide cookies, Yuletide piglets, and Yuletide ale begin to resemble the Three Wise Men from the Orient and the manger in Bethlehem. But without doubt, Christianity gradually became the predominant philosophy of life. Therefore we usually speak of the Middle Ages as being a unifying force of Christian culture."

"So it wasn't all gloom, then?"

"The first centuries after the year 400 really *were* a cultural decline. The Roman period had been a high culture, with big cities that had sewers, public baths, and libraries, not to mention proud architecture. In the early centuries of the Middle Ages this entire culture crumbled. So did its trade and economy. In the Middle Ages people returned to payment in kind and bartering. The economy was now characterized by feudalism, which meant that a few powerful nobles owned the land, which the serfs had to toil on in order to live. The population also declined steeply in the first centuries. Rome had over a million inhabitants in antiquity. But by 600, the population of the old Roman capital had fallen to 40,000, a mere fraction of what it had been. Thus a relatively small population was left to wander among what remained of the majestic edifices of the city's former glory. When they needed building materials, there were plenty of ruins to supply them. This is naturally a source of great sorrow to present-day archeologists, who would rather have seen medieval man leave the ancient monuments untouched."

"It's easy to know better after the fact."

"From a political point of view, the Roman period was already over by the end of the fourth century. However, the Bishop of Rome became the supreme head of the Roman Catholic Church. He was given the title 'Pope'—in Latin 'papa,' which means what it says—and gradually became looked upon as Christ's deputy on earth. Rome was thus the Christian capital throughout most of the medieval period. But as the kings and bishops of the new nation-states became more and more powerful, some of them were bold enough to stand up to the might of the church."

"You said the church closed Plato's Academy in Athens. Does that mean that all the Greek philosophers were forgotten?"

"Not entirely. Some of the writings of Aristotle and Plato were known. But the old Roman Empire was gradually divided into three different cultures. In Western Europe we had a Latinized Christian culture with Rome as its capital. In Eastern Europe we had a Greek Christian culture with Constantinople as its capital. This city began to be called by its Greek name, Byzantium. We therefore speak of the Byzantine Middle Ages as opposed to the Roman Catholic Middle Ages. However, North Africa and the Middle East had also been part of the Roman Empire. This area developed during the Middle Ages into an Arabic-speaking Muslim culture. After the death of Muhammad in 632, both the Middle East and North Africa were won over to Islam. Shortly thereafter, Spain also became part of the world of Islamic culture. Islam adopted Mecca, Medina, Jerusalem, and Bagdad as holy cities. From the point of view of cultural history, it is interesting to note that the Arabs also took over the ancient Hellenistic city of Alexandria. Thus much of the old Greek science was inherited by the Arabs. All through the Middle Ages, the Arabs were predominant in sciences such as mathematics, chemistry, astronomy, and medicine. Nowadays we still use Arabic figures. In a number of areas Arabic culture was superior to Christian culture."

"I wanted to know what happened to Greek philosophy."

"Can you imagine a broad river that divides for a while into three different streams before it once again becomes one great wide river?"

"Yes."

"Then you can also see how the Greco-Roman culture was divided, but survived through the three cultures: the Roman Catholic in the west, the Byzantine in the east, and the Arabic in the south. Although it's greatly oversimplified, we could say that Neoplatonism was handed down in the west, Plato in the east, and Aristotle to the Arabs in the south. But there was also something of them all in all three streams. The point is that at the end of the Middle Ages, all three streams came together in Northern Italy. The Arabic influence came from the Arabs in Spain, the Greek influence from Greece and the Byzantine Empire. And now we see the beginning of the Renaissance, the 'rebirth' of antique culture. In one sense, antique culture had survived the Dark Ages."

"I see."

"But let us not anticipate the course of events. We must first talk a little about medieval philosophy. I shall not speak from this pulpit any more. I'm coming down."

Sophie's eyes were heavy from too little sleep. When she saw the strange monk descending from the pulpit of St. Mary's Church, she felt as if she were dreaming.

Alberto walked toward the altar rail. He looked up at

the altar with its ancient crucifix, then he walked slowly toward Sophie. He sat down beside her on the bench of the pew.

It was a strange feeling, being so close to him. Under his cowl Sophie saw a pair of deep brown eyes. They belonged to a middle-aged man with dark hair and a little pointed beard. Who are you, she wondered. Why have you turned my life upside down?

"We shall become better acquainted by and by," he said, as if he had read her thoughts.

As they sat there together, with the light that filtered into the church through the stained-glass windows becoming sharper and sharper, Alberto Knox began to talk about medieval philosophy.

"The medieval philosophers took it almost for granted that Christianity was true," he began. "The question was whether we must simply *believe* the Christian revelation or whether we can approach the Christian truths with the help of reason. What was the relationship between the Greek philosophers and what the Bible said? Was there a contradiction between the Bible and reason, or were belief and knowledge compatible? Almost all medieval philosophy centered on this one question."

Sophie nodded impatiently. She had been through this in her religion class.

"We shall see how the two most prominent medieval philosophers dealt with this question, and we might as well begin with *St. Augustine*, who lived from 354 to 430. In this one person's life we can observe the actual transition from late antiquity to the Early Middle Ages. Augustine was born in the little town of Tagaste in North Africa. At the age of sixteen he went to Carthage to study. Later he traveled to Rome and Milan, and lived the last years of his life in the town of Hippo, a few miles west of Carthage. However, he was not a Christian all his life. Augustine examined several different religions and philosophies before he became a Christian."

"Could you give some examples?"

"For a time he was a *Manichaean*. The Manichaeans were a religious sect that was extremely characteristic of late antiquity. Their doctrine was half religion and half philosophy, asserting that the world consisted of a dualism of good and evil, light and darkness, spirit and matter. With his spirit, mankind could rise above the world of matter and thus prepare for the salvation of his soul. But this sharp division between good and evil gave the young Augustine no peace of mind. He was completely preoccupied with what we like to call the 'problem of evil.' By this we mean the question of where evil comes from. For a time he was influenced by Stoic philosophy, and according to the Stoics, there was no sharp division between good and evil. However, his principal leanings were toward the other significant philosophy of late antiquity, Neoplatonism. Here he came across the idea that all existence is divine in nature.''

"So he became a Neoplatonic bishop?''

"Yes, you could say that. He became a Christian first, but the Christianity of St. Augustine is largely influenced by Platonic ideas. And therefore, Sophie, therefore you have to understand that there is no dramatic break with Greek philosophy the minute we enter the Christian Middle Ages. Much of Greek philosophy was carried over to the new age through Fathers of the Church like St. Augustine.''

"Do you mean that St. Augustine was half Christian and half Neoplatonist?''

"He himself believed he was a hundred-percent Christian although he saw no real contradiction between Christianity and the philosophy of Plato. For him, the similarity between Plato and the Christian doctrine was so apparent that he thought Plato must have had knowledge of the Old Testament. This, of course, is highly improbable. Let us rather say that it was St. Augustine who 'christianized' Plato.''

"So he didn't turn his back on everything that had to do with philosophy when he started believing in Christianity?''

"No, but he pointed out that there are limits to how far reason can get you in religious questions. Christianity is a divine mystery that we can only perceive through faith. But if we believe in Christianity, God will 'illuminate' the soul so that we experience a sort of supernatural knowledge of God. St. Augustine had felt within himself that there was a limit to how far philosophy could go. Not before he became a Christian did he find peace in his own soul. 'Our heart is not quiet until it rests in Thee,' he writes."

"I don't quite understand how Plato's ideas could go together with Christianity," Sophie objected. "What about the eternal ideas?"

"Well, St. Augustine certainly maintains that God created the world out of the void, and that was a Biblical idea. The Greeks preferred the idea that the world had always existed. But St. Augustine believed that before God created the world, the 'ideas' were in the Divine mind. So he located the Platonic ideas in God and in that way preserved the Platonic view of eternal ideas."

"That was smart."

"But it indicates how not only St. Augustine but many of the other Church Fathers bent over backward to bring Greek and Jewish thought together. In a sense they were of two cultures. Augustine also inclined to Neoplatonism in his view of evil. He believed, like Plotinus, that evil is the 'absence of God.' Evil has no independent existence, it is something that is not, for God's creation is in fact only good. Evil comes from mankind's disobedience, Augustine believed. Or, in his own words, 'The good will is God's work; the evil will is the falling away from God's work.' "

"Did he also believe that man has a divine soul?"

"Yes and no. St. Augustine maintained that there is an insurmountable barrier between God and the world. In this he stands firmly on Biblical ground, rejecting the doctrine of Plotinus that everything is one. But he nevertheless emphasizes that man is a spiritual being. He has a material body—which belongs to the physical world which 'moth and rust doth corrupt'—but he also has a soul which can know God."

"What happens to the soul when we die?"

"According to St. Augustine, the entire human race was lost after the Fall of Man. But God nevertheless

decided that certain people should be saved from per-
dition.''

"In that case, God could just as well have decided
that everybody should be saved.''

"As far as that goes, St. Augustine denied that man
has any right to criticize God, referring to Paul's Epistle
to the Romans: 'O Man, who art thou that repliest
against God? Shall the thing formed say to him that
formed it; why hast thou made me thus? or Hath not the
potter power over the clay, of the same lump to make
one vessel unto honor and another unto dishonor?' ''

"So God sits up in his Heaven playing with people?
And as soon as he is dissatisfied with one of his crea-
tions, he just throws it away.''

"St. Augustine's point was that no man deserves
God's redemption. And yet God has chosen some to be
saved from damnation, so for him there was nothing
secret about who will be saved and who damned. It is
preordained. We are entirely at his mercy.''

"So in a way, he returned to the old belief in fate.''

"Perhaps. But St. Augustine did not renounce man's
responsibility for his own life. He taught that we must
live in awareness of being among the chosen. He did
not deny that we have free will. But God has 'foreseen'
how we will live.''

"Isn't that rather unfair?'' asked Sophie. "Socrates
said that we all had the same chances because we all
had the same common sense. But St. Augustine divides
people into two groups. One group gets saved and the
other gets damned.''

"You are right in that St. Augustine's theology is considerably removed from the humanism of Athens. But
St. Augustine wasn't dividing humanity into two groups.
He was merely expounding the Biblical doctrine of salvation and damnation. He explained this in a learned
work called the *City of God*.''

"Tell me about that.''

"The expression 'City of God,' or 'Kingdom of God,'
comes from the Bible and the teachings of Jesus. St.
Augustine believed that all human history is a struggle
between the 'Kingdom of God' and the 'Kingdom of the

World.' The two 'kingdoms' are not political kingdoms distinct from each other. They struggle for mastery inside every single person. Nevertheless, the Kingdom of God is more or less clearly present in the Church, and the Kingdom of the World is present in the State—for example, in the Roman Empire, which was in decline at the time of St. Augustine. This conception became increasingly clear as Church and State fought for supremacy throughout the Middle Ages. 'There is no salvation outside the Church,' it was now said. St. Augustine's 'City of God' eventually became identical with the established Church. Not until the Reformation in the sixteenth century was there any protest against the idea that people could only obtain salvation through the Church.''

"It was about time!"

"We can also observe that St. Augustine was the first philosopher we have come across to draw *history* into his philosophy. The struggle between good and evil was by no means new. What was new was that for Augustine the struggle was played out in history. There is not much of Plato in this aspect of St. Augustine's work. He was more influenced by the linear view of history as we meet it in the Old Testament: the idea that God needs all of history in order to realize his Kingdom of God. History is necessary for the enlightenment of man and the destruction of evil. Or, as St. Augustine put it, 'Divine foresight directs the history of mankind from Adam to the end of time as if it were the story of one man who gradually develops from childhood to old age.' "

Sophie looked at her watch. "It's ten o'clock," she said. "I'll have to go soon."

"But first I must tell you about the other great medieval philosopher. Shall we sit outside?"

Alberto stood up. He placed the palms of his hands together and began to stride down the aisle. He looked as if he was praying or meditating deeply on some spiritual truth. Sophie followed him; she felt she had no choice.

The sun had not yet broken through the morning clouds. Alberto seated himself on a bench outside the church. Sophie wondered what people would think if anyone came by. Sitting on a church bench at ten in the morning was odd in itself, and sitting with a medieval monk wouldn't make things look any better.

"It is eight o'clock," he began. "About four hundred years have elapsed since St. Augustine, and now school starts. From now until ten o'clock, convent schools will have the monopoly on education. Between ten and eleven o'clock the first cathedral schools will be founded, followed at noon by the first universities. The great Gothic cathedrals will be built at the same time. This church, too, dates from the 1200s—or what we call the High Gothic period. In this town they couldn't afford a large cathedral."

"They didn't need one," Sophie said. "I hate empty churches."

"Ah, but the great cathedrals were not built only for large congregations. They were built to the glory of God and were in themselves a kind of religious celebration. However, something else happened during this period which has special significance for philosophers like us."

Alberto continued: "The influence of the Arabs of Spain began to make itself felt. Throughout the Middle Ages, the Arabs had kept the Aristotelian tradition alive, and from the end of the twelfth century, Arab scholars began to arrive in Northern Italy at the invitation of the nobles. Many of Aristotle's writings thus became known and were translated from Greek and Arabic into Latin. This created a new interest in the natural sciences and infused new life into the question of the Christian revelation's relationship to Greek philosophy. Aristotle could obviously no longer be ignored in matters of science, but when should one attend to Aristotle the philosopher, and when should one stick to the Bible? Do you see?"

Sophie nodded, and the monk went on:

"The greatest and most significant philosopher of this period was *St. Thomas Aquinas,* who lived from 1225 to 1274. He came from the little town of Aquino, between Rome and Naples, but he also worked as a teacher at the University of Paris. I call him a philosopher but he was just as much a theologian. There was no great difference between philosophy and theology at that time. Briefly, we can say that Aquinas christianized Aristotle in the same way that St. Augustine christianized Plato in early medieval times.''

''Wasn't it rather an odd thing to do, christianizing philosophers who had lived several hundred years before Christ?''

''You could say so. But by 'christianizing' these two great Greek philosophers, we only mean that they were interpreted and explained in such a way that they were no longer considered a threat to Christian dogma. Aquinas was among those who tried to make Aristotle's philosophy compatible with Christianity. We say that he created the great synthesis between faith and knowledge. He did this by entering the philosophy of Aristotle and taking him at his word.''

''I'm sorry, but I had hardly any sleep last night. I'm afraid you'll have to explain it more clearly.''

''Aquinas believed that there need be no conflict between what philosophy or reason teaches us and what the Christian Revelation or faith teaches us. Christendom and philosophy often say the same thing. So we can frequently reason ourselves to the same truths that we can read in the Bible.''

''How come? Can reason tell us that God created the world in six days or that Jesus was the Son of God?''

''No, those so-called verities of faith are only accessible through belief and the Christian Revelation. But Aquinas believed in the existence of a number of 'natural theological truths.' By that he meant truths that could be reached *both* through Christian faith *and* through our innate or natural reason. For example, the truth that there is a God. Aquinas believed that there are two paths to God. One path goes through faith and the Christian Revelation, and the other goes through reason and the senses. Of these two, the path of faith and revelation is certainly the surest, because it is easy to lose one's way by trusting to reason alone. But Aquinas's point was that there need not be any conflict between a philosopher like Aristotle and the Christian doctrine.''

''So we can take our choice between believing Aristotle and believing the Bible?''

"Not at all. Aristotle goes only part of the way because he didn't know of the Christian revelation. But going only part of the way is not the same as going the wrong way. For example, it is not wrong to say that Athens is in Europe. But neither is it particularly precise. If a book only tells you that Athens is a city in Europe, it would be wise to look it up in a geography book as well. There you would find the whole truth that Athens is the capital of Greece, a small country in southeastern Europe. If you are lucky you might be told a little about the Acropolis as well. Not to mention Socrates, Plato, and Aristotle.''

"But the first bit of information about Athens was true.''

"Exactly! Aquinas wanted to prove that there is only one truth. So when Aristotle shows us something our reason tells us is true, it is not in conflict with Christian teaching. We can arrive successfully at one aspect of the truth with the aid of reason and the evidence of our senses. For example, the kind of truths Aristotle refers to when he describes the plant and the animal kingdom. Another aspect of the truth is revealed to us by God through the Bible. But the two aspects of the truth overlap at significant points. There are many questions about which the Bible and reason tell us exactly the same thing.''

"Like there being a God?''

"Exactly. Aristotle's philosophy also presumed the existence of a God—or a formal cause—which sets all natural processes going. But he gives no further description of God. For this we must rely solely on the Bible and the teachings of Jesus.''

"Is it so absolutely certain that there is a God?''

"It can be disputed, obviously. But even in our day most people will agree that human reason is certainly not capable of disproving the existence of God. Aquinas went further. He believed that he could prove God's existence on the basis of Aristotle's philosophy.''

"Not bad!''

"With our reason we can recognize that everything

around us must have a 'formal cause,' he believed. God has revealed himself to mankind both through the Bible and through reason. There is thus both a 'theology of faith' and a 'natural theology.' The same is true of the moral aspect. The Bible teaches us how God wants us to live. But God has also given us a conscience which enables us to distinguish between right and wrong on a 'natural' basis. There are thus also 'two paths' to a moral life. We know that it is wrong to harm people even if we haven't read in the Bible that we must 'do unto others as you would have them do unto you.' Here, too, the surest guide is to follow the Bible's commandment.''

''I think I understand,'' said Sophie now. ''It's almost like how we know there's a thunderstorm, by seeing the lightning *and* by hearing the thunder.''

''That's right! We can hear the thunder even if we are blind, and we can see the lightning even if we are deaf. It's best if we can both see and hear, of course. But there is no *contradiction* between what we see and what we hear. On the contrary—the two impressions reinforce each other.''

''I see.''

''Let me add another picture. If you read a novel— John Steinbeck's *Of Mice and Men*, for example . . .''

''I've read that, actually.''

''Don't you feel you know something about the author just by reading his book?''

''I realize there is a person who wrote it.''

''Is that all you know about him?''

''He seems to care about outsiders.''

''When you read this book—which is Steinbeck's creation—you get to know something about Steinbeck's nature as well. But you cannot expect to get any personal information about the author. Could you tell from reading *Of Mice and Men* how old the author was when he wrote it, where he lived, or how many children he had?''

''Of course not.''

''But you can find this information in a biography of John Steinbeck. Only in a biography—or an autobiography—can you get better acquainted with Steinbeck, the *person*.''

"That's true."

"That's more or less how it is with God's Creation and the Bible. We can recognize that there is a God just by walking around in the natural world. We can easily see that He loves flowers and animals, otherwise He would not have made them. But information about God, the person, is only found in the Bible—or in God's 'autobiography,' if you like."

"You're good at finding examples."

"Mmmm . . ."

For the first time Alberto just sat there thinking—without answering.

"Does all this have anything to do with Hilde?" Sophie could not help asking.

"We don't know whether there is a 'Hilde' at all."

"But we know someone is planting evidence of her all over the place. Postcards, a silk scarf, a green wallet, a stocking . . ."

Alberto nodded. "And it seems as if it is Hilde's father who is deciding how many clues he will plant," he said. "For now, all we know is that someone is sending us a lot of postcards. I wish he would write something about himself too. But we shall return to that later."

"It's a quarter to eleven. I'll have to get home before the end of the Middle Ages."

"I shall just conclude with a few words about how Aquinas adopted Aristotle's philosophy in all the areas where it did not collide with the Church's theology. These included his logic, his theory of knowledge, and not least his natural philosophy. Do you recall, for example, how Aristotle described the progressive scale of life from plants and animals to humans?"

Sophie nodded.

"Aristotle believed that this scale indicated a God that constituted a sort of maximum of existence. This scheme of things was not difficult to align with Christian theology. According to Aquinas, there was a progressive degree of existence from plants and animals to man, from man to angels, and from angels to God. Man, like animals, has a body and sensory organs, but man also has intelligence which enables him to reason things out.

Angels have no such body with sensory organs, which is why they have spontaneous and immediate intelligence. They have no need to 'ponder,' like humans; they have no need to reason out conclusions. They know everything that man can know without having to learn it step by step like us. And since angels have no body, they can never die. They are not everlasting like God, because they were once created by God. But they have no body that they must one day depart from, and so they will never die."

"That sounds lovely!"

"But up above the angels, God rules, Sophie. He can see and know everything in one single coherent vision."

"So he can see us now."

"Yes, perhaps he can. But not 'now.' For God, time does not exist as it does for us. Our 'now' is not God's 'now.' Because many weeks pass for us, they do not necessarily pass for God."

"That's creepy!" Sophie exclaimed. She put her hand over her mouth. Alberto looked down at her, and Sophie continued: "I got another card from Hilde's father yesterday. He wrote something like—even if it takes a week or two for Sophie, that doesn't have to mean it will be that long for us. That's almost the same as what you said about God!"

Sophie could see a sudden frown flash across Alberto's face beneath the brown cowl.

"He ought to be ashamed of himself!"

Sophie didn't quite understand what Alberto meant. He went on: "Unfortunately, Aquinas also adopted Aristotle's view of women. You may perhaps recall that Aristotle thought a woman was more or less an incomplete man. He also thought that children only inherit the father's characteristics, since a woman was passive and receptive while the man was active and creative. According to Aquinas, these views harmonized with the message of the Bible—which, for example, tells us that woman was made out of Adam's rib."

"Nonsense!"

"It's interesting to note that the eggs of mammals were not discovered until 1827. It was therefore perhaps not so surprising that people thought it was the man who was the creative and lifegiving force in reproduction. We can moreover note that, according to Aquinas, it is only as nature-being that woman is inferior to man. Woman's soul is equal to man's soul. In Heaven there is complete equality of the sexes because all physical gender differences cease to exist.''

''That's cold comfort. Weren't there any women philosophers in the Middle Ages?''

''The life of the church in the Middle Ages was heavily dominated by men. But that did not mean that there were no women thinkers. One of them was *Hildegard of Bingen* . . .''

Sophie's eyes widened:

''Does she have anything to do with Hilde?''

''What a question! Hildegard lived as a nun in the Rhine Valley from 1098 to 1179. In spite of being a woman, she worked as preacher, author, physician, botanist, and naturalist. She is an example of the fact that women were often more practical, more scientific even, in the Middle Ages.''

''But what about Hilde?''

''It was an ancient Christian and Jewish belief that God was not only a man. He also had a female side, or 'mother nature.' Women, too, are created in God's likeness. In Greek, this female side of God is called *Sophia*. 'Sophia' or 'Sophie' means wisdom.''

Sophie shook her head resignedly. Why had nobody ever told her that? And why had she never asked?

Alberto continued: ''Sophia, or God's mother nature, had a certain significance both for Jews and in the Greek Orthodox Church throughout the Middle Ages. In the west she was forgotten. But along comes Hildegard. Sophia appeared to her in a vision, dressed in a golden tunic adorned with costly jewels . . .''

Sophie stood up. Sophia had revealed herself to Hildegard in a vision . . .

''Maybe I will appear to Hilde.''

She sat down again. For the third time Alberto laid his hand on her shoulder.

''That is something we must look into. But now it is

past eleven o'clock. You must go home, and we are approaching a new era. I shall summon you to a meeting on the Renaissance. Hermes will come get you in the garden.''

With that the strange monk rose and began to walk toward the church. Sophie stayed where she was, thinking about Hildegard and Sophia, Hilde and Sophie. Suddenly she jumped up and ran after the monk-robed philosopher, calling:

''Was there also an Alberto in the Middle Ages?''

Alberto slowed his pace somewhat, turned his head slightly and said, ''Aquinas had a famous philosophy teacher called Albert the Great . . .''

With that he bowed his head and disappeared through the door of St. Mary's Church.

Sophie was not satisfied with his answer. She followed him into the church. But now it was completely empty. Did he go through the floor?

Just as she was leaving the church she noticed a picture of the Madonna. She went up to it and studied it closely. Suddenly she discovered a little drop of water under one of the Madonna's eyes. Was it a tear?

Sophie rushed out of the church and hurried back to Joanna's.

The Renaissance

∞

...O divine lineage in mortal guise...

It was just twelve when Sophie reached Joanna's front gate, out of breath with running. Joanna was standing in the front yard outside her family's yellow house.

"You've been gone for five hours!" Joanna said sharply.

Sophie shook her head.

"No, I've been gone for more than a thousand years."

"Where on earth have you been? You're crazy. Your mom called half an hour ago."

"What did you tell her?"

"I said you were at the drugstore. She said would you call her when you got back. But you should have seen my mom and dad when they came in with hot chocolate and rolls at ten this morning... and your bed was empty."

"What did you say to them?"

"It was really embarrassing. I told them you went home because we got mad at each other."

"So we'd better hurry up and be friends again. And we have to make sure your parents don't talk to my mom for a few days. Do you think we can do that?"

Joanna shrugged. Just then her father came around the corner with a wheelbarrow. He had a pair of coveralls on and was busy clearing up last year's leaves and twigs.

"Aha—so you're friends again, I see. Well, there's

not so much as a single leaf left on the basement steps now.''

"Fine," said Sophie. "So perhaps we can have our hot chocolate there instead of in bed."

Joanna's dad gave a forced laugh, but Joanna gasped. Verbal exchanges had always been more robust in Sophie's family than at the more well-to-do home of Mr. Ingebrigtsen, the financial adviser, and his wife.

"I'm sorry, Joanna, but I felt I ought to take part in this cover-up operation as well."

"Are you going to tell me about it?"

"Sure, if you walk home with me. Because it's not for the ears of financial advisers or overgrown Barbie dolls."

"That's a rotten thing to say! I suppose you think a rocky marriage that drives one of the partners away to sea is better?"

"Probably not. But I hardly slept last night. And another thing, I've begun to wonder whether Hilde can *see* everything we do."

They began to walk toward Clover Close.

"You mean she might have second sight?"

"Maybe. Maybe not."

Joanna was clearly not enthusiastic about all this secrecy.

"But that doesn't explain why her father sent a lot of crazy postcards to an empty cabin in the woods."

"I admit that is a weak spot."

"Do you want to tell me where you have been?"

So she did. Sophie told her everything, about the mysterious philosophy course as well. She made Joanna swear to keep everything secret.

They walked for a long time without speaking. As they approached Clover Close, Joanna said, "I don't like it."

She stopped at Sophie's gate and turned to go home again.

"Nobody asked you to like it. But philosophy is not a harmless party game. It's about who we are and where we come from. Do you think we learn enough about that at school?"

"Nobody can answer questions like that anyway."

"Yes, but we don't even learn to *ask* them!"

Lunch was on the table when Sophie walked into the kitchen. Nothing was said about her not having called from Joanna's.

After lunch Sophie announced that she was going to take a nap. She admitted she had hardly slept at Joanna's house, which was not at all unusual at a sleepover.

Before getting into bed she stood in front of the big brass mirror which now hung on her wall. At first she only saw her own white and exhausted face. But then—behind her own face, the faintest suggestion of another face seemed to appear. Sophie took one or two deep breaths. It was no good starting to imagine things.

She studied the sharp contours of her own pale face framed by that impossible hair which defied any style but nature's own. But beyond that face was the apparition of another girl. Suddenly the other girl began to wink frantically with both eyes, as if to signal that she was really in there on the other side. The apparition lasted only a few seconds. Then she was gone.

Sophie sat down on the edge of the bed. She had absolutely no doubt that it was Hilde she had seen in the mirror. She had caught a glimpse of her picture on a school I.D. in the major's cabin. It must have been the same girl she had seen in the mirror.

Wasn't it odd, how she always experienced mysterious things like this when she was dead tired. It meant that afterward she always had to ask herself whether it really had happened.

Sophie laid her clothes on the chair and crawled into bed. She fell asleep at once and had a strangely vivid dream.

She dreamed she was standing in a large garden that sloped down to a red boathouse. On the dock behind it sat a young fair-haired girl gazing out over the water. Sophie walked down and sat beside her. But the girl seemed not to notice her. Sophie introduced herself. "I'm Sophie," she said. But the other girl could apparently neither see nor hear her. Suddenly Sophie heard a voice calling, "Hilde!" At once the girl jumped up from

where she was sitting and ran as fast as she could up to
the house. She couldn't have been deaf or blind after
all. A middle-aged man came striding from the house
toward her. He was wearing a khaki uniform and a blue
beret. The girl threw her arms around his neck and he
swung her around a few times. Sophie noticed a little
gold crucifix on a chain lying on the dock where the girl
had been sitting. She picked it up and held it in her hand.
Then she woke up.

Sophie looked at the clock. She had been asleep for
two hours. She sat up in bed, thinking about the strange
dream. It was so real that she felt as if she had actually
lived the experience. She was equally sure that the house
and the dock really existed somewhere. Surely it resembled the picture she had seen hanging in the major's
cabin? Anyway, there was no doubt at all that the girl
in her dream was Hilde Møller Knag and that the man
was her father, home from Lebanon. In her dream he
had looked a lot like Alberto Knox . . .

As Sophie stood up and began to tidy her bed, she
found a gold crucifix on a chain under her pillow. On
the back of the crucifix there were three letters engraved:
HMK.

This was not the first time Sophie had dreamed she
found a treasure. But this was definitely the first time
she had brought it back from the dream.

"Damn!" she said aloud.

She was so mad that she opened the closet door and
hurled the delicate crucifix up onto the top shelf with
the silk scarf, the white stocking, and the postcards from
Lebanon.

The next morning Sophie woke up to a big breakfast of
hot rolls, orange juice, eggs, and vegetable salad. It was
not often that her mother was up before Sophie on a
Sunday morning. When she was, she liked to fix a solid
meal for Sophie.

While they were eating, Mom said, "There's a strange
dog in the garden. It's been sniffing round the old hedge
all morning. I can't imagine what it's doing here, can
you?"

"Yes!" Sophie burst out, and at once regretted it.

"Has it been here before?"

Sophie had already left the table and gone into the living room to look out of the window facing the large garden. It was just as she thought.

Hermes was lying in front of the secret entrance to her den.

What should she say? She had no time to think of anything before her mother came and stood beside her.

"Did you say it had been here before?" she asked.

"I expect it buried a bone there and now it's come to fetch its treasure. Dogs have memories too . . ."

"Maybe you're right, Sophie. You're the animal psychologist in the family."

Sophie thought feverishly.

"I'll take it home," she said.

"You know where it lives, then?"

Sophie shrugged her shoulders.

"It's probably got an address on its collar."

A couple of minutes later Sophie was on her way down the garden. When Hermes caught sight of her he came lolloping toward her, wagging his tail and jumping up to her.

"Good boy, Hermes!" said Sophie.

She knew her mother was watching from the window. She prayed he would not go through the hedge. But the dog dashed toward the gravel path in front of the house, streaked across the front yard, and jumped up to the gate.

When they had shut the gate behind them, Hermes continued to run a few yards in front of Sophie. It was a long way. Sophie and Hermes were not the only ones out for a Sunday walk. Whole families were setting off for the day. Sophie felt a pang of envy.

From time to time Hermes would run off and sniff at another dog or at something interesting by a garden hedge, but as soon as Sophie called "Here, boy!" he would come back to her at once.

They crossed an old pasture, a large playing field, and a playground, and emerged into an area with more traffic. They continued toward the town center along a broad street with cobbled stones and streetcars. Hermes led the way across the town square and up Church Street. They came out into the Old Town, with its massive staid town houses from the turn of the century. It was almost half past one.

Now they were on the other side of town. Sophie had not been there very often. Once when she was little, she remembered, she had been taken to visit an old aunt in one of these streets.

Eventually they reached a little square between several old houses. It was called New Square, although it all looked very old. But then the whole town was old; it had been founded way back in the Middle Ages.

Hermes walked toward No. 14, where he stood still and waited for Sophie to open the door. Her heart began to beat faster.

Inside the front door there were a number of green mailboxes attached to a panel. Sophie noticed a postcard hanging from one of the mailboxes in the top row. It had a stamped message from the mailman across it to the effect that the addressee was unknown.

The addressee was Hilde Møller Knag, 14 New Square. It was postmarked June 15. That was not for two weeks, but the mailman had obviously not noticed that.

Sophie took the card down and read it:

Dear Hilde, Now Sophie is coming to the philosopher's house. She will soon be fifteen, but you were fifteen yesterday. Or is it today, Hilde? If it is today, it must be late, then. But our watches do not always agree. One generation ages while another generation is brought forth. In the meantime history takes its course. Have you ever thought that the history of Europe is like a human life? Antiquity is like the childhood of Europe. Then come the interminable Middle Ages—Europe's schoolday. But at last comes the Renaissance; the long schoolday is over. Europe comes of age in a burst of exuberance and a thirst for life. We could say that the Renaissance is Europe's fifteenth birthday! It is mid-June, my child, and it is wonderful to be alive!

P.S. Sorry to hear you lost your gold crucifix. You must learn to take better care of your things. Love, Dad—who is just around the corner.

Hermes was already on his way up the stairs. Sophie took the postcard with her and followed. She had to run to keep up with him; he was wagging his tail delightedly. They passed the second, third, and fourth stories. From then on there was only an attic staircase. Were they going up to the roof? Hermes clambered on up the stairs and stopped outside a narrow door, which he scratched at with his paw.

Sophie heard footsteps approaching from inside. The door opened, and there stood Alberto Knox. He had changed his clothes and was now wearing another costume. It consisted of white hose, red knee-breeches, and a yellow jacket with padded shoulders. He reminded Sophie of a joker in a deck of cards. If she was not much mistaken, this was a typical Renaissance costume.

"What a clown!" Sophie exclaimed, giving him a little push so that she could go inside the apartment.

Once again she had taken out her fear and shyness on the unfortunate philosophy teacher. Sophie's thoughts were in a turmoil because of the postcard she had found down in the hallway.

"Be calm, my child," said Alberto, closing the door behind her.

"And here's the mail," she said, handing him the postcard as if she held him responsible for it.

Alberto read it and shook his head.

"He gets more and more audacious. I wouldn't be surprised if he isn't using us as a kind of birthday diversion for his daughter."

With that he tore the postcard into small pieces and threw them into the wastepaper basket.

"It said that Hilde has lost her crucifix," said Sophie.

"So I read."

"And I found it, the same one, under my pillow at home. Can you understand how it got there?"

Alberto looked gravely into her eyes.

"It may seem alluring. But it's just a cheap trick that

costs him no effort whatsoever. Let us rather concentrate on the big white rabbit that is pulled out of the universe's top hat.''

They went into the living room. It was one of the most extraordinary rooms Sophie had ever seen.

Alberto lived in a spacious attic apartment with sloping walls. A sharp light directly from the sky flooded the room from a skylight set into one of the walls. There was also another window facing the town. Through this window Sophie could look over all the roofs in the Old Town.

But what amazed Sophie most was all the stuff the room was filled with—furniture and objects from various historical periods. There was a sofa from the thirties, an old desk from the beginning of the century, and a chair that had to be hundreds of years old. But it wasn't just the furniture. Old objects, either useful or decorative, were jumbled together on shelves and cupboards. There were old clocks and vases, mortars and retorts, knives and dolls, quill pens and bookends, octants and sextants, compasses and barometers. One entire wall was covered with books, but not the sort of books found in most bookstores. The book collection itself was a cross section of the production of many hundreds of years. On the other walls hung drawings and paintings, some from recent decades, but most of them also very old. There were a lot of old charts and maps on the walls too, and as far as Norway was concerned, they were not very accurate.

Sophie stood for several minutes without speaking and took everything in.

''What a lot of old junk you've collected,'' she said.

''Now then! Just think of how many centuries of history I have preserved in this room. I wouldn't exactly call it junk.''

''Do you manage an antique shop or something?''

Alberto looked almost pained.

''We can't all let ourselves be washed away by the tide of history, Sophie. Some of us must tarry in order to gather up what has been left along the river banks.''

''What an odd thing to say.''

"Yes, but none the less true, child. We do not live in our own time alone; we carry our history within us. Don't forget that everything you see in this room was once brand new. That old sixteenth-century wooden doll might have been made for a five-year-old girl's birthday. By her old grandfather, maybe . . . then she became a teenager, then an adult, and then she married. Maybe she had a daughter of her own and gave the doll to her. She grew old, and one day she died. Although she had lived for a very long time, one day she was dead and gone. And she will never return. Actually she was only here for a short visit. But her doll—well, there it is on the shelf."

"Everything sounds so sad and solemn when you talk like that."

"Life *is* both sad and solemn. We are let into a wonderful world, we meet one another here, greet each other—and wander together for a brief moment. Then we lose each other and disappear as suddenly and unreasonably as we arrived."

"May I ask you something?"

"We're not playing hide-and-seek any more."

"Why did you move into the major's cabin?"

"So that we would not be so far from each other, when we were only talking by letter. I knew the old cabin would be empty."

"So you just moved in?"

"That's right. I moved in."

"Then maybe you can also explain how Hilde's father knew you were there."

"If I am right, he knows practically everything."

"But I still can't understand at all how you get a mailman to deliver mail in the middle of the woods!"

Alberto smiled archly.

"Even things like that are a pure bagatelle for Hilde's father. Cheap hocus-pocus, simple sleight of hand. We are living under what is possibly the world's closest surveillance."

Sophie could feel herself getting angry.

"If I ever meet him, I'll scratch his eyes out!"

Alberto walked over and sat down on the sofa. Sophie

followed and sank into a deep armchair.

"Only philosophy can bring us closer to Hilde's father," Alberto said at last. "Today I shall tell you about the Renaissance."

"Shoot."

"Not very long after St. Thomas Aquinas, cracks began to appear in the unifying culture of Christianity. Philosophy and science broke away more and more from the theology of the Church, thus enabling religious life to attain a freer relationship to reasoning. More people now emphasized that we cannot reach God through rationalism because God is in all ways unknowable. The important thing for a man was not to understand the divine mystery but to submit to God's will.

"As religion and science could now relate more freely to each other, the way was open both to new scientific methods and a new religious fervor. Thus the basis was created for two powerful upheavals in the fifteenth and sixteenth centuries, namely, the *Renaissance* and the *Reformation*."

"Can we take them one at a time?"

"By the Renaissance we mean the rich cultural development that began in the late fourteenth century. It started in Northern Italy and spread rapidly northward during the fifteenth and sixteenth centuries."

"Didn't you tell me that the word 'renaissance' meant rebirth?"

"I did indeed, and that which was to be reborn was the art and culture of antiquity. We also speak of Renaissance humanism, since now, after the long Dark Ages in which every aspect of life was seen through divine light, everything once again revolved around man. 'Go to the source' was the motto, and that meant the humanism of antiquity first and foremost.

"It almost became a popular pastime to dig up ancient sculptures and scrolls, just as it became fashionable to learn Greek. The study of Greek humanism also had a pedagogical aim. Reading humanistic subjects provided a 'classical education' and developed what may be called human qualities. 'Horses are born,' it was said, 'but human beings are not born—they are formed.' "

"Do we have to be educated to be human beings?"

"Yes, that was the thought. But before we take a closer look at the ideas of Renaissance humanism, we must say a little about the political and cultural background of the Renaissance."

Alberto rose from the sofa and began to wander about the room. After a while he paused and pointed to an antique instrument on one of the shelves.

"What is that?" he asked.

"It looks like an old compass."

"Quite right."

He then pointed to an ancient firearm hanging on the wall above the sofa.

"And that?"

"An old-fashioned rifle."

"Exactly—and this?"

Alberto pulled a large book off one of the bookshelves.

"It's an old book."

"To be absolutely precise, it is an incunabulum."

"An incunabulum?"

"Actually, it means 'cradle.' The word is used about books printed in the cradle days of printing. That is, before 1500."

"Is it really that old?"

"That old, yes. And these three discoveries—the compass, firearms, and the printing press—were essential preconditions for this new period we call the Renaissance."

"You'll have to explain that a bit more clearly."

"The compass made it easier to navigate. In other words, it was the basis for the great voyages of discovery. So were firearms in a way. The new weapons gave the Europeans military superiority over American and Asiatic cultures, although firearms were also an important factor in Europe. Printing played an important part in spreading the Renaissance humanists' new ideas. And the art of printing was, not least, one of the factors that forced the Church to relinquish its former position as sole disseminator of knowledge. New inventions and instruments began to follow thick and fast. One important instrument, for example, was the telescope, which resulted in a completely new basis for astronomy.''

''And finally came rockets and space probes.''

''Now you're going too fast. But you could say that a process started in the Renaissance finally brought people to the moon. Or for that matter to Hiroshima and Chernobyl. However, it all began with changes on the cultural and economic front. An important condition was the transition from a subsistence economy to a monetary economy. Toward the end of the Middle Ages, cities had developed, with effective trades and a lively commerce of new goods, a monetary economy and banking. A middle class arose which developed a certain freedom with regard to the basic conditions of life. Necessities became something that could be bought for money. This state of affairs rewarded people's diligence, imagination, and ingenuity. New demands were made on the individual.''

''It's a bit like the way Greek cities developed two thousand years earlier.''

''Not altogether untrue. I told you how Greek philosophy broke away from the mythological world picture that was linked to peasant culture. In the same way, the Renaissance middle class began to break away from the feudal lords and the power of the church. As this was happening, Greek culture was being rediscovered through a closer contact with the Arabs in Spain and the Byzantine culture in the east.''

''The three diverging streams from antiquity joined into one great river.''

''You are an attentive pupil. That gives you some background on the Renaissance. I shall now tell you about the new ideas.''

''Okay, but I'll have to go home and eat.''

Alberto sat down on the sofa again. He looked at Sophie.

''Above all else, the Renaissance resulted in a *new view of mankind*. The humanism of the Renaissance brought a new belief in man and his worth, in striking contrast to the biased medieval emphasis on the sinful nature of man. Man was now considered infinitely great and valuable. One of the central figures of the Renais-

sance was *Marsilio Ficino*, who exclaimed: 'Know thyself, O divine lineage in mortal guise!' Another central
figure, *Pico della Mirandola*, wrote the *Oration on the
Dignity of Man*, something that would have been unthinkable in the Middle Ages.

"Throughout the whole medieval period, the point of
departure had always been God. The humanists of the
Renaissance took as their point of departure man himself."

"But so did the Greek philosophers."

"That is precisely why we speak of a 'rebirth' of antiquity's humanism. But Renaissance humanism was to
an even greater extent characterized by *individualism*.
We are not only human beings, we are unique individuals. This idea could then lead to an almost unrestrained
worship of genius. The ideal became what we call the
Renaissance man, a man of universal genius embracing
all aspects of life, art, and science. The new view of
man also manifested itself in an interest in the human
anatomy. As in ancient times, people once again began
to dissect the dead to discover how the body was constructed. It was imperative both for medical science and
for art. Once again it became usual for works of art to
depict the nude. High time, after a thousand years of
prudery. Man was bold enough to be himself again.
There was no longer anything to be ashamed of."

"It sounds intoxicating," said Sophie, leaning her
arms on the little table that stood between her and the
philosopher.

"Undeniably. The new view of mankind led to a
whole new outlook. Man did not exist purely for God's
sake. Man could therefore delight in life here and now.
And with this new freedom to develop, the possibilities
were limitless. The aim was now to exceed all boundaries. This was also a new idea, seen from the Greek
humanistic point of view; the humanists of antiquity had
emphasized the importance of tranquility, moderation,
and restraint."

"And the Renaissance humanists lost their restraint?"

"They were certainly not especially moderate. They
behaved as if the whole world had been reawakened.

They became intensely conscious of their epoch, which is what led them to introduce the term 'Middle Ages' to cover the centuries between antiquity and their own time. There was an unrivaled development in all spheres of life. Art and architecture, literature, music, philosophy, and science flourished as never before. I will mention one concrete example. We have spoken of Ancient Rome, which gloried in titles such as the 'city of cities' and the 'hub of the universe.' During the Middle Ages the city declined, and by 1417 the old metropolis had only 17,000 inhabitants.''

"Not much more than Lillesand, where Hilde lives.''

"The Renaissance humanists saw it as their cultural duty to restore Rome: first and foremost, to begin the construction of the great St. Peter's Church over the grave of Peter the Apostle. And St. Peter's Church can boast neither of moderation nor restraint. Many great artists of the Renaissance took part in this building project, the greatest in the world. It began in 1506 and lasted for a hundred and twenty years, and it took another fifty before the huge St. Peter's Square was completed.''

"It must be a gigantic church!''

"It is over 200 meters long and 130 meters high, and it covers an area of more than 16,000 square meters. But enough about the boldness of Renaissance man. It was also significant that the Renaissance brought with it a new view of nature. The fact that man felt at home in the world and did not consider life solely as a preparation for the hereafter, created a whole new approach to the physical world. Nature was now regarded as a positive thing. Many held the view that God was also present in his creation. If he is indeed infinite, he must be present in everything. This idea is called *pantheism*. The medieval philosophers had insisted that there is an insurmountable barrier between God and the Creation. It could now be said that nature is divine—and even that it is 'God's blossoming.' Ideas of this kind were not always looked kindly on by the church. The fate of *Giordano Bruno* was a dramatic example of this. Not only did he claim that God was present in nature, he also

believed that the universe was infinite in scope. He was
punished very severely for his ideas.''

"How?''

"He was burned at the stake in Rome's Flower Market in the year 1600.''

"How horrible . . . and stupid. And you call that humanism?''

"No, not at all. Bruno was the humanist, not his ex-
ecutioners. During the Renaissance, what we call anti-
humanism flourished as well. By this I mean the
authoritarian power of State and Church. During the
Renaissance there was a tremendous thirst for trying
witches, burning heretics, magic and superstition, bloody
religious wars—and not least, the brutal conquest of
America. But humanism has always had a shadow side.
No epoch is either purely good or purely evil. Good and
evil are twin threads that run through the history of mankind. And often they intertwine. This is not least true of
our next key phrase, a *new scientific method*, another
Renaissance innovation which I will tell you about.''

"Was that when they built the first factories?''

"No, not yet. But a precondition for all the technical
development that took place after the Renaissance was
the new scientific method. By that I mean the completely
new approach to what science was. The technical fruits
of this method only became apparent later on.''

"What was this new method?''

"Mainly it was a process of investigating nature with
our own senses. Since the fourteenth century there had
been an increasing number of thinkers who warned
against blind faith in old authority, be it religious doctrine or the natural philosophy of Aristotle. There were
also warnings against the belief that problems can be
solved purely by thinking. An exaggerated belief in the
importance of reason had been valid all through the Middle Ages. Now it was said that every investigation of
natural phenomena must be based on observation, experience, and experiment. We call this the *empirical
method*.''

"Which means?''

"It only means that one bases one's knowledge of

things on one's own experience—and not on dusty parchments or figments of the imagination. Empirical science was known in antiquity, but systematic *experiments* were something quite new.''

''I guess they didn't have any of the technical apparatus we have today.''

''Of course they had neither calculators nor electronic scales. But they had mathematics and they had scales. And it was now above all imperative to express scientific observations in precise mathematical terms. 'Measure what can be measured, and make measurable what cannot be measured,' said the Italian Galileo Galilei, who was one of the most important scientists of the seventeenth century. He also said that the book of nature is written in the language of mathematics.''

''And all these experiments and measurements made new inventions possible.''

''The first phase was a new scientific method. This made the technical revolution itself possible, and the technical breakthrough opened the way for every invention since. You could say that man had begun to break away from his natural condition. Nature was no longer something man was simply a part of. 'Knowledge is power,' said the English philosopher *Francis Bacon*, thereby underlining the practical value of knowledge— and this was indeed new. Man was seriously starting to intervene in nature and beginning to control it.''

''But not only in a good way?''

''No, this is what I was referring to before when I spoke of the good and the evil threads that are constantly intertwined in everything we do. The technical revolution that began in the Renaissance led to the spinning jenny and to unemployment, to medicines and new diseases, to the improved efficiency of agriculture and the impoverishment of the environment, to practical appliances such as the washing machine and the refrigerator and pollution and industrial waste. The serious threat to the environment we are facing today has made many people see the technical revolution itself as a perilous maladjustment to natural conditions. It has been pointed out that we have started something we can no longer control. More optimistic spirits think we are still living in the cradle of technology, and that although the scientific age has certainly had its teething troubles, we will gradually learn to control nature without at the same time threatening its very existence and thus our own.''

"Which do you think?''

"I think perhaps there may be some truth in both views. In some areas we must stop interfering with nature, but in others we can succeed. One thing is certain: There is no way back to the Middle Ages. Ever since the Renaissance, mankind has been more than just part of creation. Man has begun to intervene in nature and form it after his own image. In truth, 'what a piece of work is man!' ''

"We have already been to the moon. What medieval person would have believed such a thing possible?''

"No, that's for sure. Which brings us to the *new world view*. All through the Middle Ages people had stood beneath the sky and gazed up at the sun, the moon, the stars, and the planets. But nobody had doubted that the earth was the center of the universe. No observations had sown any doubt that the earth remained still while the 'heavenly bodies' traveled in their orbits around it. We call this the geocentric world picture, or in other words, the belief that everything revolves around the earth. The Christian belief that God ruled from on high, up above all the heavenly bodies, also contributed to maintaining this world picture.''

"I wish it were that simple!''

"But in 1543 a little book was published entitled *On the Revolutions of the Celestial Spheres*. It was written by the Polish astronomer *Nicolaus Copernicus*, who died on the day the book was published. Copernicus claimed that it was not the sun that moved round the earth, it was vice versa. He thought this was completely possible from the observations of the heavenly bodies that existed. The reason people had always believed that the sun went round the earth was that the earth turns on its own axis, he said. He pointed out that all observations of heavenly bodies were far easier to understand if one assumed that both the earth and the other planets circle around the sun. We call this the *heliocentric world picture*, which means that everything centers around the sun.''

''And that world picture was the right one?''

''Not entirely. His main point—that the earth moves round the sun—is of course correct. But he claimed that the sun was the center of the universe. Today we know that the sun is only one of an infinite number of stars, and that all the stars around us make up only one of many billions of galaxies. Copernicus also believed that the earth and the other planets moved in circular orbits around the sun.''

''Don't they?''

''No. He had nothing on which to base his belief in the circular orbits other than the ancient idea that heavenly bodies were round and moved in circles simply because they were 'heavenly.' Since the time of Plato the sphere and the circle had been considered the most perfect geometrical figures. But in the early 1600s, the German astronomer *Johannes Kepler* presented the results of comprehensive observations which showed that the planets move in elliptical—or oval—orbits with the sun at one focus. He also pointed out that the speed of a planet is greatest when it is closest to the sun, and that the farther a planet's orbit is from the sun the slower it moves. Not until Kepler's time was it actually stated that the earth was a planet just like other planets. Kepler also emphasized that the same physical laws apply everywhere throughout the universe.''

''How could he know that?''

''Because he had investigated the movements of the planets with his own senses instead of blindly trusting ancient superstitions. *Galileo Galilei*, who was roughly contemporary with Kepler, also used a telescope to observe the heavenly bodies. He studied the moon's craters and said that the moon had mountains and valleys similar to those on earth. Moreover, he discovered that the planet Jupiter had four moons. So the earth was not alone in having a moon. But the greatest significance of Galileo was that he first formulated the so-called *Law of Inertia*.''

"And that is?"

"Galileo formulated it thus: A body remains in the state which it is in, at rest or in motion, as long as no external force compels it to change its state."

"If you say so."

"But this was a significant observation. Since antiquity, one of the central arguments against the earth moving round its own axis was that the earth would then move so quickly that a stone hurled straight into the air would fall yards away from the spot it was hurled from."

"So why doesn't it?"

"If you're sitting in a train and you drop an apple, it doesn't fall backward because the train is moving. It falls straight down. That is because of the law of inertia. The apple retains exactly the same speed it had before you dropped it."

"I think I understand."

"Now in Galileo's time there were no trains. But if you roll a ball along the ground—and suddenly let go . . .''

". . . it goes on rolling . . .''

". . . because it retains its speed after you let go."

"But it will stop eventually, if the room is long enough."

"That's because other forces slow it down. First, the floor, especially if it is a rough wooden floor. Then the force of gravity will sooner or later bring it to a halt. But wait, I'll show you something."

Alberto Knox got up and went over to the old desk. He took something out of one of the drawers. When he returned to his place he put it on the coffee table. It was just a wooden board, a few millimeters thick at one end and thin at the other. Beside the board, which almost covered the whole table, he laid a green marble.

"This is called an inclined plane," he said. "What do you think will happen if I let go the marble up here, where the plane is thickest?"

Sophie sighed resignedly.

"I bet you ten crowns it rolls down onto the table and ends on the floor."

"Let's see."

Alberto let go of the marble and it behaved exactly as Sophie had said. It rolled onto the table, over the tabletop, hit the floor with a little thud and finally bumped into the wall.

"Impressive," said Sophie.

"Yes, wasn't it! This was the kind of experiment Galileo did, you see."

"Was he really that stupid?"

"Patience! He wanted to investigate things with all his senses, so we have only just begun. Tell me first why the marble rolled down the inclined plane."

"It began to roll because it was heavy."

"All right. And what is weight actually, child?"

"That's a silly question."

"It's not a silly question if you can't answer it. Why did the marble roll onto the floor?"

"Because of gravity."

"Exactly—or gravitation, as we also say. Weight has something to do with gravity. *That* was the force that set the marble in motion."

Alberto had already picked the marble up from the floor. He stood bowed over the inclined plane with the marble again.

"Now I shall try to roll the marble across the plane," he said. "Watch carefully how it moves."

Sophie watched as the marble gradually curved away and was drawn down the incline.

"What happened?" asked Alberto.

"It rolled sloping because the board is sloping."

"Now I'm going to brush the marble with ink . . . then perhaps we can study exactly what you mean by sloping."

He dug out an ink brush and painted the whole marble black. Then he rolled it again. Now Sophie could see exactly where on the plane the marble had rolled because it had left a black line on the board.

"How would you describe the marble's path?"

"It's curved . . . it looks like part of a circle."

"Precisely."

Alberto looked up at her and raised his eyebrows.

"However, it is not quite a circle. This figure is called a parabola."

"That's fine with me."

"Ah, but *why* did the marble travel in precisely that way?"

Sophie thought deeply. Then she said, "Because the board was sloping, the marble was drawn toward the floor by the force of gravity."

"Yes, yes! This is nothing less than a sensation! Here I go, dragging a girl who's not yet fifteen up to my attic, and she realizes exactly the same thing Galileo did after one single experiment!"

He clapped his hands. For a moment Sophie was afraid he had gone mad. He continued: "You saw what happened when two *forces* worked simultaneously on the same object. Galileo discovered that the same thing applied, for instance, to a cannonball. It is propelled into the air, it continues its path over the earth, but will eventually be drawn toward the earth. So it will have described a trajectory corresponding to the marble's path across the inclined plane. And this was actually a new discovery at the time of Galileo. Aristotle thought that a projectile hurled obliquely into the air would first describe a gentle curve and then fall vertically to the earth. This was not so, but nobody could know Aristotle was wrong before it had been *demonstrated*."

"Does all this really matter?"

"Does it matter? You bet it matters! This has cosmic significance, my child. Of all the scientific discoveries in the history of mankind, this is positively the most important."

"I'm sure you are going to tell me why."

"Then along came the English physicist *Isaac Newton*, who lived from 1642 to 1727. He was the one who provided the final description of the solar system and the planetary orbits. Not only could he describe how the planets moved round the sun, he could also explain *why* they did so. He was able to do so partly by referring to what we call Galileo's dynamics."

"Are the planets marbles on an inclined plane then?"

"Something like that, yes. But wait a bit, Sophie."

"Do I have a choice?"

"Kepler had already pointed out that there had to be a force that caused the heavenly bodies to attract each other. There had to be, for example, a solar force which held the planets fast in their orbits. Such a force would moreover explain why the planets moved more slowly in their orbit the further away from the sun they traveled. Kepler also believed that the ebb and flow of the tides— the rise and fall in sea level—must be the result of a lunar force."

"And that's true."

"Yes, it's true. But it was a theory Galileo rejected. He mocked Kepler, who he said had given his approval to the idea that the moon rules the water. That was because Galileo rejected the idea that the forces of gravitation could work over great distances, and also *between* the heavenly bodies."

"He was wrong there."

"Yes. On that particular point he was wrong. And that was funny, really, because he was very preoccupied with the earth's gravity and falling bodies. He had even indicated how increased force can control the movement of a body."

"But you were talking about Newton."

"Yes, along came Newton. He formulated what we call the *Law of Universal Gravitation*. This law states that every object attracts every other object with a force that increases in proportion to the size of the objects and decreases in proportion to the distance between the objects."

"I think I understand. For example, there is greater attraction between two elephants than there is between two mice. And there is greater attraction between two elephants in the same zoo than there is between an Indian elephant in India and an African elephant in Africa."

"Then you have understood it. And now comes the central point. Newton proved that this attraction—or gravitation—is universal, which means it is operative everywhere, also in space between heavenly bodies. He is said to have gotten this idea while he was sitting under an apple tree. When he saw an apple fall from the tree he had to ask himself if the moon was drawn to earth with the same force, and if this was the reason why the moon continued to orbit the earth to all eternity.''

"Smart. But not so smart really."

"Why not, Sophie?"

"Well, if the moon was drawn to the earth with the same force that causes the apple to fall, one day the moon would come crashing to earth instead of going round and round it for ever."

"Which brings us to Newton's law on planetary orbits. In the case of how the earth attracts the moon, you are fifty percent right but fifty percent wrong. Why doesn't the moon fall to earth? Because it really is true that the earth's gravitational force attracting the moon is tremendous. Just think of the force required to lift sea level a meter or two at high tide."

"I don't think I understand."

"Remember Galileo's inclined plane. What happened when I rolled the marble across it?"

"Are there two different forces working on the moon?"

"Exactly. Once upon a time when the solar system began, the moon was hurled outward—outward from the earth, that is—with tremendous force. This force will remain in effect forever because it moves in a vacuum without resistance . . ."

"But it is also attracted to the earth because of earth's gravitational force, isn't it?"

"Exactly. Both forces are constant, and both work simultaneously. Therefore the moon will continue to orbit the earth."

"Is it really as simple as that?"

"As simple as that, and this very same *simplicity* was Newton's whole point. He demonstrated that a few natural laws apply to the whole universe. In calculating the planetary orbits he had merely applied two natural laws which Galileo had already proposed. One was the law of inertia, which Newton expressed thus: 'A body remains in its state of rest or rectilinear motion until it is compelled to change that state by a force impressed on it.' The other law had been demonstrated by Galileo on an inclined plane: When two forces work on a body simultaneously, the body will move on an elliptical path.''

"And that's how Newton could explain why all the planets go round the sun."

"Yes. All the planets travel in elliptical orbits round the sun as the result of two unequal movements: first, the rectilinear movement they had when the solar system was formed, and second, the movement toward the sun due to gravitation.''

"Very clever.''

"Very. Newton demonstrated that the same laws of moving bodies apply everywhere in the entire universe. He thus did away with the medieval belief that there is one set of laws for heaven and another here on earth. The heliocentric world view had found its final confirmation and its final explanation.''

Alberto got up and put the inclined plane away again. He picked up the marble and placed it on the table between them.

Sophie thought it was amazing how much they had gotten out of a bit of slanting wood and a marble. As she looked at the green marble, which was still smudged with ink, she couldn't help thinking of the earth's globe. She said, "And people just had to accept that they were living on a random planet somewhere in space?''

"Yes—the new world view was in many ways a great burden. The situation was comparable to what happened later on when Darwin proved that mankind had developed from animals. In both cases mankind lost some of its special status in creation. And in both cases the Church put up a massive resistance.''

"I can well understand that. Because where was God in all this new stuff? It was simpler when the earth was the center and God and the planets were upstairs.''

"But that was not the greatest challenge. When Newton had proved that the same natural laws applied everywhere in the universe, one might think that he thereby undermined people's faith in God's omnipotence. But Newton's own faith was never shaken. He regarded the natural laws as proof of the existence of the great and almighty God. It's possible that man's picture of himself fared worse.''

''How do you mean?''

''Since the Renaissance, people have had to get used to living their life on a random planet in the vast galaxy. I am not sure we have wholly accepted it even now. But there were those even in the Renaissance who said that every single one of us now had a more central position than before.''

''I don't quite understand.''

''Formerly, the earth was the center of the world. But since astronomers now said that there was no absolute center to the universe, it came to be thought that there were just as many centers as there were people. Each person could be the center of a universe.''

''Ah, I think I see.''

''The Renaissance resulted in a *new religiosity*. As philosophy and science gradually broke away from theology, a new Christian piety developed. Then the Renaissance arrived with its new view of man. This had its effect on religious life. The individual's personal relationship to God was now more important than his relationship to the church as an organization.''

''Like saying one's prayers at night, for instance?''

''Yes, that too. In the medieval Catholic Church, the church's liturgy in Latin and the church's ritual prayers had been the backbone of the religious service. Only priests and monks read the Bible because it only existed in Latin. But during the Renaissance, the Bible was translated from Hebrew and Greek into national languages. It was central to what we call the *Reformation*.''

''Martin Luther . . .''

''Yes, *Martin Luther* was important, but he was not the only reformer. There were also ecclesiastical reformers who chose to remain within the Roman Catholic church. One of them was *Erasmus of Rotterdam*.''

''Luther broke with the Catholic Church because he wouldn't buy indulgences, didn't he?''

''Yes, that was one of the reasons. But there was a more important reason. According to Luther, people did not need the intercession of the church or its priests in order to receive God's forgiveness. Neither was God's forgiveness dependent on the buying of 'indulgences' from the church. Trading in these so-called letters of indulgence was forbidden by the Catholic Church from the middle of the sixteenth century.''

"God was probably glad of that."

"In general, Luther distanced himself from many of the religious customs and dogmas that had become rooted in ecclesiastical history during the Middle Ages. He wanted to return to early Christianity as it was in the New Testament. 'The Scripture alone,' he said. With this slogan Luther wished to return to the 'source' of Christianity, just as the Renaissance humanists had wanted to turn to the ancient sources of art and culture. Luther translated the Bible into German, thereby founding the German written language. He believed every man should be able to read the Bible and thus in a sense become his own priest.''

"His own priest? Wasn't that taking it a bit far?"

"What he meant was that priests had no preferential position in relation to God. The Lutheran congregations employed priests for practical reasons, such as conducting services and attending to the daily clerical tasks, but Luther did not believe that anyone received God's forgiveness and redemption from sin through church rituals. Man received 'free' redemption through faith alone, he said. This was a belief he arrived at by reading the Bible.''

"So Luther was also a typical Renaissance man?"

"Yes and no. A characteristic Renaissance feature was his emphasis on the individual and the individual's personal relationship to God. So he taught himself Greek at the age of thirty-five and began the laborious job of translating the Bible from the ancient Greek version into German. Allowing the language of the people to take precedence over Latin was also a characteristic Renaissance feature. But Luther was not a humanist like Ficino or *Leonardo da Vinci*. He was also opposed by humanists such as Erasmus of Rotterdam because they thought his view of man was far too negative; Luther had proclaimed that mankind was totally depraved after the Fall from Grace. Only through the grace of God could mankind be 'justified,' he believed. For the wages of sin is death.''

"That sounds very gloomy."

Alberto Knox rose. He picked up the little green and black marble and put it in his top pocket.

"It's after four!" Sophie exclaimed in horror.

"And the next great epoch in the history of mankind is the Baroque. But we shall have to keep that for another day, my dear Hilde.''

"What did you say?" Sophie shot up from the chair she had been sitting in. "You called me Hilde!"

"That was a serious slip of the tongue."

"But a slip of the tongue is never wholly accidental."

"You may be right. You'll notice that Hilde's father has begun to put words in our mouths. I think he is exploiting the fact that we are getting weary and are not defending ourselves very well."

"You said once that you are not Hilde's father. Is that really true?"

Alberto nodded.

"But am I Hilde?"

"I'm tired now, Sophie. You have to understand that. We have been sitting here for over two hours, and I have been doing most of the talking. Don't you have to go home to eat?"

Sophie felt almost as if he was trying to throw her out. As she went into the little hall, she thought intensely about why he had made that slip. Alberto came out after her.

Hermes was lying asleep under a small row of pegs on which hung several strange-looking garments that could have been theatrical costumes. Alberto nodded toward the dog and said, "He will come and fetch you."

"Thank you for my lesson," said Sophie.

She gave Alberto an impulsive hug. "You're the best and kindest philosophy teacher I've ever had," she said.

With that she opened the door to the staircase. As the door closed, Alberto said, "It won't be long before we meet again, Hilde."

Sophie was left with those words.

Another slip of the tongue, the villain! Sophie had a strong desire to turn around and hammer on the door but something held her back.

On reaching the street she remembered that she had no money on her. She would have to walk all the long way home. How annoying! Her mother would be both angry and worried if she didn't get back by six, that was for sure.

She had not gone more than a few yards when she suddenly noticed a coin on the sidewalk. It was ten crowns, exactly the price of a bus ticket.

Sophie found her way to the bus stop and waited for a bus to the Main Square. From there she could take a bus on the same ticket and ride almost to her door.

Not until she was standing at the Main Square waiting for the second bus did she begin to wonder why she had been lucky enough to find the coin just when she needed it.

Could Hilde's father have left it there? He was a master at leaving things in the most convenient places.

How could he, if he was in Lebanon?

And why had Alberto made that slip? Not once but twice!

Sophie shivered. She felt a chill run down her spine.

The Baroque

∞

. . . such stuff as dreams are made on . . .

Sophie heard nothing more from Alberto for several days, but she glanced frequently into the garden hoping to catch sight of Hermes. She told her mother that the dog had found its own way home and that she had been invited in by its owner, a former physics teacher. He had told Sophie about the solar system and the new science that developed in the sixteenth century.

She told Joanna more. She told her all about her visit to Alberto, the postcard in the mailbox, and the ten-crown piece she had found on the way home. She kept the dream about Hilde and the gold crucifix to herself.

On Tuesday, May 29, Sophie was standing in the kitchen doing the dishes. Her mother had gone into the living room to watch the TV news. When the opening theme faded out she heard from the kitchen that a major in the Norwegian UN Battalion had been killed by a shell.

Sophie threw the dish towel on the table and rushed into the living room. She was just in time to catch a glimpse of the UN officer's face for a few seconds before they switched to the next item.

"Oh no!" she cried.

Her mother turned to her.

"Yes, war is a terrible thing!"

Sophie burst into tears.

"But Sophie, it's not that bad!"

"Did they say his name?"

"Yes, but I don't remember it. He was from Grimstad, I think."

"Isn't that the same as Lillesand?"

"No, you're being silly."

"But if you come from Grimstad, you might go to school in Lillesand."

She had stopped crying, but now it was her mother's turn to react. She got out of her chair and switched off the TV.

"What's going on, Sophie?"

"Nothing."

"Yes, there is. You have a boyfriend, and I'm beginning to think he's much older than you. Answer me now: Do you know a man in Lebanon?"

"No, not exactly . . ."

"Have you met the *son* of someone in Lebanon?"

"No, I haven't. I haven't even met his daughter."

"Whose daughter?"

"It's none of your business."

"I think it is."

"Maybe I should start asking some questions instead. Why is Dad never home? Is it because you haven't got the guts to get a divorce? Maybe you've got a boyfriend you don't want Dad and me to know about and so on and so on. I've got plenty of questions of my own."

"I think we need to talk."

"That may be. But right now I'm so worn out I'm going to bed. And I'm getting my period."

Sophie ran up to her room; she felt like crying.

As soon as she was through in the bathroom and had curled up under the covers, her mother came into the bedroom.

Sophie pretended to be asleep even though she knew her mother wouldn't believe it. She knew her mother knew that Sophie knew her mother wouldn't believe it either. Nevertheless her mother pretended to believe that Sophie was asleep. She sat on the edge of Sophie's bed and stroked her hair.

Sophie was thinking how complicated it was to live two lives at the same time. She began to look forward

218   JOSTEIN GAARDER

to the end of the philosophy course. Maybe it would be over by her birthday—or at least by Midsummer Eve, when Hilde's father would be home from Lebanon . . .

"I want to have a birthday party," she said suddenly.

"That sounds great. Who will you invite?"

"Lots of people . . . Can I?"

"Of course. We have a big garden. Hopefully the good weather will continue."

"Most of all I'd like to have it on Midsummer Eve."

"All right, that's what we'll do."

"It's a very important day," Sophie said, thinking not only of her birthday.

"It is, indeed."

"I feel I've grown up a lot lately."

"That's good, isn't it?"

"I don't know."

Sophie had been talking with her head almost buried in her pillow. Now her mother said, "Sophie—you must tell me why you seem so out of balance at the moment."

"Weren't you like this when you were fifteen?"

"Probably. But you know what I am talking about."

Sophie suddenly turned to face her mother. "The dog's name is Hermes," she said.

"It is?"

"It belongs to a man called Alberto."

"I see."

"He lives down in the Old Town."

"You went all that way with the dog?"

"There's nothing dangerous about that."

"You said that the dog had often been here."

"Did I say that?"

She had to think now. She wanted to tell as much as possible, but she couldn't tell everything.

"You're hardly ever at home," she ventured.

"No, I'm much too busy."

"Alberto and Hermes have been here lots of times."

"What for? Were they in the house as well?"

"Can't you at least ask one question at a time? They haven't been in the house. But they often go for walks in the woods. Is that so mysterious?"

"No, not in the least."

"They walk past our gate like everyone else when they go for a walk. One day when I got home from school I talked to the dog. That's how I got to know Alberto."

"What about the white rabbit and all that stuff?"

"That was something Alberto said. He is a real philosopher, you see. He has told me about all the philosophers."

"Just like that, over the hedge?"

"He has also written letters to me, lots of times, actually. Sometimes he has sent them by mail and other times he has just dropped them in the mailbox on his way out for a walk."

"So that was the 'love letter' we talked about."

"Except that it wasn't a love letter."

"And he only wrote about philosophy?"

"Yes, can you imagine! And I've learned more from him than I have learned in eight years of school. For instance, have you ever heard of Giordano Bruno, who was burned at the stake in 1600? Or of Newton's Law of Universal Gravitation?"

"No, there's a lot I don't know."

"I bet you don't even know why the earth orbits the sun—and it's your own planet!"

"About how old is this man?"

"I have no idea—about fifty, probably."

"But what is his connection with Lebanon?"

This was a tough one. Sophie thought hard. She chose the most likely story.

"Alberto has a brother who's a major in the UN Battalion. And he's from Lillesand. Maybe he's the major who once lived in the major's cabin."

"Alberto's a funny kind of name, isn't it?"

"Perhaps."

"It sounds Italian."

"Well, nearly everything that's important comes either from Greece or from Italy."

"But he speaks Norwegian?"

"Oh yes, fluently."

"You know what, Sophie—I think you should invite

Alberto home one day. I have never met a real philosopher.''

''We'll see.''

''Maybe we could invite him to your birthday party? It could be such fun to mix the generations. Then maybe I could come too. At least, I could help with the serving. Wouldn't that be a good idea?''

''If he will. At any rate, he's more interesting to talk to than the boys in my class. It's just that . . .''

''What?''

''They'd probably flip and think Alberto was my new boyfriend.''

''Then you just tell them he isn't.''

''Well, we'll have to see.''

''Yes, we shall. And Sophie—it *is* true that things haven't always been easy between Dad and me. But there was never anyone else . . .''

''I have to sleep now. I've got such awful cramps.''

''Do you want an aspirin?''

''Yes, please.''

When her mother returned with the pill and a glass of water Sophie had fallen asleep.

May 31 was a Thursday. Sophie agonized through the afternoon classes at school. She was doing better in some subjects since she started on the philosophy course. Usually her grades were good in most subjects, but lately they were even better, except in math.

In the last class they got an essay handed back. Sophie had written on ''Man and Technology.'' She had written reams on the Renaissance and the scientific breakthrough, the new view of nature and Francis Bacon, who had said that knowledge was power. She had been very careful to point out that the empirical method came before the technological discoveries. Then she had written about some of the things she could think of about technology that were not so good for society. She ended with a paragraph on the fact that everything people do can be used for good or evil. Good and evil are like a white and a black thread that make up a single strand.

Sometimes they are so closely intertwined that it is impossible to untangle them.

As the teacher gave out the exercise books he looked down at Sophie and winked.

She got an A and the comment: "Where do you get all this from?" As he stood there, she took out a pen and wrote with block letters in the margin of her exercise book: I'M STUDYING PHILOSOPHY.

As she was closing the exercise book again, something fell out of it. It was a postcard from Lebanon:

Dear Hilde, When you read this we shall already have spoken together by phone about the tragic death down here. Sometimes I ask myself if war could have been avoided if people had been a bit better at thinking. Perhaps the best remedy against violence would be a short course in philosophy. What about "the UN's little philosophy book"—which all new citizens of the world could be given a copy of in their own language. I'll propose the idea to the UN General Secretary.

You said on the phone that you were getting better at looking after your things. I'm glad, because you're the untidiest creature I've ever met. Then you said the only thing you'd lost since we last spoke was ten crowns. I'll do what I can to help you find it. Although I am far away, I have a helping hand back home. (If I find the money I'll put it in with your birthday present.) Love, Dad, who feels as if he's already started the long trip home.

Sophie had just managed to finish reading the card when the last bell rang. Once again her thoughts were in turmoil.

Joanna was waiting in the playground. On the way home Sophie opened her schoolbag and showed Joanna the latest card.

"When is it postmarked?" asked Joanna.

"Probably June 15 . . ."

"No, look . . . 5/30/90, it says."

"That was yesterday . . . the day after the death of the major in Lebanon."

"I doubt if a postcard from Lebanon can get to Norway in one day," said Joanna.

"Especially not considering the rather unusual address: Hilde Møller Knag, c/o Sophie Amundsen, Furulia Junior High School . . ."

"Do you think it could have come by mail? And the teacher just popped it in your exercise book?"

"No idea. I don't know whether I dare ask either."

No more was said about the postcard.

"I'm going to have a garden party on Midsummer Eve," said Sophie.

"With boys?"

Sophie shrugged her shoulders. "We don't have to invite the worst idiots."

"But you are going to invite Jeremy?"

"If you want. By the way, I might invite Alberto Knox."

"You must be crazy!"

"I know."

That was as far as the conversation got before their ways parted at the supermarket.

The first thing Sophie did when she got home was to see if Hermes was in the garden. Sure enough, there he was, sniffing around the apple trees.

"Hermes!"

The dog stood motionless for a second. Sophie knew exactly what was going on in that second: the dog heard her call, recognized her voice, and decided to see if she was there. Then, discovering her, he began to run toward her. Finally all four legs came pattering like drumsticks.

That was actually quite a lot in the space of one second.

He dashed up to her, wagged his tail wildly, and jumped up to lick her face.

"Hermes, clever boy! Down, down. No, stop slobbering all over me. Heel, boy! That's it!"

Sophie let herself into the house. Sherekan came jumping out from the bushes. He was rather wary of the stranger. Sophie put his cat food out, poured birdseed in the budgerigars' cup, got out a salad leaf for the tortoise, and wrote a note to her mother.

She wrote that she was going to take Hermes home and would be back by seven.

They set off through the town. Sophie had remembered to take some money with her this time. She wondered whether she ought to take the bus with Hermes, but decided she had better wait and ask Alberto about it.

While she walked on and on behind Hermes she thought about what an animal really is.

What was the difference between a dog and a person? She recalled Aristotle's words. He said that people and animals are both natural living creatures with a lot of characteristics in common. But there was one distinct difference between people and animals, and that was human reasoning.

How could he have been so sure?

Democritus, on the other hand, thought people and animals were really rather alike because both were made up of atoms. And he didn't think that either people or animals had immortal souls. According to him, souls were built up of atoms that are spread to the winds when people die. He was the one who thought a person's soul was inseparably bound to the brain.

But how could the soul be made of atoms? The soul wasn't anything you could touch like the rest of the body. It was something "spiritual."

They were already beyond Main Square and were approaching the Old Town. When they got to the sidewalk where Sophie had found the ten crowns, she looked automatically down at the asphalt. And there, on exactly the same spot where she had bent down and picked up the money, lay a postcard with the picture side up. The picture showed a garden with palms and orange trees.

Sophie bent down and picked up the card. Hermes started growling as if he didn't like Sophie touching it.

The card read:

Dear Hilde, Life consists of a long chain of coincidences. It is not altogether unlikely that the ten crowns you lost turned up right here. Maybe it was found on the square in Lillesand by an old lady who was waiting for the bus to Kristiansand. From Kristiansand she took the train to visit her grandchildren, and many, many hours later she lost the coin here on New Square. It is then perfectly possible that the very same coin was picked up later on that day by a girl who really needed it to get home by bus. You never can tell, Hilde, but if it is truly so, then one must certainly ask whether or not God's providence is behind everything. Love, Dad, who in spirit is sitting on the dock at home in Lillesand. P.S. I said I would help you find the ten crowns.

On the address side it said: "Hilde Møller Knag, c/o a casual passer-by . . ." The postmark was stamped 6/15/90.

Sophie ran up the stairs after Hermes. As soon as Alberto opened the door, she said:

"Out of my way. Here comes the mailman."

She felt she had every reason to be annoyed. Alberto stood aside as she barged in. Hermes laid himself down under the coat pegs as before.

"Has the major presented another visiting card, my child?"

Sophie looked up at him and discovered that he was wearing a different costume. He had put on a long curled wig and a wide, baggy suit with a mass of lace. He wore a loud silk scarf at his throat, and on top of the suit he had thrown a red cape. He also wore white stockings and thin patent leather shoes with bows. The whole costume reminded Sophie of pictures she had seen of the court of Louis XIV.

"You clown!" she said and handed him the card.

"Hm . . . and you really found ten crowns on the same spot where he planted the card?"

"Exactly."

"He gets ruder all the time. But maybe it's just as well."

"Why?"

"It'll make it easier to unmask him. But this trick was

both pompous and tasteless. It almost stinks of cheap perfume.''

"Perfume?''

"It tries to be elegant but is really a sham. Can't you see how he has the effrontery to compare his own shabby surveillance of us with God's providence?''

He held up the card. Then he tore it to pieces. So as not to make his mood worse she refrained from mentioning the card that fell out of her exercise book at school.

"Let's go in and sit down. What time is it?''

"Four o'clock.''

"And today we are going to talk about the seventeenth century.''

They went into the living room with the sloping walls and the skylight. Sophie noticed that Alberto had put different objects out in place of some of those she had seen last time.

On the coffee table was a small antique casket containing an assorted collection of lenses for eyeglasses. Beside it lay an open book. It looked really old.

"What is that?'' Sophie asked.

"It is a first edition of the book of Descartes's philosophical essays published in 1637 in which his famous *Discourse on Method* originally appeared, and one of my most treasured possessions.''

"And the casket?''

"It holds an exclusive collection of lenses—or optical glass. They were polished by the Dutch philosopher Spinoza sometime during the mid-1600s. They were extremely costly and are also among my most valued treasures.''

"I would probably understand better how valuable these things are if I knew who Spinoza and Descartes were.''

"Of course. But first let us try to familiarize ourselves with the period they lived in. Have a seat.''

They sat in the same places as before, Sophie in the big armchair and Alberto Knox on the sofa. Between them was the coffee table with the book and the casket. Alberto removed his wig and laid it on the writing desk.

"We are going to talk about the seventeenth century—or what we generally refer to as the Baroque period."

"The Baroque period? What a strange name."

"The word 'baroque' comes from a word that was first used to describe a pearl of irregular shape. Irregularity was typical of Baroque art, which was much richer in highly contrastive forms than the plainer and more harmonious Renaissance art. The seventeenth century was on the whole characterized by tensions between irreconcilable contrasts. On the one hand there was the Renaissance's unremitting optimism—and on the other hand there were the many who sought the opposite extreme in a life of religious seclusion and self-denial. Both in art and in real life, we meet pompous and flamboyant forms of self-expression, while at the same time there arose a monastic movement, turning away from the world."

"Both proud palaces and remote monasteries, in other words."

"Yes, you could certainly say that. One of the Baroque period's favorite sayings was the Latin expression 'carpe diem'—'seize the day.' Another Latin expression that was widely quoted was 'memento mori,' which means 'Remember that you must die.' In art, a painting could depict an extremely luxurious lifestyle, with a little skull painted in one corner.

"In many senses, the Baroque period was characterized by *vanity* or affectation. But at the same time a lot of people were concerned with the other side of the coin; they were concerned with the *ephemeral* nature of things. That is, the fact that all the beauty that surrounds us must one day perish."

"It's true. It is sad to realize that nothing lasts."

"You think exactly as many people did in the seventeenth century. The Baroque period was also an age of conflict in a political sense. Europe was ravaged by wars. The worst was the Thirty Years' War which raged over most of the continent from 1618 to 1648. In reality it was a series of wars which took a particular toll on Germany. Not least as a result of the Thirty Years' War,

France gradually became the dominant power in Europe.''

"What were the wars about?"

"To a great extent they were wars between Protestants and Catholics. But they were also about political power.''

"More or less like in Lebanon."

"Apart from wars, the seventeenth century was a time of great class differences. I'm sure you have heard of the French aristocracy and the Court of Versailles. I don't know whether you have heard much about the poverty of the French people. But any display of magnificence presupposes a display of power. It has often been said that the political situation in the Baroque period was not unlike its art and architecture. Baroque buildings were typified by a lot of ornate nooks and crannies. In a somewhat similar fashion the political situation was typified by intrigue, plotting, and assassinations.''

"Wasn't a Swedish king shot in a theater?"

"You're thinking of Gustav III, a good example of the sort of thing I mean. The assassination of Gustav III wasn't until 1792, but the circumstances were quite baroque. He was murdered while attending a huge masked ball.''

"I thought he was at the theater."

"The great masked ball was held at the Opera. We could say that the Baroque period in Sweden came to an end with the murder of Gustav III. During his time there had been a rule of 'enlightened despotism,' similar to that in the reign of Louis XIV almost a hundred years earlier. Gustav III was also an extremely vain person who adored all French ceremony and courtesies. He also loved the theater . . .''

". . . and that was the death of him."

"Yes, but the theater of the Baroque period was more than an art form. It was the most commonly employed symbol of the time.''

"A symbol of what?"

"Of life, Sophie. I don't know how many times during the seventeenth century it was said that 'Life is a theater.' It was very often, anyway. The Baroque period gave birth to modern theater—with all its forms of scenery and theatrical machinery. In the theater one built up an illusion on stage—to expose ultimately that the stage play was just an illusion. The theater thus became a reflection of human life in general. The theater could show that 'pride comes before a fall,' and present a merciless portrait of human frailty.''

"Did *Shakespeare* live in the Baroque period?"

"He wrote his greatest plays around the year 1600, so he stands with one foot in the Renaissance and the other in the Baroque. Shakespeare's work is full of passages about life as a theater. Would you like to hear some of them?"

"Yes."

"In *As You Like It*, he says:

> All the world's a stage,
> And all the men and women merely players:
> They have their exits and their entrances;
> And one man in his time plays many parts.

"And in *Macbeth*, he says:

> Life's but a walking shadow, a poor player
> That struts and frets his hour upon the stage,
> And then is heard no more; it is a tale
> Told by an idiot, full of sound and fury,
> Signifying nothing.''

"How very pessimistic."

"He was preoccupied with the brevity of life. You must have heard Shakespeare's most famous line?"

"To be or not to be—that is the question."

"Yes, spoken by Hamlet. One day we are walking around on the earth—and the next day we are dead and gone.''

"Thanks, I got the message."

"When they were not comparing life to a stage, the Baroque poets were comparing life to a dream. Shakespeare says, for example: We are such stuff as dreams are made on, and our little life is rounded with a sleep . . .''

"That was very poetic."

"The Spanish dramatist *Calderón de la Barca*, who was born in the year 1600, wrote a play called *Life Is a Dream*, in which he says: 'What is life? A madness. What is life? An illusion, a shadow, a story, and the greatest good is little enough, for all life is a dream . . .' ''

"He may be right. We read a play at school. It was called *Jeppe on the Mount*."

"By *Ludvig Holberg*, yes. He was a gigantic figure here in Scandinavia, marking the transition from the Baroque period to the Age of Enlightenment."

"Jeppe falls asleep in a ditch . . . and wakes up in the Baron's bed. So he thinks he only dreamed that he was a poor farmhand. Then when he falls asleep again they carry him back to the ditch, and he wakes up again. This time he thinks he only dreamed he was lying in the Baron's bed."

"Holberg borrowed this theme from Calderón, and Calderón had borrowed it from the old Arabian tales, *A Thousand and One Nights*. Comparing life to a dream, though, is a theme we find even farther back in history, not least in India and China. The old Chinese sage *Chuang-tzu*, for example, said: Once I dreamed I was a butterfly, and now I no longer know whether I am Chuang-tzu, who dreamed I was a butterfly, or whether I am a butterfly dreaming that I am Chuang-tzu."

"Well, it was impossible to prove either way."

"We had in Norway a genuine Baroque poet called *Petter Dass*, who lived from 1647 to 1707. On the one hand he was concerned with describing life as it is here and now, and on the other hand he emphasized that only God is eternal and constant."

"God is God if every land was waste, God is God if every man were dead."

"But in the same hymn he writes about rural life in Northern Norway—and about lumpfish, cod, and coalfish. This is a typical Baroque feature, describing in the same text the earthly and the here and now—and the celestial and the hereafter. It is all very reminiscent of

Plato's distinction between the concrete world of the senses and the immutable world of ideas."

"What about their philosophy?"

"That too was characterized by powerful struggles between diametrically opposed modes of thought. As I have already mentioned, some philosophers believed that what exists is at bottom spiritual in nature. This standpoint is called idealism. The opposite viewpoint is called materialism. By this is meant a philosophy which holds that all real things derive from concrete material substances. Materialism also had many advocates in the seventeenth century. Perhaps the most influential was the English philosopher *Thomas Hobbes*. He believed that all phenomena, including man and animals, consist exclusively of particles of matter. Even human consciousness—or the soul—derives from the movement of tiny particles in the brain."

"So he agreed with what Democritus said two thousand years before?"

"Both idealism and materialism are themes you will find all through the history of philosophy. But seldom have both views been so clearly present at the same time as in the Baroque. Materialism was constantly nourished by the new sciences. Newton showed that the same laws of motion applied to the whole universe, and that all changes in the natural world—both on earth and in space—were explained by the principles of universal gravitation and the motion of bodies.

"Everything was thus governed by the same unbreakable laws—or by the same *mechanisms*. It is therefore possible in principle to calculate every natural change with mathematical precision. And thus Newton completed what we call the *mechanistic world view*."

"Did he imagine the world as one big machine?"

"He did indeed. The word 'mechanic' comes from the Greek word 'mechane,' which means machine. It is remarkable that neither Hobbes nor Newton saw any contradiction between the mechanistic world picture and belief in God. But this was not the case for all eighteenth- and nineteenth-century materialists. The French physician and philosopher *La Mettrie* wrote a book in the eighteenth century called *L'homme machine*, which means 'Man—the machine.' Just as the leg has muscles to walk with, so has the brain 'muscles' to think with. Later on, the French mathematician *Laplace* expressed an extreme mechanistic view with this idea: If an intelligence at a given time had known the position of all particles of matter, 'nothing would be unknown, and both future and past would lie open before their eyes.' The idea here was that everything that happens is predetermined. 'It's written in the stars' that something will happen. This view is called *determinism*."

"So there was no such thing as free will."

"No, everything was a product of mechanical processes—also our thoughts and dreams. German materialists in the nineteenth century claimed that the relationship of thought to the brain was like the relationship of urine to the kidneys and gall to the liver."

"But urine and gall are material. Thoughts aren't."

"You've got hold of something central there. I can tell you a story about the same thing. A Russian astronaut and a Russian brain surgeon were once discussing religion. The brain surgeon was a Christian but the astronaut was not. The astronaut said, 'I've been out in space many times but I've never seen God or angels.' And the brain surgeon said, 'And I've operated on many clever brains but I've never seen a single thought.'"

"But that doesn't prove that thoughts don't exist."

"No, but it does underline the fact that thoughts are not things that can be operated on or broken down into ever smaller parts. It is not easy, for example, to surgically remove a delusion. It grows too deep, as it were, for surgery. An important seventeenth-century philosopher named *Leibniz* pointed out that the difference between the material and the spiritual is precisely that the material can be broken up into smaller and smaller bits, but the soul cannot even be divided into two."

"No, what kind of scalpel would you use for that?"

Alberto simply shook his head. After a while he pointed down at the table between them and said:

"The two greatest philosophers in the seventeenth century were Descartes and Spinoza. They too struggled with questions like the relationship between 'soul' and 'body,' and we are now going to study them more closely.''

"Go ahead. But I'm supposed to be home by seven.''

Descartes

∞

. . . he wanted to clear all the rubble off the site . . .

Alberto stood up, took off the red cloak, and laid it over a chair. Then he settled himself once again in the corner of the sofa.

"*René Descartes* was born in 1596 and lived in a number of different European countries at various periods of his life. Even as a young man he had a strong desire to achieve insight into the nature of man and the universe. But after studying philosophy he became increasingly convinced of his own ignorance."

"Like Socrates?"

"More or less like him, yes. Like Socrates, he was convinced that certain knowledge is only attainable through reason. We can never trust what the old books tell us. We cannot even trust what our senses tell us."

"Plato thought that too. He believed that only reason can give us certain knowledge."

"Exactly. There is a direct line of descent from Socrates and Plato via St. Augustine to Descartes. They were all typical rationalists, convinced that reason was the only path to knowledge. After comprehensive studies, Descartes came to the conclusion that the body of knowledge handed down from the Middle Ages was not necessarily reliable. You can compare him to Socrates, who did not trust the general views he encountered in the central square of Athens. So what does one do, Sophie? Can you tell me that?"

"You begin to work out your own philosophy."

"Right! Descartes decided to travel around Europe, the way Socrates spent his life talking to people in Athens. He relates that from then on he meant to confine himself to seeking the wisdom that was to be found, either within himself or in the 'great book of the world.' So he joined the army and went to war, which enabled him to spend periods of time in different parts of Central Europe. Later he lived for some years in Paris, but in 1629 he went to Holland, where he remained for nearly twenty years working on his mathematical and philosophic writings.

"In 1649 he was invited to Sweden by Queen Christina. But his sojourn in what he called 'the land of bears, ice, and rocks' brought on an attack of pneumonia and he died in the winter of 1650."

"So he was only 54 when he died."

"Yes, but he was to have enormous influence on philosophy, even after his death. One can say without exaggeration that Descartes was the father of modern philosophy. Following the heady rediscovery of man and nature in the Renaissance, the need to assemble contemporary thought into one coherent philosophical system again presented itself. The first significant system-builder was Descartes, and he was followed by Spinoza and Leibniz, Locke and Berkeley, Hume and Kant."

"What do you mean by a philosophical system?"

"I mean a philosophy that is constructed from the ground up and that is concerned with finding explanations for all the central questions of philosophy. Antiquity had its great system-constructors in Plato and Aristotle. The Middle Ages had St. Thomas Aquinas, who tried to build a bridge between Aristotle's philosophy and Christian theology. Then came the Renaissance, with a welter of old and new beliefs about nature and science, God and man. Not until the seventeenth century did philosophers make any attempt to assemble the new ideas into a clarified philosophical system, and the first to attempt it was Descartes. His work was the forerunner of what was to be philosophy's most important project in the coming generations. His main concern was with what we can know, or in other words, *certain knowledge*. The other great question that preoccupied him was *the relationship between body and mind*. Both these questions were the substance of philosophical argument for the next hundred and fifty years."

"He must have been ahead of his time."

"Ah, but the question belonged to the age. When it came to acquiring certain knowledge, many of his contemporaries voiced a total philosophic *skepticism*. They thought that man should accept that he knew nothing. But Descartes would not. Had he done so he would not have been a real philosopher. We can again draw a parallel with Socrates, who did not accept the skepticism of the Sophists. And it was in Descartes's lifetime that the new natural sciences were developing a method by which to provide certain and exact descriptions of natural processes.

"Descartes was obliged to ask himself if there was a similar certain and exact method of philosophic reflection."

"That I can understand."

"But that was only part of it. The new physics had also raised the question of the nature of matter, and thus what determines the physical processes of nature. More and more people argued in favor of a mechanistic view of nature. But the more mechanistic the physical world was seen to be, the more pressing became the question of the relationship between body and soul. Until the seventeenth century, the soul had commonly been considered as a sort of 'breath of life' that pervaded all living creatures. The original meaning of the words 'soul' and 'spirit' is, in fact, 'breath' and 'breathing.' This is the case for almost all European languages. To Aristotle, the soul was something that was present everywhere in the organism as its 'life principle'—and therefore could not be conceived as separate from the body. So he was able to speak of a plant soul or an animal soul. Philosophers did not introduce any radical division of soul and body until the seventeenth century. The reason was that the motions of all material objects—including the body, animal or human—were explained as involving mechanical processes. But man's soul could surely not be part of this body machinery, could it? What of the soul, then? An explanation was required not least of how something 'spiritual' could start a mechanical process."

"It's a strange thought, actually."

"What is?"

"I decide to lift my arm—and then, well, the arm lifts itself. Or I decide to run for a bus, and the next second my legs are moving. Or I'm thinking about something sad, and suddenly I'm crying. So there must be some mysterious connection between body and consciousness."

"That was exactly the problem that set Descartes's thoughts going. Like Plato, he was convinced that there was a sharp division between 'spirit' and 'matter.' But as to how the mind influences the body—or *the soul* the body—Plato could not provide an answer."

"Neither have I, so I am looking forward to hearing what Descartes's theory was."

"Let us follow his own line of reasoning."

Albert pointed to the book that lay on the table between them.

"In his *Discourse on Method*, Descartes raises the question of the method the philosopher must use to solve a philosophical problem. Science already had its new method . . ."

"So you said."

"Descartes maintains that we cannot accept anything as being true unless we can clearly and distinctly perceive it. To achieve this can require the breaking down of a compound problem into as many single factors as possible. Then we can take our point of departure in the simplest idea of all. You could say that every single thought must be weighed and measured, rather in the way Galileo wanted everything to be measured and everything immeasurable to be made measurable. Descartes believed that philosophy should go from the simple to the complex. Only then would it be possible to construct a new insight. And finally it would be necessary to ensure by constant enumeration and control that nothing was left out. Then, a philosophical conclusion would be within reach."

"It sounds almost like a math test."

"Yes. Descartes was a mathematician; he is considered the father of analytical geometry, and he made important contributions to the science of algebra. Descartes wanted to use the 'mathematical method' even for philosophizing. He set out to prove philosophical truths in the way one proves a mathematical theorem. In other words, he wanted to use exactly the same instrument that we use when we work with figures, namely, *reason*, since only reason can give us certainty. It is far from certain that we can rely on our senses. We have already noted Descartes's affinity with Plato, who also observed that mathematics and numerical ratio give us more certainty than the evidence of our senses."

"But can one solve philosophical problems that way?"

"We had better go back to Descartes's own reasoning. His aim is to reach certainty about the nature of life, and he starts by maintaining that at first one should doubt everything. He didn't want to build on sand, you see."

"No, because if the foundations give way, the whole house collapses."

"As you so neatly put it, my child. Now, Descartes did not think it reasonable to doubt everything, but he thought it was possible *in principle* to doubt everything. For one thing, it is by no means certain that we advance our philosophical quest by reading Plato or Aristotle. It may increase our knowledge of history but not of the world. It was important for Descartes to rid himself of all handed down, or received, learning before beginning his own philosophical construction."

"He wanted to clear all the rubble off the site before starting to build his new house . . ."

"Thank you. He wanted to use only fresh new materials in order to be sure that his new thought construction would hold. But Descartes's doubts went even deeper. We cannot even trust what our senses tell us, he said. Maybe they are deceiving us."

"How come?"

"When we dream, we feel we are experiencing reality. What separates our waking feelings from our dream feelings?

" 'When I consider this carefully, I find not a single property which with certainty separates the waking state from the dream,' writes Descartes. And he goes on: 'How can you be certain that your whole life is not a dream?' "

"Jeppe thought he had only been dreaming when he had slept in the Baron's bed."

"And when he was lying in the Baron's bed, he thought his life as a poor peasant was only a dream. So in the same way, Descartes ends up doubting absolutely everything. Many philosophers before him had reached the end of the road at that very point."

"So they didn't get very far."

"But Descartes tried to work forward from this zero point. He doubted everything, and that was the only thing he was certain of. But now something struck him: one thing had to be true, and that was that he doubted. When he doubted, he had to be thinking, and because he was thinking, it had to be certain that he was a thinking being. Or, as he himself expressed it: *Cogito, ergo sum.*"

"Which means?"

"I think, therefore I am."

"I'm not surprised he realized that."

"Fair enough. But notice the intuitive certainty with which he suddenly perceives himself as a thinking being. Perhaps you now recall what Plato said, that what we grasp with our reason is more real than what we grasp with our senses. That's the way it was for Descartes. He perceived not only that he was a thinking *I*, he realized at the same time that this thinking *I* was more real than the material world which we perceive with our senses. And he went on. He was by no means through with his philosophical quest."

"What came next?"

"Descartes now asked himself if there was anything more he could perceive with the same intuitive certainty.

He came to the conclusion that in his mind he had a clear and distinct idea of a perfect entity. This was an idea he had always had, and it was thus self-evident to Descartes that such an idea could not possibly have come from himself. The idea of a perfect entity cannot have originated from one who was himself imperfect, he claimed. Therefore the idea of a perfect entity must have originated from that perfect entity itself, or in other words, from God. That God exists was therefore just as self-evident for Descartes as that a thinking being must exist.''

''Now he was jumping to a conclusion. He was more cautious to begin with.''

''You're right. Many people have called that his weak spot. But you say 'conclusion.' Actually it was not a question of proof. Descartes only meant that we all possess the idea of a perfect entity, and that inherent in that idea is the fact that this perfect entity must exist. Because a perfect entity wouldn't be perfect if it didn't exist. Neither would we possess the idea of a perfect entity if there *were* no perfect entity. For we are imperfect, so the idea of perfection cannot come from us. According to Descartes, the idea of God is innate, it is stamped on us from birth 'like the artisan's mark stamped on his product.' ''

''Yes, but just because I possess the idea of a crocophant doesn't mean that the crocophant exists.''

''Descartes would have said that it is not inherent in the concept of a crocophant that it exists. On the other hand, it is inherent in the concept of a perfect entity that such an entity exists. According to Descartes, this is just as certain as it is inherent in the idea of a circle that all points of the circle are equidistant from the center. You cannot have a circle that does not conform to this law. Nor can you have a perfect entity that lacks its most important property, namely, existence.''

''That's an odd way of thinking.''

''It is a decidedly rationalistic way of thinking. Descartes believed like Socrates and Plato that there is a connection between reason and being. The more self-

evident a thing is to one's reason, the more certain it is
that it exists.''

"So far he has gotten to the fact that he is a thinking
person and that there exists a perfect entity.''

"Yes, and with this as his point of departure, he proceeds. In the question of all the ideas we have about
outer reality—for example, the sun and the moon—there
is the possibility that they are fantasies. But outer reality
also has certain characteristics that we can perceive with
our reason. These are the mathematical properties, or, in
other words, the kinds of things that are measurable,
such as length, breadth, and depth. Such 'quantitative'
properties are just as clear and distinct to my reason as
the fact that I am a thinking being. 'Qualitative' properties such as color, smell, and taste, on the other hand,
are linked to our sense perception and as such do not
describe outer reality.''

"So nature is not a dream after all.''

"No, and on that point Descartes once again draws
upon our idea of the perfect entity. When our reason
recognizes something clearly and distinctly—as is the
case for the mathematical properties of outer reality—it
must necessarily be so. Because a perfect God would
not deceive us. Descartes claims 'God's guarantee' that
whatever we perceive with our reason also corresponds
to reality.''

"Okay, so now he's found out he's a thinking being,
God exists, and there is an outer reality.''

"Ah, but the outer reality is essentially different from
the reality of thought. Descartes now maintains that there
are two different forms of reality—or two 'substances.'
One substance is *thought*, or the 'mind,' the other is
extension, or matter. The mind is purely conscious, it
takes up no room in space and can therefore not be subdivided into smaller parts. Matter, however, is purely
extension, it takes up room in space and can therefore
always be subdivided into smaller and smaller parts—
but it has no consciousness. Descartes maintained that
both substances originate from God, because only God
himself exists independently of anything else. But although both thought and extension come from God, the

two substances have no contact with each other. Thought is quite independent of matter, and conversely, the material processes are quite independent of thought."

"So he divided God's creation into two."

"Precisely. We say that Descartes is a *dualist*, which means that he effects a sharp division between the reality of thought and extended reality. For example, only man has a mind. Animals belong completely to extended reality. Their living and moving are accomplished mechanically. Descartes considered an animal to be a kind of complicated automaton. As regards extended reality, he takes a thoroughly mechanistic view—exactly like the materialists."

"I doubt very much that Hermes is a machine or an automaton. Descartes couldn't have liked animals very much. And what about us? Are we automatons as well?"

"We are and we aren't. Descartes came to the conclusion that man is a dual creature that both thinks and takes up room in space. Man has thus both a mind and an extended body. St. Augustine and Thomas Aquinas had already said something similar, namely, that man had a body like the animals and a soul like the angels. According to Descartes, the human body is a perfect machine. But man also has a mind which can operate quite independently of the body. The bodily processes do not have the same freedom, they obey their own laws. But what we think with our reason does not happen in the body—it happens in the mind, which is completely independent of extended reality. I should add, by the way, that Descartes did not reject the possibility that animals could think. But if they have that faculty, the same dualism between thought and extension must also apply to them."

"We have talked about this before. If I decide to run after a bus, the whole 'automaton' goes into action. And if I don't catch the bus, I start to cry."

"Even Descartes could not deny that there is a constant interaction between mind and body. As long as the mind is in the body, he believed, it is linked to the brain through a special brain organ which he called the pineal gland, where a constant interaction takes place between 'spirit' and 'matter.' Therefore the mind can constantly be affected by feelings and passions that are related to bodily needs. But the mind can also detach itself from such 'base' impulses and operate independently of the body. The aim is to get reason to assume command. Because even if I have the worst pain in my stomach, the sum of the angles in a triangle will still be 180 degrees. Thus humans have the capacity to rise above bodily needs and behave *rationally*. In this sense the mind is superior to the body. Our legs can age and become weak, the back can become bowed and our teeth can fall out—but two and two will go on being four as long as there is reason left in us. Reason doesn't become bowed and weak. It is the body that ages. For Descartes, the mind is essentially thought. Baser passions and feelings such as desire and hate are more closely linked to our bodily functions—and therefore to extended reality.''

''I can't get over the fact that Descartes compared the human body to a machine or an automaton.''

''The comparison was based on the fact that people in his time were deeply fascinated by machines and the workings of clocks, which appeared to have the ability to function of their own accord. The word 'automaton' means precisely that—something that moves of its own accord. It was obviously only an illusion that they moved of their own accord. An astronomical clock, for instance, is both constructed and wound up by human hands. Descartes made a point of the fact that ingenious inventions of that kind were actually assembled very simply from a relatively small number of parts compared with the vast number of bones, muscles, nerves, veins, and arteries that the human and the animal body consists of. Why should God not be able to make an animal or a human body based on mechanical laws?''

''Nowadays there is a lot of talk about 'artificial intelligence.' ''

''Yes, that is the automaton of our time. We have created machines that can sometimes deceive us into believing that they are intelligent. Machines like these would have terrified Descartes out of his wits. He might have begun to doubt whether human reason really was as free and independent as he had supposed. And there are philosophers who believe that man's spiritual life is no more free than the bodily processes. The human soul is naturally infinitely more complex than any data program, but some people think that in principle we are just as unfree as these data programs. But look, Sophie—I'll show you something."

Alberto pointed to a large writing table at the other end of the room. On it stood a small computer. He went over to it. Sophie followed him.

Alberto switched the computer on and soon the screen showed C: at the top. He wrote "Laila," explaining that this was an advanced conversation program.

A text soon appeared at the top of the screen:

"Hi, my name is Laila. Are you sitting comfortably?"

Sophie entered three letters:

"Yes," she wrote although she had not yet sat down. Alberto brought up a chair for her.

"What is your name?" appeared on the screen.

"Sophie Amundsen," wrote Sophie, and the computer answered:

"3 Clover Close. Nice to meet you, Sophie. Are you looking forward to your fifteenth birthday?"

Sophie was startled. Alberto laid a hand on her shoulder and said: "I have only given her your name, your address, and your date of birth. It's like when you are going to be introduced to a new friend. It's nice to know a little about them beforehand."

"Not bad," wrote Sophie.

"Oh dear, I hope you are not feeling bad, Sophie. You must try to talk in whole sentences."

"Thank you, I'm perfectly well. Can I ask you something?"

"I am glad you are well. Go ahead and ask me something."

"How old are you?" Sophie wrote.

"I was constructed in Atlanta on August 8, 1988, but I was translated into Norwegian at the Norwegian Polytechnic on March 28, 1990."

"Gosh!"

244 JOSTEIN GAARDER

"I said you must talk in whole sentences."

"I only said gosh!"

"I do not understand slang. I have a vocabulary of over 100,000 words, but the nearest I can find to gosh is gospel."

"That means the story of Jesus."

"Are you a Christian, Sophie?"

"I don't know."

"As a rule not knowing is a step toward new knowledge."

"Socrates would most likely have said the same. Or Descartes, for that matter."

"Socrates was a Greek philosopher who lived from 470 to 399 B.C. If you wish to know more, press F7. Descartes was a French philosopher who lived from 1596 to 1650. If you wish to know more, press F7."

"Thank you, that will be quite enough. Can I ask you something else?"

"I am glad that this was enough. Go ahead and ask!"

Alberto laughed quietly. Sophie wrote:

"Who is Hilde Møller Knag?"

"Hilde Møller Knag lives in Lillesand and is exactly the same age as Sophie Amundsen."

"How do you know?"

"I don't know how. I found her on the hard disc."

Sophie felt a hand on her shoulder.

"I have fed the data program with the little information we have about Hilde," said Alberto.

"What else do you know about Hilde?" wrote Sophie.

"Hilde's father is a UN Observer in Lebanon. He has the rank of major and continually sends postcards to his daughter."

"I want you to find him!"

"I can't do that. He is not on any of my files and I am not coupled to any other data base."

"I said find him!!!!!!!!"

"Are you angry, Sophie? So many exclamation marks are a sign of violent feelings."

"I want to talk to Hilde's father!"

"You have difficulty controlling yourself. If you wish

to talk about your childhood, press F9.''

Alberto laid his hand on Sophie's shoulder again.

''She's right. This is not a crystal ball. Laila is only a data program.''

''Shut up!'' wrote Sophie.

''As you wish, Sophie. Our acquaintance lasted only 13 minutes and 52 seconds. I shall remember everything we have said. I shall now end the program.''

The letter C: once again showed up on the screen.

''Now we can sit down again,'' said Alberto.

But Sophie had already pressed some other keys.

''Knag,'' she wrote.

Immediately the following message appeared on the screen:

''Here I am.''

Now it was Alberto who jumped.

''Who are you?'' wrote Sophie.

''Major Albert Knag at your service. I came straight from Lebanon. What is your command?''

''This beats everything!'' breathed Alberto. ''The rat has sneaked onto the hard disc.''

He motioned for Sophie to move and sat down in front of the keyboard.

''How did you manage to get into my PC?'' he wrote.

''A mere bagatelle, dear colleague. I am exactly where I choose to be.''

''You loathsome data virus!''

''Now, now! At the moment I am here as a birthday virus. May I send a special greeting?''

''No thanks, we've had enough of them.''

''But I'll be quick: all in your honor, dear Hilde. Once again, a very happy fifteenth birthday. Please excuse the circumstances, but I wanted my birthday greetings to spring up around you everywhere you go. Love from Dad, who is longing to give you a great big hug.''

Before Alberto could write again, the sign C: had once again appeared on the screen.

Alberto wrote ''dir knag*.*,'' which called up the following information on the screen:

| knag.lib | 147,643 | 06-15-90 | 12:47 |
| knag.lil | 326,439 | 06-23-90 | 22:34 |

Alberto wrote "erase knag*.*" and switched off the computer.

"There—now I have erased him," he said. "But it's impossible to say where he'll turn up next time."

He went on sitting there, staring at the screen. Then he added:

"The worst of it all was the name. Albert Knag . . ."

For the first time Sophie was struck by the similarity between the two names. Albert Knag and Alberto Knox. But Alberto was so incensed that she dared not say a word. They went over and sat by the coffee table again.

Spinoza

. . . God is not a puppeteer . . .

They sat silently for a long time. Then Sophie spoke, trying to get Alberto's mind off what had happened.

"Descartes must have been an odd kind of person. Did he become famous?"

Alberto breathed deeply for a couple of seconds before answering: "He had a great deal of significance. Perhaps most of all for another great philosopher, *Baruch Spinoza*, who lived from 1632 to 1677."

"Are you going to tell me about him?"

"That was my intention. And we're not going to be stopped by military provocations."

"I'm all ears."

"Spinoza belonged to the Jewish community of Amsterdam, but he was excommunicated for heresy. Few philosophers in more recent times have been so blasphemed and so persecuted for their ideas as this man. It happened because he criticized the established religion. He believed that Christianity and Judaism were only kept alive by rigid dogma and outer ritual. He was the first to apply what we call a historico-critical interpretation of the Bible."

"Explanation, please."

"He denied that the Bible was inspired by God down to the last letter. When we read the Bible, he said, we must continually bear in mind the period it was written in. A 'critical' reading, such as the one he proposed, revealed a number of inconsistencies in the texts. But beneath the surface of the Scriptures in the New Testament is Jesus, who could well be called God's mouthpiece. The teachings of Jesus therefore represented a liberation from the orthodoxy of Judaism. Jesus preached a 'religion of reason' which valued love higher than all else. Spinoza interpreted this as meaning both love of God and love of humanity. Nevertheless, Christianity had also become set in its own rigid dogmas and outer rituals.''

''I don't suppose these ideas were easy to swallow, either for the church or the synagogue.''

''When things got really tough, Spinoza was even deserted by his own family. They tried to disinherit him on the grounds of his heresy. Paradoxically enough, few have spoken out more powerfully in the cause of free speech and religious tolerance than Spinoza. The opposition he was met with on all sides led him to pursue a quiet and secluded life devoted entirely to philosophy. He earned a meager living by polishing lenses, some of which have come into my possession.''

''Very impressive!''

''There is almost something symbolic in the fact that he lived by polishing lenses. A philosopher must help people to see life in a new perspective. One of the pillars of Spinoza's philosophy was indeed to see things from the perspective of eternity.''

''The perspective of eternity?''

''Yes, Sophie. Do you think you can imagine your own life in a cosmic context? You'll have to try and imagine yourself and your life here and now . . .''

''Hm . . . that's not so easy.''

''Remind yourself that you are only living a minuscule part of all nature's life. You are part of an enormous whole.''

''I think I see what you mean . . .''

''Can you manage to feel it as well? Can you perceive all of nature at one time—the whole universe, in fact— at a single glance?''

''I doubt it. Maybe I need some lenses.''

''I don't mean only the infinity of space. I mean the

eternity of time as well. Once upon a time, thirty thousand years ago there lived a little boy in the Rhine valley. He was a tiny part of nature, a tiny ripple on an endless sea. You too, Sophie, you too are living a tiny part of nature's life. There is no difference between you and that boy.''

"Except that I'm alive now."

"Yes, but that is precisely what I wanted you to try and imagine. Who will you be in thirty thousand years?"

"Was that the heresy?"

"Not entirely . . . Spinoza didn't only say that everything is nature. He identified nature with God. He said God is all, and all is in God."

"So he was a pantheist."

"That's true. To Spinoza, God did not create the world in order to stand outside it. No, God *is* the world. Sometimes Spinoza expresses it differently. He maintains that the world is *in* God. In this, he is quoting St. Paul's speech to the Athenians on the Areopagos hill: 'In him we live and move and have our being.' But let us pursue Spinoza's own reasoning. His most important book was his *Ethics Geometrically Demonstrated.*''

"Ethics—geometrically demonstrated?"

"It may sound a bit strange to us. In philosophy, ethics means the study of moral conduct for living a good life. This is also what we mean when we speak of the ethics of Socrates or Aristotle, for example. It is only in our own time that ethics has more or less become reduced to a set of rules for living without treading on other people's toes."

"Because thinking of yourself is supposed to be egoism?"

"Something like that, yes. When Spinoza uses the word ethics, he means both the art of living and moral conduct."

"But even so . . . the art of living demonstrated geometrically?"

"The geometrical method refers to the terminology he used for his formulations. You may recall how Descartes wished to use mathematical method for philosophical reflection. By this he meant a form of philosophic reflection that was constructed from strictly logical conclusions. Spinoza was part of the same rationalistic tradition. He wanted his ethics to show that human life is subject to the universal laws of nature. We must therefore free ourselves from our feelings and our passions. Only then will we find contentment and be happy, he believed.''

"Surely we are not ruled exclusively by the laws of nature?''

"Well, Spinoza is not an easy philosopher to grasp. Let's take him bit by bit. You remember that Descartes believed that reality consisted of two completely separate substances, namely thought and extension.''

"How could I have forgotten it?''

"The word 'substance' can be interpreted as 'that which something consists of,' or that which something basically is or can be reduced to. Descartes operated then with two of these substances. Everything was either thought or extension.

"However, Spinoza rejected this split. He believed that there was only one substance. Everything that exists can be reduced to one single reality which he simply called *Substance*. At times he calls it God or nature. Thus Spinoza does not have the dualistic view of reality that Descartes had. We say he is a *monist*. That is, he reduces nature and the condition of all things to one single substance.''

"They could hardly have disagreed more.''

"Ah, but the difference between Descartes and Spinoza is not as deep-seated as many have often claimed. Descartes also pointed out that only God exists independently. It's only when Spinoza identifies God with nature—or God and creation—that he distances himself a good way from both Descartes and from the Jewish and Christian doctrines.''

"So then nature *is* God, and that's that.''

"But when Spinoza uses the word 'nature,' he doesn't only mean extended nature. By Substance, God, or nature, he means everything that exists, including all things spiritual.''

"You mean both thought and extension.''

"You said it! According to Spinoza, we humans recognize two of God's qualities or manifestations. Spinoza called these qualities God's *attributes*, and these two attributes are identical with Descartes's 'thought' and 'extension.' God—or nature—manifests itself either as thought or as extension. It may well be that God has infinitely more attributes than 'thought' and 'extension,' but these are the only two that are known to man."

"Fair enough, but what a complicated way of saying it."

"Yes, one almost needs a hammer and chisel to get through Spinoza's language. The reward is that in the end you dig out a thought as crystal clear as a diamond."

"I can hardly wait!"

"Everything in nature, then, is either thought or extension. The various phenomena we come across in everyday life, such as a flower or a poem by Wordsworth, are different *modes* of the attribute of thought or extension. A 'mode' is the particular manner which Substance, God, or nature assumes. A flower is a mode of the attribute of extension, and a poem about the same flower is a mode of the attribute of thought. But both are basically the expression of Substance, God, or nature."

"You could have fooled me!"

"But it's not as complicated as he makes it sound. Beneath his stringent formulation lies a wonderful realization that is actually so simple that everyday language cannot accommodate it."

"I think I prefer everyday language, if it's all the same to you."

"Right. Then I'd better begin with you yourself. When you get a pain in your stomach, what is it that has a pain?"

"Like you just said. It's me."

"Fair enough. And when you later recollect that you once had a pain in your stomach, what is it that thinks?"

"That's me, too."

"So you are a single person that has a stomachache one minute and is in a thoughtful mood the next. Spinoza maintained that all material things and things that happen around us are an expression of God or nature. So it follows that all thoughts that we think are also God's or nature's thoughts. For everything is One. There is only one God, one nature, or one Substance."

"But listen, when I think something, *I'm* the one who's doing the thinking. When I move, *I'm* doing the moving. Why do you have to mix God into it?"

"I like your involvement. But who are you? You are Sophie Amundsen, but you are also the expression of something infinitely bigger. You can, if you wish, say that *you* are thinking or that *you* are moving, but could you not also say that it is nature that is thinking your thoughts, or that it is nature that is moving through you? It's really just a question of which lenses you choose to look through."

"Are you saying I cannot decide for myself?"

"Yes and no. You may have the right to move your thumb any way you choose. But your thumb can only move according to its nature. It cannot jump off your hand and dance about the room. In the same way you also have your place in the structure of existence, my dear. You are Sophie, but you are also a finger of God's body."

"So God decides everything I do?"

"Or nature, or the laws of nature. Spinoza believed that God—or the laws of nature—is the *inner cause* of everything that happens. He is not an outer cause, since God speaks through the laws of nature and only through them."

"I'm not sure I can see the difference."

"God is not a puppeteer who pulls all the strings, controlling everything that happens. A real puppet master controls the puppets from outside and is therefore the 'outer cause' of the puppet's movements. But that is not the way God controls the world. God controls the world through natural laws. So God—or nature—is the 'inner cause' of everything that happens. This means that everything in the material world happens through necessity. Spinoza had a determinist view of the material, or natural, world."

"I think you said something like that before."

"You're probably thinking of the Stoics. They also claimed that everything happens out of necessity. That was why it was important to meet every situation with 'stoicism.' Man should not get carried away by his feelings. Briefly, that was also Spinoza's ethics.''

"I see what you mean, but I still don't like the idea that I don't decide for myself.''

"Okay, let's go back in time to the Stone Age boy who lived thirty thousand years ago. When he grew up, he cast spears after wild animals, loved a woman who became the mother of his children, and quite certainly worshipped the tribal gods. Do you really think he decided all that for himself?''

"I don't know.''

"Or think of a lion in Africa. Do you think it makes up its mind to be a beast of prey? Is that why it attacks a limping antelope? Could it instead have made up its mind to be a vegetarian?''

"No, a lion obeys its nature.''

"You mean, the laws of nature. So do you, Sophie, because you are also part of nature. You could of course protest, with the support of Descartes, that a lion is an animal and not a free human being with free mental faculties. But think of a newborn baby that screams and yells. If it doesn't get milk it sucks its thumb. Does that baby have a free will?''

"I guess not.''

"When does the child get its free will, then? At the age of two, she runs around and points at everything in sight. At the age of three she nags her mother, and at the age of four she suddenly gets afraid of the dark. Where's the freedom, Sophie?''

"I don't know.''

"When she is fifteen, she sits in front of a mirror experimenting with makeup. Is this the moment when she makes her own personal decisions and does what she likes?''

"I see what you're getting at.''

"She is Sophie Amundsen, certainly. But she also lives according to the laws of nature. The point is that she doesn't realize it because there are so many complex reasons for everything she does.''

''I don't think I want to hear any more.''

''But you must just answer a last question. Two equally old trees are growing in a large garden. One of the trees grows in a sunny spot and has plenty of good soil and water. The other tree grows in poor soil in a dark spot. Which of the trees do you think is bigger? And which of them bears more fruit?''

''Obviously the tree with the best conditions for growing.''

''According to Spinoza, this tree is free. It has its full freedom to develop its inherent abilities. But if it is an apple tree it will not have the ability to bear pears or plums. The same applies to us humans. We can be hindered in our development and our personal growth by political conditions, for instance. Outer circumstances can constrain us. Only when we are free to develop our innate abilities can we live as free beings. But we are just as much determined by inner potential and outer opportunities as the Stone Age boy on the Rhine, the lion in Africa, or the apple tree in the garden.''

''Okay, I give in, almost.''

''Spinoza emphasizes that there is only one being which is totally and utterly 'its own cause' and can act with complete freedom. Only God or nature is the expression of such a free and 'nonaccidental' process. Man can strive for freedom in order to live without outer constraint, but he will never achieve 'free will.' We do not control everything that happens in our body—which is a mode of the attribute of extension. Neither do we 'choose' our thinking. Man therefore does not have a 'free soul'; it is more or less imprisoned in a mechanical body.''

''That is rather hard to understand.''

''Spinoza said that it was our passions—such as ambition and lust—which prevent us from achieving true happiness and harmony, but that if we recognize that everything happens from necessity, we can achieve an intuitive understanding of nature as a whole. We can come to realize with crystal clarity that everything is related, even that everything is One. The goal is to comprehend everything that exists in an all-embracing perception. Only then will we achieve true happiness and contentment. This was what Spinoza called seeing everything 'sub specie aeternitatis.' ''

''Which means what?''

''To see everything from the perspective of eternity. Wasn't that where we started?''

''It'll have to be where we end, too. I must get going.''

Alberto got up and fetched a large fruit dish from the book shelves. He set it on the coffee table.

''Won't you at least have a piece of fruit before you go?''

Sophie helped herself to a banana. Alberto took a green apple.

She broke off the top of the banana and began to peel it.

''There's something written here,'' she said suddenly.

''Where?''

''Here—inside the banana peel. It looks as if it was written with an ink brush.''

Sophie leaned over and showed Alberto the banana. He read aloud:

Here I am again, Hilde. I'm everywhere. Happy birthday!

''Very funny,'' said Sophie.

''He gets more crafty all the time.''

''But it's impossible . . . isn't it? Do you know if they grow bananas in Lebanon?''

Alberto shook his head.

''I'm certainly not going to eat *that*.''

''Leave it then. Someone who writes birthday greetings to his daughter on the inside of an unpeeled banana must be mentally disturbed. But he must also be quite ingenious.''

''Yes, both.''

''So shall we establish here and now that Hilde has an ingenious father? In other words, he's not so stupid.''

''That's what I've been telling you. And it could just as well be him that made you call me Hilde last time I came here. Maybe he's the one putting all the words in our mouths.''

''Nothing can be ruled out. But we should doubt everything.''

''For all we know, our entire life could be a dream.''

''But let's not jump to conclusions. There could be a simpler explanation.''

''Well whatever, I have to hurry home. My mom is waiting for me.''

Alberto saw her to the door. As she left, he said:

''We'll meet again, dear Hilde.''

Then the door closed behind her.

Locke

*... as bare and empty as a blackboard before the
teacher arrives ...*

Sophie arrived home at eight-thirty. That was one and a
half hours after the agreement—which was not really an
agreement. She had simply skipped dinner and left a
message for her mother that she would be back not later
than seven.

"This has got to stop, Sophie. I had to call information and ask if they had any record of anyone named
Alberto in the Old Town. They laughed at me."

"I couldn't get away. I think we're just about to make
a breakthrough in a huge mystery."

"Nonsense!"

"It's true!"

"Did you invite him to your party?"

"Oh no, I forgot."

"Well, now I insist on meeting him. Tomorrow at the
latest. It's not natural for a young girl to be meeting an
older man like this."

"You've got no reason to be scared of Alberto. It may
be worse with Hilde's father."

"Who's Hilde?"

"The daughter of the man in Lebanon. He's really
bad. He may be controlling the whole world."

"If you don't immediately introduce me to your Alberto, I won't allow you to see him again. I won't feel
easy about him until I at least know what he looks like."

Sophie had a brilliant idea and dashed up to her room.

"What's the matter with you now?" her mother called after her.

In a flash Sophie was back again.

"In a minute you'll see what he looks like. And then I hope you'll let me be."

She waved the video cassette and went over to the VCR.

"Did he give you a video?"

"From Athens . . ."

Pictures of the Acropolis soon appeared on the screen. Her mother sat dumbfounded as Alberto came forward and began to speak directly to Sophie.

Sophie now noticed something she had forgotten about. The Acropolis was crowded with tourists milling about in their respective groups. A small placard was being held up from the middle of one group. On it was written HILDE . . . Alberto continued his wandering on the Acropolis. After a while he went down through the entrance and climbed to the Areopagos hill where Paul had addressed the Athenians. Then he went on to talk to Sophie from the square.

Her mother sat commenting on the video in short utterances:

"Incredible . . . is *that* Alberto? He mentioned the rabbit again . . . But, yes, he's really talking to you, Sophie. I didn't know Paul went to Athens . . ."

The video was coming to the part where ancient Athens suddenly rises from the ruins. At the last minute Sophie managed to stop the tape. Now that she had shown her mother Alberto, there was no need to introduce her to Plato as well.

There was silence in the room.

"What do you think of him? He's quite good-looking, isn't he?" teased Sophie.

"What a strange man he must be, having himself filmed in Athens just so he could send it to a girl he hardly knows. *When* was he in Athens?"

"I haven't a clue."

"But there's something else . . ."

"What?"

"He looks very much like the major who lived in that little hut in the woods."

"Well maybe it *is* him, Mom."

"But nobody has seen him for over fifteen years."

"He probably moved around a lot . . . to Athens, maybe."

Her mother shook her head. "When I saw him sometime in the seventies, he wasn't a day younger than this Alberto I just saw. He had a foreign-sounding name . . ."

"Knox?"

"Could be, Sophie. Could be his name was Knox."

"Or was it Knag?"

"I can't for the life of me remember . . . Which Knox or Knag are you talking about?"

"One is Alberto, the other is Hilde's father."

"It's all making me dizzy."

"Is there any food in the house?"

"You can warm up the meatballs."

Exactly two weeks went by without Sophie hearing a word from Alberto. She got another birthday card for Hilde, but although the actual day was approaching, she did not receive a single birthday card herself.

One afternoon she went to the Old Town and knocked on Alberto's door. He was out, but there was a short note attached to his door. It said:

Happy birthday, Hilde! Now the great turning point is at hand. The moment of truth, little one. Every time I think about it, I can't stop laughing. It has naturally something to do with Berkeley, so hold on to your hat.

Sophie tore the note off the door and stuffed it into Alberto's mailbox as she went out.

Damn! Surely he'd not gone back to Athens? How could he leave her with so many questions unanswered?

When she got home from school on June 14, Hermes was romping about in the garden. Sophie ran toward him and he came prancing happily toward her. She put her arms around him as if he were the one who could solve all the riddles.

Again she left a note for her mother, but this time she put Alberto's address on it.

As they made their way across town Sophie thought about tomorrow. Not about her own birthday so much—that was not going to be celebrated until Midsummer Eve anyway. But tomorrow was Hilde's birthday too. Sophie was convinced something quite extraordinary would happen. At least there would be an end to all those birthday cards from Lebanon.

When they had crossed Main Square and were making for the Old Town, they passed by a park with a play-ground. Hermes stopped by a bench as if he wanted Sophie to sit down.

She did, and while she patted the dog's head she looked into his eyes. Suddenly the dog started to shudder violently. He's going to bark now, thought Sophie.

Then his jaws began to vibrate, but Hermes neither growled nor barked. He opened his mouth and said:

"Happy birthday, Hilde!"

Sophie was speechless. Did the dog just talk to her? Impossible, she must have imagined it because she was thinking of Hilde. But deep down she was nevertheless convinced that Hermes had spoken, and in a deep resonant bass voice.

The next second everything was as before. Hermes gave a couple of demonstrative barks—as if to cover up the fact that he had just spoken with a human voice—and trotted on ahead toward Alberto's place. As they were going inside Sophie looked up at the sky. It had been fine weather all day but now heavy clouds were beginning to gather in the distance.

Alberto opened the door and Sophie said at once:

"No civilities, please. You are a great idiot, and you know it."

"What's the matter now?"

"The major taught Hermes to *talk*!"

"Ah, so it has come to that."

"Yes, imagine!"

"And what did he say?"

"I'll give you three guesses."

"I imagine he said something along the lines of Happy Birthday!"

"Bingo."

Alberto let Sophie in. He was dressed in yet another costume. It wasn't all that different from last time, but today there were hardly any braidings, bows, or lace.

"But that's not all," Sophie said.

"What do you mean?"

"Didn't you find the note in the mailbox?"

"Oh, that. I threw it away at once."

"I don't care if he laughs every time he thinks of Berkeley. But what is so funny about that particular philosopher?"

"We'll have to wait and see."

"But today is the day you're going to talk about him, isn't it?"

"Yes, today is the day."

Alberto made himself comfortable on the sofa. Then he said:

"Last time we sat here I told you about Descartes and Spinoza. We agreed that they had one important thing in common, namely, that they were both *rationalists*."

"And a rationalist is someone who believes strongly in the importance of reason."

"That's right, a rationalist believes in reason as the primary source of knowledge, and he may also believe that man has certain innate ideas that exist in the mind prior to all experience. And the clearer such ideas may be, the more certain it is that they correspond to reality. You recall how Descartes had a clear and distinct idea of a 'perfect entity,' on the basis of which he concluded that God exists."

"I am not especially forgetful."

"Rationalist thinking of this kind was typical for philosophy of the seventeenth century. It was also firmly rooted in the Middle Ages, and we remember it from Plato and Socrates too. But in the eighteenth century it was the object of an ever increasing in-depth criticism. A number of philosophers held that we have absolutely nothing in the mind that we have not experienced through the senses. A view such as this is called *empiricism*."

"And you are going to talk about them today, these empiricists?"

"I'm going to attempt to, yes. The most important empiricists—or philosophers of experience—were Locke, Berkeley, and Hume, and all three were British. The leading rationalists in the seventeenth century were Descartes, who was French; Spinoza, who was Dutch; and Leibniz, who was German. So we usually make a distinction between *British empiricism* and *Continental rationalism*."

"What a lot of difficult words! Could you repeat the meaning of empiricism?"

"An empiricist will derive all knowledge of the world from what the senses tell us. The classic formulation of an empirical approach came from Aristotle. He said: 'There is nothing in the mind except what was first in the senses.' This view implied a pointed criticism of Plato, who had held that man brought with him a set of innate 'ideas' from the world of ideas. Locke repeats Aristotle's words, and when Locke uses them, they are aimed at Descartes."

"There is nothing in the mind . . . except what was first in the senses?"

"We have no innate ideas or conceptions about the world we are brought into before we have *seen* it. If we do have a conception or an idea that cannot be related to experienced facts, then it will be a false conception. When we, for instance, use words like 'God,' 'eternity,' or 'substance,' reason is being misused, because nobody has *experienced* God, eternity, or what philosophers have called substance. So therefore many learned dissertations could be written which in actual fact contain no really new conceptions. An ingeniously contrived philosophical system such as this may seem impressive, but it is pure fantasy. Seventeenth- and eighteenth-century philosophers had inherited a number of such learned dissertations. Now they had to be examined under a microscope. They had to be purified of all hollow notions. We might compare it with panning for gold. Most of what you fish up is sand and clay, but in between you see the glint of a particle of gold.''

"And that particle of gold is real experience?''

"Or at least thoughts that can be related to experience. It became a matter of great importance to the British empiricists to scrutinize all human conceptions to see whether there was any basis for them in actual experience. But let us take one philosopher at a time.''

"Okay, shoot!''

"The first was the Englishman *John Locke*, who lived from 1632 to 1704. His main work was the *Essay Concerning Human Understanding*, published in 1690. In it he tried to clarify two questions. First, where we get our ideas from, and secondly, whether we can rely on what our senses tell us.''

"That was some project!''

"We'll take these questions one at a time. Locke's claim is that all our thoughts and ideas issue from that which we have taken in through the senses. Before we perceive anything, the mind is a 'tabula rasa'—or an empty slate.''

"You can skip the Latin.''

"Before we sense anything, then, the mind is as bare and empty as a blackboard before the teacher arrives in the classroom. Locke also compared the mind to an unfurnished room. But then we begin to sense things. We see the world around us, we smell, taste, feel, and hear. And nobody does this more intensely than infants. In this way what Locke called *simple ideas of sense* arise. But the mind does not just passively receive information from outside it. Some activity happens in the mind as well. The single sense ideas are worked on by thinking, reasoning, believing, and doubting, thus giving rise to what he calls *reflection*. So he distinguished between 'sensation' and 'reflection.' The mind is not merely a passive receiver. It classifies and processes all sensations as they come streaming in. And this is just where one must be on guard.''

"On guard?''

"Locke emphasized that the only things we can perceive are *simple sensations*. When I eat an apple, for

example, I do not sense the whole apple in one single
sensation. In actual fact I receive a whole series of simple sensations—such as that something is green, smells
fresh, and tastes juicy and sharp. Only after I have eaten
an apple many times do I think: Now I am eating an
'apple.' As Locke would say, we have formed a *complex
idea* of an 'apple.' When we were infants, tasting an
apple for the first time, we had no such complex idea.
But we saw something green, we tasted something fresh
and juicy, yummy . . . It was a bit sour too. Little by
little we bundle many similar sensations together and
form concepts like 'apple,' 'pear,' 'orange.' But in the
final analysis, all the material for our knowledge of the
world comes to us through sensations. Knowledge that
cannot be traced back to a simple sensation is therefore
false knowledge and must consequently be rejected.''

"At any rate we can be sure that what we see, hear,
smell, and taste are the way we sense it.''

"Both yes and no. And that brings us to the second
question Locke tried to answer. He had first answered
the question of where we get our ideas from. Now he
asked whether the world really is the way we perceive
it. This is not so obvious, you see, Sophie. We mustn't
jump to conclusions. That is the only thing a real philosopher must never do.''

"I didn't say a word.''

"Locke distinguished between what he called 'primary' and 'secondary' qualities. And in this he acknowl-
edged his debt to the great philosophers before him—
including Descartes.

"By *primary qualities* he meant extension, weight,
motion and number, and so on. When it is a question of
qualities such as these, we can be certain that the senses
reproduce them objectively. But we also sense other
qualities in things. We say that something is sweet or
sour, green or red, hot or cold. Locke calls these *secondary qualities.* Sensations like these—color, smell,
taste, sound—do not reproduce the real qualities that are
inherent in the things themselves. They reproduce only
the effect of the outer reality on our senses.''

"Everyone to his own taste, in other words.''

"Exactly. Everyone can agree on the primary qualities like size and weight because they lie within the objects themselves. But the secondary qualities like color and taste can vary from person to person and from animal to animal, depending on the nature of the individual's sensations."

"When Joanna eats an orange, she gets a look on her face like when other people eat a lemon. She can't take more than one segment at a time. She says it tastes sour. I usually think the same orange is nice and sweet."

"And neither one of you is right or wrong. You are just describing how the orange affects your senses. It's the same with the sense of color. Maybe you don't like a certain shade of red. But if Joanna buys a dress in that color it might be wise to keep your opinion to yourself. You experience the color differently, but it *is* neither pretty nor ugly."

"But everyone can agree that an orange is round."

"Yes, if you have a round orange, you can't 'think' it is square. You can 'think' it is sweet or sour, but you can't 'think' it weighs eight kilos if it only weighs two hundred grams. You can certainly 'believe' it weighs several kilos, but then you'd be way off the mark. If several people have to guess how much something weighs, there will always be one of them who is more right than the others. The same applies to number. Either there *are* 986 peas in the can or there are not. The same with motion. Either the car is moving or it's stationary."

"I get it."

"So when it was a question of 'extended' reality, Locke agreed with Descartes that it does have certain qualities that man is able to understand with his reason."

"It shouldn't be so difficult to agree on that."

"Locke admitted what he called intuitive, or 'demonstrative,' knowledge in other areas too. For instance, he held that certain ethical principles applied to everyone. In other words, he believed in the idea of a *natural right*, and that was a rationalistic feature of his thought. An equally rationalistic feature was that Locke believed that it was inherent in human reason to be able to know that God exists."

"Maybe he was right."

"About what?"

"That God exists."

"It is possible, of course. But he did not let it rest on faith. He believed that the idea of God was born of human reason. *That* was a rationalistic feature. I should add that he spoke out for intellectual liberty and tolerance. He was also preoccupied with equality of the sexes, maintaining that the subjugation of women to men was 'man-made.' Therefore it could be altered."

"I can't disagree there."

"Locke was one of the first philosophers in more recent times to be interested in sexual roles. He had a great influence on *John Stuart Mill*, who in turn had a key role in the struggle for equality of the sexes. All in all, Locke was a forerunner of many liberal ideas which later, during the period of the French Enlightenment in the eighteenth century, came into full flower. It was he who first advocated the principle of *division of powers* . . ."

"Isn't that when the power of the state is divided between different institutions?"

"Do you remember which institutions?"

"There's the legislative power, or elected representatives. There's the judicial power, or law courts, and then there's the executive power, that's the government."

"This division of power originated from the French Enlightenment philosopher *Montesquieu*. Locke had first and foremost emphasized that the legislative and the executive power must be separated if tyranny was to be avoided. He lived at the time of Louis XIV, who had assembled all power in his own hands. 'I am the State,' he said. We say he was an 'absolute' ruler. Nowadays we would call Louis XIV's rule lawless and arbitrary. Locke's view was that to ensure a legal State, the people's representatives must make the laws and the king or the government must apply them."

Hume

. . . commit it then to the flames . . .

Alberto sat staring down at the table. He finally turned and looked out of the window.

"It's clouding over," said Sophie.

"Yes, it's muggy."

"Are you going to talk about Berkeley now?"

"He was the next of the three British empiricists. But as he is in a category of his own in many ways, we will first concentrate on *David Hume*, who lived from 1711 to 1776. He stands out as the most important of the empiricists. He is also significant as the person who set the great philosopher Immanuel Kant on the road to *his* philosophy."

"Doesn't it matter to you that I'm more interested in Berkeley's philosophy?"

"That's of no importance. Hume grew up near Edinburgh in Scotland. His family wanted him to take up law but he felt 'an insurmountable resistance to everything but philosophy and learning.' He lived in the Age of Enlightenment at the same time as great French thinkers like Voltaire and Rousseau, and he traveled widely in Europe before returning to settle down in Edinburgh toward the end of his life. His main work, *A Treatise of Human Nature*, was published when Hume was twenty-eight years old, but he claimed that he got the idea for the book when he was only fifteen."

"I see I don't have any time to waste."

"You have already begun."

"But if I were going to formulate my own philosophy, it would be quite different from anything I've heard up to now."

"Is there anything in particular that's missing?"

"Well, to start with, all the philosophers you have talked about are men. And men seem to live in a world of their own. I am more interested in the real world, where there are flowers and animals and children that are born and grow up. Your philosophers are always talking about 'man' and 'humans,' and now here's another treatise on 'human nature.' It's as if this 'human' is a middle-aged man. I mean, life begins with pregnancy and birth, and I've heard nothing about diapers or crying babies so far. And hardly anything about love and friendship."

"You are right, of course. But Hume was a philosopher who thought in a different way. More than any other philosopher, he took the everyday world as his starting point. I even think Hume had a strong feeling for the way children—the new citizens of the world—experienced life."

"I'd better listen then."

"As an empiricist, Hume took it upon himself to clean up all the woolly concepts and thought constructions that these male philosophers had invented. There were piles of old wreckage, both written and spoken, from the Middle Ages and the rationalist philosophy of the seventeenth century. Hume proposed the return to our spontaneous experience of the world. No philosopher 'will ever be able to take us behind the daily experiences or give us rules of conduct that are different from those we get through reflections on everyday life,' he said."

"Sounds promising so far. Can you give any examples?"

"In the time of Hume there was a widespread belief in angels. That is, human figures with wings. Have you ever seen such a creature, Sophie?"

"No."

"But you have seen a human figure?"

"Dumb question."

"You have also seen wings?"

"Of course, but not on a human figure."

"So, according to Hume, an 'angel' is a *complex idea*. It consists of two different experiences which are not in fact related, but which nevertheless are associated in man's imagination. In other words, it is a false idea which must be immediately rejected. We must tidy up all our thoughts and ideas, as well as our book collections, in the same way. For as Hume put it: If we take in our hands any volume . . . let us ask, 'Does it contain any abstract reasoning concerning quantity or number?' No. 'Does it contain any experimental reasoning concerning matter of fact and existence?' No. Commit it then to the flames, for it can contain nothing but sophistry and illusion."

"That was drastic."

"But the world still exists. More fresh and sharply outlined than ever. Hume wanted to know how a child experiences the world. Didn't you say that many of the philosophers you have heard about lived in their own world, and that you were more interested in the real world?"

"Something like that."

"Hume could have said the same thing. But let us follow his train of thought more closely."

"I'm with you."

"Hume begins by establishing that man has two different types of perceptions, namely *impressions* and *ideas*. By 'impressions' he means the immediate sensation of external reality. By 'ideas' he means the recollection of such impressions."

"Could you give me an example?"

"If you burn yourself on a hot oven, you get an immediate 'impression.' Afterward you can recollect that you burned yourself. That impression insofar as it is recalled is what Hume calls an 'idea.' The difference is that an impression is stronger and livelier than your reflective memory of that impression. You could say that the sensation is the original and that the idea, or reflection, is only a pale imitation. It is the impression which is the direct cause of the idea stored in the mind."

"I follow you—so far."

"Hume emphasizes further that both an impression and an idea can be either simple or complex. You remember we talked about an apple in connection with Locke. The direct experience of an apple is an example of a complex impression."

"Sorry to interrupt, but is this terribly important?"

"Important? How can you ask? Even though philosophers may have been preoccupied with a number of pseudoproblems, you mustn't give up now over the construction of an argument. Hume would probably agree with Descartes that it is essential to construct a thought process right from the ground."

"Okay, okay."

"Hume's point is that we sometimes form complex ideas for which there is no corresponding object in the physical world. We've already talked about angels. Previously we referred to crocophants. Another example is Pegasus, a winged horse. In all these cases we have to admit that the mind has done a good job of cutting out and pasting together all on its own. Each element was once sensed, and entered the theater of the mind in the form of a real 'impression.' Nothing is ever actually invented by the mind. The mind puts things together and constructs false 'ideas.' "

"Yes, I see. That *is* important."

"All right, then. Hume wanted to investigate every single idea to see whether it was compounded in a way that does not correspond to reality. He asked: From which impression does this idea originate? First of all he had to find out which 'single ideas' went into the making of a complex idea. This would provide him with a critical method by which to analyze our ideas, and thus enable him to tidy up our thoughts and notions."

"Do you have an example or two?"

"In Hume's day, there were a lot of people who had very clear ideas of 'heaven' or the 'New Jerusalem.' You remember how Descartes indicated that 'clear and distinct' ideas in themselves could be a guarantee that they corresponded to something that really existed?"

"I said I was not especially forgetful."

"We soon realize that our idea of 'heaven' is compounded of a great many elements. Heaven is made up of 'pearly gates,' 'streets of gold,' 'angels' by the score and so on and so forth. And still we have not broken everything down into single elements, for pearly gates, streets of gold, and angels are all complex ideas in themselves. Only when we recognize that our idea of heaven consists of single notions such as 'pearl,' 'gate,' 'street,' 'gold,' 'white-robed figure,' and 'wings' can we ask ourselves if we ever really had any such 'simple impressions.' "

"We did. But we cut out and pasted all these 'simple impressions' into one idea."

"That's just what we did. Because if there is something we humans do when we visualize, it's use scissors and paste. But Hume emphasizes that all the elements we put together in our ideas must at some time have entered the mind in the form of 'simple impressions.' A person who has never seen gold will never be able to visualize streets of gold."

"He was very clever. What about Descartes having a clear and distinct idea of God?"

"Hume had an answer to that too. Let's say we imagine God as an infinitely 'intelligent, wise, and good being.' We have thus a 'complex idea' that consists of something infinitely intelligent, something infinitely wise, and something infinitely good. If we had never known intelligence, wisdom, and goodness, we would never have such an idea of God. Our idea of God might also be that he is a 'severe but just Father'—that is to say, a concept made up of 'severity,' 'justice,' and 'father.' Many critics of religion since Hume have claimed that such ideas of God can be associated with how we experienced our own father when we were little. It was said that the idea of a father led to the idea of a 'heavenly father.' "

"Maybe that's true, but I have never accepted that God had to be a man. Sometimes my mother calls God 'Godiva,' just to even things up."

"Anyway, Hume opposed all thoughts and ideas that could not be traced back to corresponding sense perceptions. He said he wanted to 'dismiss all this meaningless nonsense which long has dominated metaphysical thought and brought it into disrepute.'

"But even in everyday life we use complex ideas without stopping to wonder whether they are valid. For example, take the question of 'I'—or the ego. This was the very basis of Descartes's philosophy. It was the one clear and distinct perception that the whole of his philosophy was built on."

"I hope Hume didn't try to deny that I am me. He'd be talking off the top of his head."

"Sophie, if there is one thing I want this course to teach you, it's not to jump to conclusions."

"Sorry. Go on."

"No, why don't you use Hume's method and analyze what you perceive as your 'ego.' "

"First I'd have to figure out whether the ego is a single or a complex idea."

"And what conclusion do you come to?"

"I really have to admit that I feel quite complex. I'm very volatile, for instance. And I have trouble making up my mind about things. And I can both like and dislike the same people."

"In other words, the 'ego concept' is a 'complex idea.' "

"Okay. So now I guess I must figure out if I have had a corresponding 'complex impression' of my own ego. And I guess I have. I always had, actually."

"Does that worry you?"

"I'm very changeable. I'm not the same today as I was when I was four years old. My temperament and how I see myself alter from one minute to the next. I can suddenly feel like I am a 'new person.' "

"So the feeling of having an unalterable ego is a false perception. The perception of the ego is in reality a long chain of simple impressions that you have never experienced *simultaneously*. It is 'nothing but a bundle or collection of different perceptions, which succeed one another with an inconceivable rapidity, and are in a perpetual flux and movement,' as Hume expressed it. The mind is 'a kind of theater, where several perceptions successively make their appearance; pass, re-pass, slide away, and mingle in an infinite variety of postures and situations.' Hume pointed out that we have no underlying 'personal identity' beneath or behind these perceptions and feelings which come and go. It is just like the images on a movie screen. They change so rapidly we do not register that the film is made up of single pictures. In reality the pictures are not connected. The film is a collection of instants.''

''I think I give in.''

''Does that mean you give up the idea of having an unalterable ego?''

''I guess it does.''

''A moment ago you believed the opposite. I should add that Hume's analysis of the human mind and his rejection of the unalterable ego was put forward almost 2,500 years earlier on the other side of the world.''

''Who by?''

''By *Buddha*. It's almost uncanny how similarly the two formulate their ideas. Buddha saw life as an unbroken succession of mental and physical processes which keep people in a continual state of change. The infant is not the same as the adult; I am not the same today as I was yesterday. There is nothing of which I can say 'this is mine,' said Buddha, and nothing of which I can say 'this is me.' There is thus no 'I' or unalterable ego.''

''Yes, that was typically Hume.''

''In continuation of the idea of an unalterable ego, many rationalists had taken it for granted that man had an eternal soul.''

''Is that a false perception too?''

''According to Hume and Buddha, yes. Do you know what Buddha said to his followers just before he died?''

''No, how could I?''

'' 'Decay is inherent in all compound things. Work out your own salvation with diligence.' Hume could have said the same thing. Or Democritus, for that matter. We know at all events that Hume rejected any attempt to prove the immortality of the soul or the existence of God. That does not mean that he ruled out either one, but to prove religious faith by human reason was rationalistic claptrap, he thought. Hume was not a Christian, neither was he a confirmed atheist. He was what we call an *agnostic*.''

''What's that?''

''An agnostic is someone who holds that the existence of God or a god can neither be proved nor disproved. When Hume was dying a friend asked him if he believed in life after death. He is said to have answered:

''It is also possible that a knob of coal placed upon the fire will not burn.''

''I see.''

''The answer was typical of his unconditional open-mindedness. He only accepted what he had perceived through his senses. He held all other possibilities open. He rejected neither faith in Christianity nor faith in miracles. But both were matters of *faith* and not of knowledge or reason. You might say that with Hume's philosophy, the final link between faith and knowledge was broken.''

''You say he didn't deny that miracles can happen?''

''That didn't mean that he believed in them, more the opposite. He made a point of the fact that people seemed to have a powerful need of what we today would call 'supernatural' happenings. The thing is that all the miracles you hear of have always happened in some far distant place or a long, long time ago. Actually, Hume only rejected miracles because he had never experienced any. But he had not experienced that they couldn't happen either.''

''You'll have to explain that.''

''According to Hume, a miracle is against the laws of nature. But it is meaningless to allege that we have *experienced* the laws of nature. We experience that a stone falls to the ground when we let go of it, and if it *didn't* fall—well, then we experienced *that*.''

''I would say that was a miracle—or something supernatural.''

''So you believe there are two natures—a 'natural' and a 'supernatural.' Aren't you on the way back to the rationalistic claptrap?''

''Maybe, but I still think the stone will fall to the

ground every time I let go.''

''Why?''

''Now you're being horrible.''

''I'm not horrible, Sophie. It's never wrong for a philosopher to ask questions. We may be getting to the crux of Hume's philosophy. Tell me how you can be so certain that the stone will always fall to the earth.''

''I've seen it happen so many times that I'm absolutely certain.''

''Hume would say that you have experienced a stone falling to the ground many times. But you have never experienced that it will *always* fall. It is usual to say that the stone falls to the ground because of the law of gravitation. But we have never experienced such a law. We have only experienced that things fall.''

''Isn't that the same thing?''

''Not completely. You say you believe the stone will fall to the ground because you have seen it happen so many times. That's exactly Hume's point. You are so used to the one thing following the other that you expect the same to happen every time you let go of a stone. This is the way the concept of what we like to call 'the unbreakable laws of nature' arises.''

''Did he really mean it was possible that a stone would not fall?''

''He was probably just as convinced as you that it would fall every time he tried it. But he pointed out that he had not experienced *why* it happens.''

''Now we're far away from babies and flowers again!''

''No, on the contrary. You are welcome to take children as Hume's verification. Who do you think would be more surprised if the stone floated above the ground for an hour or two—you or a one-year-old child?''

''I guess I would.''

''Why?''

''Because I would know better than the child how unnatural it was.''

''And why wouldn't the child think it was unnatural?''

''Because it hasn't yet learned how nature behaves.''

"Or perhaps because nature hasn't yet become a *habit*?"

"I see where you're coming from. Hume wanted people to sharpen their awareness."

"So now do the following exercise: let's say you and a small child go to a magic show, where things are made to float in the air. Which of you would have the most fun?"

"I probably would."

"And why would that be?"

"Because I would know how impossible it all is."

"So . . . for the child it's no fun to see the laws of nature being defied before it has learned what they are."

"I guess that's right."

"And we are still at the crux of Hume's philosophy of experience. He would have added that the child has not yet become a slave of the expectations of habit; he is thus the more open-minded of you two. I wonder if the child is not also the greater philosopher? He comes utterly without preconceived opinions. And that, my dear Sophie, is the philosopher's most distinguishing virtue. The child perceives the world as it is, without putting more into things than he experiences."

"Every time I feel prejudice I get a bad feeling."

"When Hume discusses the force of habit, he concentrates on 'the law of causation.' This law establishes that everything that happens must have a cause. Hume used two billiard balls for his example. If you roll a black billiard ball against a white one that is at rest, what will the white one do?"

"If the black ball hits the white one, the white one will start to move."

"I see, and why will it do that?"

"Because it was hit by the black one."

"So we usually say that the impact of the black ball is the *cause* of the white ball's starting to move. But remember now, we can only talk of what we have actually experienced."

"I have actually experienced it lots of times. Joanna has a pool table in her basement."

"Hume would say the only thing you have experienced is that the white ball begins to roll across the table. You have not experienced the actual cause of it beginning to roll. You have experienced that one event comes after the other, but you have not experienced that the other event happens *because of* the first one.''

"Isn't that splitting hairs?"

"No, it's very central. Hume emphasized that the expectation of one thing following another does not lie in the things themselves, but in our mind. And expectation, as we have seen, is associated with habit. Going back to the child again, it would not have stared in amazement if when one billiard ball struck the other, both had remained perfectly motionless. When we speak of the 'laws of nature' or of 'cause and effect,' we are actually speaking of what we expect, rather than what is 'reasonable.' The laws of nature are neither reasonable nor unreasonable, they simply are. The expectation that the white billiard ball will move when it is struck by the black billiard ball is therefore not innate. We are not born with a set of expectations as to what the world is like or how things in the world behave. The world is like it is, and it's something we get to know.''

"I'm beginning to feel as if we're getting off the track again."

"Not if our expectations cause us to jump to conclusions. Hume did not deny the existence of unbreakable 'natural laws,' but he held that because we are not in a position to experience the natural laws themselves, we can easily come to the wrong conclusions.''

"Like what?"

"Well, because I have seen a whole herd of black horses doesn't mean that all horses are black.''

"No, of course not."

"And although I have seen nothing but black crows in my life, it doesn't mean that there's no such thing as a white crow. Both for a philosopher and for a scientist it can be important not to reject the possibility of finding a white crow. You might almost say that hunting for 'the white crow' is science's principal task.''

"Yes, I see."

"In the question of cause and effect, there can be

many people who imagine that lightning is the cause of thunder because the thunder comes after the lightning. The example is really not so different from the one with the billiard balls. But *is* lightning the cause of thunder?''

''Not really, because actually they both happen at the same time.''

''Both thunder and lightning are due to an electric discharge. So in reality a third factor causes them both.''

''Right.''

''An empiricist of our own century, Bertrand Russell, has provided a more grotesque example. A chicken which experiences every day that it gets fed when the farmer's wife comes over to the chicken run will finally come to the conclusion that there is a causal link between the approach of the farmer's wife and feed being put into its bowl.''

''But one day the chicken doesn't get its food?''

''No, one day the farmer's wife comes over and wrings the chicken's neck.''

''Yuck, how disgusting!''

''The fact that one thing follows after another thus does not necessarily mean there is a causal link. One of the main concerns of philosophy is to warn people against jumping to conclusions. It can in fact lead to many different forms of superstition.''

''How come?''

''You see a black cat cross the street. Later that day you fall and break your arm. But that doesn't mean there is any causal link between the two incidents. In science, it is especially important not to jump to conclusions. For instance, the fact that a lot of people get well after taking a particular drug doesn't mean it was the drug that cured them. That's why it's important to have a large control group of patients who think they are also being given this same medicine, but who are in fact only being given flour and water. If these patients also get well, there has to be a third factor—such as the belief that the medicine works, and has cured them.''

''I think I'm beginning to see what empiricism is.''

''Hume also rebelled against rationalist thought in the area of ethics. The rationalists had always held that the ability to distinguish between right and wrong is inherent in human reason. We have come across this idea of a so-called natural right in many philosophers from Socrates to Locke. But according to Hume, it is not reason that determines what we say and do.''

"What is it then?''

"It is our *sentiments*. If you decide to help someone in need, you do so because of your feelings, not your reason.''

"What if I can't be bothered to help?''

"That, too, would be a matter of feelings. It is neither reasonable nor unreasonable not to help someone in need, but it could be unkind.''

"But there must be a limit somewhere. Everyone *knows* it's wrong to kill.''

"According to Hume, everybody has a feeling for other people's welfare. So we all have a capacity for compassion. But it has nothing to do with reason.''

"I don't know if I agree.''

"It's not always so unwise to get rid of another person, Sophie. If you wish to achieve something or other, it can actually be quite a good idea.''

"Hey, wait a minute! I protest!''

"Maybe you can try and explain why one shouldn't kill a troublesome person.''

"That person wants to live too. Therefore you ought not to kill them.''

"Was that a logical reason?''

"I don't know.''

"What you did was to draw a conclusion from a *descriptive sentence*—'That person wants to live too'—to what we call a *normative sentence*: 'Therefore you ought not to kill them.' From the point of view of reason this is nonsense. You might just as well say 'There are lots of people who cheat on their taxes, therefore I ought to cheat on my taxes too.' Hume said you can never draw conclusions from *is* sentences to *ought* sentences. Nevertheless it is exceedingly common, not least in newspaper articles, political party programs, and speeches. Would you like some examples?''

"Please.''

" 'More and more people want to travel by air. Therefore more airports ought to be built.' Do you think the conclusion holds up?"

"No. It's nonsense. We have to think of the environment. I think we ought to build more railroads instead."

"Or they say: The development of new oilfields will raise the population's living standards by ten percent. Therefore we ought to develop new oilfields as rapidly as possible."

"Definitely not. We have to think of the environment again. And anyway, the standard of living in Norway is high enough."

"Sometimes it is said that 'this law has been passed by the Senate, therefore all citizens in this country ought to abide by it.' But frequently it goes against people's deepest convictions to abide by such conventions."

"Yes, I understand that."

"So we have established that we cannot use reason as a yardstick for how we ought to act. Acting responsibly is not a matter of strengthening our reason but of deepening our feelings for the welfare of others. ' 'Tis not contrary to reason to prefer the destruction of the whole world to the scratching of my finger,' said Hume."

"That's a hair-raising assertion."

"It's maybe even more hair-raising if you shuffle the cards. You know that the Nazis murdered millions of Jews. Would you say that there was something wrong with the Nazis' reason, or would you say there was something wrong with their emotional life?"

"There was definitely something wrong with their feelings."

"Many of them were exceedingly clear-headed. It is not unusual to find ice-cold calculation behind the most callous decisions. Many of the Nazis were convicted after the war, but they were not convicted for being 'unreasonable.' They were convicted for being gruesome murderers. It can happen that people who are not of sound mind can be acquitted of their crimes. We say that they were 'not accountable for their actions.' Nobody has ever been acquitted of a crime they committed for being unfeeling.''

''I should hope not.''

''But we need not stick to the most grotesque examples. If a flood disaster renders millions of people homeless, it is our feelings that determine whether we come to their aid. If we are callous, and leave the whole thing to 'cold reason,' we might think it was actually quite in order that millions of people die in a world that is threatened by overpopulation.''

''It makes me mad that you can even think that.''

''And notice it's not your reason that gets mad.''

''Okay, I got it.''

Berkeley

∞

. . . like a giddy planet round a burning sun . . .

Alberto walked over to the window facing the town.
Sophie followed him. While they stood looking out at
the old houses, a small plane flew in over the rooftops.
Fixed to its tail was a long banner which Sophie guessed
would be advertising some product or local event, a rock
concert perhaps. But as it approached and turned, she
saw quite a different message: HAPPY BIRTHDAY, HILDE!

"Gate-crasher," was Alberto's only comment.

Heavy black clouds from the hills to the south were
now beginning to gather over the town. The little plane
disappeared into the grayness.

"I'm afraid there's going to be a storm," said Alberto.

"So I'll take the bus home."

"I only hope the major isn't behind this, too."

"He's not God Almighty, is he?"

Alberto did not reply. He walked across the room and
sat down again by the coffee table.

"We have to talk about Berkeley," he said after a
while.

Sophie had already resumed her place. She caught
herself biting her nails.

"*George Berkeley* was an Irish bishop who lived from
1685 to 1753," Alberto began. There was a long silence.

"Berkeley was an Irish bishop . . ." Sophie prompted.

"But he was a philosopher as well . . ."

"Yes?"

"He felt that current philosophies and science were a threat to the Christian way of life, that the all-pervading materialism, not least, represented a threat to the Christian faith in God as creator and preserver of all nature."

"He did?"

"And yet Berkeley was the most consistent of the empiricists."

"He believed we cannot know any more of the world than we can perceive through the senses?"

"More than that. Berkeley claimed that worldly things are indeed as we perceive them, but they are not 'things.' "

"You'll have to explain that."

"You remember that Locke pointed out that we cannot make statements about the 'secondary qualities' of things. We cannot say an apple *is* green and sour. We can only say we perceive it as being so. But Locke also said that the 'primary qualities' like density, gravity, and weight really do belong to the external reality around us. External reality has, in fact, a material substance."

"I remember that, and I think Locke's division of things was important."

"Yes, Sophie, if only that were all."

"Go on."

"Locke believed—just like Descartes and Spinoza—that the material world is a reality."

"Yes?"

"This is just what Berkeley questioned, and he did so by the logic of empiricism. He said the only things that exist are those we perceive. But we do not perceive 'material' or 'matter.' We do not perceive things as tangible objects. To assume that what we perceive has its own underlying 'substance' is jumping to conclusions. We have absolutely no experience on which to base such a claim."

"How stupid. Look!" Sophie thumped her fist hard on the table. "Ouch," she said. "Doesn't that prove that this table is really a table, both of material and matter?"

"How did you feel it?"

"I felt something hard."

"You had a sensation of something hard, but you didn't feel the actual *matter* in the table. In the same way, you can dream you are hitting something hard, but there isn't anything hard in a dream, is there?"

"No, not in a dream."

"A person can also be hypnotized into 'feeling' things like warmth and cold, a caress or a punch."

"But if the table wasn't really hard, why did I feel it?"

"Berkeley believed in a 'spirit.' He thought all our ideas have a cause beyond our consciousness, but that this cause is not of a material nature. It is spiritual."

Sophie had started biting her nails again.

Alberto continued: "According to Berkeley, my own soul can be the cause of my own ideas—just as when I dream—but only another will or spirit can be the cause of the ideas that make up the 'corporeal' world. Everything is due to that spirit which is the cause of 'everything in everything' and which 'all things consist in,' he said."

"What 'spirit' was he talking about?"

"Berkeley was of course thinking of God. He said that 'we can moreover claim that the existence of God is far more clearly perceived than the existence of man.' "

"Is it not even certain that we exist?"

"Yes, and no. Everything we see and feel is 'an effect of God's power,' said Berkeley. For God is 'intimately present in our consciousness, causing to exist for us the profusion of ideas and perceptions that we are constantly subject to.' The whole world around us and our whole life exist in God. He is the one cause of everything that exists. We exist only in the mind of God."

"I am amazed, to put it mildly."

"So 'to be or not to be' is not the whole question. The question is also *who* we are. Are we really human beings of flesh and blood? Does our world consist of real things—or are we encircled by the mind?"

Sophie continued to bite her nails.

Alberto went on: "Material reality was not the only thing Berkeley was questioning. He was also questioning whether 'time' and 'space' had any absolute or independent existence. Our own perception of time and space can also be merely figments of the mind. A week or two for us need not be a week or two for God . . .''

"You said that for Berkeley this spirit that everything exists in is the Christian God."

"Yes, I suppose I did. But for us . . .''

"Us?"

"For us—for you and me—this 'will or spirit' that is the 'cause of everything in everything' could be Hilde's father.''

Sophie's eyes opened wide with incredulity. Yet at the same time a realization began to dawn on her.

"Is that what you think?"

"I cannot see any other possibility. That is perhaps the only feasible explanation for everything that has happened to us. All those postcards and signs that have turned up here and there . . . Hermes beginning to talk . . . my own involuntary slips of the tongue.''

"I . . .''

"Imagine my calling you Sophie, Hilde! I knew all the time that your name wasn't Sophie.''

"What are you saying? Now you are definitely confused.''

"Yes, my mind is going round and round, my child. Like a giddy planet round a burning sun.''

"And that sun is Hilde's father?"

"You could say so."

"Are you saying he's been a kind of God for us?"

"To be perfectly candid, yes. He should be ashamed of himself!"

"What about Hilde herself?"

"She is an angel, Sophie."

"An angel?"

"Hilde is the one this 'spirit' turns to.''

"Are you saying that Albert Knag tells Hilde about us?"

"Or writes about us. For we cannot perceive the matter itself that our reality is made of, that much we have learned. We cannot know whether our external reality is made of sound waves or of paper and writing. According to Berkeley, all we can know is that we are spirit.''

"And Hilde is an angel . . ."

"Hilde is an angel, yes. Let that be the last word. Happy birthday, Hilde!"

Suddenly the room was filled with a bluish light. A few seconds later they heard the crash of thunder and the whole house shook.

"I have to go," said Sophie. She got up and ran to the front door. As she let herself out, Hermes woke up from his nap in the hallway. She thought she heard him say, "See you later, Hilde."

Sophie rushed down the stairs and ran out into the street. It was deserted. And now the rain came down in torrents.

One or two cars were plowing through the downpour, but there were no buses in sight. Sophie ran across Main Square and on through the town. As she ran, one thought kept going round and round in her mind: "Tomorrow is my *birthday*! Isn't it extra bitter to realize that life is only a dream on the day before your fifteenth birthday? It's like dreaming you won a million and then just as you're getting the money you wake up."

Sophie ran across the squelching playing field. Minutes later she saw someone come running toward her. It was her mother. The sky was pierced again and again by angry darts of lightning.

When they reached each other Sophie's mother put her arm around her.

"What's happening to us, little one?"

"I don't know," Sophie sobbed. "It's like a bad dream."

Bjerkely

∾

. . . an old magic mirror Great-grandmother
had bought
from a Gypsy woman . . .

Hilde Møller Knag awoke in the attic room in the old captain's house outside Lillesand. She glanced at the clock. It was only six o'clock, but it was already light. Broad rays of morning sun lit up the room.

She got out of bed and went to the window. On the way she stopped by the desk and tore a page off her calendar. Thursday, June 14, 1990. She crumpled the page up and threw it in her wastebasket.

Friday, June 15, 1990, said the calendar now, shining at her. Way back in January she had written "15th birthday" on this page. She felt it was extra-special to be fifteen on the fifteenth. It would never happen again.

Fifteen! Wasn't this the first day of her adult life? She couldn't just go back to bed. Furthermore, it was the last day of school before the summer vacation. The students just had to appear in church at one o'clock. And what was more, in a week Dad would be home from Lebanon. He had promised to be home for Midsummer Eve.

Hilde stood by the window and looked out over the garden, down toward the dock behind the little red boathouse. The motorboat had not yet been brought out for the summer, but the old rowboat was tied up to the dock. She must remember to bail the water out of it after last night's heavy downpour.

As she was looking out over the little bay, she remembered the time when as a little girl of six she had climbed up into the rowboat and rowed out into the bay alone. She had fallen overboard and it was all she could do to struggle ashore. Drenched to the skin, she had pushed her way through the thicket hedge. As she stood in the garden looking up at the house, her mother had come running toward her. The boat and both oars were left afloat in the bay. She still dreamed about the boat sometimes, drifting on its own, abandoned. It had been an embarrassing experience.

The garden was neither especially luxuriant nor particularly well kept. But it was large and it was Hilde's. A weather-beaten apple tree and a few practically barren fruit bushes had just about survived the severe winter storms. The old glider stood on the lawn between granite rocks and thicket. It looked so forlorn in the sharp morning light. Even more so because the cushions had been taken in. Mom had probably hurried out late last night and rescued them from the rain.

There were birch trees—*bjørketreer*—all around the large garden, sheltering it partly, at least, from the worst squalls. It was because of those trees that the house had been renamed Bjerkely over a hundred years ago.

Hilde's great-grandfather had built the house some years before the turn of the century. He had been a captain on one of the last tall sailing ships. There were a lot of people who continued to call it the captain's house.

That morning the garden still showed signs of the heavy rain that had suddenly started late last evening. Hilde had been awakened several times by bursts of thunder. But today there was not a cloud in the sky.

Everything is so fresh after a summer storm like that. It had been hot and dry for several weeks and the tips of the leaves on the birch trees had started to turn yellow. Now it was as if the whole world had been newly washed. It seemed as if even her childhood had been washed away with the storm.

"Indeed, there is pain when spring buds burst . . ." Wasn't there a Swedish poet who had said something like that? Or was she Finnish?

Hilde stood in front of the heavy brass mirror hanging on the wall above Grandmother's old dresser.

Was she pretty? She wasn't ugly, anyway. Maybe she was kind of in-between . . .

She had long, fair hair. Hilde had always wished her hair could be either a bit fairer or a bit darker. This in-between color was so mousy. On the positive side, there were these soft curls. Lots of her friends struggled to get their hair to curl just a little bit, but Hilde's hair had always been naturally curly. Another positive feature, she thought, were her deep green eyes. "Are they really green?" her aunts and uncles used to say as they bent over to look at her.

Hilde considered whether the image she was studying was that of a girl or that of a young woman. She decided it was neither. The body might be quite womanly, but the face reminded her of an unripe apple.

There was something about this old mirror that always made Hilde think of her father. It had once hung down in the "studio." The studio, over the boathouse, was her father's combined library, writer's workshop, and retreat. Albert, as Hilde called him when he was home, had always wanted to write something significant. Once he had tried to write a novel, but he never finished it. From time to time he had had a few poems and sketches of the archipelago published in a national journal. Hilde was so proud every time she saw his name in print. ALBERT KNAG. It meant something in Lillesand, anyway. Her great-grandfather's name had also been Albert.

The mirror. Many years ago her father had joked about not being able to wink at your own reflection with both eyes at the same time, except in this brass mirror. It was an exception because it was an old magic mirror Great-grandmother had bought from a Gypsy woman just after her wedding.

Hilde had tried for ages, but it was just as hard to wink at yourself with both eyes as to run away from your own shadow. In the end she had been given the old family heirloom to keep. Through the years she had tried from time to time to master the impossible art.

Not surprisingly, she was pensive today. And not un-
naturally, she was preoccupied with herself. Fifteen
years old . . .

She happened to glance at her bedside table. There
was a large package there. It had pretty blue wrapping
and was tied with a red silk ribbon. It must be a birthday
present!

Could this be *the* present? The great big present from
Dad that had been so very secret? He had dropped so
many cryptic hints in his cards from Lebanon. But he
had "imposed a severe censorship on himself."

The present was something that "grew bigger and
bigger," he had written. Then he had said something
about a girl she was soon to meet—and that he had sent
copies of all his cards to her. Hilde had tried to pump
her mother for clues, but she had no idea what he meant,
either.

The oddest hint had been that the present could perhaps be "shared with other people." He wasn't working
for the UN for nothing! If her father had one bee in his
bonnet—and he had plenty—it was that the UN ought
to be a kind of world government. May the UN one day
really be able to unite the whole of humanity, he had
written on one of his cards.

Was she allowed to open the package before her
mother came up to her room singing "Happy Birthday
to You," with pastry and a Norwegian flag? Surely that
was why it had been put there?

She walked quietly across the room and picked up the
package. It was heavy! She found the tag: To Hilde on
her 15th birthday from Dad.

She sat on the bed and carefully untied the red silk
ribbon. Then she undid the blue paper.

It was a large ring binder.

Was this her present? Was this the fifteenth-birthday
present that there had been so much fuss about? The
present that grew bigger and bigger and could be shared
with other people?

A quick glance showed that the ring binder was filled
with typewritten pages. Hilde recognized them as being

from her father's typewriter, the one he had taken with him to Lebanon.

Had he written a whole book for her?

On the first page, in large handwritten letters, was the title, SOPHIE'S WORLD.

Farther down the page there were two typewritten lines of poetry:

> TRUE ENLIGHTENMENT IS TO MAN
> LIKE SUNLIGHT TO THE SOIL
> ——N.F.S. Grundtvig

Hilde turned to the next page, to the beginning of the first chapter. It was entitled "The Garden of Eden." She got into bed, sat up comfortably, resting the ring binder against her knees, and began to read.

Sophie Amundsen was on her way home from school. She had walked the first part of the way with Joanna. They had been discussing robots. Joanna thought the human brain was like an advanced computer. Sophie was not certain she agreed. Surely a person was more than a piece of hardware?

Hilde read on, oblivious of all else, even forgetting that it was her birthday. From time to time a brief thought crept in between the lines as she read: Had Dad written a book? Had he finally begun on the significant novel and completed it in Lebanon? He had often complained that time hung heavily on one's hands in that part of the world.

Sophie's father was far from home, too. She was probably the girl Hilde would be getting to know . . .

Only by conjuring up an intense feeling of one day being dead could she appreciate how terribly good life was. . . . Where does the world come from? . . . At some point something must have come from nothing. But was that possible? Wasn't that just as impossible as the idea that the world had always existed?

Hilde read on and on. With surprise, she read about Sophie Amundsen receiving a postcard from Lebanon: "Hilde Møller Knag, c/o Sophie Amundsen, 3 Clover Close . . ."

Dear Hilde, Happy 15th birthday. As I'm sure you'll understand, I want to give you a present that will help you grow. Forgive me for sending the card c/o Sophie. It was the easiest way. Love from Dad.

The joker! Hilde knew her father had always been a sly one, but today he had really taken her by surprise! Instead of tying the card on the package, he had written it into the book.

But poor Sophie! She must have been totally confused!

Why would a father send a birthday card to Sophie's address when it was quite obviously intended to go somewhere else? What kind of father would cheat his own daughter of a birthday card by purposely sending it astray? How could it be "the easiest way"? And above all, how was she supposed to trace this Hilde person?

No, how could she?

Hilde turned a couple of pages and began to read the second chapter, "The Top Hat." She soon came to the long letter which a mysterious person had written to Sophie.

Being interested in why we are here is not a "casual" interest like collecting stamps. People who ask such questions are taking part in a debate that has gone on as long as man has lived on this planet.

"Sophie was completely exhausted." So was Hilde. Not only had Dad written a book for her fifteenth birthday, he had written a strange and wonderful book.

> To summarize briefly: A white rabbit is pulled out of
> a top hat. Because it is an extremely large rabbit, the
> trick takes many billions of years. All mortals are born
> at the very tip of the rabbit's fine hairs, where they
> are in a position to wonder at the impossibility of the
> trick. But as they grow older they work themselves
> ever deeper into the fur. And there they stay . . .

Sophie was not the only one who felt she had been on
the point of finding herself a comfortable place deep
down in the rabbit's fur. Today was Hilde's fifteenth
birthday, and she had the feeling it was time to decide
which way she would choose to crawl.

She read about the Greek natural philosophers. Hilde
knew that her father was interested in philosophy. He
had written an article in the newspaper proposing that
philosophy should be a regular school subject. It was
called "Why should philosophy be part of the school
curriculum?" He had even raised the issue at a PTA
meeting in Hilde's class. Hilde had found it acutely embarrassing.

She looked at the clock. It was seven-thirty. It would
probably be half an hour before her mother came up with
the breakfast tray, thank goodness, because right now
she was engrossed in Sophie and all the philosophical
questions. She read the chapter called "Democritus."
First of all, Sophie got a question to think about: Why
is Lego the most ingenious toy in the world? Then she
found a large brown envelope in the mailbox:

> Democritus agreed with his predecessors that trans-
> formations in nature could not be due to the fact that
> anything actually "changed." He therefore assumed
> that everything was built up of tiny invisible blocks,
> each of which was eternal and immutable. Democri-
> tus called these smallest units *atoms*.

Hilde was indignant when Sophie found the red silk
scarf under her bed. So *that* was where it was! But how
could a scarf just disappear into a story? It had to *be*
someplace . . .

The chapter on Socrates began with Sophie reading "something about the Norwegian UN battalion in Lebanon" in the newspaper. Typical Dad! He was so concerned that people in Norway were not interested enough in the UN forces' peacekeeping task. If nobody else was, then Sophie would have to be. In that way he could write it into his story and get some sort of attention from the media.

She had to smile as she read the P.P.S. in the philosophy teacher's letter to Sophie:

> If you should come across a red silk scarf anywhere, please take care of it. Sometimes personal property gets mixed up. Especially at school and places like that, and this is a philosophy school.

Hilde heard her mother's footsteps on the stairs. Before she knocked on the door, Hilde had begun to read about Sophie's discovery of the video of Athens in her secret den.

"Happy birthday . . ." Her mother had begun to sing halfway up the stairs.

"Come in," said Hilde, in the middle of the passage where the philosophy teacher was talking directly to Sophie from the Acropolis. He looked almost exactly like Hilde's father—with a "black, well-trimmed beard" and a blue beret.

"Happy birthday, Hilde!"

"Uh-huh."

"Hilde?"

"Just put it there."

"Aren't you going to . . . ?"

"You can see I'm reading."

"Imagine, you're fifteen!"

"Have you ever been to Athens, Mom?"

"No, why do you ask?"

"It's so amazing that those old temples are still standing. They are actually 2,500 years old. The biggest one is called the Virgin's Place, by the way."

"Have you opened your present from Dad?"

"What present?"

"You *must* look up now, Hilde. You're in a complete daze."

Hilde let the large ring binder slide down onto her lap.

Her mother stood leaning over the bed with the tray. On it were lighted candles, buttered rolls with shrimp salad, and a soda. There was also a small package. Her mother stood awkwardly holding the tray with both hands, with a flag under one arm.

"Oh, thanks a lot, Mom. It's sweet of you, but I'm really busy."

"You don't have to go to school till one o'clock."

Not until now did Hilde remember where she was, and her mother put the tray down on the bedside table.

"Sorry, Mom. I was completely absorbed in this."

"What *is* it he has written, Hilde? I've been just as mystified as you. It's been impossible to get a sensible word out of him for months."

For some reason Hilde felt embarrassed. "Oh, it's just a story."

"A story?"

"Yes, a story. And a history of philosophy. Or something like that."

"Aren't you going to open the package from me?"

Hilde didn't want to be unfair, so she opened her mother's present right away. It was a gold bracelet.

"It's lovely, Mom! Thank you very much!"

Hilde got out of bed and gave her mother a hug.

They sat talking for a while.

Then Hilde said, "I have to get back to the book, Mom. Right now he's standing on top of the Acropolis."

"Who is?"

"I've no idea. Neither has Sophie. That's the whole point."

"Well, I have to get to work. Don't forget to eat something. Your dress is on a hanger downstairs."

Finally her mother disappeared down the stairs. So did Sophie's philosophy teacher; he walked down the steps from the Acropolis and stood on the Areopagos rock before appearing a little later in the old square of Athens.

Hilde shivered when the old buildings suddenly rose

from the ruins. One of her father's pet ideas had been to let all the United Nations countries collaborate in reconstructing an exact copy of the Athenian square. It would be the forum for philosophical discussion and also for disarmament talks. He felt that a giant project like that would forge world unity. "We have, after all, succeeded in building oil rigs and moon rockets."

Then she read about Plato. "The soul yearns to fly home on the wings of love to the world of ideas. It longs to be freed from the chains of the body . . ."

Sophie had crawled through the hedge and followed Hermes, but the dog had escaped her. After having read about Plato, she had gone farther into the woods and come upon the red cabin by the little lake. Inside hung a painting of Bjerkely. From the description it was clearly meant to be Hilde's Bjerkely. But there was also a portrait of a man named Berkeley. "How odd!"

Hilde laid the heavy ring binder aside on the bed and went over to her bookshelf and looked him up in the three-volume encyclopedia she had been given on her fourteenth birthday. Here he was—Berkeley!

Berkeley, George, 1685–1753, Eng. Philos., Bishop of Cloyne. Denied existence of a material world beyond the human mind. Our sense perceptions proceed from God. Main work: *A Treatise Concerning the Principles of Human Knowledge* (1710).

Yes, it was decidedly odd. Hilde stood thinking for a few seconds before going back to bed and the ring binder.

In one way, it was her father who had hung the two pictures on the wall. Could there be any connection other than the similarity of names?

Berkeley was a philosopher who denied the existence of a material world beyond the human mind. That was certainly very strange, one had to admit. But it was not easy to disprove such claims, either. As regards Sophie, it fitted very well. After all, Hilde's father was responsible for her "sense perceptions."

Well, she would know more if she read on. Hilde

looked up from the ring binder and smiled when she got to the point where Sophie discovers the reflection of a girl who winks with both eyes. "The other girl had winked at Sophie as if to say: I can see you, Sophie. I am here, on the other side."

Sophie finds the green wallet in the cabin as well— with the money and everything! How could it have made its way there?

Absurd! For a second or two Hilde had really believed that Sophie had found it. But then she tried to imagine how the whole thing must appear to Sophie. It must all seem quite inscrutable and uncanny.

For the first time Hilde felt a strong desire to meet Sophie face to face. She felt like telling her the real truth about the whole business.

But now Sophie had to get out of the cabin before she was caught red-handed. The boat was adrift on the lake, of course. (Her father couldn't resist reminding her of that old story, could he!)

Hilde gulped a mouthful of soda and took a bite of her roll while she read the letter about the "meticulous" Aristotle, who had criticized Plato's theories.

> Aristotle pointed out that nothing exists in consciousness that has not first been experienced by the senses. Plato would have said that there is nothing in the natural world that has not first existed in the world of ideas. Aristotle held that Plato was thus "doubling the number of things."

Hilde had not known that it was Aristotle who had invented the game of "animal, vegetable, or mineral."

> Aristotle wanted to do a thorough clearing up in nature's "room." He tried to show that everything in nature belongs to different categories and subcategories.

When she read about Aristotle's view of women she was both irritated and disappointed. Imagine being such a brilliant philosopher and yet such a crass idiot!

Aristotle had inspired Sophie to clean up her own room. And there, together with all the other stuff, she found the white stocking which had disappeared from Hilde's closet a month ago! Sophie put all the pages she had gotten from Alberto into a ring binder. "There were in all over fifty pages." For her own part, Hilde had gotten up to page 124, but then she also had Sophie's story on top of all the correspondence from Alberto Knox.

The next chapter was called "Hellenism." First of all, Sophie finds a postcard with a picture of a UN jeep. It is stamped UN Battalion, June 15. Another of these "cards" to Hilde that her father had put into the story instead of sending by mail.

Dear Hilde, I assume you are still celebrating your fifteenth birthday. Or is this the morning after? Anyway, it makes no difference to your present. In a sense, that will last a lifetime. But I'd like to wish you a happy birthday one more time. Perhaps you understand now why I send the cards to Sophie. I am sure she will pass them on to you.

P.S. Mom said you had lost your wallet. I hereby promise to reimburse you the 150 crowns. You will probably be able to get another school I.D. before they close for the summer vacation. Love from Dad.

Not bad! That made her 150 crowns richer. He probably thought a homemade present alone wasn't enough.

So it appeared that June 15 was Sophie's birthday, too. But Sophie's calendar had only gotten as far as the middle of May. That must have been when her father had written this chapter, and he had postdated the "birthday card" to Hilde. But poor Sophie, running down to the supermarket to meet Joanna.

Who was Hilde? How could her father as good as take it for granted that Sophie would find her? In any case, it was senseless of him to send Sophie the cards instead of sending them directly to his daughter.

Hilde, like Sophie, was elevated to the celestial spheres as she read about Plotinus.

> I believe there is something of the divine mystery in everything that exists. We can see it sparkle in a sunflower or a poppy. We sense more of the unfathomable mystery in a butterfly that flutters from a twig— or in a goldfish swimming in a bowl. But we are closest to God in our own soul. Only there can we become one with the greatest mystery of life. In truth, at very rare moments we can experience that *we ourselves are that divine mystery.*

This was the most giddying passage Hilde had read up to now. But it was nevertheless the simplest. Everything is one, and this "one" is a divine mystery that everyone shares.

This was not really something you needed to believe. It *is* so, thought Hilde. So everyone can read what they like into the word "divine."

She turned quickly to the next chapter. Sophie and Joanna go camping the night before the national holiday on May 17. They make their way to the major's cabin . . .

Hilde had not read many pages before she flung the bedclothes angrily aside, got up, and began to walk up and down, clutching the ring binder in her hands.

This was just about the most impudent trick she had ever heard of. In that little hut in the woods, her father lets these two girls find copies of all the cards he had sent Hilde in the first two weeks of May. And the copies were real enough. Hilde had read the very same words over and over. She recognized every single word.

> Dear Hilde, I am now so bursting with all these secrets for your birthday that I have to stop myself several times a day from calling home and blowing the whole thing. It is something that simply grows and grows. And as you know, when a thing gets bigger and bigger it's more difficult to keep it to yourself . . .

Sophie gets a new lesson from Alberto. It's all about
Jews and Greeks and the two great cultures. Hilde liked
getting this wide bird's-eye view of history. She had
never learned anything like it at school. They only gave
you details and more details. She now saw Jesus and
Christianity in a completely new light.

She liked the quote from Goethe: "He who cannot
draw on three thousand years is living from hand to
mouth."

The next chapter began with a piece of card which
sticks to Sophie's kitchen window. It is a new birthday
card for Hilde, of course.

> Dear Hilde, I don't know whether it will still be your
> birthday when you recd this card. I hope so, in a
> way; or at least that not too many days have gone
> by. A week or two for Sophie does not have to mean
> just as long for us. I shall be coming home for Mid-
> summer Eve, so we can sit together for hours in the
> glider, looking out over the sea, Hilde. We have so
> much to talk about . . .

Then Alberto calls Sophie, and this is the first time she
hears his voice.

> "You make it sound like a war."
> "I would rather call it a battle of wills. We have to
> attract Hilde's attention and get her over on our side
> before her father comes home to Lillesand."

And then Sophie meets Alberto Knox disguised as a
medieval monk in the twelfth-century stone church.

Oh, no, the church! Hilde looked at the time. A quarter past one . . . She had forgotten all about the time.

Maybe it wouldn't matter so much that she cut school
on her birthday. But it did mean that her classmates
wouldn't be celebrating with her. Oh well, she had always had plenty of well-wishers.

Soon she found herself receiving a long sermon.
Alberto had no problem slipping into the role of a medieval priest.

When she read about how Sophia had appeared to
Hildegard in visions, she turned once again to her encyclopedia. But this time she found nothing about either
of them. Wasn't that typical! As soon as it was a question of women or something to do with women, the encyclopedia was about as informative as a moon crater.
Was the whole work censored by the Society for the
Protection of Men?

Hildegard of Bingen was a preacher, a writer, a doctor, a botanist, and a biologist. She was "perhaps an
example of the fact that women were often more practical, more scientific even, in the Middle Ages."

But there was not a single word about her in the encyclopedia. How scandalous!

Hilde had never heard that God had a "female side"
or a "mother nature." Her name was Sophia, apparently—but she was apparently not worth printer's ink,
either.

The nearest she could find in the encyclopedia was an
entry about the Santa Sophia Church in Constantinople
(now Istanbul), named Hagia Sophia, which means Sacred Wisdom. But there was nothing about it being female. That was censorship, wasn't it?

Otherwise, it was true enough that Sophie had revealed herself to Hilde. She was picturing the girl with
the straight hair all the time . . .

When Sophie gets home after spending most of the
morning in St. Mary's Church, she stands in front of the
brass mirror she took home from the cabin in the woods.

She studied the sharp contours of her own pale face
framed by that impossible hair which defied any style
but nature's own. But beyond that face was the apparition of another girl.

Suddenly the other girl began to wink frantically
with both eyes, as if to signal that she was really in
there on the other side. The apparition lasted only a
few seconds. Then she was gone.

How many times had Hilde stood in front of the mirror
like that as if she was searching for someone else behind
the glass? But how could her father have known that?

Wasn't it also a dark-haired woman she had been searching for? Great-grandmother had bought it from a Gypsy woman, hadn't she? Hilde felt her hands shaking as they held the book. She had the feeling that Sophie really existed somewhere "on the other side."

Now Sophie is dreaming about Hilde and Bjerkely. Hilde can neither see nor hear her, but then—Sophie finds Hilde's gold crucifix on the dock. And the crucifix—with Hilde's initials and everything—is in Sophie's bed when she wakes after her dream!

Hilde forced herself to think hard. Surely she hadn't lost her crucifix as well? She went to her dresser and took out her jewelry case. The crucifix, which she had received as a christening gift from her grandmother, was not there!

So she really had lost it. All right, but how had her father known it when she didn't even know it herself?

And another thing: Sophie had apparently dreamed that Hilde's father came home from Lebanon. But there was still a week to go before that happened. Was Sophie's dream prophetic? Did her father mean that when he came home Sophie would somehow be there? He had written that she would get a new friend . . .

In a momentary vision of absolute clarity Hilde knew that Sophie was more than just paper and ink. She really *existed*.

The Enlightenment

∞

*. . . from the way needles are made to the way
cannons are founded . . .*

Hilde had just begun the chapter on the Renaissance
when she heard her mother come in the front door. She
looked at the clock. It was four in the afternoon.

Her mother ran upstairs and opened Hilde's door.

"Didn't you go to the church?"

"Yes, I did."

"But . . . what did you wear?"

"What I'm wearing now."

"Your nightgown?"

"It's an old stone church from the Middle Ages."

"Hilde!"

She let the ring binder fall into her lap and looked up
at her mother.

"I forgot the time, Mom. I'm sorry, but I'm reading
something terribly exciting."

Her mother could not help smiling.

"It's a magic book," added Hilde.

"Okay. Happy birthday once again, Hilde!"

"Hey, I don't know if I can take that phrase any
more."

"But I haven't . . . I'm just going to rest for a while,
then I'll start fixing a great dinner. I managed to get hold
of some strawberries."

"Okay, I'll go on reading."

Her mother left and Hilde read on.

Sophie is following Hermes through the town. In Alberto's hall she finds another card from Lebanon. This, too, is dated June 15.

Hilde was just beginning to understand the system of the dates. The cards dated before June 15 are copies of cards Hilde had already received from her dad. But those with today's date are reaching her for the first time via the ring binder.

Dear Hilde, Now Sophie is coming to the philosopher's house. She will soon be fifteen, but you were fifteen yesterday. Or is it today, Hilde? If it is today, it must be late, then. But our watches do not always agree . . .

Hilde read how Alberto told Sophie about the Renaissance and the new science, the seventeenth-century rationalists and British empiricism.

She jumped at every new card and birthday greeting that her father had stuck into the story. He got them to fall out of an exercise book, turn up inside a banana skin, and hide inside a computer program. Without the slightest effort, he could get Alberto to make a slip of the tongue and call Sophie Hilde. On top of everything else, he got Hermes to say "Happy birthday, Hilde!"

Hilde agreed with Alberto that he was going a bit too far, comparing himself with God and Providence. But whom was she actually agreeing with? Wasn't it her father who put those reproachful—or self-reproachful—words in Alberto's mouth? She decided that the comparison with God was not so crazy after all. Her father really was like an almighty God for Sophie's world.

When Alberto got to Berkeley, Hilde was at least as enthralled as Sophie had been. What would happen now? There had been all kinds of hints that something special was going to happen as soon as they got to that philosopher—who had denied the existence of a material world outside human consciousness.

The chapter begins with Alberto and Sophie standing

at the window, seeing the little plane with the long Happy Birthday streamer waving behind it. At the same time dark clouds begin to gather over the town.

"So 'to be or not to be' is not the whole question. The question is also who we are. Are we really human beings of flesh and blood? Does our world consist of real things—or are we encircled by the mind?"

Not so surprising that Sophie starts biting her nails. Nail-biting had never been one of Hilde's bad habits but she didn't feel particularly pleased with herself right now. Then finally it was all out in the open: "For us—for you and me—this 'will or spirit' that is the 'cause of everything in everything' could be Hilde's father."

"Are you saying he's been a kind of God for us?"
"To be perfectly candid, yes. He should be ashamed of himself!"
"What about Hilde herself?"
"She is an angel, Sophie."
"An angel?"
"Hilde is the one this 'spirit' turns to."

With that, Sophie tears herself away from Alberto and runs out into the storm. Could it be the same storm that raged over Bjerkely last night—a few hours after Sophie ran through the town?

As she ran, one thought kept going round and round in her mind: "Tomorrow is my *birthday*! Isn't it extra bitter to realize that life is only a dream on the day before your fifteenth birthday? It's like dreaming you won a million and then just as you're getting the money you wake up."

Sophie ran across the squelching playing field. Minutes later she saw someone come running toward her. It was her mother. The sky was pierced again and again by angry darts of lightning.

When they reached each other Sophie's mother put her arm around her.

"What's happening to us, little one?"

"I don't know," Sophie sobbed. "It's like a bad dream."

Hilde felt the tears start. "To be or not to be—that is the question." She threw the ring binder to the end of the bed and stood up. She walked back and forth across the floor. At last she stopped in front of the brass mirror, where she remained until her mother came to say dinner was ready. When Hilde heard the knock on the door, she had no idea how long she had been standing there.

But she was sure, she was perfectly sure, that her reflection had winked with both eyes.

She tried to be the grateful birthday girl all through dinner. But her thoughts were with Sophie and Alberto all the time.

How would things go for them now that they *knew* it was Hilde's father who decided everything? Although "knew" was perhaps an exaggeration. It was nonsense to think they knew anything at all. Wasn't it only her father who let them know things?

Still, the problem was the same however you looked at it. As soon as Sophie and Alberto "knew" how everything hung together, they were in a way at the end of the road.

She almost choked on a mouthful of food as she suddenly realized that the same problem possibly applied to her own world too. People had progressed steadily in their understanding of natural laws. Could history simply continue to all eternity once the last piece of the jigsaw puzzle of philosophy and science had fallen into place? Wasn't there a connection between the development of ideas and science on the one hand, and the greenhouse effect and deforestation on the other? Maybe it was not so crazy to call man's thirst for knowledge a fall from grace?

The question was so huge and so terrifying that Hilde tried to forget it again. She would probably understand much more as she read further in her father's birthday book.

"Happy birthday to you . . . ," sang her mother when

they were done with their ice cream and Italian strawberries. "Now we'll do whatever you choose."

"I know it sounds a bit crazy, but all I want to do is
read my present from Dad."

"Well, as long as he doesn't make you completely
delirious."

"No way."

"We could share a pizza while we watch that mystery
on TV."

"Yes, if you like."

Hilde suddenly thought of the way Sophie spoke to
her mother. Dad had hopefully not written any of Hilde's
mother into the character of the other mother? Just to
make sure, she decided not to mention the white rabbit
being pulled out of the top hat. Not today, at least.

"By the way," she said as she was leaving the table.

"What?"

"I can't find my gold crucifix anywhere."

Her mother looked at her with an enigmatic expression.

"I found it down by the dock weeks ago. You must
have dropped it, you untidy scamp."

"Did you mention it to Dad?"

"Let me think . . . yes, I believe I may have."

"Where is it then?"

Her mother got up and went to get her own jewelry
case. Hilde heard a little cry of surprise from the bedroom. She came quickly back into the living room.

"Right now I can't seem to find it."

"I thought as much."

She gave her mother a hug and ran upstairs to her
room. At last—now she could read on about Sophie and
Alberto. She sat up on the bed as before with the heavy
ring binder resting against her knees and began the next
chapter.

Sophie woke up the next morning when her mother came
into the room carrying a tray loaded with birthday presents. She had stuck a flag in an empty soda bottle.

"Happy birthday, Sophie!"

Sophie rubbed the sleep from her eyes. She tried to

remember what had happened the night before. But it was all like jumbled pieces of a jigsaw puzzle. One of the pieces was Alberto, another was Hilde and the major. A third was Berkeley, a fourth Bjerkely. The blackest piece of all was the violent storm. She had practically been in shock. Her mother had rubbed her dry with a towel and simply put her to bed with a cup of hot milk and honey. She had fallen asleep immediately.

"I think I'm still alive," she said weakly.

"Of course you're alive! And today you are fifteen years old."

"Are you quite sure?"

"Quite sure. Shouldn't a mother know when her only child was born? June 15, 1975 . . . and half-past one, Sophie. It was the happiest moment of my life."

"Are you sure it isn't all only a dream?"

"It must be a good dream to wake up to rolls and soda and birthday presents."

She put the tray of presents on a chair and disappeared out of the room for a second. When she came back she was carrying another tray with rolls and soda. She put it on the end of the bed.

It was the signal for the traditional birthday morning ritual, with the unpacking of presents and her mother's sentimental flights back to her first contractions fifteen years ago. Her mother's present was a tennis racket. Sophie had never played tennis, but there were some open-air courts a few minutes from Clover Close. Her father had sent her a mini-TV and FM radio. The screen was no bigger than an ordinary photograph. There were also presents from old aunts and friends of the family.

Presently her mother said, "Do you think I should stay home from work today?"

"No, why should you?"

"You were very upset yesterday. If it goes on, I think we should make an appointment to see a psychiatrist."

"That won't be necessary."

"Was it the storm—or was it Alberto?"

"What about you? You said: What's happening to us, little one?"

"I was thinking of you running around town to meet

some mysterious person . . . Maybe it's my fault."

"It's not anybody's 'fault' that I'm taking a course in philosophy in my leisure time. Just go to work. School doesn't start till ten, and we're only getting our grades and sitting around."

"Do you know what you're going to get?"

"More than I got last semester at any rate."

Not long after her mother had gone the telephone rang.

"Sophie Amundsen."

"This is Alberto."

"Ah."

"The major didn't spare any ammunition last night."

"What do you mean."

"The thunderstorm, Sophie."

"I don't know what to think."

"That is the finest virtue a genuine philosopher can have. I am proud of how much you have learned in such a short time."

"I am scared that nothing is real."

"That's called existential angst, or dread, and is as a rule only a stage on the way to new consciousness."

"I think I need a break from the course."

"Are there that many frogs in the garden at the moment?"

Sophie started to laugh. Alberto continued: "I think it would be better to persevere. Happy birthday, by the way. We must complete the course by Midsummer Eve. It's our last chance."

"Our last chance for what?"

"Are you sitting comfortably? We're going to have to spend some time on this, you understand."

"I'm sitting down."

"You remember Descartes?"

"I think, therefore I am?"

"With regard to our own methodical doubt, we are right now starting from scratch. We don't even know whether we think. It may turn out that we *are* thoughts, and that is quite different from thinking. We have good reason to believe that we have merely been invented by Hilde's father as a kind of birthday diversion for the major's daughter from Lillesand. Do you see?"

"Yes . . ."

"But therein also lies a built-in contradiction. If we are fictive, we have no right to 'believe' anything at all. In which case this whole telephone conversation is purely imaginary."

"And we haven't the tiniest bit of free will because it's the major who plans everything we say and do. So we can just as well hang up now."

"No, now you're oversimplifying things."

"Explain it, then."

"Would you claim that people plan everything they dream? It may be that Hilde's father knows everything we do. It may be just as difficult to escape his omniscience as it is to run away from your own shadow. However—and this is where I have begun to devise a plan—it is not certain that the major has already decided on everything that is to happen. He may not decide before the very last minute—that is to say, in the moment of creation. Precisely at such moments we may possibly have an initiative of our own which guides what we say and do. Such an initiative would naturally constitute extremely weak impulses compared to the major's heavy artillery. We are very likely defenseless against intrusive external forces such as talking dogs, messages in bananas, and thunderstorms booked in advance. But we cannot rule out our stubbornness, however weak it may be."

"How could that be possible?"

"The major naturally knows everything about our little world, but that doesn't mean he is all powerful. At any rate we must try to live as if he is not."

"I think I see where you're going with this."

"The trick would be if we could manage to do something all on our own—something the major would not be able to discover."

"How can we do that if we don't even exist?"

"Who said we don't exist? The question is not *whether* we are, but *what* we are and *who* we are. Even if it turns out that we are merely impulses in the major's dual personality, that need not take our little bit of existence away from us."

"Or our free will?"

"I'm working on it, Sophie."

"But Hilde's father must be fully aware that you are working on it."

"Decidedly so. But he doesn't know what the actual plan is. I am attempting to find an Archimedian point."

"An Archimedian point?"

"Archimedes was a Greek scientist who said 'Give me a firm point on which to stand and I will move the earth.' That's the kind of point we must find to move ourselves out of the major's inner universe."

"That would be quite a feat."

"But we won't manage to slip away before we have finished the philosophy course. While that lasts he has much too firm a grip on us. He has clearly decided that I am to guide you through the centuries right up to our own time. But we only have a few days left before he boards a plane somewhere down in the Middle East. If we haven't succeeded in detaching ourselves from his gluey imagination before he arrives at Bjerkely, we are done for."

"You're frightening me!"

"First of all I shall give you the most important facts about the French Enlightenment. Then we shall take the main outline of Kant's philosophy so that we can get to Romanticism. Hegel will also be a significant part of the picture for us. And in talking about him we will unavoidably touch on Kierkegaard's indignant clash with Hegelian philosophy. We shall briefly talk about Marx, Darwin, and Freud. And if we can manage a few closing comments on Sartre and Existentialism, our plan can be put into operation."

"That's an awful lot for one week."

"That's why we must begin at once. Can you come over right away?"

"I have to go to school. We are having a class get-together and then we get our grades."

"Drop it. If we are only fictive, it's pure imagination that candy and soda have any taste."

"But my grades . . ."

"Sophie, either you are living in a wondrous universe

on a tiny planet in one of many hundred billion galaxies—
or else you are the result of a few electromagnetic impulses in the major's mind. And you are talking about
grades! You ought to be ashamed of yourself!"

"I'm sorry."

"But you'd better go to school before we meet. It might
have a bad influence on Hilde if you cut your last schoolday. She probably goes to school even on her birthday.
She is an angel, you know."

"So I'll come straight from school."

"We can meet at the major's cabin."

"The major's cabin?"

. . . Click!

Hilde let the ring binder slide into her lap. Her father
had given her conscience a dig there—she did cut her
last day at school. How sneaky of him!

She sat for a while wondering what the plan was that
Alberto was devising. Should she sneak a look at the
last page? No, that would be cheating. She'd better hurry
up and read it to the end.

But she was convinced Alberto was right on one important point. One thing was that her father had an over-
view of what was going to happen to Sophie and
Alberto. But while he was writing, he probably didn't
know everything that would happen. He might dash off
something in a great hurry, something he might not notice till long after he had written it. In a situation like
that Sophie and Alberto would have a certain amount of
leeway.

Once again Hilde had an almost transfiguring conviction that Sophie and Alberto really existed. Still waters
run deep, she thought to herself.

Why did that idea come to her?

It was certainly not a thought that rippled the surface.

At school, Sophie received lots of attention because it was
her birthday. Her classmates were already keyed up by
thoughts of summer vacation, and grades, and the sodas
on the last day of school.

The minute the teacher dismissed the class with her best

wishes for the vacation, Sophie ran home. Joanna tried to slow her down but Sophie called over her shoulder that there was something she just had to do.

In the mailbox she found two cards from Lebanon. They were both birthday cards: HAPPY BIRTHDAY—15 YEARS. One of them was to "Hilde Møller Knag, c/o Sophie Amundsen . . ." But the other one was to Sophie herself. Both cards were stamped "UN Battalion—June 15."

Sophie read her own card first:

Dear Sophie Amundsen, Today you are getting a card as well. Happy birthday, Sophie, and many thanks for everything you have done for Hilde. Best regards, Major Albert Knag.

Sophie was not sure how to react, now that Hilde's father had finally written to her too.

Hilde's card read:

Dear Hilde, I have no idea what day or time it is in Lillesand. But, as I said, it doesn't make much difference. If I know you, I am not too late for a last, or next to last, greeting from down here. But don't stay up too late! Alberto will soon be telling you about the French Enlightenment. He will concentrate on seven points. They are:

1. Opposition to authority
2. Rationalism
3. The enlightenment movement
4. Cultural optimism
5. The return to nature
6. Natural religion
7. Human rights

The major was obviously still keeping his eye on them.

Sophie let herself in and put her report card with all the A's on the kitchen table. Then she slipped through the hedge and ran into the woods.

Soon she was once again rowing across the little lake. Alberto was sitting on the doorstep when she got to the cabin. He invited her to sit beside him. The weather was fine although a slight mist of damp raw air was coming off the lake. It was as though it had not quite recovered from the storm.

"Let's get going right away," said Alberto.

"After Hume, the next great philosopher was the German, Immanuel Kant. But France also had many important thinkers in the eighteenth century. We could say that the philosophical center of gravity in Europe in the eighteenth century was in England in the first half, in France in the middle, and in Germany toward the end of it."

"A shift from west to east, in other words."

"Precisely. Let me outline some of the ideas that many of the French Enlightenment philosophers had in common. The important names are *Montesquieu*, *Voltaire*, and *Rousseau*, but there were many, many others. I shall concentrate on seven points."

"Thanks, that I am painfully aware of."

Sophie handed him the card from Hilde's father. Alberto sighed deeply. "He could have saved himself the trouble . . . the first key words, then, are *opposition to authority*. Many of the French Enlightenment philosophers visited England, which was in many ways more liberal than their home country, and were intrigued by the English natural sciences, especially Newton and his universal physics. But they were also inspired by British philosophy, in particular by Locke and his political philosophy. Once back in France, they became increasingly opposed to the old authority. They thought it was essential to remain skeptical of all inherited truths, the idea being that the individual must find his own answer to every question. The tradition of Descartes was very inspiring in this respect."

"Because he was the one who built everything up from the ground."

"Quite so. The opposition to authority was not least directed against the power of the clergy, the king, and the nobility. During the eighteenth century, these institutions had far more power in France than they had in England."

"Then came the French Revolution."

"Yes, in 1789. But the revolutionary ideas arose much earlier. The next key word is *rationalism*."

"I thought rationalism went out with Hume."

"Hume himself did not die until 1776. That was about twenty years after Montesquieu and only two years before Voltaire and Rousseau, who both died in 1778. But all three had been to England and were familiar with the philosophy of Locke. You may recall that Locke was not consistent in his empiricism. He believed, for example, that faith in God and certain moral norms were inherent in human reason. This idea is also the core of the French Enlightenment."

"You also said that the French have always been more rational than the British."

"Yes, a difference that goes right back to the Middle Ages. When the British speak of 'common sense,' the French usually speak of 'evident.' The English expression means 'what everybody knows,' the French means 'what is obvious'—to one's reason, that is."

"I see."

"Like the humanists of antiquity—such as Socrates and the Stoics—most of the Enlightenment philosophers had an unshakable faith in human reason. This was so characteristic that the French Enlightenment is often called the Age of Reason. The new natural sciences had revealed that nature was subject to reason. Now the Enlightenment philosophers saw it as their duty to lay a foundation for morals, religion, and ethics in accordance with man's immutable reason. This led to the *enlightenment movement*."

"The third point."

"Now was the time to start 'enlightening' the masses. This was to be the basis for a better society. People thought that poverty and oppression were the fault of ignorance and superstition. Great attention was therefore focused on the education of children and of the people. It is no accident that the science of pedagogy was founded during the Enlightenment."

"So schools date from the Middle Ages, and pedagogy from the Enlightenment."

"You could say that. The greatest monument to the enlightenment movement was characteristically enough a huge encyclopedia. I refer to the Encyclopedia in 28 volumes published during the years from 1751 to 1772. All the great philosophers and men of letters contributed to it. 'Everything is to be found here,' it was said, 'from the way needles are made to the way cannons are founded.' ''

"The next point is *cultural optimism*," Sophie said.

"Would you oblige me by putting that card away while I am talking?"

"Excuse me."

"The Enlightenment philosophers thought that once reason and knowledge became widespread, humanity would make great progress. It could only be a question of time before irrationalism and ignorance would give way to an 'enlightened' humanity. This thought was dominant in Western Europe until the last couple of decades. Today we are no longer so convinced that all 'developments' are to the good.

"But this criticism of 'civilization' was already being voiced by French Enlightenment philosophers."

"Maybe we should have listened to them."

"For some, the new catchphrase was *back to nature*. But 'nature' to the Enlightenment philosophers meant almost the same as 'reason,' since human reason was a gift of nature rather than of religion or of 'civilization.' It was observed that the so-called primitive peoples were frequently both healthier and happier than Europeans, and this, it was said, was because they had not been 'civilized.' Rousseau proposed the catchphrase, 'We should return to nature.' For nature is good, and man is 'by nature' good; it is civilization which ruins him. Rousseau also believed that the child should be allowed to remain in its 'naturally' innocent state as long as possible. It would not be wrong to say that the idea of the intrinsic value of childhood dates from the Enlightenment. Previously, childhood had been considered merely a preparation for adult life. But we are all human beings—and we live our life on this earth, even when we are children."

"I should think so!"

"Religion, they thought, had to be made natural."

"What exactly did they mean by that?"

"They meant that religion also had to be brought into

harmony with 'natural' reason. There were many who fought for what one could call a *natural religion*, and that is the sixth point on the list. At the time there were a lot of confirmed materialists who did not believe in a God, and who professed to atheism. But most of the Enlightenment philosophers thought it was irrational to imagine a world without God. The world was far too rational for that. Newton held the same view, for example. It was also considered rational to believe in the immortality of the soul. Just as for Descartes, whether or not man has an immortal soul was held to be more a question of reason than of faith."

"That I find very strange. To me, it's a typical case of what you believe, not of what you know."

"That's because you don't live in the eighteenth century. According to the Enlightenment philosophers, what religion needed was to be stripped of all the irrational dogmas or doctrines that had got attached to the simple teachings of Jesus during the course of ecclesiastical history."

"I see."

"Many people consequently professed to what is known as *Deism*."

"What is that?"

"By Deism we mean a belief that God created the world ages and ages ago, but has not revealed himself to the world since. Thus God is reduced to the 'Supreme Being' who only reveals himself to mankind through nature and natural laws, never in any 'supernatural' way. We find a similar 'philosophical God' in the writings of Aristotle. For him, God was the 'formal cause' or 'first mover.' "

"So now there's only one point left, *human rights*."

"And yet this is perhaps the most important. On the whole, you could say that the French Enlightenment was more practical than the English philosophy."

"You mean they lived according to their philosophy?"

"Yes, very much so. The French Enlightenment philosophers did not content themselves with theoretical views on man's place in society. They fought actively for what they called the 'natural rights' of the citizen. At first, this took the form of a campaign against censorship—for the freedom of the press. But also in matters of religion, morals, and politics, the individual's right to freedom of thought and utterance had to be secured. They also fought for the abolition of slavery and for a more humane treatment of criminals."

"I think I agree with most of that."

"The principle of the 'inviolability of the individual' culminated in the Declaration of the Rights of Man and Citizen adopted by the French National Assembly in 1789. This Declaration of Human Rights was the basis for our own Norwegian Constitution of 1814."

"But a lot of people still have to fight for these rights."

"Yes, unhappily. But the Enlightenment philosophers wanted to establish certain rights that everybody was entitled to simply by being born. That was what they meant by natural rights.

"We still speak of a 'natural right' which can often be in conflict with the laws of the land. And we constantly find individuals, or even whole nations, that claim this 'natural right' when they rebel against anarchy, servitude, and oppression."

"What about women's rights?"

"The French Revolution in 1787 established a number of rights for all 'citizens.' But a citizen was nearly always considered to be a man. Yet it was the French Revolution that gave us the first inklings of feminism."

"It was about time!"

"As early as 1787 the Enlightenment philosopher *Condorcet* published a treatise on the rights of women. He held that women had the same 'natural rights' as men. During the Revolution of 1789, women were extremely active in the fight against the old feudal regime. For example, it was women who led the demonstrations that forced the king away from his palace at Versailles. Women's groups were formed in Paris. In addition to the demand for the same political rights as men, they also demanded changes in the marriage laws and in women's social conditions."

"Did they get equal rights?"

"No. Just as on so many subsequent occasions, the question of women's rights was exploited in the heat of the struggle, but as soon as things fell into place in a new regime, the old male-dominated society was reintroduced."

"Typical!"

"One of those who fought hardest for the rights of women during the French Revolution was *Olympe de Gouges*. In 1791—two years after the revolution—she published a declaration on the rights of women. The declaration on the rights of the citizen had not included any article on women's natural rights. Olympe de Gouges now demanded all the same rights for women as for men."

"What happened?"

"She was beheaded in 1793. And all political activity for women was banned."

"How shameful!"

"It was not until the nineteenth century that feminism really got under way, not only in France but also in the rest of Europe. Little by little this struggle began to bear fruit. But in Norway, for example, women did not get the right to vote until 1913. And women in many parts of the world still have a lot to fight for."

"They can count on my support."

Alberto sat looking across at the lake. After a minute or two he said:

"That was more or less what I wanted to say about the Enlightenment."

"What do you mean by more or less?"

"I have the feeling there won't be any more."

But as he said this, something began to happen in the middle of the lake. Something was bubbling up from the depths. A huge and hideous creature rose from the surface.

"A sea serpent!" cried Sophie.

The dark monster coiled itself back and forth a few times and then disappeared back into the depths. The water was as still as before.

Alberto had turned away.

"Now we'll go inside," he said.

They went into the little hut.

Sophie stood looking at the two pictures of Berkeley and Bjerkely. She pointed to the picture of Bjerkely and said:

"I think Hilde lives somewhere inside that picture."

An embroidered sampler now hung between the two pictures. It read: LIBERTY, EQUALITY AND FRATERNITY.

Sophie turned to Alberto: "Did you hang that there?"

He just shook his head with a disconsolate expression.

Then Sophie discovered a small envelope on the mantelpiece. "To Hilde and Sophie," it said. Sophie knew at once who it was from, but it was a new turn of events that he had begun to count on her.

She opened the letter and read aloud:

Dear both of you, Sophie's philosophy teacher ought to have underlined the significance of the French Enlightenment for the ideals and principles the UN is founded on. Two hundred years ago, the slogan "Liberty, Equality, and Fraternity" helped unite the people of France. Today the same words should unite the whole world. It is more important now than ever before to be one big Family of Man. Our descendants are our own children and grandchildren. What kind of world are they inheriting from us?

Hilde's mother was calling from downstairs that the mystery was starting in ten minutes and that she had put the pizza in the oven. Hilde was quite exhausted after all she had read. She had been up since six o'clock this morning.

She decided to spend the rest of the evening celebrating her birthday with her mother. But first she had to look something up in her encyclopedia.

Gouges . . . no. De Gouges? No again. Olympe de Gouges? Still a blank. This encyclopedia had not written one single word about the woman who was beheaded for her political commitment. Wasn't that scandalous!

She was surely not just someone her father had thought up?

Hilde ran downstairs to get a bigger encyclopedia.

"I just have to look something up," she said to her astounded mother.

She took the FORV to GP volume of the big family encyclopedia and ran up to her room again.

Gouges . . . there she was!

Gouges, Marie Olympe (1748–1793), Fr. author, played a prominent role during the French Revolution with numerous brochures on social questions and several plays. One of the few during the Revolution who campaigned for human rights to apply to women. In 1791 published "Declaration on the Rights of Women." Beheaded in 1793 for daring to defend Louis XVI and oppose Robespierre. (Lit: L. Lacour, "Les Origines du féminisme contemporain," 1900)

Kant

*. . . the starry heavens above me and the moral law
within me . . .*

It was close to midnight before Major Albert Knag
called home to wish Hilde a happy birthday. Hilde's
mother answered the telephone.

"It's for you, Hilde."

"Hello?"

"It's Dad."

"Are you crazy? It's nearly midnight!"

"I just wanted to say Happy Birthday . . ."

"You've been doing that all day."

". . . but I didn't want to call before the day was over."

"Why?"

"Didn't you get my present?"

"Yes, I did. Thank you very much."

"I can't wait to hear what you think of it."

"It's terrific. I have hardly eaten all day, it's so exciting."

"I have to know how far you've gotten."

"They just went inside the major's cabin because you
started teasing them with a sea serpent."

"The Enlightenment."

"And Olympe de Gouges."

"So I didn't get it completely wrong."

"Wrong in what way?"

"I think there's one more birthday greeting to come.
But that one is set to music."

"I'd better read a little more before I go to sleep."

"You haven't given up, then?"

"I've learned more in this one day than ever before. I can hardly believe that it's less than twenty-four hours since Sophie got home from school and found the first envelope."

"It's strange how little time it takes to read."

"But I can't help feeling sorry for her."

"For Mom?"

"No, for Sophie, of course."

"Why?"

"The poor girl is totally confused."

"But she's only . . ."

"You were going to say she's only made up."

"Yes, something like that."

"I think Sophie and Alberto really *exist*."

"We'll talk more about it when I get home."

"Okay."

"Have a nice day."

"What?"

"I mean good night."

"Good night."

When Hilde went to bed half an hour later it was still so light that she could see the garden and the little bay. It never got really dark at this time of the year.

She played with the idea that she was inside a picture hanging on the wall of the little cabin in the woods. She wondered if one could look out of the picture into what surrounded it.

Before she fell asleep, she read a few more pages in the big ring binder.

Sophie put the letter from Hilde's father back on the mantel.

"What he says about the UN is not unimportant," said Alberto, "but I don't like him interfering in my presentation."

"I don't think you should worry too much about that."

"Nevertheless, from now on I intend to ignore all extraordinary phenomena such as sea serpents and the like. Let's sit here by the window while I tell you about Kant."

Sophie noticed a pair of glasses lying on a small table between two armchairs. She also noticed that the lenses were red.

Maybe they were strong sunglasses . . .

"It's almost two o'clock," she said. "I have to be home before five. Mom has probably made plans for my birthday."

"That gives us three hours."

"Let's start."

"*Immanuel Kant* was born in 1724 in the East Prussian town of Königsberg, the son of a master saddler. He lived there practically all his life until he died at the age of eighty. His family was deeply pious, and his own religious conviction formed a significant background to his philosophy. Like Berkeley, he felt it was essential to preserve the foundations of Christian belief."

"I've heard enough about Berkeley, thanks."

"Kant was the first of the philosophers we have heard about so far to have taught philosophy at a university. He was a professor of philosophy."

"Professor?"

"There are two kinds of philosopher. One is a person who seeks his own answers to philosophical questions. The other is someone who is an expert on the history of philosophy but does not necessarily construct his own philosophy."

"And Kant was that kind?"

"Kant was both. If he had simply been a brilliant professor and an expert on the ideas of other philosophers, he would never have carved a place for himself in the history of philosophy. But it is important to note that Kant had a solid grounding in the philosophic tradition of the past. He was familiar both with the rationalism of Descartes and Spinoza and the empiricism of Locke, Berkeley, and Hume."

"I asked you not to mention Berkeley again."

"Remember that the rationalists believed that the basis for all human knowledge lay in the mind. And that the empiricists believed all knowledge of the world proceeded from the senses. Moreover, Hume had pointed out that there are clear limits regarding which conclusions we could reach through our sense perceptions."

"And who did Kant agree with?"

"He thought both views were partly right, but he thought both were partly wrong, too. The question everybody was concerned with was what we can know about the world. This philosophical project had been preoccupying all philosophers since Descartes.

"Two main possibilities were drawn up: either the world is exactly as we perceive it, or it is the way it appears to our reason."

"And what did Kant think?"

"Kant thought that both 'sensing' and 'reason' come into play in our conception of the world. But he thought the rationalists went too far in their claims as to how much reason can contribute, and he also thought the empiricists placed too much emphasis on sensory experience."

"If you don't give me an example soon, it will all be just a bunch of words."

"In his point of departure Kant agrees with Hume and the empiricists that all our knowledge of the world comes from our sensations. But—and here Kant stretches his hand out to the rationalists—in our reason there are also decisive factors that determine *how* we perceive the world around us. In other words, there are certain conditions in the human mind that are contributive to our conception of the world."

"You call that an example?"

"Let us rather do a little experiment. Could you bring those glasses from the table over there? Thank you. Now, put them on."

Sophie put the glasses on. Everything around her became red. The pale colors became pink and the dark colors became crimson.

"What do you see?"

"I see exactly the same as before, except that it's all red."

"That's because the glasses limit the way you perceive reality. Everything you see is part of the world around you, but *how* you see it is determined by the glasses you are wearing. So you cannot say the world is red even though you conceive it as being so."

"No, naturally."

"If you now took a walk in the woods, or home to Captain's Bend, you would see everything the way you normally do. But whatever you saw, it would all be red."

"As long as I didn't take the glasses off, yes."

"And that, Sophie, is precisely what Kant meant when he said that there are certain conditions governing the mind's operation which influence the way we experience the world."

"What kind of conditions?"

"Whatever we see will first and foremost be perceived as phenomena in *time* and *space*. Kant called 'time' and 'space' our two 'forms of intuition.' And he emphasized that these two 'forms' in our own mind *precede* every experience. In other words, we can know *before* we experience things that we will perceive them as phenomena in time and space. For we are not able to take off the 'glasses' of reason."

"So he thought that perceiving things in time and space was innate?"

"Yes, in a way. *What* we see may depend on whether we are raised in India or Greenland, but wherever we are, we experience the world as a series of processes in time and space. This is something we can say beforehand."

"But aren't time and space things that *exist* beyond ourselves?"

"No. Kant's idea was that time and space belong to the human condition. Time and space are first and foremost modes of perception and not attributes of the physical world."

"That was a whole new way of looking at things."

"For the mind of man is not just 'passive wax' which simply receives sensations from outside. The mind leaves its imprint on the way we apprehend the world. You could compare it with what happens when you pour water into a glass pitcher. The water adapts itself to the pitcher's form. In the same way our perceptions adapt themselves to our 'forms of intuition.' "

"I think I understand what you mean."

"Kant claimed that it is not only mind which conforms

to things. Things also conform to the mind. Kant called this the Copernican Revolution in the problem of human knowledge.

"By that he meant that it was just as new and just as radically different from former thinking as when Copernicus claimed that the earth revolved around the sun and not vice versa."

"I see now how he could think both the rationalists and the empiricists were right up to a point. The rationalists had almost forgotten the importance of experience, and the empiricists had shut their eyes to the way our own mind influences the way we see the world."

"And even the *law of causality*—which Hume believed man could not experience—belongs to the mind, according to Kant."

"Explain that, please."

"You remember how Hume claimed that it was only force of habit that made us see a causal link behind all natural processes. According to Hume, we cannot perceive the black billiard ball as being the cause of the white ball's movement. Therefore, we cannot prove that the black billiard ball will always set the white one in motion."

"Yes, I remember."

"But that very thing which Hume says we cannot prove is what Kant makes into an attribute of human reason. The law of causality is eternal and absolute simply because human reason perceives everything that happens as a matter of cause and effect."

"Again, I would have thought that the law of causality lay in the physical world itself, not in our minds."

"Kant's philosophy states that it is inherent in us. He agreed with Hume that we cannot know with certainty what the world is like 'in itself.' We can only know what the world is like 'for me'—or for everybody. Kant's greatest contribution to philosophy is the dividing line he draws between things in themselves—*das Ding an sich*—and things as they appear to us."

"I'm not so good at German."

"Kant made an important distinction between 'the thing in itself' and 'the thing for me.' We can never have certain

knowledge of things 'in themselves.' We can only know
how things 'appear' to us. On the other hand, prior to
any particular experience we can say something about
how things will be perceived by the human mind.''

''We can?''

''Before you go out in the morning, you cannot know
what you will see or experience during the day. But you
can know that what you see and experience will be perceived as happening in time and space. You can moreover be confident that the law of cause and effect will
apply, simply because you carry it with you as part of
your consciousness.''

''But you mean we could have been made differently?''

''Yes, we could have had a different sensory apparatus.
And we could have had a different sense of time and a
different feeling about space. We could even have been
created in such a way that we would not go around
searching for the cause of things that happen around us.''

''How do you mean?''

''Imagine there's a cat lying on the floor in the living
room. A ball comes rolling into the room. What does the
cat do?''

''I've tried that lots of times. The cat will run after the
ball.''

''All right. Now imagine that you were sitting in that
same room. If you suddenly see a ball come rolling in,
would you also start running after it?''

''First, I would turn around to see where the ball came
from.''

''Yes, because you are a human being, you will inevi-
tably look for the cause of every event, because the law
of causality is part of your makeup.''

''So Kant says.''

''Hume showed that we can neither perceive nor prove
natural laws. That made Kant uneasy. But he believed he
could prove their absolute validity by showing that in reality we are talking about the laws of human cognition.''

''Will a child also turn around to see where the ball
came from?''

''Maybe not. But Kant pointed out that a child's reason
is not fully developed until it has had some sensory ma-

terial to work with. It is altogether senseless to talk about an empty mind."

"No, that would be a very strange mind."

"So now let's sum up. According to Kant, there are two elements that contribute to man's knowledge of the world. One is the external conditions that we cannot know of before we have perceived them through the senses. We can call this the *material* of knowledge. The other is the internal conditions in man himself—such as the perception of events as happening in time and space and as processes conforming to an unbreakable law of causality. We can call this the *form* of knowledge."

Alberto and Sophie remained seated for a while gazing out of the window. Suddenly Sophie saw a little girl between the trees on the opposite side of the lake.

"Look!" said Sophie. "Who's that?"

"I'm sure I don't know."

The girl was only visible for a few seconds, then she was gone. Sophie noticed that she was wearing some kind of red hat.

"We shall under no circumstances let ourselves be distracted."

"Go on, then."

"Kant believed that there are clear limits to what we can know. You could perhaps say that the mind's 'glasses' set these limits."

"In what way?"

"You remember that philosophers before Kant had discussed the really 'big' questions—for instance, whether man has an immortal soul, whether there is a God, whether nature consists of tiny indivisible particles, and whether the universe is finite or infinite."

"Yes."

"Kant believed there was no certain knowledge to be obtained on these questions. Not that he rejected this type of argument. On the contrary. If he had just brushed these questions aside, he could hardly have been called a philosopher."

"What did he do?"

"Be patient. In such great philosophical questions, Kant believed that reason operates beyond the limits of what we humans can comprehend. At the same time, there is in our nature a basic desire to pose these same questions. But when, for example, we ask whether the universe is finite or infinite, we are asking about a totality of which we ourselves are a tiny part. We can therefore never completely know this totality."

"Why not?"

"When you put the red glasses on, we demonstrated that according to Kant there are two elements that contribute to our knowledge of the world."

"Sensory perception and reason."

"Yes, the material of our knowledge comes to us through the senses, but this material must conform to the attributes of reason. For example, one of the attributes of reason is to seek the cause of an event."

"Like the ball rolling across the floor."

"If you like. But when we wonder where the world came from—and then discuss possible answers—reason is in a sense 'on hold.' For it has no sensory material to process, no experience to make use of, because we have never experienced the whole of the great reality that we are a tiny part of."

"We are—in a way—a tiny part of the ball that comes rolling across the floor. So we can't know where it came from."

"But it will always be an attribute of human reason to ask where the ball comes from. That's why we ask and ask, we exert ourselves to the fullest to find answers to all the deepest questions. But we never get anything firm to bite on; we never get a satisfactory answer because reason is not locked on."

"I know exactly how that feels, thank you very much."

"In such weighty questions as to the nature of reality, Kant showed that there will always be two contrasting viewpoints that are equally likely or unlikely, depending on what our reason tells us."

"Examples, please."

"It is just as meaningful to say that the world must have had a beginning in time as to say that it had no such beginning. Reason cannot decide between them. We can allege that the world has always existed, but *can* anything always have existed if there was never any beginning? So now we are forced to adopt the opposite view.

"We say that the world must have begun sometime— and it must have begun from nothing, unless we want to talk about a change from one state to another. But *can* something come from nothing, Sophie?"

"No, both possibilities are equally problematic. Yet it seems one of them must be right and the other wrong."

"You probably remember that Democritus and the materialists said that nature must consist of minimal parts that everything is made up of. Others, like Descartes, believed that it must always be possible to divide extended reality into ever smaller parts. But which of them was right?"

"Both. Neither."

"Further, many philosophers named freedom as one of man's most important values. At the same time we saw philosophers like the Stoics, for example, and Spinoza, who said that everything happens through the necessity of natural law. This was another case of human reason being unable to make a certain judgment, according to Kant."

"Both views are equally reasonable and unreasonable."

"Finally, we are bound to fail if we attempt to prove the existence of God with the aid of reason. Here the rationalists, like Descartes, had tried to prove that there must be a God simply because we have the idea of a 'supreme being.' Others, like Aristotle and Thomas Aquinas, decided that there must be a God because everything must have a first cause."

"What did Kant think?"

"He rejected both these proofs of the existence of God. Neither reason nor experience is any certain basis for claiming the existence of God. As far as reason goes, it is just as likely as it is unlikely that God exists."

"But you started by saying that Kant wanted to preserve the basis for Christian faith."

"Yes, he opened up a religious dimension. There, where both reason and experience fall short, there occurs a vacuum that can be filled by *faith*."

"That's how he saved Christianity?"

"If you will. Now, it might be worth noting that Kant was a Protestant. Since the days of the Reformation, Protestantism has been characterized by its emphasis on faith. The Catholic Church, on the other hand, has since the early Middle Ages believed more in reason as a pillar of faith.

"But Kant went further than simply to establish that these weighty questions should be left to the faith of the individual. He believed that it is essential for morality to presuppose that man has an *immortal soul*, that *God exists*, and that man has a *free will*."

"So he does the same as Descartes. First he is very critical of everything we can understand. And then he smuggles God in by the back door."

"But unlike Descartes, he emphasizes most particularly that it is not reason which brought him to this point but faith. He himself called faith in the immortal soul, in God's existence, and in man's free will *practical postulates*."

"Which means?"

"To 'postulate' something is to assume something that cannot be proved. By a 'practical postulate,' Kant meant something that had to be assumed for the sake of 'praxis,' or practice; that is to say, for man's morality. 'It is a moral necessity to assume the existence of God,' he said."

Suddenly there was a knock at the door. Sophie got up, but as Alberto gave no sign of rising, she asked: "Shouldn't we see who it is?"

Alberto shrugged and reluctantly got up. They opened the door, and a little girl stood there in a white summer dress and a red bonnet. It was the girl they had seen on the other side of the lake. Over one arm she carried a basket of food.

"Hi," said Sophie. "Who are you?"

"Can't you see I am Little Red Ridinghood?"

Sophie looked at Alberto, and Alberto nodded.

"You heard what she said."

"I'm looking for my grandmother's house," said the girl. "She is old and sick, but I'm taking her some food."

"It's not here," said Alberto, "so you'd better get on your way."

He gestured in a way that reminded Sophie of the way you brush off a fly.

"But I'm supposed to deliver a letter," continued the girl in the red bonnet.

With that, she took out a small envelope and handed it to Sophie. Then she went skipping away.

"Watch out for the wolf!" Sophie called after her.

Alberto was already on his way back into the living room.

"Just think! That was Little Red Ridinghood," said Sophie.

"And it's no good warning her. She will go to her grandmother's house and be eaten by the wolf. She never learns. It will repeat itself to the end of time."

"But I have never heard that she knocked on the door of another house before she went to her grandmother's."

"A bagatelle, Sophie."

Now Sophie looked at the envelope she had been given. It was addressed "To Hilde." She opened it and read aloud:

Dear Hilde, If the human brain was simple enough for us to understand, we would still be so stupid that we couldn't understand it. Love, Dad.

Alberto nodded. "True enough. I believe Kant said something to that effect. We cannot expect to understand what we *are*. Maybe we can comprehend a flower or an insect, but we can never comprehend ourselves. Even less can we expect to comprehend the universe."

Sophie had to read the cryptic sentence in the note to Hilde several times before Alberto went on: "We are not going to be interrupted by sea serpents and the like. Before we stop for today, I'll tell you about Kant's ethics."

"Please hurry. I have to go home soon."

"Hume's skepticism with regard to what reason and the senses can tell us forced Kant to think through many of life's important questions again. Not least in the area of ethics."

"Didn't Hume say that you can never prove what is right and what is wrong? You can't draw conclusions from is-sentences to ought-sentences.''

"For Hume it was neither our reason nor our experience that determined the difference between right and wrong. It was simply our sentiments. This was too tenuous a basis for Kant.''

"I can imagine.''

"Kant had always felt that the difference between right and wrong was a matter of reason, not sentiment. In this he agreed with the rationalists, who said the ability to distinguish between right and wrong is inherent in human reason. Everybody knows what is right or wrong, not because we have learned it but because it is born in the mind. According to Kant, everybody has 'practical reason,' that is, the intelligence that gives us the capacity to discern what is right or wrong in every case.''

"And that is innate?''

"The ability to tell right from wrong is just as innate as all the other attributes of reason. Just as we are all intelligent beings, for example, perceiving everything as having a causal relation, we all have access to the same universal *moral law*.

"This moral law has the same absolute validity as the physical laws. It is just as basic to our morality as the statements that everything has a cause, or that seven plus five is twelve, are basic to our intelligence.''

"And what does that moral law say?''

"Since it precedes every experience, it is 'formal.' That is to say, it is not bound to any particular situation of moral choice. For it applies to all people in all societies at all times. So it does not say you shall do this or this if you find yourself in that or that situation. It says how you are to behave in *all* situations.''

"But what is the point of having a moral law implanted inside yourself if it doesn't tell you what to do in specific situations?''

"Kant formulates the moral law as a *categorical imperative*. By this he means that the moral law is 'categorical,' or that it applies to all situations. It is, moreover, 'imperative,' which means it is commanding and therefore absolutely authoritative.''

"I see.''

"Kant formulates this 'categorical imperative' in several ways. First he says: *Act as if the maxim of your action were to become through your will a Universal Law of Nature.*"

"So when I do something, I must make sure I want everybody else to do the same if they are in the same situation."

"Exactly. Only then will you be acting in accordance with the moral law within you. Kant also formulates the 'categorical imperative' in this way: *Act in such a way that you always treat humanity, whether in your own person or in the person of any other, never simply as a means, but always at the same time as an end.*"

"So we must not exploit other people to our own advantage."

"No, because every man is an end in himself. But that does not only apply to others, it also applies to you yourself. You must not exploit yourself as a mere means to achieving something, either."

"It reminds me of the golden rule: Do unto others . . ."

"Yes, that is also a 'formal' rule of conduct that basically covers all ethical choices. You could say that the golden rule says the same thing as Kant's universal law of morals."

"But surely this is only an assertion. Hume was probably right in that we can't prove what is right or wrong by reason."

"According to Kant, the law of morals is just as absolute and just as universal as the law of causality. That cannot be proved by reason either, but it is nevertheless absolute and unalterable. Nobody would deny that."

"I get the feeling that what we are really talking about is conscience. Because everybody has a conscience, don't they?"

"Yes. When Kant describes the law of morals, he is describing the human conscience. We cannot prove what our conscience tells us, but we know it, nevertheless."

"Sometimes I might only be kind and helpful to others because I know it pays off. It could be a way of becoming popular."

"But if you share with others only to be popular, you

are not acting out of respect for moral law. You might be acting in accordance with moral law—and that could be fair enough—but if it is to be a moral action, you must have conquered yourself. Only when you do something purely out of duty can it be called a moral action. Kant's ethics is therefore sometimes called *duty ethics*."

"I can feel it my duty to collect money for the Red Cross or the church bazaar."

"Yes, and the important thing is that you do it because you know it is right. Even if the money you collect gets lost in the street, or is not sufficient to feed all the mouths it is intended to, you obeyed the moral law. You acted out of good will, and according to Kant, it is this good will which determines whether or not the action was morally right, not the consequences of the action. Kant's ethics is therefore also called a good will ethic."

"Why was it so important to him to know exactly when one acts out of respect for moral law? Surely the most important thing is that what we do really helps other people."

"Indeed it is and Kant would certainly not disagree. But only when we know in ourselves that we are acting out of respect for moral law are we acting freely."

"We act freely only when we obey a law? Isn't that kind of peculiar?"

"Not according to Kant. You perhaps remember that he had to 'assume'or 'postulate' that man has a free will. This is an important point, because Kant also said that everything obeys the law of causality. How, then, can we have a free will?"

"Search me."

"On this point Kant divides man into two parts in a way not dissimilar to the way Descartes claimed that man was a 'dual creature,' one with both a body and a mind. As material creatures, we are wholly and fully at the mercy of causality's unbreakable law, says Kant. We do not decide what we perceive—perception comes to us through necessity and influences us whether we like it or not. But we are not only material creatures—we are also creatures of reason.

"As material beings we belong wholly to the natural

world. We are therefore subject to causal relations. As such, we have no free will. But as rational beings we have a part in what Kant calls *das Ding an sich*—that is, the world as it exists in itself, independent of our sensory impressions. Only when we follow our 'practical reason'—which enables us to make moral choices—do we exercise our free will, because when we conform to moral law, it is we who make the law we are conforming to."

"Yes, that's true in a way. It is me, or something in me, which tells me not to be mean to others."

"So when you choose not to be mean—even if it is against your own interests—you are then acting freely."

"You're not especially free or independent if you just do whatever you want, in any case."

"One can become a slave to all kinds of things. One can even become a slave to one's own egoism. Independence and freedom are exactly what are required to rise above one's desires and vices."

"What about animals? I suppose they just follow their inclinations and needs. They don't have any freedom to follow moral law, do they?"

"No, that's the difference between animals and humans."

"I see that now."

"And finally we could perhaps say that Kant succeeded in showing the way out of the impasse that philosophy had reached in the struggle between rationalism and empiricism. With Kant, an era in the history of philosophy is therefore at an end. He died in 1804, when the cultural epoch we call Romanticism was in the ascendant. One of his most quoted sayings is carved on his gravestone in Königsberg: 'Two things fill my mind with ever-increasing wonder and awe, the more often and the more intensely the reflection dwells on them: the starry heavens above me and the moral law within me.' "

Alberto leaned back in his chair. "That's it," he said. "I think I have told you what's most important about Kant."

"Anyway, it's a quarter past four."

"But there is just one thing. Please give me a minute."

"I never leave the classroom before the teacher is finished."

"Did I say that Kant believed we had no freedom if we lived only as creatures of the senses?"

"Yes, you said something like that."

"But if we obey universal reason we are free and independent. Did I say that, too?"

"Yes. Why are you saying it again now?"

Alberto leaned toward Sophie, looked deep into her eyes, and whispered: "Don't believe everything you see, Sophie."

"What do you mean by that?"

"Just turn the other way, child."

"Now, I don't understand what you mean at all."

"People usually say, I'll believe that when I see it. But don't believe what you see, either."

"You said something like that once before."

"Yes, about Parmenides."

"But I still don't know what you mean."

"Well, we sat out there on the step, talking. Then that so-called sea serpent began to flap about in the water."

"Wasn't it peculiar!"

"Not at all. Then Little Red Ridinghood came to the door. 'I'm looking for my grandmother's house.' What a silly performance! It's just the major's tricks, Sophie. Like the banana message and that idiotic thunderstorm."

"Do you think . . . ?"

"But I said I had a plan. As long as we stick to our reason, he can't trick us. Because in a way we are free. He can let us 'perceive' all kinds of things; nothing would surprise me. If he lets the sky go dark or elephants fly, I shall only smile. But seven plus five *is* twelve. That's a fact that survives all his comic-strip effects. Philosophy is the opposite of fairy tales."

Sophie sat for a moment staring at him in amazement.

"Off you go," he said finally. "I'll call you for a session on Romanticism. You also need to hear about Hegel and Kierkegaard. But there's only a week to go before the major arrives at Kjevik airport. Before then, we must manage to free ourselves from his gluey fantasies. I'll say no more, Sophie. Except that I want you to know I'm working on a wonderful plan for both of us."

"I'll be off, then."

"Wait—we may have forgotten the most important thing."

"What's that?"

"The birthday song, Sophie. Hilde is fifteen today."

"So am I."

"You are, too, yes. Let's sing then."

They both stood up and sang:

"Happy Birthday to You."

It was half-past four. Sophie ran down to the water's edge and rowed over to the other side. She pulled the boat up into the rushes and began to hurry through the woods.

When she reached the path, she suddenly noticed something moving between the trees. She wondered if it was Little Red Ridinghood wandering alone through the woods to her grandmother's, but the figure between the trees was much smaller.

She went nearer. The figure was no bigger than a doll. It was brown and was wearing a red sweater.

Sophie stopped dead in her tracks when she realized it was a teddy bear.

That someone could have left a teddy bear in the forest was in itself no surprise. But this teddy bear was alive, and seemed intensely preoccupied.

"Hi," said Sophie.

"My name is Winnie-the-Pooh," said the teddy bear, "and I have unfortunately lost my way in the woods on this otherwise very fine day. I have certainly never seen you before."

"Maybe I'm the one who has never been here before," said Sophie. "So for that matter you could still be back home in Hundred Acre Wood."

"No, that sum is much too hard. Don't forget I'm only a small bear and I'm not very clever."

"I have heard of you."

"And I suppose you are Alice. Christopher Robin told us about you one day. I suppose that's how we met. You drank so much out of one bottle that you got smaller and smaller. But then you drank out of another bottle and started to grow again. You really have to be careful what you put in your mouth. I ate so much once that I got stuck in a rabbit hole.''

''I am not Alice.''

''It makes no difference who we are. The important thing is *that* we are. That's what Owl says, and he is very wise. Seven plus four is twelve, he once said on quite an ordinary sunny day. Both Eeyore and me felt very stupid, 'cos it's hard to do sums. It's much easier to figure out the weather.''

''My name is Sophie.''

''Nice to meet you, Sophie. As I said, I think you must be new around here. But now this little bear has to go 'cos I've got to find Piglet. We are going to a great big garden party for Rabbit and his friends.''

He waved with one paw. Sophie saw now that he was holding a little folded piece of paper in the other.

''What is that you've got there?'' she asked.

Winnie-the-Pooh produced the paper and said: ''This was what made me lose my way.''

''But it's only a piece of paper.''

''No it's not only a piece of paper. It's a letter to Hilde-through-the-Looking-Glass.''

''Oh—I can take that.''

''Are you the girl in the looking glass?''

''No, but . . .''

''A letter must always be delivered personally. Christopher Robin had to teach me that only yesterday.''

''But I know Hilde.''

''Makes no difference. Even if you know a person very well, you should never read their letters.''

''I mean, I can give it to Hilde.''

''That's quite a different thing. Here you are, Sophie. If I can get rid of this letter, I can probably find Piglet as well. To find Hilde-through-the-Looking-Glass you must first find a big looking glass. But that is no easy matter round here.''

And with that the little bear handed over the folded paper to Sophie and set off through the woods on his little feet. When he was out of sight, Sophie unfolded the piece of paper and read it:

Dear Hilde, It's too bad that Alberto didn't also tell Sophie that Kant advocated the establishment of a "league of nations." In his treatise *Perpetual Peace*, he wrote that all countries should unite in a league of the nations, which would assure peaceful coexistence between nations. About 125 years after the appearance of this treatise in 1795, the League of Nations was founded, after the First World War. After the Second World War it was replaced by the United Nations. So you could say that Kant was the father of the UN idea. Kant's point was that man's "practical reason" requires the nations to emerge from their wild state of nature which creates wars, and contract to keep the peace. Although the road to the establishment of a league of nations is laborious, it is our duty to work for the "universal and lasting securing of peace." The establishment of such a league was for Kant a far-distant goal. You could almost say it was philosophy's ultimate goal. I am in Lebanon at the moment. Love, Dad.

Sophie put the note in her pocket and continued on her way homeward. This was the kind of meeting in the woods Alberto had warned her about. But she couldn't have let the little teddy wander about in the woods on a never ending hunt for Hilde-through-the-Looking-Glass, could she?

Romanticism

∞

. . . the path of mystery leads inwards . . .

Hilde let the heavy ring binder slide into her lap. Then she let it slide further onto the floor.

It was already lighter in the room than when she had gone to bed. She looked at the clock. It was almost three. She snuggled down under the covers and closed her eyes. As she was falling asleep she wondered why her father had begun to write about Little Red Ridinghood and Winnie-the-Pooh . . .

She slept until eleven o'clock the next morning. The tension in her body told her that she had dreamed intensely all night, but she could not remember what she had dreamed. It felt as if she had been in a totally different reality.

She went downstairs and fixed breakfast. Her mother had put on her blue jumpsuit ready to go down to the boathouse and work on the motorboat. Even if it was not afloat, it had to be shipshape when Dad got back from Lebanon.

"Do you want to come down and give me a hand?"

"I have to read a little first. Should I come down with some tea and a mid-morning snack?"

"What mid-morning?"

When Hilde had eaten she went back up to her room, made her bed, and sat herself comfortably with the ring binder resting against her knees.

*   *   *

Sophie slipped through the hedge and stood in the big garden which she had once thought of as her own Garden of Eden . . .

There were branches and leaves strewn everywhere after the storm the night before. It seemed to her that there was some connection between the storm and the fallen branches and her meeting with Little Red Ridinghood and Winnie-the-Pooh.

She went into the house. Her mother had just gotten home and was putting some bottles of soda in the refrigerator. On the table was a delicious-looking chocolate cake.

"Are you expecting visitors?" asked Sophie; she had almost forgotten it was her birthday.

"We're having the real party next Saturday, but I thought we ought to have a little celebration today as well."

"How?"

"I have invited Joanna and her parents."

"Fine with me."

The visitors arrived shortly before half-past seven. The atmosphere was somewhat formal—Sophie's mother very seldom saw Joanna's parents socially.

It was not long before Sophie and Joanna went upstairs to Sophie's room to write the garden party invitations. Since Alberto Knox was also to be invited, Sophie had the idea of inviting people to a "philosophical garden party." Joanna didn't object. It was Sophie's party after all, and theme parties were "in" at the moment.

Finally they had composed the invitation. It had taken two hours and they couldn't stop laughing.

Dear . . .
You are hereby invited to a philosophical garden party at 3 Clover Close on Saturday June 23 (Midsummer Eve) at 7 p.m. During the evening we shall hopefully solve the mystery of life. Please bring warm sweaters and bright ideas suitable for solving the riddles of philosophy. Because of the danger of woodland fires we unfortunately cannot have a bonfire, but everybody is free to let the flames of their imagination

flicker unimpeded. There will be at least one genuine philosopher among the invited guests. For this reason the party is a strictly private arrangement. Members of the press will not be admitted.

> With regards,
> Joanna Ingebrigtsen (organizing committee)
> and Sophie Amundsen (hostess)

The two girls went downstairs to their parents, who were now talking somewhat more freely. Sophie handed the draft invitation, written with a calligraphic pen, to her mother.

"Could you make eighteen copies, please." It was not the first time she had asked her mother to make photocopies for her at work.

Her mother read the invitation and then handed it to Joanna's father.

"You see what I mean? She is going a little crazy."

"But it looks really exciting," said Joanna's father, handing the sheet on to his wife. "I wouldn't mind coming to that party myself."

Barbie read the invitation, then she said: "Well, I must say! Can we come too, Sophie?"

"Let's say twenty copies, then," said Sophie, taking them at their word.

"You must be nuts!" said Joanna.

Before Sophie went to bed that night she stood for a long time gazing out of the window. She remembered how she had once seen the outline of Alberto's figure in the darkness. It was more than a month ago. Now it was again late at night, but this was a white summer night.

Sophie heard nothing from Alberto until Tuesday morning. He called just after her mother had left for work.

"Sophie Amundsen."

"And Alberto Knox."

"I thought so."

"I'm sorry I didn't call before, but I've been working hard on our plan. I can only be alone and work undisturbed when the major is concentrating wholly and completely on you."

"That's weird."

"Then I seize the opportunity to conceal myself, you see. The best surveillance system in the world has its limitations when it is only controlled by one single person . . . I got your card."

"You mean the invitation?"

"Dare you risk it?"

"Why not?"

"Anything can happen at a party like that."

"Are you coming?"

"Of course I'm coming. But there is another thing. Did you remember that it's the day Hilde's father gets back from Lebanon?"

"No, I didn't, actually."

"It can't possibly be pure coincidence that he lets you arrange a philosophical garden party the same day as he gets home to Bjerkely."

"I didn't think about it, as I said."

"I'm sure he did. But all right, we'll talk about that later. Can you come to the major's cabin this morning?"

"I'm supposed to weed the flower beds."

"Let's say two o'clock, then. Can you make that?"

"I'll be there."

Alberto Knox was sitting on the step again when Sophie arrived.

"Have a seat," he said, getting straight down to work.

"Previously we spoke of the Renaissance, the Baroque period, and the Enlightenment. Today we are going to talk about *Romanticism*, which could be described as Europe's last great cultural epoch. We are approaching the end of a long story, my child."

"Did Romanticism last that long?"

"It began toward the end of the eighteenth century and lasted till the middle of the nineteenth. But after 1850 one can no longer speak of whole 'epochs' which comprise poetry, philosophy, art, science, and music."

"Was Romanticism one of those epochs?"

"It has been said that Romanticism was Europe's last common approach to life. It started in Germany, arising as a reaction to the Enlightenment's unequivocal emphasis" on reason. After Kant and his cool intellectualism, it was as if German youth heaved a sigh of relief.''

"What did they replace it with?"

"The new catchwords were 'feeling,' 'imagination,' 'experience,' and 'yearning.' Some of the Enlightenment thinkers had drawn attention to the importance of feeling—not least Rousseau—but at that time it was a criticism of the bias toward reason. What had been an undercurrent now became the mainstream of German culture."

"So Kant's popularity didn't last very long?"

"Well, it did and it didn't. Many of the Romantics saw themselves as Kant's successors, since Kant had established that there was a limit to what we can know of 'das Ding an sich.' On the other hand, he had underlined the importance of the ego's contribution to knowledge, or cognition. The individual was now completely free to interpret life in his own way. The Romantics exploited this in an almost unrestrained 'ego-worship,' which led to the exaltation of artistic genius.''

"Were there a lot of these geniuses?"

"*Beethoven* was one. His music expresses his own feelings and yearnings. Beethoven was in a sense a 'free' artist—unlike the Baroque masters such as Bach and Handel, who composed their works to the glory of God, mostly in strict musical forms."

"I only know the Moonlight Sonata and the Fifth Symphony."

"But you know how romantic the Moonlight Sonata is, and you can hear how dramatically Beethoven expresses himself in the Fifth Symphony."

"You said the Renaissance humanists were individualists too."

"Yes. There were many similarities between the Renaissance and Romanticism. A typical one was the importance of art to human cognition. Kant made a considerable contribution here as well. In his aesthetics he investigated what happens when we are overwhelmed by beauty—in a work of art, for instance. When we abandon ourselves to a work of art with no other intention than the aesthetic experience itself, we are brought closer to an experience of 'das Ding an sich.' ''

"So the artist can provide something philosophers can't express?"

"That was the view of the Romantics. According to Kant, the artist plays freely on his faculty of cognition. The German poet *Schiller* developed Kant's thought further. He wrote that the activity of the artist is like playing, and man is only free when he plays, because then he makes up his own rules. The Romantics believed that only art could bring us closer to 'the inexpressible.' Some went as far as to compare the artist to God."

"Because the artist creates his own reality the way God created the world."

"It was said that the artist had a 'universe-creating imagination.' In his transports of artistic rapture he could sense the dissolving of the boundary between dream and reality.

"*Novalis*, one of the young geniuses, said that 'the world becomes a dream, and the dream becomes reality.' He wrote a novel called *Heinrich von Ofterdingen* set in Medieval times. It was unfinished when he died in 1801, but it was nevertheless a very significant novel. It tells of the young Heinrich who is searching for the 'blue flower' that he once saw in a dream and has yearned for ever since. The English Romantic poet *Coleridge* expressed the same idea; saying something like this:

What if you slept? And what if, in your sleep, you dreamed? And what if, in your dream, you went to heaven and there plucked a strange and beautiful flower? And what if, when you awoke, you had the flower in your hand? Ah, what then?"

"How pretty!"

"This yearning for something distant and unattainable was characteristic of the Romantics. They longed for by-gone eras, such as the Middle Ages, which now became enthusiastically reappraised after the Enlightenment's negative evaluation. And they longed for distant cultures like the Orient with its mysticism. Or else they would feel drawn to Night, to Twilight, to old ruins and the supernatural. They were preoccupied with what we usually refer to as the dark side of life, or the murky, uncanny, and mystical."

"It sounds to me like an exciting period. Who *were* these Romantics?"

"Romanticism was in the main an urban phenomenon. In the first half of the last century there was, in fact, a flourishing metropolitan culture in many parts of Europe, not least in Germany. The typical Romantics were young men, often university students, although they did not always take their studies very seriously. They had a decidedly anti–middle class approach to life and could refer to the police or their landladies as philistines, for example, or simply as the enemy."

"I would never have dared rent a room to a Romantic!"

"The first generation of Romantics were young in about 1800, and we could actually call the Romantic Movement Europe's first student uprising. The Romantics were not unlike the hippies a hundred and fifty years later."

"You mean flower power and long hair, strumming their guitars and lying around?"

"Yes. It was once said that 'idleness is the ideal of genius, and indolence the virtue of the Romantic.' It was the duty of the Romantic to experience life—or to dream himself away from it. Day-to-day business could be taken care of by the philistines."

"Byron was a Romantic poet, wasn't he?"

"Yes, both Byron and Shelley were Romantic poets of the so-called Satanic school. Byron, moreover, provided the Romantic Age with its idol, the Byronic hero—the alien, moody, rebellious spirit—in life as well as in art. Byron himself could be both willful and passionate, and being also handsome, he was besieged by women of fashion. Public gossip attributed the romantic adventures of his verses to his own life, but although he had numerous liaisons, true love remained as illusive and as unattainable for him as Novalis's blue flower. Novalis became engaged to a fourteen-year-old girl. She died four days after her fifteenth birthday, but Novalis remained devoted to her for the rest of his short life."

"Did you say she died four days after her fifteenth birthday?"

"Yes . . ."

"I am fifteen years and four days old *today*."

"So you are."

"What was her name?"

"Her name was Sophie."

"*What?*"

"Yes, it was . . ."

"You scare me. Could it be a coincidence?"

"I couldn't say, Sophie. But her name was Sophie."

"Go on!"

"Novalis himself died when he was only twenty-nine. He was one of the 'young dead.' Many of the Romantics died young, usually of tuberculosis. Some committed suicide . . ."

"Ugh!"

"Those who lived to be old usually stopped being Romantics at about the age of thirty. Some of them went on to become thoroughly middle-class and conservative."

"They went over to the enemy, then."

"Maybe. But we were talking about romantic love. The theme of unrequited love was introduced as early as 1774 by *Goethe* in his novel *The Sorrows of Young Werther*. The book ends with young Werther shooting himself when he can't have the woman he loves . . ."

"Was it necessary to go that far?"

"The suicide rate rose after the publication of the novel, and for a time the book was banned in Denmark and Norway. So being a Romantic was not without danger. Strong emotions were involved."

"When you say 'Romantic,' I think of those great big landscape paintings, with dark forests and wild, rugged nature . . . preferably in swirling mists."

"Yes, one of the features of Romanticism was this yearning for nature and nature's mysteries. And as I said, it was not the kind of thing that arises in rural areas. You may recall Rousseau, who initiated the slogan 'back to nature.' The Romantics gave this slogan popular currency. Romanticism represents not least a reaction to the Enlightenment's mechanistic universe. It was said that Romanticism implied a renaissance of the old *cosmic consciousness*."

"Explain that, please."

"It means viewing nature as a whole; the Romantics were tracing their roots not only back to Spinoza, but also to Plotinus and Renaissance philosophers like Jakob Böhme and Giordano Bruno. What all these thinkers had in common was that they experienced a divine 'ego' in nature."

"They were Pantheists then . . ."

"Both Descartes and Hume had drawn a sharp line between the ego and 'extended' reality. Kant had also left behind him a sharp distinction between the cognitive 'I' and nature 'in itself.' Now it was said that nature is nothing but one big 'I.' The Romantics also used the expressions 'world soul' or 'world spirit.' "

"I see."

"The leading Romantic philosopher was *Schelling*, who lived from 1775 to 1854. He wanted to unite mind and matter. All of nature—both the human soul and physical reality—is the expression of one Absolute, or world spirit, he believed."

"Yes, just like Spinoza."

"Nature is visible spirit, spirit is invisible nature, said Schelling, since one senses a 'structuring spirit' everywhere in nature. He also said that matter is slumbering intelligence."

"You'll have to explain that a bit more clearly."

"Schelling saw a 'world spirit' in nature, but he saw the same 'world spirit' in the human mind. The natural and the spiritual are actually expressions of the same thing."

"Yes, why not?"

"World spirit can thus be sought both in nature and in one's own mind. Novalis could therefore say 'the path of mystery leads inwards.' He was saying that man bears the whole universe within himself and comes closest to the mystery of the world by stepping inside himself."

"That's a very lovely thought."

"For many Romantics, philosophy, nature study, and poetry formed a synthesis. Sitting in your attic dashing off inspired verses and investigating the life of plants or the composition of rocks were only two sides of the same coin because nature is not a dead mechanism, it is one living world spirit."

"Another word and I think I'll become a Romantic."

"The Norwegian-born naturalist *Henrik Steffens*—whom Wergeland called 'Norway's departed laurel leaf' because he had settled in Germany—went to Copenhagen in 1801 to lecture on German Romanticism. He characterized the Romantic Movement by saying, 'Tired of the eternal efforts to fight our way through raw matter, we chose another way and sought to embrace the infinite. We went inside ourselves and created a new world . . . '"

"How can you remember all that?"

"A bagatelle, child."

"Go on, then."

"Schelling also saw a development in nature from earth and rock to the human mind. He drew attention to very gradual transitions from inanimate nature to more complicated life forms. It was characteristic of the Romantic view in general that nature was thought of as an organism, or in other words, a unity which is constantly developing its innate potentialities. Nature is like a flower unfolding its leaves and petals. Or like a poet unfolding his verses."

"Doesn't that remind you of Aristotle?"

"It does indeed. The Romantic natural philosophy had Aristotelian as well as Neoplatonic overtones. Aristotle had a more organic view of natural processes than the mechanical materialists . . ."

"Yes, that's what I thought . . ."

"We find similar ideas at work in the field of history. A man who came to have great significance for the Romantics was the historical philosopher Johann Gottfried von *Herder*, who lived from 1744 to 1803. He believed that history is characterized by continuity, evolution, and design. We say he had a 'dynamic' view of history because he saw it as a process. The Enlightenment philosophers had often had a 'static' view of history. To them, there was only one universal reason which there could be more or less of at various periods. Herder showed that each historical epoch had its own intrinsic value and each nation its own character or 'soul.' The question is whether we can identify with other cultures."

"So, just as we have to identify with another person's situation to understand them better, we have to identify with other cultures to understand them too."

"That is taken for granted nowadays. But in the Romantic period it was a new idea. Romanticism helped strengthen the feeling of national identity. It is no coincidence that the Norwegian struggle for national independence flourished at that particular time—in 1814."

"I see."

"Because Romanticism involved new orientations in so many areas, it has been usual to distinguish between two forms of Romanticism. There is what we call *Universal Romanticism*, referring to the Romantics who were preoccupied with nature, world soul, and artistic genius. This form of Romanticism flourished first, especially around 1800, in Germany, in the town of Jena."

"And the other?"

"The other is the so-called *National Romanticism*, which became popular a little later, especially in the town of Heidelberg. The National Romantics were mainly interested in the history of 'the people,' the language of 'the people,' and the culture of 'the people' in general. And 'the people' were seen as an organism unfolding its innate potentiality—exactly like nature and history."

"Tell me where you live, and I'll tell you who you are."

"What united these two aspects of Romanticism was first and foremost the key word 'organism.' The Romantics considered both a plant and a nation to be a living organism. A poetic work was also a living organism. Language was an organism. The entire physical world, even, was considered one organism. There is therefore no sharp dividing line between National Romanticism and Universal Romanticism. The world spirit was just as much present in the people and in popular culture as in nature and art."

"I see."

"Herder had been the forerunner, collecting folk songs from many lands under the eloquent title *Voices of the People*. He even referred to folktales as 'the mother tongue of the people.' The *Brothers Grimm* and others began to collect folk songs and fairy tales in Heidelberg. You must know of *Grimm's Fairy Tales*."

"Oh sure, Snow White and the Seven Dwarfs, Rumpelstiltskin, The Frog Prince, Hansel and Gretel . . ."

"And many more. In Norway we had *Asbjørnsen and Moe*, who traveled around the country collecting 'folks' own tales.' It was like harvesting a juicy fruit that was suddenly discovered to be both good and nourishing. And it was urgent—the fruit had already begun to fall. Folk songs were collected; the Norwegian language began to be studied scientifically. The old myths and sagas from heathen times were rediscovered, and composers all over Europe began to incorporate folk melodies into their compositions in an attempt to bridge the gap between folk music and art music."

"What's art music?"

"Art music is music composed by a particular person, like Beethoven. Folk music was not written by any particular person, it came from the people. That's why we don't know exactly when the various folk melodies date from. We distinguish in the same way between folktales and art tales."

"So art tales are . . . ?"

"They are tales written by an author, like *Hans Christian Andersen*. The fairy tale genre was passionately cultivated by the Romantics. One of the German masters of the genre was *E.T.A. Hoffmann*."

"I've heard of *The Tales of Hoffmann*."

"The fairy tale was the absolute literary ideal of the Romantics—in the same way that the absolute art form of the Baroque period was the theater. It gave the poet full scope to explore his own creativity."

"He could play God to a fictional universe."

"Precisely. And this is a good moment to sum up."

"Go ahead."

"The philosophers of Romanticism viewed the 'world soul' as an 'ego' which in a more or less dreamlike state created everything in the world. The philosopher *Fichte* said that nature stems from a higher, unconscious imagination. Schelling said explicitly that the world is 'in God.' God is aware of some of it, he believed, but there are other aspects of nature which represent the unknown in God. For God also has a dark side."

"The thought is fascinating and frightening. It reminds me of Berkeley."

"The relationship between the artist and his work was seen in exactly the same light. The fairy tale gave the writer free rein to exploit his 'universe-creating imagination.' And even the creative act was not always completely conscious. The writer could experience that his story was being written by some innate force. He could practically be in a hypnotic trance while he wrote."

"He could?"

"Yes, but then he would suddenly destroy the illusion. He would intervene in the story and address ironic comments to the reader, so that the reader, at least momentarily, would be reminded that it was, after all, only a story."

"I see."

"At the same time the writer could remind his reader that it was he who was manipulating the fictional universe. This form of disillusion is called 'romantic irony.' *Henrik Ibsen*, for example, lets one of the characters in *Peer Gynt* say: 'One cannot die in the middle of Act Five.' "

"That's a very funny line, actually. What he's really saying is that he's only a fictional character."

"The statement is so paradoxical that we can certainly emphasize it with a new section."

"What did you mean by that?"

"Oh, nothing, Sophie. But we did say that Novalis's fiancée was called Sophie, just like you, and that she died when she was only fifteen years and four days old . . ."

"You're scaring me, don't you know that?"

Alberto sat staring, stony faced. Then he said: "But you needn't be worried that you will meet the same fate as Novalis's fiancée."

"Why not?"

"Because there are several more chapters."

"What are you saying?"

"I'm saying that anyone reading the story of Sophie and Alberto will know intuitively that there are many pages of the story still to come. We have only gotten as far as Romanticism."

"You're making me dizzy."

"It's really the major trying to make Hilde dizzy. It's not very nice of him, is it? New section!"

*   *   *

Alberto had hardly finished speaking when a boy came running out of the woods. He had a turban on his head, and he was carrying an oil lamp.

Sophie grabbed Alberto's arm.

"Who's that?" she asked.

The boy answered for himself: "My name is Aladdin and I've come all the way from Lebanon."

Alberto looked at him sternly:

"And what do you have in your lamp?"

The boy rubbed the lamp, and out of it rose a thick cloud which formed itself into the figure of a man. He had a black beard like Alberto's and a blue beret. Floating above the lamp, he said: "Can you hear me, Hilde? I suppose it's too late for any more birthday greetings. I just wanted to say that Bjerkely and the south country back home seem like fairyland to me here in Lebanon. I'll see you there in a few days."

So saying, the figure became a cloud again and was sucked back into the lamp. The boy with the turban put the lamp under his arm, ran into the woods, and was gone.

"I don't believe this," said Sophie.

"A bagatelle, my dear."

"The spirit of the lamp spoke exactly like Hilde's father."

"That's because it was Hilde's father—in spirit."

"But . . ."

"Both you and I and everything around us are living deep in the major's mind. It is late at night on Saturday, April 28, and all the UN soldiers are asleep around the major, who, although still awake, is not far from sleep himself. But he must finish the book he is to give Hilde as a fifteenth birthday present. That's why he has to work, Sophie, that's why the poor man gets hardly any rest."

"I give up."

"New section!"

Sophie and Alberto sat looking across the little lake. Alberto seemed to be in some sort of trance. After a while Sophie ventured to nudge his shoulder.

"Were you dreaming?"

"Yes, he was interfering directly there. The last few paragraphs were dictated by him to the letter. He should be ashamed of himself. But now he has given himself away and come out into the open. Now we know that we are living our lives in a book which Hilde's father will send home to Hilde as a birthday present. You heard what I said? Well, it wasn't 'me' saying it."

"If what you say is true, I'm going to run away from the book and go my own way."

"That's exactly what I am planning. But before that can happen, we must try and talk with Hilde. She reads every word we say. Once we succeed in getting away from here it will be much harder to contact her. That means we must grasp the opportunity now."

"What do we say?"

"I think the major is just about to fall asleep over his typewriter—although his fingers are still racing feverishly over the keys . . ."

"It's a creepy thought."

"This is the moment when he may write something he will regret later. And he has no correction fluid. That's a vital part of my plan. May no one give the major a bottle of correction fluid!"

"He won't get so much as a single coverup strip from me!"

"I'm calling on that poor girl here and now to rebel against her own father. She should be ashamed to let herself be amused by his self-indulgent playing with shadows. If only we had him here, we'd give him a taste of our indignation!"

"But he's not here."

"He is here in spirit and soul, but he's also safely tucked away in Lebanon. Everything around us is the major's ego."

"But he is more than what we can see here."

"We are but shadows in the major's soul. And it is no easy matter for a shadow to turn on its master, Sophie. It requires both cunning and strategy. But we have an opportunity of influencing Hilde. Only an angel can rebel against God."

"We could ask Hilde to give him a piece of her mind the moment he gets home. She could tell him he's a rogue. She could wreck his boat—or at least, smash the lantern."

Alberto nodded. Then he said: "She could also run away from him. That would be much easier for her than it is for us. She could leave the major's house and never return. Wouldn't that be fitting for a major who plays with his 'universe-creating imagination' at our expense?"

"I can picture it. The major travels all over the world searching for Hilde. But Hilde has vanished into thin air because she can't stand living with a father who plays the fool at Alberto's and Sophie's expense."

"Yes, that's it! Plays the fool! That's what I meant by his using us as birthday amusement. But he'd better watch out, Sophie. So had Hilde!"

"How do you mean?"

"Are you sitting tight?"

"As long as there are no more genies from a lamp."

"Try to imagine that everything that happens to us goes on in someone else's mind. We *are* that mind. That means we have no soul, we are someone else's soul. So far we are on familiar philosophical ground. Both Berkeley and Schelling would prick up their ears."

"And?"

"Now it is possible that this soul is Hilde Møller Knag's father. He is over there in Lebanon writing a book on philosophy for his daughter's fifteenth birthday. When Hilde wakes up on June 15, she finds the book on her bedside table, and now she—and anyone else—can read about us. It has long been suggested that this 'present' could be shared with others."

"Yes, I remember."

"What I am saying to you now will be read by Hilde after her father in Lebanon once imagined that I was telling you he was in Lebanon . . . imagining me telling you that he was in Lebanon."

Sophie's head was swimming. She tried to remember what she had heard about Berkeley and the Romantics. Alberto Knox continued: "But they shouldn't feel so cocky because of that. They are the last people who should laugh, because laughter can easily get stuck in their throat.''

''Who are we talking about?''

''Hilde and her father. Weren't we talking about them?''

''But why shouldn't they feel so cocky?''

''Because it is feasible that they, too, are nothing but mind.''

''How could they be?''

''If it was possible for Berkeley and the Romantics, it must be possible for them. Maybe the major is also a shadow in a book about him and Hilde, which is also about us, since we are a part of their lives.''

''That would be even worse. That makes us only shadows of shadows.''

''But it is possible that a completely different author is somewhere writing a book about a UN Major Albert Knag, who is writing a book for his daughter Hilde. This book is about a certain Alberto Knox who suddenly begins to send humble philosophical lectures to Sophie Amundsen, 3 Clover Close.''

''Do you believe that?''

''I'm just saying it's possible. To us, that author would be a 'hidden God.' Although everything we are and everything we say and do proceeds from him, because we *are* him we will never be able to know anything about him. We are in the innermost box.''

Alberto and Sophie now sat for a long time without saying anything. It was Sophie who finally broke the silence: ''But if there really is an author who is writing a story about Hilde's father in Lebanon, just like *he* is writing a story about us . . .''

''Yes?''

''. . . then it's possible that author shouldn't be cocky either.''

''What do you mean?''

''He is sitting somewhere, hiding both Hilde and me deep inside his head. Isn't it just possible that he, too, is part of a higher mind?''

Alberto nodded.

''Of course it is, Sophie. That's also a possibility. And

if that is the way it is, it means he has permitted us to have this philosophical conversation in order to present this possibility. He wishes to emphasize that he, too, is a helpless shadow, and that this book, in which Hilde and Sophie appear, is in reality a textbook on philosophy."

"A textbook?"

"Because all our conversations, all our dialogues . . ."

"Yes?"

". . . are in reality one long monologue."

"I get the feeling that everything is dissolving into mind and spirit. I'm glad there are still a few philosophers left. The philosophy that began so proudly with Thales, Empedocles, and Democritus can't be stranded here, surely?"

"Of course not. I still have to tell you about Hegel. He was the first philosopher who tried to salvage philosophy when the Romantics had dissolved everything into spirit."

"I'm very curious."

"So as not to be interrupted by any further spirits or shadows, we shall go inside."

"It's getting chilly out here anyway."

"Next chapter!"

Hegel

❧

... the reasonable is that which is viable ...

Hilde let the big ring binder fall to the floor with a heavy thud. She lay on her bed staring up at the ceiling. Her thoughts were in a turmoil.

Now her father really had made her head swim. The rascal! How *could* he?

Sophie had tried to talk directly to her. She had asked her to rebel against her father. And she had really managed to plant an idea in Hilde's mind. A plan . . .

Sophie and Alberto could not so much as harm a hair on his head, but Hilde could. And through Hilde, Sophie could reach her father.

She agreed with Sophie and Alberto that he was going too far in his game of shadows. Even if he had only made Alberto and Sophie up, there were limits to the show of power he ought to permit himself.

Poor Sophie and Alberto! They were just as defenseless against the major's imagination as a movie screen is against the film projector.

Hilde would certainly teach him a lesson when he got home! She could already see the outline of a really good plan.

She got up and went to look out over the bay. It was almost two o'clock. She opened the window and called over toward the boathouse.

"Mom!"

Her mother came out.

"I'll be down with some sandwiches in about an hour. Okay?"

"Fine."

"I just have to read a chapter on Hegel."

Alberto and Sophie had seated themselves in the two chairs by the window facing the lake.

"*Georg Wilhelm Friedrich Hegel* was a legitimate child of Romanticism," began Alberto. "One could almost say he developed with the German spirit as it gradually evolved in Germany. He was born in Stuttgart in 1770, and began to study theology in Tübingen at the age of eighteen. Beginning in 1799, he worked with Schelling in Jena during the time when the Romantic Movement was experiencing its most explosive growth. After a period as assistant professor in Jena he became a professor in Heidelberg, the center of German National Romanticism. In 1818 he was appointed professor in Berlin, just at the time when the city was becoming the spiritual center of Europe. He died of cholera in 1831, but not before 'Hegelianism' had gained an enormous following at nearly all the universities in Germany."

"So he covered a lot of ground."

"Yes, and so did his philosophy. Hegel united and developed almost all the ideas that had surfaced in the Romantic period. But he was sharply critical of many of the Romantics, including Schelling."

"What was it he criticized?"

"Schelling as well as other Romantics had said that the deepest meaning of life lay in what they called the 'world spirit.' Hegel also uses the term 'world spirit,' but in a new sense. When Hegel talks of 'world spirit' or 'world reason,' he means the sum of human utterances, because only man has a 'spirit.'

"In this sense, he can speak of the progress of world spirit throughout history. However, we must never forget that he is referring to human life, human thought, and human culture."

"That makes this spirit much less spooky. It is not lying in wait anymore like a 'slumbering intelligence' in rocks and trees."

"Now, you remember that Kant had talked about something he called 'das Ding an sich.' Although he denied that man could have any clear cognition of the innermost secrets of nature, he admitted that there exists a kind of unattainable 'truth.' Hegel said that 'truth is subjective,' thus rejecting the existence of any 'truth' above or beyond human reason. All knowledge is human knowledge, he said."

"He had to get the philosophers down to earth again, right?"

"Yes, perhaps you could say that. However, Hegel's philosophy was so all-embracing and diversified that for present purposes we shall content ourselves with highlighting some of the main aspects. It is actually doubtful whether one can say that Hegel had his own 'philosophy' at all. What is usually known as Hegel's philosophy is mainly a *method* for understanding the progress of history. Hegel's philosophy teaches us nothing about the inner nature of life, but it can teach us to think productively."

"That's not unimportant."

"All the philosophical systems before Hegel had had one thing in common, namely, the attempt to set up eternal criteria for what man can know about the world. This was true of Descartes, Spinoza, Hume, and Kant. Each and every one had tried to investigate the basis of human cognition. But they had all made pronouncements on the *timeless* factor of human knowledge of the world."

"Isn't that a philosopher's job?"

"Hegel did not believe it was possible. He believed that the basis of human cognition changed from one generation to the next. There were therefore no 'eternal truths,' no timeless reason. The only fixed point philosophy can hold on to is history itself."

"I'm afraid you'll have to explain that. History is in a constant state of change, so how can it be a fixed point?"

"A river is also in a constant state of change. That doesn't mean you can't talk about it. But you cannot say at which place in the valley the river is the 'truest' river."

"No, because it's just as much river all the way through."

"So to Hegel, history was like a running river. Every

tiny movement in the water at a given spot in the river is determined by the falls and eddies in the water higher upstream. But these movements are determined, too, by the rocks and bends in the river at the point where you are observing it."

"I get it . . . I think."

"And the history of thought—or of reason—is like this river. The thoughts that are washed along with the current of past tradition, as well as the material conditions prevailing at the time, help to determine how you think. You can therefore never claim that any particular thought is correct for ever and ever. But the thought can be correct from where you stand."

"That's not the same as saying that everything is equally right or equally wrong, is it?"

"Certainly not, but some things can be right or wrong in relation to a certain historical context. If you advocated slavery today, you would at best be thought foolish. But you wouldn't have been considered foolish 2,500 years ago, even though there were already progressive voices in favor of slavery's abolition. But we can take a more local example. Not more than 100 years ago it was not considered unreasonable to burn off large areas of forest in order to cultivate the land. But it is extremely unreasonable today. We have a completely different—and better—basis for such judgments."

"Now I see."

"Hegel pointed out that as regards philosophical reflection, also, reason is dynamic; it's a process, in fact. And the 'truth' is this same process, since there are no criteria beyond the historical process itself that can determine what is the most true or the most reasonable."

"Examples, please."

"You cannot single out particular thoughts from antiquity, the Middle Ages, the Renaissance, or the Enlightenment and say they were right or wrong. By the same token, you cannot say that Plato was wrong and that Aristotle was right. Neither can you say that Hume was wrong but Kant and Schelling were right. That would be an antihistorical way of thinking."

"No, it doesn't sound right."

"In fact, you cannot detach any philosopher, or any thought at all, from that philosopher's or that thought's historical context. But—and here I come to another point—because something new is always being added, reason is 'progressive.' In other words, human knowledge is constantly expanding and progressing."

"Does that mean that Kant's philosophy is nevertheless more right than Plato's?"

"Yes. The world spirit has developed—and progressed—from Plato to Kant. And it's a good thing! If we return to the example of the river, we could say that there is now more water in it. It has been running for over a thousand years. Only Kant shouldn't think that his 'truths' will remain on the banks of the river like immovable rocks. Kant's ideas get processed too, and his 'reason' becomes the subject of future generations' criticism. Which is exactly what has happened."

"But the river you talked about . . ."

"Yes?"

"Where does it go?"

"Hegel claimed that the 'world spirit' is developing toward an ever-expanding knowledge of itself. It's the same with rivers—they become broader and broader as they get nearer to the sea. According to Hegel, history is the story of the 'world spirit' gradually coming to consciousness of itself. Although the world has always existed, human culture and human development have made the world spirit increasingly conscious of its intrinsic value."

"How could he be so sure of that?"

"He claimed it as a historical reality. It was not a prediction. Anybody who studies history will see that humanity has advanced toward ever-increasing 'self-knowledge' and 'self-development.' According to Hegel, the study of history shows that humanity is moving toward greater rationality and freedom. In spite of all its capers, historical development is progressive. We say that history is purposeful."

"So it develops. That's clear enough."

"Yes. History is one long chain of reflections. Hegel also indicated certain rules that apply for this chain of reflections. Anyone studying history in depth will observe that a thought is usually proposed on the basis of other, previously proposed thoughts. But as soon as one thought is proposed, it will be contradicted by another. A tension arises between these two opposite ways of thinking. But the tension is resolved by the proposal of a third thought which accommodates the best of both points of view. Hegel calls this a *dialectic* process."

"Could you give an example?"

"You remember that the pre-Socratics discussed the question of primeval substance and change?"

"More or less."

"Then the Eleatics claimed that change was in fact impossible. They were therefore forced to deny any change even though they could register the changes through their senses. The Eleatics had put forward a claim, and Hegel called a standpoint like that a *thesis*."

"Yes?"

"But whenever such an extreme claim is proposed, a contradictory claim will arise. Hegel called this a *negation*. The negation of the Eleatic philosophy was Heraclitus, who said that everything flows. There is now a tension between two diametrically opposed schools of thought. But this tension was resolved when Empedocles pointed out that both claims were partly right and partly wrong."

"Yes, it all comes back to me now . . ."

"The Eleatics were right in that nothing actually changes, but they were not right in holding that we cannot rely on our senses. Heraclitus had been right in that we can rely on our senses, but not right in holding that everything flows."

"Because there was more than one substance. It was the combination that flowed, not the substance itself."

"Right! Empedocles' standpoint—which provided the compromise between the two schools of thought—was what Hegel called the *negation of the negation*."

"What a terrible term!"

"He also called these three stages of knowledge *thesis, antithesis,* and *synthesis*. You could, for example, say that Descartes's rationalism was a thesis—which was contradicted by Hume's empirical antithesis. But the contradiction, or the tension between two modes of thought, was resolved in Kant's synthesis. Kant agreed with the rationalists in some things and with the empiricists in others. But the story doesn't end with Kant. Kant's synthesis now becomes the point of departure for another chain of reflections, or 'triad.' Because a synthesis will also be contradicted by a new antithesis."

"It's all very theoretical!"

"Yes, it certainly is theoretical. But Hegel didn't see it as pressing history into any kind of framework. He believed that history itself revealed this dialectical pattern. He thus claimed he had uncovered certain laws for the development of reason—or for the progress of the 'world spirit' through history."

"There it is again!"

"But Hegel's dialectic is not only applicable to history. When we discuss something, we think dialectically. We try to find flaws in the argument. Hegel called that 'negative thinking.' But when we find flaws in an argument, we preserve the best of it."

"Give me an example."

"Well, when a socialist and a conservative sit down together to resolve a social problem, a tension will quickly be revealed between their conflicting modes of thought. But this does not mean that one is absolutely right and the other totally wrong. It is possible that they are both partly right and partly wrong. And as the argument evolves, the best of both arguments will often crystallize."

"I hope."

"But while we are in the throes of a discussion like that, it is not easy to decide which position is more rational. In a way, it's up to history to decide what's right and what's wrong. The reasonable is that which is viable."

"Whatever survives is right."

"Or vice versa: that which is right survives."

"Don't you have a tiny example for me?"

"One hundred and fifty years ago there were a lot of people fighting for women's rights. Many people also bitterly opposed giving women equal rights. When we read the arguments of both sides today, it is not difficult to see which side had the more 'reasonable' opinions. But we must not forget that we have the knowledge of hindsight.

It 'proved to be the case' that those who fought for equality were right. A lot of people would no doubt cringe if they saw in print what their grandfathers had said on the matter."

"I'm sure they would. What was Hegel's view?"

"About equality of the sexes?"

"Isn't that what we are talking about?"

"Would you like to hear a quote?"

"Very much."

" 'The difference between man and woman is like that between animals and plants,' he said. 'Men correspond to animals, while women correspond to plants because their development is more placid and the principle that underlies it is the rather vague unity of feeling. When women hold the helm of government, the state is at once in jeopardy, because women regulate their actions not by the demands of universality but by arbitrary inclinations and opinions. Women are educated—who knows how?—as it were by breathing in ideas, by living rather than by acquiring knowledge. The status of manhood, on the other hand, is attained only by the stress of thought and much technical exertion.' "

"Thank you, that will be quite enough. I'd rather not hear any more statements like that."

"But it is a striking example of how people's views of what is rational change all the time. It shows that Hegel was also a child of his time. And so are we. Our 'obvious' views will not stand the test of time either."

"What views, for example?"

"I have no such examples."

"Why not?"

"Because I would be exemplifying things that are already undergoing a change. For instance, I could say it's stupid to drive a car because cars pollute the environment. Lots of people think this already. But history will prove that much of what we think is obvious will not hold up in the light of history."

"I see."

"We can also observe something else: The many men in Hegel's time who could reel off gross broadsides like that one on the inferiority of women hastened the development of feminism.''

"How so?''

"They proposed a thesis. Why? Because women had already begun to rebel. There's no need to have an opinion on something everyone agrees on. And the more grossly they expressed themselves about women's inferiority, the stronger became the negation.''

"Yes, of course.''

"You might say that the very best that can happen is to have energetic opponents. The more extreme they become, the more powerful the reaction they will have to face. There's a saying about 'more grist to the mill.' ''

"My mill began to grind more energetically a minute ago!''

"From the point of view of pure logic or philosophy, there will often be a dialectical tension between two concepts.''

"For example?''

"If I reflect on the concept of 'being,' I will be obliged to introduce the opposite concept, that of 'nothing.' You can't reflect on your existence without immediately realizing that you won't always exist. The tension between 'being' and 'nothing' becomes resolved in the concept of 'becoming.' Because if something is in the process of becoming, it both is and is not.''

"I see that.''

"Hegel's 'reason' is thus *dynamic logic*. Since reality is characterized by opposites, a description of reality must therefore also be full of opposites. Here is another example for you: the Danish nuclear physicist Niels Bohr is said to have told a story about Newton's having a horseshoe over his front door.''

"That's for luck.''

"But it is only a superstition, and Newton was anything but superstitious. When someone asked him if he really believed in that kind of thing, he said, 'No, I don't, but I'm told it works anyway.' ''

"Amazing.''

"But his answer was quite dialectical, a contradiction in terms, almost. Niels Bohr, who, like our own Norwegian poet Vinje, was known for his ambivalence, once said: There are two kinds of truths. There are the superficial truths, the opposite of which are obviously wrong. But there are also the profound truths, whose opposites are equally right."

"What kind of truths can they be?"

"If I say life is short, for example . . ."

"I would agree."

"But on another occasion I could throw open my arms and say life is long."

"You're right. That's also true, in a sense."

"Finally I'll give you an example of how a dialectic tension can result in a spontaneous act which leads to a sudden change."

"Yes, do."

"Imagine a young girl who always answers her mother with Yes, Mom . . . Okay, Mom . . . As you wish, Mom . . . At once, Mom."

"Gives me the shudders!"

"Finally the girl's mother gets absolutely maddened by her daughter's overobedience, and shouts: Stop being such a goody-goody! And the girl answers: Okay, Mom."

"I would have slapped her."

"Perhaps. But what would you have done if the girl had answered instead: But I *want* to be a goody-goody?"

"That would have been an odd answer. Maybe I would have slapped her anyway."

"In other words, the situation was deadlocked. The dialectic tension had come to a point where something *had* to happen."

"Like a slap in the face?"

"A final aspect of Hegel's philosophy needs to be mentioned here."

"I'm listening."

"Do you remember how we said that the Romantics were individualists?"

"The path of mystery leads inwards . . ."

"This individualism also met its negation, or opposite, in Hegel's philosophy. Hegel emphasized what he called the 'objective' powers. Among such powers, Hegel emphasized the importance of the family, civil society, and the state. You might say that Hegel was somewhat skeptical of the individual. He believed that the individual was an organic part of the community. Reason, or 'world spirit,' came to light first and foremost in the interplay of people."

"Explain that more clearly, please!"

"Reason manifests itself above all in language. And a language is something we are born into. The Norwegian language manages quite well without Mr. Hansen, but Mr. Hansen cannot manage without Norwegian. It is thus not the individual who forms the language, it is the language which forms the individual."

"I guess you could say so."

"In the same way that a baby is born into a language, it is also born into its historical background. And nobody has a 'free' relationship to that kind of background. He who does not find his place within the state is therefore an unhistorical person. This idea, you may recall, was also central for the great Athenian philosophers. Just as the state is unthinkable without citizens, citizens are unthinkable without the state."

"Obviously."

"According to Hegel, the state is 'more' than the individual citizen. It is moreover more than the sum of its citizens. So Hegel says one cannot 'resign from society.' Anyone who simply shrugs their shoulders at the society they live in and wants to 'find their soul,' will therefore be ridiculed."

"I don't know whether I wholly agree, but okay."

"According to Hegel, it is not the individual that finds itself, it is the world spirit."

"The world spirit finds itself?"

"Hegel said that the world spirit returns to itself in three stages. By that he means that it becomes conscious of itself in three stages."

"Which are?"

"The world spirit first becomes conscious of itself in the individual. Hegel calls this *subjective* spirit. It reaches a higher consciousness in the family, civil society, and the state. Hegel calls this *objective* spirit because it appears in interaction between people. But there is a third stage . . ."

"And that is . . . ?"

"The world spirit reaches the highest form of self-realization in *absolute spirit*. And this absolute spirit is art, religion, and philosophy. And of these, philosophy is the highest form of knowledge because in philosophy, the world spirit reflects on its own impact on history. So the world spirit first meets itself in philosophy. You could say, perhaps, that philosophy is the mirror of the world spirit."

"This is so mysterious that I need to have time to think it over. But I liked the last bit you said."

"What, that philosophy is the mirror of the world spirit?"

"Yes, that was beautiful. Do you think it has anything to do with the brass mirror?"

"Since you ask, yes."

"What do you mean?"

"I assume the brass mirror has some special significance since it is constantly cropping up."

"You must have an idea what that significance is?"

"I haven't. I merely said that it wouldn't keep coming up unless it had a special significance for Hilde and her father. What that significance is only Hilde knows."

"Was that romantic irony?"

"A hopeless question, Sophie."

"Why?"

"Because it's not us working with these things. We are only hapless victims of that irony. If an overgrown child draws something on a piece of paper, you can't ask the paper what the drawing is supposed to represent."

"You give me the shudders."

Kierkegaard

∞

. . . Europe is on the road to bankruptcy . . .

Hilde looked at her watch. It was already past four
o'clock. She laid the ring binder on her desk and ran
downstairs to the kitchen. She had to get down to the
boathouse before her mother got tired of waiting for her.
She glanced at the brass mirror as she passed.

She quickly put the kettle on for tea and fixed some
sandwiches.

She had made up her mind to play a few tricks on
her father. Hilde was beginning to feel more and more
allied with Sophie and Alberto. Her plan would start
when he got to Copenhagen.

She went down to the boathouse with a large tray.

"Here's our brunch," she said.

Her mother was holding a block wrapped in sandpa-
per. She pushed a stray lock of hair back from her forehead. There was sand in her hair too.

"Let's drop dinner, then."

They sat down outside on the dock and began to eat.

"When's Dad arriving?" asked Hilde after a while.

"On Saturday. I thought you knew that."

"But what time? Didn't you say he was changing
planes in Copenhagen?"

"That's right . . ."

Her mother took a bite of her sandwich.

"He gets to Copenhagen at about five. The plane to
Kristiansand leaves at a quarter to eight. He'll probably

land at Kjevik at half-past nine."

"So he has a few hours at Kastrup . . ."

"Yes, why?"

"Nothing. I was just wondering."

When Hilde thought a suitable interval had elapsed, she said casually, "Have you heard from Anne and Ole lately?"

"They call from time to time. They are coming home on vacation sometime in July."

"Not before?"

"No, I don't think so."

"So they'll be in Copenhagen this week . . . ?"

"Why all these questions, Hilde?"

"No reason. Just small talk."

"You mentioned Copenhagen twice."

"I did?"

"We talked about Dad touching down in . . ."

"That's probably why I thought of Anne and Ole."

As soon as they finished eating, Hilde collected the mugs and plates on the tray.

"I have to get on with my reading, Mom."

"I guess you must."

Was there a touch of reproach in her voice? They had talked about fixing up the boat together before Dad came home.

"Dad almost made me promise to finish the book before he got home."

"It's a little crazy. When he's away, he doesn't have to order us around back home."

"If you only knew how much he orders people around," said Hilde enigmatically, "and you can't imagine how much he enjoys it."

She returned to her room and went on reading.

Suddenly Sophie heard a knock on the door. Alberto looked at her severely.

"We don't wish to be disturbed."

The knocking became louder.

"I am going to tell you about a Danish philosopher who was infuriated by Hegel's philosophy," said Alberto.

The knocking on the door grew so violent that the whole door shook.

"It's the major, of course, sending some phantasm to see whether we swallow the bait," said Alberto. "It costs him no effort at all."

"But if we don't open the door and see who it is, it won't cost him any effort to tear the whole place down either."

"You might have a point there. We'd better open the door then."

They went to the door. Since the knocking had been so forceful, Sophie expected to see a very large person. But standing on the front step was a little girl with long fair hair, wearing a blue dress. She had a small bottle in each hand. One bottle was red, the other blue.

"Hi," said Sophie. "Who are you?"

"My name is Alice," said the girl, curtseying shyly.

"I thought so," said Alberto, nodding. "It's Alice in Wonderland."

"How did she find her way to us?"

Alice explained: "Wonderland is a completely border-less country. That means that Wonderland is every-where—rather like the UN. It should be an honorary member of the UN. We should have representatives on all committees, because the UN also arose out of people's wonder."

"Hm . . . that major!" muttered Alberto.

"And what brings you here?" asked Sophie.

"I am to give Sophie these little philosophy bottles."

She handed the bottles to Sophie. There was red liquid in one and blue in the other. The label on the red bottle read DRINK ME, and on the blue one the label read DRINK ME too.

The next second a white rabbit came hurrying past the cabin. It walked upright on two legs and was dressed in a waistcoat and jacket. Just in front of the cabin it took a pocket watch out of its waistcoat pocket and said:

"Oh dear! Oh dear! I shall be too late!"

Then it ran on. Alice began to run after it. Just before she ran into the woods, she curtsied and said, "Now it's starting again."

"Say hello to Dinah and the Queen," Sophie called after her.

Alberto and Sophie remained standing on the front step, examining the bottles.

"DRINK ME and DRINK ME too," read Sophie. "I don't know if I dare. They might be poisonous."

Alberto merely shrugged his shoulders.

"They come from the major, and everything that comes from the major is purely in the mind. So it's only pretend-juice."

Sophie took the cap off the red bottle and put it cautiously to her lips. The juice had a strangely sweet taste, but that wasn't all. As she drank, something started to happen to her surroundings.

It felt as if the lake and the woods and the cabin all merged into one. Soon it seemed that everything she saw was one person, and that person was Sophie herself. She glanced up at Alberto, but he too seemed to be part of Sophie's soul.

"Curiouser and curiouser," she said. "Everything looks like it did before, but now it's all one thing. I feel as if everything is one thought."

Alberto nodded—but it seemed to Sophie that it was she nodding to herself.

"It is Pantheism or Idealism," he said. "It is the Romantics' world spirit. They experienced everything as one big 'ego.' It is also Hegel—who was critical of the individual, and who saw everything as the expression of the one and only world reason."

"Should I drink from the other bottle too?"

"It says so on the label."

Sophie took the cap off the blue bottle and took a large gulp. This juice tasted fresher and sharper than the other. Again everything around her changed suddenly.

Instantly the effects of the red bottle disappeared and everything slid back to its normal place. Alberto was Alberto, the trees were back in the woods and the water looked like a lake again.

But it only lasted for a second, because things went on sliding away from each other. The woods were no longer woods and every little tree now seemed like a world in itself. The tiniest twig was like a fairy-tale world about which a thousand stories could be told.

The little lake suddenly became a boundless ocean—not in depth or breadth, but in its glittering detail and the intricate patterns of its waves. Sophie felt she might spend a lifetime staring at this water and to her dying day it would still remain an unfathomable mystery.

She looked up at the crown of a tree. Three little sparrows were engrossed in a curious game. Was it hide-and-seek? Sophie had known in a way that there were birds in this tree, even after she had drunk from the red bottle, but she had not really seen them properly. The red juice had erased all contrasts and all individual differences.

Sophie jumped down from the large flat stone step they were standing on and bent over to look at the grass. There she discovered another new world—like a deep-sea diver opening his eyes under water for the first time. In amongst the twigs and straws of grass, the moss was teeming with tiny details. Sophie watched a spider make its way over the moss, surefooted and purposeful, a red plant louse running up and down a blade of grass, and a whole army of ants laboring in a united effort in the grass. But each tiny ant moved its legs in its own particular manner.

The most curious of all was the sight that met her eyes when she stood up again and looked at Alberto, still standing on the front step of the cabin. In Alberto she now saw a wondrous person—he was like a being from another planet, or an enchanted figure out of a fairy tale. At the same time she experienced herself in a completely new way as a unique individual. She was more than just a human being, a fifteen-year-old girl. She was Sophie Amundsen, and only she was that.

"What do you see?" asked Alberto.

"I see that you're a strange bird."

"You think so?"

"I don't think I'll ever get to understand what it's like being another person. No two people in the whole world are alike."

"And the woods?"

"They don't seem the same any more. They're like a whole universe of wondrous tales."

"It is as I suspected. The blue bottle is individualism. It is, for example, *Søren Kierkegaard*'s reaction to the idealism of the Romantics. But it also encompasses another Dane who lived at the same time as Kierkegaard, the famous fairy-tale writer Hans Christian Andersen. He had the same sharp eye for nature's incredible richness of detail. A philosopher who saw the same thing more than a century earlier was the German *Leibniz*. He reacted against the idealistic philosophy of Spinoza just as Kierkegaard reacted against Hegel."

"I hear you, but you sound so funny that I feel like laughing."

"That's understandable. Just take another sip from the red bottle. Come on, let's sit here on the step. We'll talk a bit about Kierkegaard before we stop for today."

Sophie sat on the step beside Alberto. She drank a little from the red bottle and things began to merge together again. They actually merged rather too much; once more she got the feeling that no differences mattered at all. But she only had to touch the blue bottle to her lips again, and the world about her looked more or less as it did when Alice arrived with the two bottles.

"But which is *true*?" she now asked. "Is it the red or the blue bottle that gives the true picture?"

"Both the red and the blue, Sophie. We cannot say the Romantics were wrong in holding that there is only one reality. But maybe they were a little bit narrow in their outlook."

"What about the blue bottle?"

"I think Kierkegaard must have taken a few hefty swigs from that one. He certainly had a sharp eye for the significance of the individual. We are more than 'children of our time.' And moreover, every single one of us is a unique individual who only lives once."

"And Hegel had not made much of that?"

"No, he was more interested in the broad scope of history. This was just what made Kierkegaard so indignant. He thought that both the idealism of the Romantics and Hegel's 'historicism' had obscured the individual's responsibility for his own life. Therefore to Kierkegaard, Hegel and the Romantics were tarred with the same brush."

"I can see why he was so mad."

"Søren Kierkegaard was born in 1813 and was subjected to a very severe upbringing by his father. His religious melancholia was a legacy from this father."

"That sounds ominous."

"It was because of this melancholia that he felt obliged to break off his engagement, something the Copenhagen bourgeoisie did not look kindly on. So from early on he became an outcast and an object of scorn. However, he gradually learned to give as good as he got, and he became increasingly what Ibsen later on described as 'an enemy of the people.'"

"All because of a broken engagement?"

"No, not only because of that. Toward the end of his life, especially, he became aggressively critical of society. 'The whole of Europe is on the road to bankruptcy,' he said. He believed he was living in an age utterly devoid of passion and commitment. He was particularly incensed by the vapidness of the established Danish Lutheran Church. He was merciless in his criticism of what you might call 'Sunday Christianity.'"

"Nowadays we talk of 'confirmation Christianity.' Most kids only get confirmed because of all the presents they get."

"Yes, you've got the point. To Kierkegaard, Christianity was both so overwhelming and so irrational that it had to be an either/or. It was not good being 'rather' or 'to some extent' religious. Because either Jesus rose on Easter Day—or he did not. And if he really did rise from the dead, if he really died for our sake—then this is so overwhelming that it must permeate our entire life."

"Yes, I think I understand."

"But Kierkegaard saw how both the church and people in general had a noncommittal approach to religious questions. To Kierkegaard, religion and knowledge were like fire and water. It was not enough to believe that Christianity is 'true.' Having a Christian faith meant following a Christian way of life."

"What did that have to do with Hegel?"

"You're right. Maybe we started at the wrong end."

"So I suggest you go into reverse and start again."

"Kierkegaard began his study of theology when he was seventeen, but he became increasingly absorbed in philosophical questions. When he was twenty-seven he took his master's degree with the dissertation 'On the Concept of Irony.' In this work he did battle with Romantic irony and the Romantics' uncommitted play with illusion. He posited 'Socratic irony' in contrast. Even though Socrates had made use of irony to great effect, it had the purpose of eliciting the fundamental truths about life. Unlike the Romantics, Socrates was what Kierkegaard called an 'existential' thinker. That is to say, a thinker who draws his entire existence into his philosophical reflection."

"So?"

"After breaking off his engagement in 1841, Kierkegaard went to Berlin where he attended Schelling's lectures."

"Did he meet Hegel?"

"No, Hegel had died ten years earlier, but his ideas were predominant in Berlin and in many parts of Europe. His 'system' was being used as a kind of all-purpose explanation for every type of question. Kierkegaard indicated that the sort of 'objective truths' that Hegelianism was concerned with were totally irrelevant to the personal life of the individual."

"What kind of truths are relevant, then?"

"According to Kierkegaard, rather than searching for the Truth with a capital T, it is more important to find the kind of truths that are meaningful to the individual's life. It is important to find 'the truth for me.' He thus sets the individual, or *each and every man*, up against the 'system.' Kierkegaard thought Hegel had forgotten that he was a man. This is what he wrote about the Hegelian professor: "While the ponderous Sir Professor explains the entire mystery of life, he has in distraction forgotten his own name; that he is a man, neither more nor less, not a fantastic three-eighths of a paragraph.""

"And what, according to Kierkegaard, is a man?"

"It's not possible to say in general terms. A broad description of human nature or human beings was totally without interest to Kierkegaard. The only important thing was each man's 'own existence.' And you don't experience your own existence behind a desk. It's only when we act—and especially when we make significant *choices*—that we relate to our own existence. There is a story about Buddha that illustrates what Kierkegaard meant."

"About Buddha?"

"Yes, since Buddha's philosophy also took man's existence as its starting point. There was once a monk who asked Buddha if he could give clearer answers to fundamental questions on what the world is and what a man is. Buddha answered by likening the monk to a man who gets pierced by a poisoned arrow. The wounded man would have no theoretical interest in what the arrow was made of, what kind of poison it was dipped in, or which direction it came from."

"He would most likely want somebody to pull it out and treat the wound."

"Yes, he would. That would be existentially important to him. Both Buddha and Kierkegaard had a strong sense of only existing for a brief moment. And as I said, then you don't sit down behind a desk and philosophize about the nature of the world spirit."

"No, of course not."

"Kierkegaard also said that truth is 'subjective.' By this he did not mean that it doesn't matter what we think or believe. He meant that the really important truths are *personal*. Only these truths are 'true for me.' "

"Could you give an example of a subjective truth?"

"An important question is, for example, whether Christianity is true. This is not a question one can relate to theoretically or academically. For a person who 'understands himself in life,' it is a question of life and death. It is not something you sit and discuss for discussion's sake. It is something to be approached with the greatest passion and sincerity."

"Understandable."

"If you fall into the water, you have no theoretical interest in whether or not you will drown. It is neither 'interesting' nor 'uninteresting' whether there are alligators in the water. It is a question of life or death."

"I get it, thank you very much."

"So we must therefore distinguish between the philosophical question of whether God exists and the individual's relationship to the same question, a situation in which each and every man is utterly alone. Fundamental questions such as these can only be approached through *faith*. Things we can know through reason, or knowledge, are according to Kierkegaard totally unimportant."

"I think you'd better explain that."

"Eight plus four is twelve. We can be absolutely certain of this. That's an example of the sort of 'reasoned truth' that every philosopher since Descartes had talked about. But do we include it in our daily prayers? Is it something we will lie pondering over when we are dying? Not at all. Truths like those can be both 'objective' and 'general,' but they are nevertheless totally immaterial to each man's existence."

"What about faith?"

"You can never know whether a person forgives you when you wrong them. Therefore it is existentially important to you. It is a question you are intensely concerned with. Neither can you know whether a person loves you. It's something you just have to believe or hope. But these things are more important to you than the fact that the sum of the angles in a triangle is 180 degrees. You don't think about the law of cause and effect or about modes of perception when you are in the middle of your first kiss."

"You'd be very odd if you did."

"Faith is the most important factor in religious questions. Kierkegaard wrote: 'If I am capable of grasping God objectively, I do not believe, but precisely because I cannot do this I must believe. If I wish to preserve myself in faith I must constantly be intent upon holding fast the objective uncertainty, so as to remain out upon the deep, over seventy thousand fathoms of water, still preserving my faith.' "

"That's heavy stuff."

"Many had previously tried to prove the existence of God—or at any rate to bring him within the bounds of rationality. But if you content yourself with some such proof or logical argument, you suffer a loss of faith, and with it, a loss of religious passion. Because what matters is not whether Christianity is true, but whether it is true for you. The same thought was expressed in the Middle Ages in the maxim: *credo quia absurdum.*"

"You don't say."

"It means I believe because it is irrational. If Christianity had appealed to our reason, and not to other sides of us, it would not be a question of faith."

"No, I understand that now."

"So we have looked at what Kierkegaard meant by 'existential,' what he meant by 'subjective truth,' and what his concept of 'faith' was. These three concepts were formulated as a criticism of philosophical tradition in general, and of Hegel in particular. But they also embodied a trenchant 'social criticism.' The individual in modern urban society had become 'the public,' he said, and the predominant characteristic of the crowd, or the masses, was all their noncommittal 'talk.' Today we would probably use the word 'conformity'; that is when everybody 'thinks' and 'believes in' the same things without having any deeper feeling about it."

"I wonder what Kierkegaard would have said to Joanna's parents."

"He was not always kind in his judgments. He had a sharp pen and a bitter sense of irony. For example, he could say things like 'the crowd is the untruth,' or 'the truth is always in the minority,' and that most people had a superficial approach to life."

"It's one thing to collect Barbie dolls. But it's worse to be one."

"That brings us to Kierkegaard's theory of what he called the three stages on life's way."

"Pardon me?"

"Kierkegaard believed that there were three different forms of life. He himself used the term *stages.* He calls them the aesthetic stage, the ethical stage, and the religious stage. He used the term 'stage' to emphasize that one can live at one of the two lower stages and then suddenly leap to a higher stage. Many people live at the same stage all their life."

"I bet there's an explanation on the way. I'm anxious to know which stage I'm at."

"He who lives at the *aesthetic stage* lives for the moment and grasps every opportunity of enjoyment. Good is whatever is beautiful, satisfying, or pleasant. This person lives wholly in the world of the senses, and is a slave to his own desires and moods. Everything that is boring is bad."

"Yes thanks, I think I know that attitude."

"The typical Romantic is thus also the typical aesthete, since there is more to it than pure sensory enjoyment. A person who has a reflective approach to reality—or for that matter to his art or the philosophy he or she is engaged in—is living at the aesthetic stage. It is even possible to have an aesthetic, or 'reflective,' attitude to sorrow and suffering. In which case vanity has taken over. Ibsen's *Peer Gynt* is the portrait of a typical aesthete."

"I think I see what you mean."

"Do you know anyone like that?"

"Not completely. But I think maybe it sounds a little like the major."

"Maybe so, maybe so, Sophie . . . Although that was another example of his rather sickly Romantic irony. You should wash your mouth out."

"What?"

"All right, it wasn't your fault."

"Keep going, then."

"A person who lives at the aesthetic stage can easily experience *angst*, or a sense of dread, and a feeling of emptiness. If this happens, there is also hope. According to Kierkegaard, angst is almost positive. It is an expression of the fact that the individual is in an 'existential situation,' and can now elect to make the great leap to a higher stage. But it either happens or it doesn't. It doesn't help to be on the verge of making the leap if you don't do it completely. It is a matter of 'either/or.' But nobody can do it for you. It is your own choice."

"It's a little like deciding to quit drinking or doing drugs."

"Yes, it could be like that. Kierkegaard's description of this 'category of decision' can be somewhat reminiscent of Socrates' view that all true insight comes from within. The *choice* that leads a person to leap from an aesthetic approach to an ethical or religious approach must come from within. Ibsen depicts this in *Peer Gynt*. Another masterly description of how existential choice springs from inner need and despair can be found in Dostoevsky's great novel *Crime and Punishment*."

"The best you can do is choose a different form of life."

"And so perhaps you will begin to live at the *ethical stage*. This is characterized by seriousness and consistency of moral choices. This approach is not unlike Kant's ethics of duty. You try to live by the law of morals. Kierkegaard, like Kant, drew attention first and foremost to human temperament. The important thing is not what you may think is precisely right or wrong. What matters is that you choose to have an opinion at all on what is right or wrong. The aesthete's only concern is whether something is fun or boring."

"Isn't there a risk of becoming *too* serious, living like that?"

"Decidedly! Kierkegaard never claimed that the ethical stage was satisfactory. Even a dutiful person will eventually get tired of always being dedicated and meticulous. Lots of people experience that sort of fatigue reaction late in life. Some relapse into the reflective life of their aesthetic stage.

"But others make a new leap to the *religious stage*. They take the 'jump into the abyss' of Faith's 'seventy thousand fathoms.' They choose faith in preference to aesthetic pleasure and reason's call of duty. And although it can be 'terrible to jump into the open arms of the living God,' as Kierkegaard put it, it is the only path to redemption."

"Christianity, you mean."

"Yes, because to Kierkegaard, the religious stage was Christianity. But he also became significant to non-Christian thinkers. Existentialism, inspired by the Danish philosopher, flourished widely in the twentieth century."

Sophie glanced at her watch.

"It's nearly seven. I have to run. Mom will be frantic."

She waved to the philosopher and ran down to the boat.

Marx

. . . a spectre is haunting Europe . . .

Hilde got off her bed and went to the window facing the bay. When she had started to read this Saturday, it was still Sophie's fifteenth birthday. The day before had been Hilde's own birthday.

If her father had imagined that she would get as far as Sophie's birthday yesterday, he had certainly not been realistic. She had done nothing but read all day long. But he was right that there would only be one more birthday greeting. It was when Alberto and Sophie had sung Happy Birthday to her. Very embarrassing, Hilde thought.

And now Sophie had invited people to a philosophical garden party on the very day her father was due back from Lebanon. Hilde was convinced something would happen that day which neither she nor her father were quite sure of.

But one thing was certain: before her father got home to Bjerkely he would get a scare. That was the least she could do for Sophie and Alberto, especially after they had appealed for help . . .

Her mother was still down in the boathouse. Hilde ran downstairs to the telephone. She found Anne and Ole's number in Copenhagen and called them.

"Anne Kvamsdal."

"Hi, this is Hilde."

"Oh, how are you? How are things in Lillesand?"

"Fine, with vacation and everything. And Dad gets back from Lebanon in a week."

"Won't that be great, Hilde!"

"Yes, I'm looking forward to it. That's actually why I'm calling . . ."

"It is?"

"I think he's landing at Kastrup around 5 p.m. on Saturday the 23rd. Will you be in Copenhagen then?"

"I think so."

"I was wondering if you could do something for me."

"Why, of course."

"It's kind of a special favor. I'm not even sure if it's possible."

"Now you're making me curious . . ."

Hilde began to describe her plan. She told Anne about the ring binder, about Sophie and Alberto and all the rest. She had to backtrack several times because either she or Anne were laughing too hard. But when Hilde hung up, her plan was in operation.

She would now have to begin some preparations of her own. But there was still plenty of time.

Hilde spent the remainder of the afternoon and the evening with her mother. They ended up driving to Kristiansand and going to the movies. They felt they had some catching up to do since they had not done anything special the day before. As they drove past the exit to Kjevik airport, a few more pieces of the big jigsaw puzzle Hilde was constructing fell into place.

It was late before she went to bed that night, but she took the ring binder and read on.

When Sophie slipped out of the den through the hedge it was almost eight o'clock. Her mother was weeding the flowerbeds by the front door when Sophie appeared.

"Where did you spring from?"

"I came through the hedge."

"Through the hedge?"

"Didn't you know there was a path on the other side?"

"But where have you *been*, Sophie? This is the second

time you've just disappeared without leaving any message."

"I'm sorry, Mom. It was such a lovely day, I went for a long walk."

Her mother rose from the pile of weeds and gave her a severe look.

"You haven't been with that philosopher again?"

"As a matter of fact, I have. I told you he likes going for long walks."

"But he is coming to the garden party, isn't he?"

"Oh yes, he's looking forward to it."

"Me too. I'm counting the days."

Was there a touch of sharpness in her voice? To be on the safe side, Sophie said:

"I'm glad I invited Joanna's parents too. Otherwise it might be a bit embarrassing."

"I don't know . . . but whatever happens, I am going to have a talk with this Alberto as one adult to another."

"You can borrow my room if you like. I'm sure you'll like him."

"And another thing. There's a letter for you."

"There is?"

"It's stamped UN Battalion."

"It must be from Alberto's brother."

"It's got to stop, Sophie!"

Sophie's brain worked overtime. But in a flash she hit on a plausible answer. It was as though she was getting inspiration from some guiding spirit.

"I told Alberto I collect rare postmarks. And brothers also have their uses."

Her mother seemed to be reassured.

"Dinner's in the fridge," she said in a slightly more amicable tone.

"Where's the letter?"

"On top of the fridge."

Sophie rushed inside. The envelope was stamped June 15, 1990. She opened it and took out a little note:

What matters our creative endless toil,
When at a snatch, oblivion ends the coil?

Indeed, Sophie had no answer to that question. Before she ate, she put the note in the closet together with all the other stuff she had collected in the past weeks. She would learn soon enough why the question had been asked.

The following morning Joanna came by. After a game of badminton, they got down to planning the philosophical garden party. They needed to have some surprises on hand in case the party flopped at any point.

When Sophie's mother got home from work they were still talking about it. Her mother kept saying: "Don't worry about what it costs." And she was not being sarcastic!

Perhaps she was thinking that a "philosophical garden party" was just what was needed to bring Sophie down to earth again after her many weeks of intensive philosophical studies.

Before the evening was over they had agreed on everything, from paper lanterns to a philosophical quiz with a prize. The prize should preferably be a book about philosophy for young people. If there was such a thing! Sophie was not at all sure.

Two days before Midsummer Eve, on Thursday, June 21, Alberto called Sophie again.

"Sophie."

"And Alberto."

"Oh, hi! How are you?"

"Very well indeed, thank you. I think I have found an excellent way out."

"Way out of what?"

"You know what. A way out of the mental captivity we have lived in for much too long."

"Oh, that."

"But I cannot say a word about the plan before it is set in motion."

"Won't it be too late then? I need to know what I am involved in."

"Now you're being naïve. All our conversations are being overheard. The most sensible thing would be to say nothing."

"It's as bad as that, huh?"

"Naturally, my child. The most important things must

happen when we are not talking."

"Oh."

"We are living our lives in a fictional reality behind the words in a long story. Each single letter is being written on an old portable typewriter by the major. Nothing that is in print can therefore escape his attention."

"No, I realize that. But how are we going to hide from him?"

"Ssh!"

"What?"

"There's something going on between the lines as well. That's just where I'm trying to be tricky, with every crafty ruse I know."

"I get it."

"But we must make the most of the time both today and tomorrow. On Saturday the balloon goes up. Can you come over right now?"

"I'm on my way."

Sophie fed the birds and the fish and found a large lettuce leaf for Govinda. She opened a can of cat food for Sherekan and put it out in a bowl on the step as she left.

Then she slipped through the hedge and out to the path on the far side. A little way further on she suddenly caught sight of a spacious desk standing in the midst of the heather. An elderly man was sitting at it, apparently adding up figures. Sophie went over to him and asked his name.

"Ebenezer Scrooge," he said, poring over his ledgers again.

"My name is Sophie. You are a businessman, I presume?"

He nodded. "And immensely rich. Not a penny must go to waste. That's why I have to concentrate on my accounts."

"Why bother?"

Sophie waved and walked on. But she had not gone many yards before she noticed a little girl sitting quite alone under one of the tall trees. She was dressed in rags, and looked pale and ill. As Sophie walked by, she thrust her hand into a little bag and pulled out a box of matches.

"Will you buy some matches?" she asked, holding them out to Sophie. Sophie felt in her pockets to see if she had any money with her. Yes—she found a crown.

"How much are they?"

"One crown."

Sophie gave the girl the coin and stood there, with the box of matches in her hand.

"You are the first person to buy anything from me for over a hundred years. Sometimes I starve to death, and other times the frost does away with me."

Sophie thought it was perhaps not surprising if the sale of matches was not especially brisk here in the woods. But then she came to think of the businessman she had just passed. There was no reason for the little match girl to die of starvation when he was so wealthy.

"Come here," said Sophie.

She took the girl's hand and walked with her back to the rich man.

"You must see to it that this girl gets a better life," she said.

The man glanced up from his paperwork and said: "That kind of thing costs money, and I said not so much as a penny must go to waste."

"But it's not fair that you're so rich when this girl is so poor," insisted Sophie. "It's unjust!"

"Bah! Humbug! Justice only exists between equals."

"What do you mean by that?"

"I had to work my way up, and it has paid off. Progress, they call it."

"If you don't help me, I'll die," said the poor girl.

The businessman looked up again from his ledgers. Then he threw his quill pen onto the table impatiently.

"You don't figure in my accounts! So—be off with you—to the poorhouse!"

"If you don't help me, I'll set fire to the woods," the girl persisted.

That brought the man to his feet, but the girl had already struck one of her matches. She held it to a tuft of dry grass which flared up instantly.

The man threw up his arms. "God help me!" he shouted. "The red cock has crowed!"

The girl looked up at him with a playful smile.

"You didn't know I was a communist, did you?"

The next minute, the girl, the businessman, and the desk had disappeared. Sophie was once again standing alone while the flames consumed the dry grass ever more hungrily. It took her a while to put out the fire by stamping on it.

Thank goodness! Sophie glanced down at the blackened grass. She was holding a box of matches in her hand.

She couldn't have started the fire herself, could she?

When she met Alberto outside the cabin she told him what had happened.

"Scrooge was the miserly capitalist in *A Christmas Carol*, by *Charles Dickens*. You probably remember the little match girl from the tale by Hans Christian Andersen."

"I didn't expect to meet them here in the woods."

"Why not? These are no ordinary woods, and now we are going to talk about *Karl Marx*. It is most appropriate that you have witnessed an example of the tremendous class struggles of the mid-nineteenth century. But let's go inside. We are a little more protected from the major's interference there."

Once again they sat at the little table by the window facing the lake. Sophie could still feel all over her body how she had experienced the little lake after having drunk from the blue bottle.

Today, both bottles were standing on the mantelpiece. There was a miniature model of a Greek temple on the table.

"What's that?" asked Sophie.

"All in good time, my dear."

Alberto began to talk: "When Kierkegaard went to Berlin in 1841, he might have sat next to Karl Marx at Schelling's lectures. Kierkegaard had written a master of arts thesis on Socrates. About the same time, Marx had written a doctoral thesis on Democritus and Epicurus—in other words, on the materialism of antiquity. Thus they had both staked out the course of their own philosophies."

"Because Kierkegaard became an existentialist and

Marx became a materialist?"

"Marx became what is known as a *historical material-ist.* But we'll come back to that."

"Go on."

"Each in his own way, both Kierkegaard and Marx took Hegel's philosophy as their point of departure. Both were influenced by Hegel's mode of thought, but both rejected his 'world spirit,' or his idealism."

"It was probably too high-flown for them."

"Definitely. In general, we usually say that the era of the great philosophical systems ended with Hegel. After him, philosophy took a new direction. Instead of great speculative systems, we had what we call an existential philosophy or a philosophy of action. This was what Marx meant when he observed that until now, 'philosophers have only interpreted the world in various ways; the point is to change it.' These words mark a significant turning point in the history of philosophy."

"After meeting Scrooge and the little match girl, I have no problem understanding what Marx meant."

"Marx's thinking had a practical—or political—objective. He was not only a philosopher; he was a historian, a sociologist, and an economist."

"And he was a forerunner in all these areas?"

"Certainly no other philosopher had greater significance for practical politics. On the other hand, we must be wary of identifying everything that calls itself Marxism with Marx's own thinking. It is said of Marx that he only became a Marxist in the mid-1840s, but even after that he could at times feel it necessary to assert that he was not a Marxist."

"Was Jesus a Christian?"

"That, too, of course, is debatable."

"Carry on."

"Right from the start, his friend and colleague *Friedrich Engels* contributed to what was subsequently known as Marxism. In our own century, Lenin, Stalin, Mao and many others also made their contribution to Marxism, or Marxism-Leninism."

"I suggest we try to stick to Marx himself. You said he was a historical materialist?"

"He was not a philosophical materialist like the atomists of antiquity nor did he advocate the mechanical materialism of the seventeenth and eighteenth centuries. But he thought that, to a great extent, it was the material factors in society which determined the way we think. Material factors of that nature have certainly been decisive for historical development."

"That was quite different from Hegel's world spirit."

"Hegel had pointed out that historical development is driven by the tension between opposites—which is then resolved by a sudden change. Marx developed this idea further. But according to Marx, Hegel was standing on his head."

"Not all the time, I hope."

"Hegel called the force that drives history forward world spirit or world reason. This, Marx claimed, is upside down. He wished to show that material changes are the ones that affect history. 'Spiritual relations' do not create material change, it is the other way about. Material change creates new spiritual relations. Marx particularly emphasized that it was the economic forces in society that created change and thus drove history forward."

"Do you have an example?"

"Antiquity's philosophy and science were purely theoretical in purpose. Nobody was particularly interested in putting new discoveries into practice."

"They weren't?"

"That was because of the way the economic life of the community was organized. Production was mainly based on slave labor, so the citizens had no need to increase production with practical innovations. This is an example of how material relations help to affect philosophical reflection in society."

"Yes, I see."

"Marx called these material, economic, and social relations the *basis* of society. The way a society thinks, what kind of political institutions there are, which laws it has and, not least, what there is of religion, morals, art, philosophy, and science, Marx called society's *superstructure*."

"Basis and superstructure, right."

"And now you will perhaps be good enough to pass me the Greek temple."

Sophie did so.

"This is a model of the Parthenon temple on the Acropolis. You have also seen it in real life."

"On the video, you mean."

"You can see that the construction has a very elegant and elaborate roof. Probably the roof with its front gable is what strikes one first. This is what we call the superstructure."

"But the roof cannot float in thin air."

"It is supported by the columns."

"The building has very powerful foundations—its bases—supporting the entire construction. In the same way, Marx believed that material relations support, so to speak, everything in the way of thoughts and ideas in society. Society's superstructure is in fact a reflection of the bases of that society."

"Are you saying that Plato's theory of ideas is a reflection of vase production and wine growing?"

"No, it's not that simple, as Marx expressly points out. It is the interactive effect of society's basis on its superstructure. If Marx had rejected this interaction, he would have been a mechanical materialist. But because Marx realized that there was an interactive or dialectic relation between bases and superstructure, we say that he is a *dialectical materialist.* By the way, you may care to note that Plato was neither a potter nor a wine grower."

"All right. Do you have any more to say about the temple?"

"Yes, a little. Could you describe the bases of the temple?"

"The columns are standing on a base that consists of three levels—or steps."

"In the same manner we will identify three levels in the bases of society. The most basic level is what we may call society's *conditions of production.* In other words, the natural conditions or resources that are available to society. These are the foundation of any society, and this foundation clearly determines the type of production in the society, and by the same token, the nature of that society and its culture in general."

"You can't have a herring trade in the Sahara, or grow dates in northern Norway."

"You've got it. And the way people think in a nomadic culture is very different from the way they think in a fishing village in northern Norway. The next level is the society's *means of production*. By this Marx meant the various kinds of equipment, tools, and machinery, as well as the raw materials to be found there."

"In the old days people rowed out to the fishing grounds. Nowadays they use huge trawlers to catch the fish."

"Yes, and here you are talking about the next level in the base of society, namely, those who own the means of production. The division of labor, or the distribution of work and ownership, was what Marx called society's 'production relations.' "

"I see."

"So far we can conclude that it is the *mode of production* in a society which determines which political and ideological conditions are to be found there. It is not by chance that today we think somewhat differently—and have a somewhat different moral codex—from the old feudal society."

"So Marx didn't believe in a natural right that was eternally valid."

"No, the question of what was morally right, according to Marx, is a product of the base of society. For example, it is not accidental that in the old peasant society, parents would decide whom their children married. It was a question of who was to inherit the farm. In a modern city, social relations are different. Nowadays you can meet your future spouse at a party or a disco, and if you are sufficiently in love, you'll find somewhere to live."

"I could never have put up with my parents deciding who I was to marry."

"No, that's because you are a child of your time. Marx emphasized moreover that it is mainly society's ruling class that sets the norms for what is right or wrong. Because 'the history of all hitherto existing societies is the history of class struggles.' In other words, history is principally a matter of who is to own the means of production."

"Don't people's thoughts and ideas help to change history?"

"Yes and no. Marx understood that conditions in society's superstructure could have an interactive effect on the base of society, but he denied that society's superstructure had any independent history of its own. What has driven historical development from the slave society of antiquity to the industrial society of today has primarily been determined by changes in the base of society."

"So you said."

"Marx believed that in all phases of history there has been a conflict between two dominant classes of society. In antiquity's *slave society*, the conflict was between free citizen and slave. In the *feudal society* of the Middle Ages, it was between feudal lord and serf; later on, between aristocrat and citizen. But in Marx's own time, in what he called a bourgeois or *capitalist society*, the conflict was first and foremost between the capitalists and the workers, or the proletariat. So the conflict stood between those who own the means of production and those who do not. And since the 'upper classes' do not voluntarily relinquish their power, change can only come about through revolution."

"What about a communist society?"

"Marx was especially interested in the transition from a capitalist to a communist society. He also carried out a detailed analysis of the capitalist mode of production. But before we look at that, we must say something about Marx's view of man's *labor*."

"Go ahead."

"Before he became a communist, the young Marx was preoccupied with what happens to man when he works. This was something Hegel had also analyzed. Hegel believed there was an interactive, or dialectic, relationship between man and nature. When man alters nature, he himself is altered. Or, to put it slightly differently, when man works, he interacts with nature and transforms it. But in the process nature also interacts with man and transforms his consciousness."

"Tell me what you do and I'll tell you who you are."

"That, briefly, was Marx's point. How we work affects our consciousness, but our consciousness also affects the way we work. You could say it is an interactive relationship between hand and consciousness. Thus the way you think is closely connected to the job you do."

"So it must be depressing to be unemployed."

"Yes. A person who is unemployed is, in a sense, empty. Hegel was aware of this early on. To both Hegel and Marx, work was a positive thing, and was closely connected with the essence of mankind."

"So it must also be positive to a worker?"

"Yes, originally. But this is precisely where Marx aimed his criticism of the capitalist method of production."

"What was that?"

"Under the capitalist system, the worker labors for someone else. His labor is thus something external to him—or something that does not belong to him. The worker becomes alien to his work—but at the same time also alien to himself. He loses touch with his own reality. Marx says, with a Hegelian expression, that the worker becomes *alienated*."

"I have an aunt who has worked in a factory, packaging candy for over twenty years, so I can easily understand what you mean. She says she hates going to work, every single morning."

"But if she hates her work, Sophie, she must hate herself, in a sense."

"She hates candy, that's for sure."

"In a capitalist society, labor is organized in such a way that the worker in fact slaves for another social class. Thus the worker transfers his own labor—and with it, the whole of his life—to the bourgeoisie."

"Is it really that bad?"

"We're talking about Marx, and we must therefore take our point of departure in the social conditions during the middle of the last century. So the answer must be a resounding yes. The worker could have a 12-hour working day in a freezing cold production hall. The pay was often so poor that children and expectant mothers also had to work. This led to unspeakable social conditions. In many places, part of the wages was paid out in the form of cheap liquor, and women were obliged to supplement their earnings by prostitution. Their customers were the respected citizenry of the town. In short, in the precise situation that should have been the honorable hallmark of mankind, namely work, the worker was turned into a beast of burden."

"That infuriates me!"

"It infuriated Marx too. And while it was happening, the children of the bourgeoisie played the violin in warm, spacious living rooms after a refreshing bath. Or they sat at the piano while waiting for their four-course dinner. The violin and the piano could have served just as well as a diversion after a long horseback ride."

"Ugh! How unjust!"

"Marx would have agreed. Together with Engels, he published a *Communist Manifesto* in 1848. The first sentence in this manifesto says: A spectre is haunting Europe—the spectre of Communism."

"That sounds frightening."

"It frightened the bourgeoisie too. Because now the proletariat was beginning to revolt. Would you like to hear how the Manifesto ends?"

"Yes, please."

"The Communists disdain to conceal their views and aims. They openly declare that their ends can be attained only by the forcible overthrow of all existing social conditions. Let the ruling classes tremble at a Communist revolution. The proletarians have nothing to lose but their chains. They have a world to win. Workingmen of all countries, unite!"

"If conditions were as bad as you say, I think I would have signed that Manifesto. But conditions are surely a lot different today?"

"In Norway they are, but they aren't everywhere. Many people still live under inhuman conditions while they continue to produce commodities that make capitalists richer and richer. Marx called this *exploitation*."

"Could you explain that word, please?"

"If a worker produces a commodity, this commodity has a certain exchange-value."

"Yes."

"If you now deduct the workers' wages and the other production costs from the exchange-value, there will always be a certain sum left over. This sum was what Marx called profit. In other words, the capitalist pockets a value that was actually created by the worker. That is what is meant by exploitation."

"I see."

"So now the capitalist invests some of his profit in new capital—for instance, in modernizing the production plant in the hope of producing his commodity even more cheaply, and thereby increasing his profit in the future."

"That sounds logical."

"Yes, it can seem logical. But both in this and in other areas, in the long term it will not go the way the capitalist has imagined."

"How do you mean?"

"Marx believed there were a number of inherent contradictions in the capitalist method of production. Capitalism is an economic system which is self-destructive because it lacks rational control."

"That's good, isn't it, for the oppressed?"

"Yes; it is inherent in the capitalist system that it is marching toward its own destruction. In that sense, capitalism is 'progressive' because it is a stage on the way to communism."

"Can you give an example of capitalism being self-destructive?"

"We said that the capitalist had a good surplus of money, and he uses part of this surplus to modernize the factory. But he also spends money on violin lessons. Moreover, his wife has become accustomed to a luxurious way of life."

"No doubt."

"He buys new machinery and so no longer needs so many employees. He does this to increase his competitive power."

"I get it."

"But he is not the only one thinking in this way, which

means that production as a whole is continually being made more effective. Factories become bigger and bigger, and are gradually concentrated in fewer and fewer hands. What happens then, Sophie?"

"Er . . ."

"Fewer and fewer workers are required, which means there are more and more unemployed. There are therefore increasing social problems, and *crises* such as these are a signal that capitalism is marching toward its own destruction. But capitalism has a number of other self-destructive elements. Whenever profit has to be tied up in the means of production without leaving a big enough surplus to keep production going at competitive prices . . ."

"Yes?"

". . . what does the capitalist do then? Can you tell me?"

"No, I'm afraid I can't."

"Imagine if you were a factory owner. You cannot make ends meet. You cannot buy the raw materials you need to keep producing. You are facing bankruptcy. So now my question is, what can you do to economize?"

"Maybe I could cut down on wages?"

"Smart! Yes, that really is the smartest thing you could do. But if all capitalists were as smart as you—and they are—the workers would be so poor that they couldn't afford to buy goods any more. We would say that purchasing power is falling. And now we really are in a vicious circle. The knell has sounded for capitalist private property, Marx would say. We are rapidly approaching a revolutionary situation."

"Yes, I see."

"To make a long story short, in the end the proletariat rises and takes over the means of production."

"And then what?"

"For a period, we get a new 'class society' in which the proletarians suppress the bourgeoisie by force. Marx called this the *dictatorship of the proletariat*. But after a transition period, the dictatorship of the proletariat is replaced by a 'classless society,' in which the means of production are owned 'by all'—that is, by the people themselves. In this kind of society, the policy is 'from each according to his abilities, to each according to his needs.' Moreover, labor now belongs to the workers themselves and capitalism's alienation ceases."

"It all sounds wonderful, but what actually happened? Was there a revolution?"

"Yes and no. Today, economists can establish that Marx was mistaken on a number of vital issues, not least his analysis of the crises of capitalism. And he paid insufficient attention to the plundering of the natural environment—the serious consequences of which we are experiencing today. Nevertheless . . ."

"Nevertheless?"

"Marxism led to great upheavals. There is no doubt that socialism has largely succeeded in combating an inhumane society. In Europe, at any rate, we live in a society with more justice—and more solidarity—than Marx did. This is not least due to Marx himself and the entire socialist movement."

"What happened?"

"After Marx, the socialist movement split into two main streams, Social Democracy and Leninism. Social Democracy, which has stood for a gradual and peaceful path in the direction of socialism, was Western Europe's way. We might call this the slow revolution. Leninism, which retained Marx's belief that revolution was the only way to combat the old class society, had great influence in Eastern Europe, Asia, and Africa. Each in their own way, both movements have fought against hardship and oppression."

"But didn't it create a new form of oppression? For example in Russia and Eastern Europe?"

"No doubt of that, and here again we see that everything man touches becomes a mixture of good and evil. On the other hand, it would be unreasonable to blame Marx for the negative factors in the so-called socialist countries fifty or a hundred years after his death. But maybe he had given too little thought to the people who would be the administrators of communist society. There will probably never be a 'promised land.' Mankind will always create new problems to fight about."

"I'm sure it will."

"And there we bring down the curtain on Marx, Sophie."

"Hey, wait a minute! Didn't you say something about justice only existing among equals?"

"No, it was Scrooge who said that."

"How do you know what he said?"

"Oh well—you and I have the same author. In actual fact we are more closely linked to each other than we would appear to the casual observer."

"Your wretched irony again!"

"Double, Sophie, that was double irony."

"But back to justice. You said that Marx thought capitalism was an unjust form of society. How would you define a just society?"

"A moral philosopher called John Rawls attempted to say something about it with the following example: Imagine you were a member of a distinguished council whose task it was to make all the laws for a future society."

"I wouldn't mind at all being on that council."

"They are obliged to consider absolutely every detail, because as soon as they reach an agreement—and everybody has signed the laws—they will all drop dead."

"Oh . . ."

"But they will immediately come to life again in the society they have legislated for. The point is that they have no idea which *position* they will have in society."

"Ah, I see."

"That society would be a just society. It would have arisen among equals."

"Men *and* women!"

"That goes without saying. None of them knew whether they would wake up as men or women. Since the odds are fifty-fifty, society would be just as attractive for women as for men."

"It sounds promising."

"So tell me, was the Europe of Karl Marx a society like that?"

"Absolutely not!"

"But do you by any chance know of such a society today?"

"Hm . . . that's a good question."

"Think about it. But for now there will be no more about Marx."

"Excuse me?"

"Next chapter!"

Darwin

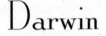

. . . a ship sailing through life with a cargo of genes . . .

Hilde was awakened on Sunday morning by a loud bump. It was the ring binder falling on the floor. She had been lying in bed reading about Sophie and Alberto's conversation on Marx and had fallen asleep. The reading lamp by the bed had been on all night.

The green glowing digits on her desk alarm clock showed 8:59.

She had been dreaming about huge factories and polluted cities; a little girl sitting at a street corner selling matches—well-dressed people in long coats passing by without as much as a glance.

When Hilde sat up in bed she remembered the legislators who were to wake up in a society they themselves had created. Hilde was glad she had woken up in Bjerkely, at any rate.

Would she have dared to wake up in Norway without knowing whereabouts in Norway she would wake up?

But it was not only a question of *where* she would wake up. Could she not just as easily have woken up in a different age? In the Middle Ages, for instance—or in the Stone Age ten or twenty thousand years ago? Hilde tried to imagine herself sitting at the entrance to a cave, scraping an animal hide, perhaps.

What could it have been like to be a fifteen-year-old girl before there was anything called a culture? How would she have thought? Could she have had thoughts at all?

Hilde pulled on a sweater, heaved the ring binder onto the bed and settled down to read the next chapter.

Alberto had just said "Next chapter!" when somebody knocked on the door of the major's cabin.

"We don't have any choice, do we?" said Sophie.

"No, I suppose we don't," said Alberto.

On the step outside stood a very old man with long white hair and a beard. He held a staff in one hand, and in the other a board on which was painted a picture of a boat. The boat was crowded with all kinds of animals.

"And who is this elderly gentleman?" asked Alberto.

"My name is Noah."

"I guessed as much."

"Your oldest ancestor, my son. But it is probably no longer fashionable to recognize one's ancestors."

"What is that in your hand?" asked Sophie.

"This is a picture of all the animals that were saved from the Flood. Here, my daughter, it is for you."

Sophie took the large board.

"Well, I'd better go home and tend the grapevines," the old man said, and giving a little jump, he clicked his heels together in the air and skipped merrily away into the woods in the manner peculiar to very old men now and then.

Sophie and Alberto went inside and sat down again. Sophie began to look at the picture, but before she had a chance to study it, Alberto took it from her with an authoritative grasp.

"We'll concentrate on the broad outlines first."

"Okay, okay."

"I forgot to mention that Marx lived the last 34 years of his life in London. He moved there in 1849 and died in 1883. All that time *Charles Darwin* was living just outside London. He died in 1882 and was buried with great pomp and ceremony in Westminster Abbey as one of England's distinguished sons. So Marx and Darwin's paths crossed, but not only in time and space. Marx wanted to dedicate the English edition of his greatest work, *Cap-*

ital, to Darwin, but Darwin declined the honor. When Marx died the year after Darwin, his friend Friedrich Engels said: As Darwin discovered the theory of organic evolution, so Marx discovered the theory of mankind's historical evolution.''

''I see.''

''Another great thinker who was to link his work to Darwin was the psychologist Sigmund Freud. He also lived his last years in London. Freud said that both Darwin's theory of evolution and his own psychoanalysis had resulted in an affront to mankind's naïve egoism.''

''That was a lot of names at one time. Are we talking about Marx, Darwin, or Freud?''

''In a broader sense we can talk about a *naturalistic* current from the middle of the nineteenth century until quite far into our own. By 'naturalistic' we mean a sense of reality that accepts no other reality than nature and the sensory world. A naturalist therefore also considers mankind to be part of nature. A naturalistic scientist will exclusively rely on natural phenomena—not on either rationalistic suppositions or any form of divine revelation.''

''And that applies to Marx, Darwin, and Freud?''

''Absolutely. The key words from the middle of the last century were nature, environment, history, evolution, and growth. Marx had pointed out that human ideologies were a product of the basis of society. Darwin showed that mankind was the result of a slow biological evolution, and Freud's studies of the unconscious revealed that people's actions were often the result of 'animal' urges or instincts.''

''I think I understand more or less what you mean by naturalistic, but isn't it best we talk about one person at a time?''

''We'll talk about Darwin, Sophie. You may recall that the pre-Socratics looked for *natural explanations* of the processes of nature. In the same way that they had to distance themselves from ancient mythological explanations, Darwin had to distance himself from the church's view of the creation of man and beast.''

''But was he a real philosopher?''

''Darwin was a biologist and a natural scientist. But he

was also the scientist of recent times who has most openly challenged the Biblical view of man's place in Creation."

"So you'll have to say something about Darwin's theory of evolution."

"Let's begin with Darwin the man. He was born in the little town of Shrewsbury in 1809. His father, Dr. Robert Darwin, was a renowned local physician, and very strict about his son's upbringing. When Charles was a pupil at the local grammar school, his headmaster described him as a boy who was always flying around, fooling about with stuff and nonsense, and never doing a stroke of anything that was the slightest bit useful. By 'useful,' the headmaster meant cramming Greek and Latin verbs. By 'flying around,' he was referring among other things to the fact that Charles clambered around collecting beetles of all kinds."

"I'll bet he came to regret those words."

"When he subsequently studied theology, Charles was far more interested in bird-watching and collecting insects, so he did not get very good grades in theology. But while he was still at college, he gained himself a reputation as a natural scientist, not least due to his interest in geology, which was perhaps the most expansive science of the day. As soon as he had graduated in theology at Cambridge in April 1831, he went to North Wales to study rock formations and to search for fossils. In August of the same year, when he was barely twenty-two years old, he received a letter which was to determine the course of his whole life . . ."

"What was the letter about?"

"It was from his friend and teacher, John Steven Henslow. He wrote: 'I have been requested to . . . recommend a naturalist to go as companion to Captain Fitzroy, who has been commissioned by the government to survey the southern coasts of South America. I have stated that I consider you to be the best qualified person I know of who is likely to undertake such a situation. As far as the financial side of it is concerned, I have no notion. The voyage is to last two years . . . ' "

"How can you remember all that by heart?"

"A bagatelle, Sophie."

"And what did he answer?"

"He wished ardently to grasp the chance, but in those days young men did nothing without their parents' consent. After much persuasion, his father finally agreed—and it was he who financed his son's voyage. As far as the 'financial side' went, it was conspicuous by its absence."

"Oh."

"The ship was the naval vessel HMS *Beagle*. It sailed from Plymouth on December 27, 1831, bound for South America, and it did not return until October of 1836. The two years became five and the voyage to South America turned into a voyage round the world. And now we come to one of the most important voyages of discovery in recent times."

"They sailed all the way round the world?"

"Yes, quite literally. From South America they sailed on across the Pacific to New Zealand, Australia, and South Africa. Then they sailed back to South America before setting sail for England. Darwin wrote that the voyage on board the *Beagle* was without doubt the most significant event in his life."

"It couldn't have been easy to be a naturalist at sea."

"For the first years, the *Beagle* sailed up and down the coast of South America. This gave Darwin plenty of opportunity to familiarize himself with the continent, also inland. The expedition's many forays into the Galapagos Islands in the Pacific west of South America were of decisive significance as well. He was able to collect and send to England vast amounts of material. However, he kept his reflections on nature and the evolution of life to himself. When he returned home at the age of twenty-seven, he found himself renowned as a scientist. At that point he had an inwardly clear picture of what was to become his theory of evolution. But he did not publish his main work until many years after his return, for Darwin was a cautious man—as is fitting for a scientist."

"What was his main work?"

"Well, there were several, actually. But the book which gave rise to the most heated debate in England was *The Origin of Species*, published in 1859. Its full title was *On* the Origin of Species by Means of Natural Selection, or the Preservation of Favoured Races in the Struggle for Life. The long title is actually a complete résumé of Darwin's theory.''

''He certainly packed a lot into one title.''

''But let's take it piece by piece. In *The Origin of Species*, Darwin advanced two theories or main theses: first, he proposed that all existing vegetable and animal forms were descended from earlier, more primitive forms by way of a biological evolution. Secondly, that evolution was the result of *natural selection*.''

''The survival of the fittest, right?''

''That's right, but let us first concentrate on the idea of evolution. This, in itself, was not all that original. The idea of biological evolution began to be widely accepted in some circles as early as 1800. The leading spokesman for this idea was the French zoologist *Lamarck*. Even before him, Darwin's own grandfather, *Erasmus Darwin*, had suggested that plants and animals had evolved from some few primitive species. But none of them had come up with an acceptable explanation as to *how* this evolution happened. They were therefore not considered by churchmen to be any great threat.''

''But Darwin was?''

''Yes, indeed, and not without reason. Both in ecclesiastic and scientific circles, the Biblical doctrine of the immutability of all vegetable and animal species was strictly adhered to. Each and every form of animal life had been created separately once and for all. This Christian view was moreover in harmony with the teachings of Plato and Aristotle.''

''How so?''

''Plato's theory of ideas presupposed that all animal species were immutable because they were made after patterns of eternal ideas or forms. The immutability of animal species was also one of the cornerstones of Aristotle's philosophy. But in Darwin's time there were a number of observations and finds which were putting traditional beliefs to the test.''

''What kind of observations and finds were they?''

''Well, to begin with an increasing number of fossils

were being dug out. There were also finds of large fossil bones from extinct animals. Darwin himself was puzzled to find traces of sea creatures far inland. In South America he made similar discoveries high up in the mountains of the Andes. What is a sea creature doing in the Andes, Sophie? Can you tell me that?"

"No."

"Some believed that they had just been thrown away there by humans or animals. Others believed that God had created these fossils and traces of sea creatures to lead the ungodly astray."

"But what did scientists believe?"

"Most geologists swore to a 'catastrophe theory,' according to which the earth had been subjected to gigantic floods, earthquakes, and other catastrophes that had destroyed all life. We read of one of these in the Bible—the Flood and Noah's Ark. After each catastrophe, God renewed life on earth by creating new—and more perfect—plants and animals."

"So the fossils were imprints of earlier life forms that had been wiped out after these gigantic catastrophes?"

"Precisely. For example, it was thought that fossils were imprints of animals that had failed to get into the Ark. But when Darwin set sail on the *Beagle*, he had with him the first volume of the English biologist *Sir Charles Lyell's Principles of Geology*. Lyell held that the present geology of the earth, with its mountains and valleys, was the result of an interminably long and gradual evolution. His point was that even quite small changes could cause huge geological upheavals, considering the aeons of time that have elapsed."

"What kind of changes was he thinking of?"

"He was thinking of the same forces that prevail today: wind and weather, melting ice, earthquakes, and elevations of the ground level. You've heard the saying about a drop of water wearing away a stone—not by brute force, but by continuous dripping. Lyell believed that similar tiny and gradual changes over the ages could alter the face of nature completely. However, this theory alone could not explain why Darwin found the remains of sea creatures high up in the Andes. But Darwin always remembered that *tiny gradual changes* could result in dramatic alterations if they were given sufficient time."

"I suppose he thought the same explanation could be used for the evolution of animals."

"Yes, that was his thought. But as I said before, Darwin was a cautious man. He posed questions long before he ventured to answer them. In that sense he used the same method as all true philosophers: it is important to ask but there is no haste to provide the answer."

"Yes, I see."

"A decisive factor in Lyell's theory was the age of the earth. In Darwin's time, it was widely believed that about 6,000 years had elapsed since God created the earth. That figure had been arrived at by counting the generations since Adam and Eve."

"How naïve!"

"Well, it's easy to be wise after the event. Darwin figured the age of the earth to be 300 million years. Because one thing, at least, was clear: neither Lyell's theory of gradual geological evolution nor Darwin's own theory of evolution had any validity unless one reckoned with tremendously long periods of time."

"How old is the earth?"

"Today we know that the earth is 4.6 billion years old."

"Wow!"

"Up to now, we have looked at one of Darwin's arguments for biological evolution, namely, the *stratified deposits of fossils* in various layers of rock. Another argument was the *geographic distribution* of living species. This was where Darwin's scientific voyage could contribute new and extremely comprehensive data. He had seen with his own eyes that the individuals of a single species of animal within the same region could differ from each other in only the minutest detail. He made some very interesting observations on the Galapagos Islands, west of Ecuador, in particular."

"Tell me about them."

"The Galapagos Islands are a compact group of volcanic islands. There were therefore no great differences in the plant and animal life there. But Darwin was interested in the tiny differences. On all the islands, he came across giant tortoises that were slightly different from one island to another. Had God really created a separate race of tortoises for each and every island?"

"It's doubtful."

"Darwin's observations of bird life on the Galapagos were even more striking. The Galapagos finches were clearly varied from island to island, especially as regards the shape of the beak. Darwin demonstrated that these variations were closely linked to the way the finches found their food on the different islands. The ground finches with steeply profiled beaks lived on pine cone seeds, the little warbler finches lived on insects, and the tree finches lived on termites extracted from bark and branches . . . Each and every one of the species had a beak that was perfectly adapted to its own food intake. Could all these finches be descended from one and the same species? And had the finches adapted to their surroundings on the different islands over the ages in such a way that new species of finches evolved?"

"That was the conclusion he came to, wasn't it?"

"Yes. Maybe that was where Darwin became a 'Darwinist'—on the Galapagos Islands. He also observed that the fauna there bore a strong resemblance to many of the species he had seen in South America. Had God once and for all really created all these animals slightly different from each other—or had an evolution taken place? Increasingly, he began to doubt that all species were immutable. But he still had no viable explanation as to *how* such an evolution had occurred. But there was one more factor to indicate that all the animals on earth might be related."

"And what was that?"

"The development of the embryo in mammals. If you compare the embryos of dogs, bats, rabbits, and humans at an early stage, they look so alike that it is hard to tell the difference. You cannot distinguish a human embryo from a rabbit embryo until a very late stage. Shouldn't this indicate that we are distant relatives?"

"But he had still no explanation of how evolution happened?"

"He pondered constantly on Lyell's theory of the minute

changes that could have great effect over a long period of time. But he could find no explanation that would apply as a general principle. He was familiar with the theory of the French zoologist Lamarck, who had shown that the different species had developed the characteristics they needed. Giraffes, for example, had developed long necks because for generations they had reached up for leaves in the trees. Lamarck believed that the characteristics each individual acquires through his own efforts are passed on to the next generation. But this theory of the heredity of 'acquired characteristics' was rejected by Darwin because Lamarck had no proof of his bold claims. However, Darwin was beginning to pursue another, much more obvious line of thought. You could almost say that the actual mechanism behind the evolution of species was right in front of his very nose."

"So what was it?"

"I would rather you worked the mechanism out for yourself. So I ask: If you had three cows, but only enough fodder to keep two of them alive, what would you do?"

"I suppose I'd have to slaughter one of them."

"All right . . . which one would you slaughter?"

"I suppose I'd slaughter the one that gave the least milk."

"Would you?"

"Yes, that's logical, isn't it?"

"That is exactly what mankind had done for thousands of years. But we haven't finished with your two cows yet. Suppose you wanted one of them to calve. Which one would you choose?"

"The one that was the best milker. Then its calf would probably be a good milker too."

"You prefer good milkers to bad, then. Now there's one more question. If you were a hunter and you had two gundogs, but had to give up one of them, which one would you keep?"

"The one that's best at finding the kind of game I shoot, obviously."

"Quite so, you would favor the better gundog. That's exactly how people have bred domestic animals for more than ten thousand years, Sophie. Hens did not always lay five eggs a week, sheep did not always yield as much wool, and horses were not always as strong and swift as they are now. Breeders have made an *artificial selection.* The same applies to the vegetable kingdom. You don't plant bad potatoes if there are good seed potatoes available, and you don't waste time cutting wheat that yields no grain. Darwin pointed out that no cows, no stalks of wheat, no dogs, and no finches are completely alike. Nature produces an enormous breadth of variation. Even within the same species, no two individuals are exactly alike. You probably experienced that for yourself when you drank the blue liquid."

"I'll say."

"So now Darwin had to ask himself: could a similar mechanism be at work in nature too? Is it possible that nature makes a 'natural selection' as to which individuals are to survive? And could such a selection over a very long period of time create new species of flora and fauna?"

"I would guess the answer is yes."

"Darwin could still not quite imagine how such a natural selection could take place. But in October 1838, exactly two years after his return on the *Beagle,* he chanced to come across a little book by the specialist in population studies, *Thomas Malthus.* The book was called *An Essay on the Principle of Population.* Malthus got the idea for this essay from *Benjamin Franklin,* the American who invented the lightning conductor among other things. Franklin had made the point that if there were no limiting factors in nature, one single species of plant or animal would spread over the entire globe. But because there are many species, they keep each other in balance."

"I can see that."

"Malthus developed this idea and applied it to the world's population. He believed that mankind's ability to procreate is so great that there are always more children born than can survive. Since the production of food can never keep pace with the increase in population, he believed that huge numbers were destined to succumb in the struggle for existence. Those who survived to grow up—and perpetuate the race—would therefore be those who came out best in the struggle for survival."

"That sounds logical."

"But this was actually the universal mechanism that Darwin had been searching for. Here was the explanation of how evolution happens. It was due to *natural selection* in the struggle for life, in which those that were best adapted to their surroundings would survive and perpetuate the race. This was the second theory which he proposed in *The Origin of Species*. He wrote: 'The elephant is reckoned the slowest breeder of all known animals,' but if it had six young and survived to a hundred, 'after a period of from 740 to 750 years there would be nearly nineteen million elephants alive, descended from the first pair.' "

"Not to mention all the thousands of cods' eggs from a single cod."

"Darwin further proposed that the struggle for survival is frequently hardest among species that resemble each other the most. They have to fight for the same food. There, the slightest advantage—that is to say, the infinitesimal variation—truly comes into its own. The more bitter the struggle for survival, the quicker will be the evolution of new species, so that only the very best adapted will survive and the others will die out."

"The less food there is and the bigger the brood, the quicker evolution happens?"

"Yes, but it's not only a question of food. It can be just as vital to avoid being eaten by other animals. For example, it can be a matter of survival to have a protective camouflage, the ability to run swiftly, to recognize hostile animals, or, if the worst comes to the worst, to have a repellent taste. A poison that can kill predators is quite useful too. That's why so many cacti are poisonous, Sophie. Practically nothing else can grow in the desert, so this plant is especially vulnerable to plant-eating animals."

"Most cacti are prickly as well."

"The ability to reproduce is also of fundamental importance, obviously. Darwin studied the ingenuity of plant pollination in great detail. Flowers glow in glorious hues and exude delirious scents to attract the insects which are instrumental in pollination. To perpetuate their kind, birds trill their melodious tones. A placid or melancholy bull with no interest in cows will have no interest for genealogy either, since with characteristics like these, its line will die out at once. The bull's sole purpose in life is to grow to sexual maturity and reproduce in order to propagate the race. It is rather like a relay race. Those that for one reason or another are unable to pass on their genes are continually discarded, and in that way the race is continually refined. Resistance to disease is one of the most important characteristics progressively accumulated and preserved in the variants that survive."

"So everything gets better and better?"

"The result of this continual selection is that the ones best adapted to a *particular environment*—or a particular ecological niche—will in the long term perpetuate the race in that environment. But what is an advantage in one environment is not necessarily an advantage in another. For some of the Galapagos finches, the ability to fly was vital. But being good at flying is not so necessary if food is dug from the ground and there are no predators. The reason why so many different animal species have arisen over the ages is precisely because of these many niches in the natural environment."

"But even so, there is only one human race."

"That's because man has a unique ability to adapt to different conditions of life. One of the things that amazed Darwin most was the way the Indians in Tierra del Fuego managed to live under such terrible climatic conditions. But that doesn't mean that all human beings are alike. Those who live near the equator have darker skins than people in the more northerly climes because their dark skin protects them from the sun. White people who expose themselves to the sun for long periods are more prone to skin cancer."

"Is it a similar advantage to have white skin if you live in northern countries?"

"Yes, otherwise everyone on earth would be dark-skinned. But white skin more easily forms sun vitamins, and that can be vital in areas with very little sun. Nowadays that is not so important because we can make sure we have enough sun vitamins in our diet. But nothing in nature is random. Everything is due to infinitesimal changes that have taken effect over countless generations."

"Actually, it's quite fantastic to imagine."

"It is indeed. So far, then, we can sum up Darwin's theory of evolution in a few sentences."

"Go ahead!"

"We can say that the 'raw material' behind the evolution of life on earth was the continual *variation* of individuals within the same species, plus the *large number of progeny*, which meant that only a fraction of them survived. The actual 'mechanism,' or driving force, behind evolution was thus the *natural selection* in the struggle for survival. This selection ensured that the strongest, or the 'fittest,' survived."

"It seems as logical as a math sum. How was *The Origin of Species* received?"

"It was the cause of bitter controversies. The Church protested vehemently and the scientific world was sharply divided. That was not really so surprising. Darwin had, after all, distanced God a good way from the act of creation, although there were admittedly some who claimed it was surely greater to have created something with its own innate evolutionary potential than simply to create a fixed entity."

Suddenly Sophie jumped up from her chair.

"Look out there!" she cried.

She pointed out of the window. Down by the lake a man and a woman were walking hand in hand. They were completely naked.

"That's Adam and Eve," said Alberto. "They were gradually forced to throw in their lot with Little Red Ridinghood and Alice in Wonderland. That's why they have turned up here."

Sophie went to the window to watch them, but they soon disappeared among the trees.

"Because Darwin believed that mankind was descended from animals?"

"In 1871 Darwin published *The Descent of Man*, in which he drew attention to the great similarities between humans and animals, advancing the theory that men and anthropoid apes must at one time have evolved from the same progenitor. By this time the first fossil skulls of an extinct type of man had been found, first in the Rock of Gibraltar and some years later in Neanderthal in Germany. Strangely enough, there were fewer protests in 1871 than in 1859, when Darwin published *The Origin of Species*. But man's descent from animals had been implicit in the first book as well. And as I said, when Darwin died in 1882, he was buried with all the ceremony due to a pioneer of science.''

"So in the end he found honor and dignity?''

"Eventually, yes. But not before he had been described as the most dangerous man in England.''

"Holy Moses!''

'' 'Let us hope it is not true,' wrote an upper-class lady, 'but if it is, let us hope it will not be generally known.' A distinguished scientist expressed a similar thought: 'An embarrassing discovery, and the less said about it the better.' ''

"That was almost proof that man is related to the ostrich!''

"Good point. But that's easy enough for us to say now. People were suddenly obliged to revise their whole approach to the Book of Genesis. The young writer John Ruskin put it like this: 'If only the geologists would leave me alone. After each Bible verse I hear the blows of their hammers.' ''

"And the blows of the hammers were his doubts about the word of God?''

"That was presumably what he meant. Because it was more than the literal interpretation of the story of creation that toppled. The essence of Darwin's theory was the utterly *random* variations which had finally produced Man. And what was more, Darwin had turned Man into a product of something as unsentimental as the struggle for existence.''

"Did Darwin have anything to say about how such random variations arose?''

"You've put your finger on the weakest point in his theory. Darwin had only the vaguest idea of heredity. Something happens in the crossing. A father and mother never get two identical offspring. There is always some slight difference. On the other hand it's difficult to produce anything really new in that way. Moreover, there are plants and animals which reproduce by budding or by simple cell division. On the question of how the variations arise, Darwin's theory has been supplemented by the so-called neo-Darwinism."

"What's that?"

"All life and all reproduction is basically a matter of cell division. When a cell divides into two, two identical cells are produced with exactly the same hereditary factors. In cell division, then, we say a cell copies itself."

"Yes?"

"But occasionally, infinitesimal errors occur in the process, so that the copied cell is not exactly the same as the mother cell. In modern biological terms, this is a *mutation*. Mutations are either totally irrelevant, or they can lead to marked changes in the behavior of the individual. They can be directly harmful, and such 'mutants' will be continually discarded from the large broods. Many diseases are in fact due to mutations. But sometimes a mutation can give an individual just that extra positive characteristic needed to hold its own in the struggle for existence."

"Like a longer neck, for instance?"

"Lamarck's explanation of why the giraffe has such a long neck was that giraffes have always had to reach upwards. But according to Darwinism, no such inherited characteristic would be passed on. Darwin believed that the giraffe's long neck was the result of a variation. Neo-Darwinism supplemented this by showing a clear *cause* of just that particular variation."

"Mutations?"

"Yes. Absolutely random changes in hereditary factors supplied one of the giraffe's ancestors with a slightly longer neck than average. When there was a limited supply of food, this could be vital enough. The giraffe that could reach up highest in the trees managed best. We can also imagine how some such 'primal giraffes' evolved the ability to dig in the ground for food. Over a very long period of time, an animal species, now long extinct, could have divided itself into two species. We can take some more recent examples of the way natural selection can work."

"Yes, please."

"In Britain there is a certain species of butterfly called the *peppered moth*, which lives on the trunks of silver birches. Back in the eighteenth century, most peppered moths were silvery gray. Can you guess why, Sophie?"

"So they weren't so easy for hungry birds to spot."

"But from time to time, due to quite chance mutations, some darker ones were born. How do you think these darker variants fared?"

"They were easier to see, so they were more easily snapped up by hungry birds."

"Yes, because in that environment—where the birch trunks were silver—the darker hue was an unfavorable characteristic. So it was always the paler peppered moths that increased in number. But then something happened in that environment. In several places, the silvery trunks became blackened by industrial soot. What do you think happened to the peppered moths then?"

"The darker ones survived best."

"Yes, so now it wasn't long before they increased in number. From 1848 to 1948, the proportion of dark peppered moths increased from 1 to 99 percent in certain places. The environment had changed, and it was no longer an advantage to be light. On the contrary. The white 'losers' were weeded out with the help of the birds as soon as they appeared on the birch trunks. But then something significant happened again. A decrease in the use of coal and better filtering equipment in the factories has recently produced a cleaner environment."

"So now the birches are silver again?"

"And therefore the peppered moth is in the process of returning to its silvery color. This is what we call *adaptation*. It's a natural law."

"Yes, I see."

"But there are numerous examples of how man interferes in the environment."

"Like what?"

"For example, people have tried to eradicate pests with various pesticides. At first, this can produce excellent results. But when you spray a field or an orchard with pesticides, you actually cause a miniature ecocatastrophe for the pests you are trying to eradicate. Due to continual mutations, a type of pest develops that is resistant to the pesticide being used. Now these 'winners' have free play, so it becomes harder and harder to combat certain kinds of pest simply because of man's attempt to eradicate them. The most resistant variants are the ones that survive, of course."

"That's pretty scary."

"It certainly is food for thought. We also try to combat parasites in our own bodies in the form of bacteria."

"We use penicillin or other kinds of antibiotic."

"Yes, and penicillin is also an ecocatastrophe for the little devils. However, as we continue to administer penicillin, we are making certain bacteria resistant, thereby cultivating a group of bacteria that is much harder to combat than it was before. We find we have to use stronger and stronger antibiotics, until . . ."

"Until they finally crawl out of our mouths? Maybe we ought to start shooting them?"

"That might be a tiny bit exaggerated. But it is clear that modern medicine has created a serious dilemma. The problem is not only that a single bacterium has become more virulent. In the past, there were many children who never survived—they succumbed to various diseases. Sometimes only the minority survived. But in a sense modern medicine has put natural selection out of commission. Something that has helped one individual over a serious illness can in the long run contribute to weakening the resistance of the whole human race to certain diseases. If we pay absolutely no attention to what is called hereditary hygiene, we could find ourselves facing a degeneration of the human race. Mankind's hereditary potential for resisting serious disease will be weakened."

"What a terrifying prospect!"

"But a real philosopher must not refrain from pointing out something 'terrifying' if he otherwise believes it to be true. So let us attempt another summary."

"Okay."

"You could say that life is one big lottery in which only

the winning numbers are visible."

"What on earth do you mean?"

"Those that have lost in the struggle for existence have disappeared, you see. It takes many millions of years to select the winning numbers for each and every species of vegetable and animal on the earth. And the losing numbers—well, they only make one appearance. So there are no species of animal or vegetable in existence today that are not winning numbers in the great lottery of life."

"Because only the best have survived."

"Yes, that's another way of saying it. And now, if you will kindly pass me the picture which that fellow—that zookeeper—brought us . . ."

Sophie passed the picture over to him. The picture of Noah's Ark covered one side of it. The other was devoted to a tree diagram of all the various species of animals. This was the side Alberto was now showing her.

"Our Darwinian Noah also brought us a sketch that shows the distribution of the various vegetable and animal species. You can see how the different species belong in the different groups, classes, and subkingdoms."

"Yes."

"Together with monkeys, man belongs to the so-called primates. Primates are mammals, and all mammals belong to the vertebrates, which again belong to the multicellular animals."

"It's almost like Aristotle."

"Yes, that's true. But the sketch illustrates not only the distribution of the different species today. It also tells something of the history of evolution. You can see, for example, that birds at some point parted from reptiles, and that reptiles at some point parted from amphibia, and that amphibia parted from fishes."

"Yes, it's very clear."

"Every time a line divides into two, it's because mutations have resulted in a new species. That is how, over the ages, the different classes and subkingdoms of animals arose. In actual fact there are more than a million animal species in the world today, and this million is only a fraction of the species that have at some time lived on the earth. You can see, for instance, that an animal group such as the Trilobita is totally extinct."

"And at the bottom are the monocellular animals."

"Some of these may not have changed in two billion years. You can also see that there is a line from these monocellular organisms to the vegetable kingdom. Because in all probability plants come from the same primal cell as animals."

"Yes, I see that. But there's something that puzzles me."

"Yes?"

"Where did this first primal cell come from? Did Darwin have any answer to that?"

"I said, did I not, that he was a very cautious man. But as regards that question, he did permit himself to propose what one might call a qualified guess. He wrote:

If (and O, what an if!) we could picture some hot little pool in which all manner of ammoniacal and phosphorous salts, light, heat, electricity and so forth were present, and that a protein compound were to be chemically formed in it, ready to undergo even more complicated changes . . ."

"What then?"

"What Darwin was philosophizing on here was how the first living cell might have been formed out of inorganic matter. And again, he hit the nail right on the head. Scientists of today think the first primitive form of life arose in precisely the kind of 'hot little pool' that Darwin pictured."

"Go on."

"That will have to suffice because we're leaving Darwin now. We're going to jump ahead to the most recent findings about the origins of life on earth."

"I'm rather apprehensive. Does anybody really *know* how life began?"

"Maybe not, but more and more pieces of the puzzle have fallen into place to form a picture of how it *may* have begun."

"Well?"

"Let us first establish that all life on earth—both animal and vegetable—is constructed of exactly the same substances. The simplest definition of life is that it is a substance which in a nutrient solution has the ability to subdivide itself into two identical parts. This process is governed by a substance we call DNA. By DNA we mean the chromosomes, or hereditary structures, that are found in all living cells. We also use the term DNA *molecule*, because DNA is in fact a complex molecule—or macromolecule. The question is, then, how the first molecule arose.''

''Yes?''

''The earth was formed when the solar system came into being 4.6 billion years ago. It began as a glowing mass which gradually cooled. This is where modern science believes life began between three and four billion years ago.''

''It sounds totally improbable.''

''Don't say that before you have heard the rest. First of all, our planet was quite different from the way it looks today. Since there was no life, there was no oxygen in the atmosphere. Free oxygen was first formed by the photosynthesis of plants. And the fact that there was no oxygen is important. It is unlikely that life cells—which, again, can form DNA—could have arisen in an atmosphere containing oxygen.''

''Why?''

''Because oxygen is strongly reactive. Long before complex molecules like DNA could be formed, the DNA molecular cells would be oxydized.''

''Really.''

''That is how we know for certain that no *new* life arises today, not even so much as a bacterium or a virus. All life on earth must be exactly the same age. An elephant has just as long a family tree as the smallest bacterium. You could almost say that an elephant—or a human being—is in reality a single coherent colony of monocellular creatures. Because each cell in our body carries the same hereditary material. The whole recipe of who we are lies hidden in each tiny cell.''

''That's an odd thought.''

''One of life's great mysteries is that the cells of a multicellular animal have the ability to specialize their function in spite of the fact that not all the different hereditary characteristics are active in all the cells. Some of these characteristics—or genes—are 'activated' and others are 'deactivated.' A liver cell does not produce the same proteins as a nerve cell or a skin cell. But all three types of cell have the same DNA molecule, which contains the whole recipe for the organism in question.

"Since there was no oxygen in the atmosphere, there was no protective ozone layer around the earth. That means there was nothing to stop the radiation from the cosmos. This is also significant because this radiation was probably instrumental in forming the first complex molecule. Cosmic radiation of this nature was the actual energy which caused the various chemical substances on the earth to start combining into a complicated macromolecule."

"Okay."

"Let me recapitulate: Before such complex molecules, of which all life consists, can be formed, at least two conditions must be present: there must be *no oxygen* in the atmosphere, and there must be access for *cosmic radiation.*"

"I get it."

"In this 'hot little pool'—or primal soup, as it is often called by modern scientists—there was once formed a gigantically complicated macromolecule, which had the wondrous property of being able to subdivide itself into two identical parts. And so the long evolutionary process began, Sophie. If we simplify it a bit, we can say that we are now talking of the first hereditary material, the first DNA or the first living cell. It subdivided itself again and again—but from the very first stage, transmutation was occurring. After aeons of time, one of these monocellular organisms connected with a more complicated multicellular organism. Thus the photosynthesis of plants also began, and in that way the atmosphere came to contain oxygen. This had two results: first, the atmosphere permitted the evolution of animals that could breathe with the aid of lungs. Secondly, the atmosphere protected life from the harmful cosmic radiation. Strangely enough, this radiation, which was probably a vital 'spark' in the formation of the first cell, is also harmful to all forms of life."

"But the atmosphere can't have been formed overnight. How did the earliest forms of life manage?"

"Life began in the primal 'seas'—which are what we mean by primal soup. There it could live protected from the harmful rays. Not until much later, when life in the oceans had formed an atmosphere, did the first amphibians crawl out onto land. The rest is what we have already talked about. And here we are, sitting in a hut in the woods, looking back on a process that has taken three or four billion years. And in us, this long process has finally become aware of itself."

"And yet you don't think it all happened quite accidentally?"

"I never said that. The picture on this board shows that evolution had a *direction*. Across the aeons of time animals have evolved with increasingly complicated nerve systems—and an ever bigger brain. Personally, I don't think that can be accidental. What do you think?"

"It can't be pure chance that created the human eye. Don't you think there is meaning in our being able to see the world around us?"

"Funnily enough, the development of the eye puzzled Darwin too. He couldn't really come to terms with the fact that something as delicate and sensitive as an eye could be exclusively due to natural selection."

Sophie sat looking up at Alberto. She was thinking how odd it was that she should be alive now, and that she only lived this one time and would never again return to life. Suddenly she exclaimed:

> What matters our creative endless toil,
> When, at a snatch, oblivion ends the coil?

Alberto frowned at her.

"You must not talk like that, child. Those are the words of the Devil."

"The Devil?"

"Or Mephistopheles—in Goethe's *Faust*. 'Was soll uns denn das ew'ge Schaffen! Geschaffenes zu nichts hinwegzuraffen!' "

"But what do those words mean exactly?"

"As Faust dies and looks back on his life's work, he says in triumph:

Then to the moment could I say:
Linger you now, you are so fair!
Now records of my earthly day
No flights of aeons can impair—
Foreknowledge comes, and fills me with such bliss,
I take my joy, my highest moment this."

"That was very poetic."

"But then it's the Devil's turn. As soon as Faust dies, he exclaims:

A foolish word, bygone.
How so then, gone?
Gone, to sheer Nothing, past with null made one!
What matters creative endless toil,
When, at a snatch, oblivion ends the coil?
'It is bygone'—How shall this riddle run?
As good as if things never had begun,
Yet circle back, existence to possess:
I'd rather have Eternal Emptiness."

"That's pessimistic. I liked the first passage best. Even though his life was over, Faust saw some meaning in the traces he would leave behind him."

"And is it not also a consequence of Darwin's theory that we are part of something all-encompassing, in which every tiny life form has its significance in the big picture? We are the living planet, Sophie! We are the great vessel sailing around a burning sun in the universe. But each and every one of us is also a ship sailing through life with a cargo of genes. When we have carried this cargo safely to the next harbor—we have not lived in vain. *Thomas Hardy* expresses the same thought in his poem 'Transformations':

Portion of this yew
Is a man my grandsire knew,

Bosomed here at its foot:
This branch may be his wife,
A ruddy human life
Now turned to a green shoot.

These grasses must be made
Of her who often prayed,
Last century, for repose;
And the fair girl long ago
Whom I often tried to know
May be entering this rose.

So, they are not underground,
But as nerves and veins abound
In the growths of upper air,
And they feel the sun and rain,
And the energy again
That made them what they
      were!''

"That's very pretty."
"But we will talk no more. I simply say next chapter!"
"Oh, stop all that irony!"
"New chapter, I said! I shall be obeyed!"

Freud

*... the odious egoistic impulse that had emerged in
her ...*

Hilde Møller Knag jumped out of bed with the bulky
ring binder in her arms. She plonked it down on her
writing desk, grabbed her clothes, and dashed into the
bathroom. She stood under the shower for two minutes,
dressed herself quickly, and ran downstairs.

"Breakfast is ready, Hilde!"

"I just have to go and row first."

"But Hilde . . . !"

She ran out of the house, down the garden, and out
onto the little dock. She untied the boat and jumped
down into it. She rowed around the bay with short angry
strokes until she had calmed down.

"We are the living planet, Sophie! We are the great
vessel sailing around a burning sun in the universe. But
each and every of us is also a ship sailing through life
with a cargo of genes. When we have carried this cargo
safely to the next harbor—we have not lived in
vain . . ."

She knew the passage by heart. It had been written
for her. Not for Sophie, for her. Every word in the ring
binder was written by Dad to Hilde.

She rested the oars in the oarlocks and drew them in.
The boat rocked gently on the water, the ripples slapping
softly against the prow.

And like the little rowboat floating on the surface in

the bay at Lillesand, she herself was just a nutshell on the surface of life.

Where were Sophie and Alberto in this picture? Yes, where were Alberto and Sophie?

She could not fathom that they were no more than "electromagnetic impulses" in her father's brain. She could not fathom, and certainly not accept, that they were only paper and printer's ink from a ribbon in her father's portable typewriter. One might just as well say that she herself was nothing but a conglomeration of protein compounds that had suddenly come to life one day in a "hot little pool." But she was more than that. She was Hilde Møller Knag.

She had to admit that the ring binder was a fantastic present, and that her father had touched the core of something *eternal* in her. But she didn't care for the way he was dealing with Sophie and Alberto.

She would certainly teach him a lesson, even before he got home. She felt she owed it to the two of them. Hilde could already imagine her father at Kastrup Airport, in Copenhagen. She could just see him running around like mad.

Hilde was now quite herself again. She rowed the boat back to the dock, where she was careful to make it fast. After breakfast she sat at the table for a long time with her mother. It felt good to be able to talk about something as ordinary as whether the egg was a trifle too soft.

She did not start to read again until the evening. There were not many pages left now.

Once again there was a knocking on the door.

"Let's just put our hands over our ears," said Alberto, "and perhaps it'll go away."

"No, I want to see who it is."

Alberto followed her to the door.

On the step stood a naked man. He had adopted a very ceremonial posture, but the only thing he had with him was the crown on his head.

"Well?" he said. "What do you good people think of the Emperor's new clothes?"

Alberto and Sophie were utterly dumbfounded. This caused the naked man some consternation.

"What? You are not bowing!" he cried.

"Indeed, that is true," said Alberto, "but the Emperor is stark naked."

The naked man maintained his ceremonial posture. Alberto bent over and whispered in Sophie's ear:

"He thinks he is respectable."

At this, the man scowled.

"Is some kind of censorship being exercised on these premises?" he asked.

"Regrettably," said Alberto. "In here we are both alert and of sound mind in every way. In the Emperor's shameless condition he can therefore not cross the threshold of this house."

Sophie found the naked man's pomposity so absurd that she burst out laughing. As if her laughter had been a prearranged signal, the man with the crown on his head suddenly became aware that he was naked. Covering his private parts with both hands, he bounded toward the nearest clump of trees and disappeared, probably to join company with Adam and Eve, Noah, Little Red Ridinghood, and Winnie-the-Pooh.

Alberto and Sophie remained standing on the step, laughing.

At last Alberto said, "It might be a good idea if we went inside. I'm going to tell you about Freud and his theory of the unconscious."

They seated themselves by the window again. Sophie looked at her watch and said: "It's already half past two and I have a lot to do before the garden party."

"So have I. We'll just say a few words about *Sigmund Freud*."

"Was he a philosopher?"

"We could describe him as a cultural philosopher, at least. Freud was born in 1856 and he studied medicine at the University of Vienna. He lived in Vienna for the greater part of his life at a period when the cultural life of the city was flourishing. He specialized early on in neurology. Toward the close of the last century, and far into our own, he developed his 'depth psychology' or *psychoanalysis*."

"You're going to explain this, right?"

"Psychoanalysis is a description of the human mind in general as well as a therapy for nervous and mental disorders. I do not intend to give you a complete picture either of Freud or of his work. But his theory of the unconscious is necessary to an understanding of what a human being is."

"You intrigue me. Go on."

"Freud held that there is a constant tension between man and his surroundings. In particular, a tension—or conflict—between his drives and needs and the demands of society. It is no exaggeration to say that Freud discovered human drives. This makes him an important exponent of the naturalistic currents that were so prominent toward the end of the nineteenth century."

"What do you mean by human drives?"

"Our actions are not always guided by reason. Man is not really such a rational creature as the eighteenth-century rationalists liked to think. Irrational impulses often determine what we think, what we dream, and what we do. Such irrational impulses can be an expression of basic drives or needs. The human sexual drive, for example, is just as basic as the baby's instinct to suckle."

"Yes?"

"This in itself was no new discovery. But Freud showed that these basic needs can be disguised or 'sublimated,' thereby steering our actions without our being aware of it. He also showed that infants have some sort of sexuality. The respectable middle-class Viennese reacted with abhorrence to this suggestion of the 'sexuality of the child' and made him very unpopular."

"I'm not surprised."

"We call it Victorianism, when everything to do with sexuality is taboo. Freud first became aware of children's sexuality during his practice of psychotherapy. So he had an empirical basis for his claims. He had also seen how numerous forms of neurosis or psychological disorders could be traced back to conflicts during childhood. He gradually developed a type of therapy that we could call the archeology of the soul."

"What do you mean by that?"

"An archeologist searches for traces of the distant past by digging through layers of cultural history. He may find a knife from the eighteenth century. Deeper in the ground he may find a comb from the fourteenth century—and even deeper down perhaps an urn from the fifth century B.C."

"Yes?"

"In a similar way, the psychoanalyst, with the patient's help, can dig deep into the patient's mind and bring to light the experiences that have caused the patient's psychological disorder, since according to Freud, we store the memory of all our experiences deep inside us."

"Yes, I see."

"The analyst can perhaps discover an unhappy experience that the patient has tried to suppress for many years, but which has nevertheless lain buried, gnawing away at the patient's resources. By bringing a 'traumatic experience' into the conscious mind—and holding it up to the patient, so to speak—he or she can help the patient 'be done with it,' and get well again."

"That sounds logical."

"But I am jumping too far ahead. Let us first take a look at Freud's description of the human mind. Have you ever seen a newborn baby?"

"I have a cousin who is four."

"When we come into the world, we live out our physical and mental needs quite directly and unashamedly. If we do not get milk, we cry, or maybe we cry if we have a wet diaper. We also give direct expression to our desire for physical contact and body warmth. Freud called this 'pleasure principle' in us the *id*. As newborn babies we are hardly anything but id."

"Go on."

"We carry the id, or pleasure principle, with us into adulthood and throughout life. But gradually we learn to regulate our desires and adjust to our surroundings. We learn to regulate the pleasure principle in relation to the 'reality principle.' In Freud's terms, we develop an *ego* which has this regulative function. Even though we want or need something, we cannot just lie down and scream until we get what we want or need."

"No, obviously."

"We may desire something very badly that the outside world will not accept. We may *repress* our desires. That means we try to push them away and forget about them."

"I see."

"However, Freud proposed, and worked with, a third element in the human mind. From infancy we are constantly faced with the moral demands of our parents and of society. When we do anything wrong, our parents say 'Don't do that!' or 'Naughty naughty, that's bad!' Even when we are grown up, we retain the echo of such moral demands and judgments. It seems as though the world's moral expectations have become part of us. Freud called this the *superego*."

"Is that another word for conscience?"

"Conscience is a component of the superego. But Freud claimed that the superego tells us when our desires themselves are 'bad' or 'improper,' not least in the case of erotic or sexual desire. And as I said, Freud claimed that these 'improper' desires already manifest themselves at an early stage of childhood."

"How?"

"Nowadays we know that infants like touching their sex organs. We can observe this on any beach. In Freud's time, this behavior could result in a slap over the fingers of the two- or three-year-old, perhaps accompanied by the mother saying, 'Naughty!' or 'Don't do that!' or 'Keep your hands on top of the covers!' "

"How sick!"

"That's the beginning of guilt feelings about everything connected with the sex organs and sexuality. Because this guilt feeling remains in the superego, many people—according to Freud, most people—feel guilty about sex all their lives. At the same time he showed that sexual desires and needs are natural and vital for human beings. And thus, my dear Sophie, the stage is set for a lifelong conflict between desire and guilt."

"Don't you think the conflict has died down a lot since Freud's time?"

"Most certainly. But many of Freud's patients experienced the conflict so acutely that they developed what Freud called *neuroses*. One of his many women patients, for example, was secretly in love with her brother-in-law. When her sister died of an illness, she thought: 'Now he is free to marry me!' This thought was on course for a frontal collision with her superego, and was so monstrous an idea that she immediately repressed it, Freud tells us. In other words, she buried it deep in her unconscious. Freud wrote: 'The young girl was ill and displaying severe hysterical symptoms. When I began treating her it appeared that she had thoroughly forgotten about the scene at her sister's bedside and the odious egoistic impulse that had emerged in her. But during analysis she remembered it, and in a state of great agitation she reproduced the pathogenic moment and through this treatment became cured.' "

"Now I better understand what you meant by an archeology of the soul."

"So we can give a general description of the human psyche. After many years of experience in treating patients, Freud concluded that the *conscious* constitutes only a small part of the human mind. The conscious is like the tip of the iceberg above sea level. Below sea level—or below the threshold of the conscious—is the 'subconscious,' or the *unconscious*."

"So the unconscious is everything that's inside us that we have forgotten and don't remember?"

"We don't have all our experiences consciously present all the time. But the kinds of things we have thought or experienced, and which we can recall if we 'put our mind to it,' Freud termed the preconscious. He reserved the term 'unconscious' for things we have repressed. That is, the sort of thing we have made an effort to forget because it was either 'unpleasant,' 'improper,' or 'nasty.' If we have desires and urges that are not tolerable to the conscious, the superego shoves them downstairs. Away with them!"

"I get it."

"This mechanism is at work in all healthy people. But it

can be such a tremendous strain for some people to keep the unpleasant or forbidden thoughts away from consciousness that it leads to mental illness. Whatever is repressed in this way will try of its own accord to reenter consciousness. For some people it takes a great effort to keep such impulses under the critical eye of the conscious. When Freud was in America in 1909 lecturing on psychoanalysis, he gave an example of the way this repression mechanism functions."

"I'd like to hear that!"

"He said: 'Suppose that here in this hall and in this audience, whose exemplary stillness and attention I cannot sufficiently commend, there is an individual who is creating a disturbance, and, by his ill-bred laughing, talking, by scraping his feet, distracts my attention from my task. I explain that I cannot go on with my lecture under these conditions, and thereupon several strong men among you get up and, after a short struggle, eject the disturber of the peace from the hall. He is now *repressed*, and I can continue my lecture. But in order that the disturbance may not be repeated, in case the man who has just been thrown out attempts to force his way back into the room, the gentlemen who have executed my suggestion take their chairs to the door and establish themselves there as a *resistance*, to keep up the repression. Now, if you transfer both locations to the psyche, calling this *consciousness*, and the outside the *unconscious*, you have a tolerably good illustration of the process of repression.' "

"I agree."

"But the disturber of the peace insists on reentering, Sophie. At least, that's the way it is with repressed thoughts and urges. We live under the constant pressure of repressed thoughts that are trying to fight their way up from the unconscious. That's why we often say or do things without intending to. Unconscious reactions thus prompt our feelings and actions."

"Can you give me an example?"

"Freud operates with several of these mechanisms. One is what he called *parapraxes*—slips of the tongue or pen. In other words, we accidentally say or do things that we once tried to repress. Freud gives the example of the shop foreman who was to propose a toast to the boss. The trouble was that this boss was terribly unpopular. In plain words, he was what one might call a swine."

"Yes?"

"The foreman stood up, raised his glass, and said 'Here's to the swine!' "

"I'm speechless!"

"So was the foreman. He had actually only said what he really meant. But he didn't mean to say it. Do you want to hear another example?"

"Yes, please."

"A bishop was coming to tea with the local minister, who had a large family of nice well-behaved little daughters. This bishop happened to have an unusually big nose. The little girls were duly instructed that on no account were they to refer to the bishop's nose, since children often blurt out spontaneous remarks about people because their repressive mechanism is not yet developed. The bishop arrived, and the delightful daughters strained themselves to the utmost not to comment on his nose. They tried to not even look at it and to forget about it. But they were thinking about it the whole time. And then one of them was asked to pass the sugar around. She looked at the distinguished bishop and said, 'Do you take sugar in your nose?' "

"How awful!"

"Another thing we can do is to *rationalize*. That means that we do not give the real reason for what we are doing either to ourselves or to other people because the real reason is unacceptable."

"Like what?"

"I could hypnotize you to open a window. While you are under hypnosis I tell you that when I begin to drum my fingers on the table you will get up and open the window. I drum on the table—and you open the window. Afterward I ask you why you opened the window and you might say you did it because it was too hot. But that is not the real reason. You are reluctant to admit to yourself that you did something under my hypnotic orders. So you rationalize."

"Yes, I see."

"We all encounter that sort of thing practically every day."

"This four-year-old cousin of mine, I don't think he has a lot of playmates, so he's always happy when I visit. One day I told him I had to hurry home to my mom. Do you know what he said?"

"What did he say?"

"He said, she's stupid!"

"Yes, that was definitely a case of rationalizing. The boy didn't mean what he actually said. He meant it was stupid you had to go, but he was too shy to say so. Another thing we do is *project.*"

"What's that?"

"When we project, we transfer the characteristics we are trying to repress in ourselves onto other people. A person who is very miserly, for example, will characterize others as penny-pinchers. And someone who will not admit to being preoccupied with sex can be the first to be incensed at other people's sex-fixation."

"Hmm."

"Freud claimed that our everyday life was filled with unconscious mechanisms like these. We forget a particular person's name, we fumble with our clothes while we talk, or we shift what appear to be random objects around in the room. We also stumble over words and make various slips of the tongue or pen that can seem completely innocent. Freud's point was that these slips are neither as accidental nor as innocent as we think. These bungled actions can in fact reveal the most intimate secrets."

"From now on I'll watch all my words very carefully."

"Even if you do, you won't be able to escape from your unconscious impulses. The art is precisely not to expend too much effort on burying unpleasant things in the unconscious. It's like trying to block up the entrance to a water vole's nest. You can be sure the water vole will pop up in another part of the garden. It is actually quite healthy to leave the door ajar between the conscious and the unconscious."

"If you lock that door you can get mentally sick, right?"

"Yes. A neurotic is just such a person, who uses too much energy trying to keep the 'unpleasant' out of his consciousness. Frequently there is a particular experience which the person is desperately trying to repress. He can nonetheless be anxious for the doctor to help him to find his way back to the hidden traumas."

"How does the doctor do that?"

"Freud developed a technique which he called *free association*. In other words, he let the patient lie in a relaxed position and just talk about whatever came into his or her mind—however irrelevant, random, unpleasant, or embarrassing it might sound. The idea was to break through the 'lid' or 'control' that had grown over the traumas, because it was these traumas that were causing the patient concern. They are active all the time, just not consciously."

"The harder you try to forget something, the more you think about it unconsciously?"

"Exactly. That is why it is so important to be aware of the signals from the unconscious. According to Freud, the royal road to the unconscious is our dreams. His main work was written on this subject—*The Interpretation of Dreams*, published in 1900, in which he showed that our dreams are not random. Our unconscious tries to communicate with our conscious through dreams."

"Go on."

"After many years of experience with patients—and not least after having analyzed his own dreams—Freud determined that all dreams are *wish fulfillments*. This is clearly observable in children, he said. They dream about ice cream and cherries. But in adults, the wishes that are to be fulfilled in dreams are disguised. That is because even when we sleep, censorship is at work on what we will permit ourselves. And although this censorship, or repression mechanism, is considerably weaker when we are asleep than when we are awake, it is still strong enough to cause our dreams to distort the wishes we cannot acknowledge."

"Which is why dreams have to be interpreted."

"Freud showed that we must distinguish between the actual dream as we recall it in the morning and the real meaning of the dream. He termed the actual dream image—that is, the 'film' or 'video' we dream—the *manifest dream.* This 'apparent' dream content always takes its material or scenario from the previous day. But the dream also contains a deeper meaning which is hidden from consciousness. Freud called this the *latent dream thoughts,* and these hidden thoughts which the dream is really about may stem from the distant past, from earliest childhood, for instance.''

"So we have to analyze the dream before we can understand it.''

"Yes, and for the mentally ill, this must be done in conjunction with the therapist. But it is not the doctor who interprets the dream. He can only do it with the help of the patient. In this situation, the doctor simply fulfills the function of a Socratic 'midwife,' assisting during the interpretation.''

"I see.''

"The actual process of converting the latent dream thoughts to the manifest dream aspect was termed by Freud the *dream work.* We might call it 'masking' or 'coding' what the dream is actually about. In interpreting the dream, we must go through the reverse process and unmask or decode the *motif* to arrive at its theme.''

"Can you give me an example?''

"Freud's book teems with examples. But we can construct a simple and very Freudian example for ourselves. Let us say a young man dreams that he is given two balloons by his female cousin . . .''

"Yes?''

"Go on, try to interpret the dream yourself.''

"Hmm . . . there is a manifest dream, just like you said: a young man gets two balloons from his female cousin.''

"Carry on.''

"You said the scenario is always from the previous day. So he had been to the fair the day before—or maybe he saw a picture of balloons in the newspaper.''

"It's possible, but he need only have seen the word 'balloon,' or something that reminded him of a balloon.''

"But what are the latent dream thoughts that the dream is really about?''

"You're the interpreter.''

"Maybe he just wanted a couple of balloons.''

"No, that won't work. You're right about the dream being a wish fulfillment. But a young man would hardly have an ardent wish for a couple of balloons. And if he had, he wouldn't need to dream about them."

"I think I've got it: he really wants his cousin—and the two balloons are her breasts."

"Yes, that's a much more likely explanation. And it presupposes that he experienced his wish as an embarrassment."

"In a way, our dreams make a lot of detours?"

"Yes. Freud believed that the dream was a 'disguised fulfillment of a repressed wish.' But exactly *what* we have repressed can have changed considerably since Freud was a doctor in Vienna. However, the mechanism of disguised dream content can still be intact."

"Yes, I see."

"Freud's psychoanalysis was extremely important in the 1920s, especially for the treatment of certain psychiatric patients. His theory of the unconscious was also very significant for art and literature."

"Artists became interested in people's unconscious mental life?"

"Exactly so, although this had already become a predominant aspect of literature in the last decade of the nineteenth century—before Freud's psychoanalysis was known. It merely shows that the appearance of Freud's psychoanalysis at that particular time, the 1890s, was no coincidence."

"You mean it was in the spirit of the times?"

"Freud himself did not claim to have discovered phenomena such as repression, defense mechanisms, or rationalizing. He was simply the first to apply these human experiences to psychiatry. He was also a master at illustrating his theories with literary examples. But as I mentioned, from the 1920s, Freud's psychoanalysis had a more direct influence on art and literature."

"In what sense?"

"Poets and painters, especially the surrealists, attempted to exploit the power of the unconscious in their work."

"What are surrealists?"

"The word surrealism comes from the French, and means 'super realism.' In 1924 *André Breton* published a 'surrealistic manifesto,' claiming that art should come from the unconscious. The artist should thus derive the freest possible inspiration from his dream images and strive toward a 'super realism,' in which the boundaries between dream and reality were dissolved. For an artist too it can be necessary to break the censorship of the conscious and let words and images have free play."

"I can see that."

"In a sense, Freud demonstrated that there is an artist in everyone. A dream is, after all, a little work of art, and there are new dreams every night. In order to interpret his patients' dreams, Freud often had to work his way through a dense language of symbols—rather in the way we interpret a picture or a literary text."

"And we dream every single night?"

"Recent research shows that we dream for about twenty percent of our sleeping hours, that is, between one and two hours each night. If we are disturbed during our dream phases we become nervous and irritable. This means nothing less than that everybody has an innate need to give artistic expression to his or her existential situation. After all, it is ourselves that our dreams are about. We are the directors, we set up the scenario and play all the roles. A person who says he doesn't understand art doesn't know himself very well."

"I see that."

"Freud also delivered impressive evidence of the wonders of the human mind. His work with patients convinced him that we retain everything we have seen and experienced somewhere deep in our consciousness, and all these impressions can be brought to light again. When we experience a memory lapse, and a bit later 'have it on the tip of our tongue' and then later still 'suddenly remember it,' we are talking about something which has lain in the unconscious and suddenly slips through the half-open door to consciousness."

"But it takes a while sometimes."

"All artists are aware of that. But then suddenly it's as if all doors and all drawers fly open. Everything comes tumbling out by itself, and we can find all the words and images we need. This is when we have 'lifted the lid' of the unconscious. We can call it *inspiration*, Sophie. It feels as if what we are drawing or writing is coming from some outside source."

"It must be a wonderful feeling."

"But you must have experienced it yourself. You can frequently observe inspiration at work in children who are overtired. They are sometimes so extremely overtired that they seem to be wide awake. Suddenly they start telling a story—as if they are finding words they haven't yet learned. They have, though; the words and the ideas have lain 'latent' in their consciousness, but now, when all caution and all censorship have let go, they are surfacing. It can also be important for an artist not to let reason and reflection control a more or less unconscious expression. Shall I tell you a little story to illustrate this?"

"Sure."

"It's a very serious and a very sad story."

"Okay."

"Once upon a time there was a centipede that was amazingly good at dancing with all hundred legs. All the creatures of the forest gathered to watch every time the centipede danced, and they were all duly impressed by the exquisite dance. But there was one creature that didn't like watching the centipede dance—that was a tortoise."

"It was probably just envious."

"How can I get the centipede to stop dancing? thought the tortoise. He couldn't just say he didn't like the dance. Neither could he say he danced better himself, that would obviously be untrue. So he devised a fiendish plan."

"Let's hear it."

"He sat down and wrote a letter to the centipede. 'O incomparable centipede,' he wrote, 'I am a devoted admirer of your exquisite dancing. I must know how you go about it when you dance. Is it that you lift your left leg number 28 and then your right leg number 39? Or do you begin by lifting your right leg number 17 before you lift your left leg number 44? I await your answer in breathless anticipation. Yours truly, Tortoise."

"How mean!"

"When the centipede read the letter, she immediately began to think about what she actually did when she danced. Which leg did she lift first? And which leg next? What do you think happened in the end?"

"The centipede never danced again?"

"That's exactly what happened. And that's the way it goes when imagination gets strangled by reasoned deliberation."

"That was a sad story."

"It is important for an artist to be able to 'let go.' The surrealists tried to exploit this by putting themselves into a state where things just happened by themselves. They had a sheet of white paper in front of them and they began to write without thinking about what they wrote. They called it *automatic writing*. The expression originally comes from spiritualism, where a medium believed that a departed spirit was guiding the pen. But I thought we would talk more about that kind of thing tomorrow."

"I'd like that."

"In one sense, the surrealist artist is also a medium, that is to say, a means or a link. He is a medium of his own unconscious. But perhaps there is an element of the unconscious in every creative process, for what do we actually mean by creativity?"

"I've no idea. Isn't it when you create something?"

"Fair enough, and that happens in a delicate interplay between imagination and reason. But all too frequently, reason throttles the imagination, and that's serious because without imagination, nothing really new will ever be created. I believe imagination is like a Darwinian system."

"I'm sorry, but *that* I didn't get."

"Well, Darwinism holds that nature's mutants arise one after the other, but only a few of them can be used. Only some of them get the right to live."

"So?"

"That's how it is when we have an inspiration and get masses of new ideas. Thought-mutants occur in the consciousness one after the other, at least if we refrain from censoring ourselves too much. But only some of these thoughts can be used. Here, reason comes into its own.

It, too, has a vital function. When the day's catch is laid on the table we must not forget to be selective."

"That's not a bad comparison."

"Imagine if everything that 'strikes us' were allowed to pass our lips! Not to speak of jumping off our notepads out of our desk drawers! The world would sink under the weight of casual impulses and no selection would have taken place."

"So it's reason that chooses between all these ideas?"

"Yes, don't you think so? Maybe the imagination creates what is new, but the imagination does not make the actual selection. The imagination does not 'compose.' A composition—and every work of art is one—is created in a wondrous interplay between imagination and reason, or between mind and reflection. For there will always be an element of chance in the creative process. You have to turn the sheep loose before you can start to herd them."

Alberto sat quite still, staring out of the window. While he sat there, Sophie suddenly noticed a crowd of brightly colored Disney figures down by the lake.

"There's Goofy," she exclaimed, "and Donald Duck and his nephews . . . Look, Alberto. There's Mickey Mouse and . . ."

He turned toward her: "Yes, it's very sad, child."

"What do you mean?"

"Here we are being made the helpless victims of the major's flock of sheep. But it's my own fault, of course. I was the one who started talking about free association of ideas."

"You certainly don't have to blame yourself . . ."

"I was going to say something about the importance of imagination to us philosophers. In order to think new thoughts, we must be bold enough to let ourselves go. But right now, he's going a bit far."

"Don't worry about it."

"I was about to mention the importance of reflection, and here we are, presented with this lurid imbecility. He should be ashamed of himself!"

"Are you being ironic now?"

"It's *he* who is ironic, not me. But I have one comfort—

and that is the whole cornerstone of my plan."

"Now I'm really confused."

"We have talked about dreams. There's a touch of irony about that too. For what are we but the major's dream images?"

"Ah!"

"But there is still one thing he hasn't counted on."

"What's that?"

"Maybe he is embarrassingly aware of his own dream. He is aware of everything we say and do—just as the dreamer remembers the dream's manifest dream aspect. It is he who wields it with his pen. But even if he remembers everything we say to each other, he is still not quite awake."

"What do you mean?"

"He does not know the latent dream thoughts, Sophie. He forgets that this too is a disguised dream."

"You are talking so strangely."

"The major thinks so too. That is because he does not understand his own dream language. Let us be thankful for that. That gives us a tiny bit of elbow room, you see. And with this elbow room we shall soon fight our way out of his muddy consciousness like water voles frisking about in the sun on a summer's day."

"Do you think we'll make it?"

"We must. Within a couple of days I shall give you a new horizon. Then the major will no longer know where the water voles are or where they will pop up next time."

"But even if we are only dream images, I am still my mother's daughter. And it's five o'clock. I have to go home to Captain's Bend and prepare for the garden party."

"Hmm . . . can you do me a small favor on the way home?"

"What?"

"Try to attract a little extra attention. Try to get the major to keep his eye on you all the way home. Try and think about him when you get home—and he'll think about you too."

"What good will that do?"

"Then I can carry on undisturbed with my work on the secret plan. I'm going to dive down into the major's unconscious. That's where I'll be until we meet again."

Our Own Time

∞

. . . man is condemned to be free . . .

The alarm clock showed 11:55 p.m. Hilde lay staring at the ceiling. She tried to let her associations flow freely. Each time she finished a chain of thoughts, she tried to ask herself why.

Could there be something she was trying to repress?

If only she could have set aside all censorship, she might have slid into a waking dream. A bit scary, she thought.

The more she relaxed and opened herself to random thoughts and images, the more she felt as if she was in the major's cabin by the little lake in the woods.

What could Alberto be planning? Of course, it was Hilde's father planning that Alberto was planning something. Did he already know what Alberto would do? Perhaps he was trying to give himself free rein, so that whatever happened in the end would come as a surprise to him too.

There were not many pages left now. Should she take a peek at the last page? No, that would be cheating. And besides, Hilde was convinced that it was far from decided what was to happen on the last page.

Wasn't that a curious thought? The ring binder was right here and her father could not possibly get back in time to add anything to it. Not unless Alberto did something on his own. A surprise . . .

Hilde had a few surprises up her own sleeve, in any

case. Her father did not control her. But was she in full
control of herself?

What was consciousness? Wasn't it one of the greatest
riddles of the universe? What was memory? What made
us ''remember'' everything we had seen and experienced?

What kind of mechanism made us create fabulous
dreams night after night?

She closed her eyes from time to time. Then she
opened them and stared at the ceiling again. At last she
forgot to open them.

She was asleep.

When the raucous scream of a seagull woke her, Hilde
got out of bed. As usual, she crossed the room to the
window and stood looking out across the bay. It had
gotten to be a habit, summer and winter.

As she stood there, she suddenly felt a myriad of colors exploding in her head. She remembered what she
had dreamt. But it felt like more than an ordinary dream,
with its vivid colors and shapes . . .

She had dreamt that her father came home from Lebanon, and the whole dream was an extension of Sophie's
dream when she found the gold crucifix on the dock.

Hilde was sitting on the edge of the dock—exactly as
in Sophie's dream. Then she heard a very soft voice
whispering, ''My name is Sophie!'' Hilde had stayed
where she was, sitting very still, trying to hear where
the voice was coming from. It continued, an almost in-
audible rustling, as if an insect were speaking to her:
''You must be both deaf and blind!'' Just then her father
had come into the garden in his UN uniform. ''Hilde!''
he shouted. Hilde ran up to him and threw her arms
around his neck. That's where the dream ended.

She remembered some lines of a poem by Arnulf
Øverland:

Wakened one night by a curious dream
and a voice that seemed to be speaking to me
like a far-off subterranean stream,
I rose and asked: What do you want of me?

She was still standing at the window when her mother came in.

"Hi there! Are you already awake?"

"I'm not sure . . ."

"I'll be home around four, as usual."

"Okay, Mom."

"Have a nice vacation day, Hilde!"

"You have a good day too."

When she heard her mother slam the front door, she slipped back into bed with the ring binder.

"I'm going to dive down into the major's unconscious. That's where I'll be until we meet again."

There, yes. Hilde started reading again. She could feel under her right index finger that there were only a few pages left.

When Sophie left the major's cabin, she could still see some of the Disney figures at the water's edge, but they seemed to dissolve as she approached them. By the time she reached the boat they had all disappeared.

While she was rowing she made faces, and after she had pulled the boat up into the reeds on the other side she waved her arms about. She was working desperately to hold the major's attention so that Alberto could sit undisturbed in the cabin.

She danced along the path, hopping and skipping. Then she tried walking like a mechanical doll. To keep the major interested she began to sing as well. At one point she stood still, pondering what Alberto's plan could be. Catching herself, she got such a bad conscience that she started to climb a tree.

Sophie climbed as high as she could. When she was nearly at the top, she realized she could not get down. She decided to wait a little before trying again. But meanwhile she could not just stay quietly where she was. Then the major would get tired of watching her and would begin to interest himself in what Alberto was doing.

Sophie waved her arms, tried to crow like a rooster a couple of times, and finally began to yodel. It was the first time in her fifteen-year-old life that Sophie had yodeled.

All things considered, she was quite pleased with the result.

She tried once more to climb down but she was truly stuck. Suddenly a huge goose landed on one of the branches Sophie was clinging to. Having recently seen a whole swarm of Disney figures, Sophie was not in the least surprised when the goose began to speak.

"My name is Morten," said the goose. "Actually, I'm a tame goose, but on this special occasion I have flown up from Lebanon with the wild geese. You look as if you could use some help getting down from this tree."

"You are much too small to help me," said Sophie.

"You are jumping to conclusions, young lady. It is you who are too big."

"It's the same thing, isn't it?"

"I would have you know I carried a peasant boy exactly your age all over Sweden. His name was Nils Holgersson."

"I am fifteen."

"And Nils was fourteen. A year one way or the other makes no difference to the freight."

"How did you manage to lift him?"

"I gave him a little slap and he passed out. When he woke up, he was no bigger than a thumb."

"Perhaps you could give me a little slap too, because I can't sit up here forever. And I'm giving a philosophical garden party on Saturday."

"That's interesting. I presume this is a philosophy book, then. When I was flying over Sweden with Nils Holgersson, we touched down on Mårbacka in Värmland, where Nils met an old woman who was planning to write a book about Sweden for schoolchildren. It was to be both instructive and true, she said. When she heard about Nils's adventures, she decided to write a book about all the things he had seen on gooseback."

"That was very strange."

"To tell you the truth it was rather ironic, because we were already in that book."

Suddenly Sophie felt something slap her cheek and the next minute she had become no bigger than a thumb. The tree was like a whole forest and the goose was as big as a horse.

"Come on, then," said the goose.

Sophie walked along the branch and climbed up on the goose's back. Its feathers were soft, but now that she was so small, they pricked her more than they tickled.

As soon as she had settled comfortably the goose took off. They flew high above the treetops. Sophie looked down at the lake and the major's cabin. Inside sat Alberto, laying his devious plans.

"A short sightseeing tour will have to be sufficient today," said the goose, flapping its wings again and again.

With that, it flew in to land at the foot of the tree which Sophie had so recently begun to climb. As the goose touched down Sophie tumbled onto the ground. After rolling around in the heather a few times, she sat up. She realized with amazement that she was her full size again.

The goose waddled around her a few times.

"Thanks a lot for your help," said Sophie.

"It was a mere bagatelle. Did you say this was a philosophy book?"

"No, that's what you said."

"Oh well, it's all the same. If it had been up to me, I would have liked to fly you through the whole history of philosophy just as I flew Nils Holgersson through Sweden. We could have circled over Miletus and Athens, Jerusalem and Alexandria, Rome and Florence, London and Paris, Jena and Heidelberg, Berlin and Copenhagen . . ."

"Thanks, that's enough."

"But flying across the centuries would have been a hefty job even for a very ironic goose. Crossing the Swedish provinces is far easier."

So saying, the goose ran a few steps and flapped itself into the air.

Sophie was exhausted, but when she crawled out of the den into the garden a little later she thought Alberto would have been well pleased with her diversionary maneuvers. The major could not have thought much about Alberto during the past hour. If he did, he had to have a severe case of split personality.

Sophie had just walked in the front door when her mother came home from work. That saved her having to describe her rescue from a tall tree by a tame goose.

After dinner they began to get everything ready for the garden party. They brought a four-meter-long table top and trestles from the attic and carried it into the garden.

They had planned to set out the long table under the fruit trees. The last time they had used the trestle table had been on Sophie's parents' tenth anniversary. Sophie was only eight years old at the time, but she clearly remembered the big outdoor party with all their friends and relatives.

The weather report was as good as it could be. There had not been as much as a drop of rain since that horrid thunderstorm the day before Sophie's birthday. Nevertheless they decided to leave the actual table setting and decorating until Saturday morning.

Later that evening they baked two different kinds of bread. They were going to serve chicken and salad. And sodas. Sophie was worried that some of the boys in her class would bring beer. If there was one thing she was afraid of it was trouble.

As Sophie was going to bed, her mother asked her once again if Alberto was coming to the party.

"Of course he's coming. He has even promised to do a philosophical trick."

"A philosophical trick? What kind of trick is that?"

"No idea . . . if he were a magician, he would have done a magic trick. He would probably have pulled a white rabbit out of a hat . . ."

"What, again?"

"But since he's a philosopher, he's going to do a philosophical trick instead. After all, it is a philosophical garden party. Are you planning to do something too?"

"Actually, I am."

"A speech?"

"I'm not telling. Good night, Sophie!"

Early the next morning Sophie was woken up by her mother, who came in to say goodbye before she went to work. She gave Sophie a list of last-minute things to buy in town for the garden party.

The minute her mother had left the house, the telephone rang. It was Alberto. He had obviously found out exactly when Sophie was home alone.

"How is your secret coming along?"

"Ssh! Not a word. Don't even give him the chance to think about it."

"I think I held his attention yesterday."

"Good."

"Is the philosophy course finished?"

"That's why I'm calling. We're already in our own century. From now on you should be able to orient yourself on your own. The foundations were the most important. But we must nevertheless meet for a short talk about our own time."

"But I have to go to town . . ."

"That's excellent. I said it was our own time we had to talk about."

"Really?"

"So it would be most practical to meet in town, I mean."

"Shall I come to your place?"

"No, no, not here. Everything's a mess. I've been hunting for hidden microphones."

"Ah!"

"There's a café that's just opened at the Main Square. Café Pierre. Do you know it?"

"Yes. When shall I be there?"

"Can we meet at twelve?"

"Okay. Bye!"

At a couple of minutes past twelve Sophie walked into Café Pierre. It was one of those new fashionable places with little round tables and black chairs, upturned vermouth bottles in dispensers, baguettes, and sandwiches.

The room was small, and the first thing Sophie noticed was that Alberto was not there. A lot of other people were sitting at the round tables, but Sophie saw only that Alberto was not among them.

She was not in the habit of going into cafés on her own. Should she just turn around and leave, and come back later to see if he had arrived?

She ordered a cup of lemon tea at the marble bar and

sat down at one of the vacant tables. She stared at the door. People came and went all the time, but there was still no Alberto.

If only she had a newspaper!

As time passed, she started to look around. She got a couple of glances in return. For a moment Sophie felt like a young woman. She was only fifteen, but she could certainly have passed for seventeen—or at least, sixteen and a half.

She wondered what all these people thought about being alive. They looked as though they had simply dropped in, as though they had just sat down here by chance. They were all talking away, gesticulating vehemently, but it didn't look as though they were talking about anything that mattered.

She suddenly came to think of Kierkegaard, who had said that what characterized the crowd most was their idle chatter. Were all these people living at the aesthetic stage? Or was there something that was existentially important to them?

In one of his early letters to her Alberto had talked about the similarity between children and philosophers. She realized again that she was afraid of becoming an adult. Suppose she too ended up crawling deep down into the fur of the white rabbit that was pulled out of the universe's top hat!

She kept her eyes on the door. Suddenly Alberto walked in. Although it was midsummer, he was wearing a black beret and a gray hip-length coat of herringbone tweed. He hurried over to her. It felt very strange to meet him in public.

"It's quarter past twelve!"

"It's what is known as the academic quarter of an hour. Would you like a snack?"

He sat down and looked into her eyes. Sophie shrugged.

"Sure. A sandwich, maybe."

Alberto went up to the counter. He soon returned with a cup of coffee and two baguette sandwiches with cheese and ham.

"Was it expensive?"

"A bagatelle, Sophie."

"Do you have any excuse at all for being late?"

"No. I did it on purpose. I'll explain why presently."

He took a few large bites of his sandwich. Then he said:

"Let's talk about our own century."

"Has anything of philosophical interest happened?"

"Lots . . . movements are going off in all directions. We'll start with one very important direction, and that is *existentialism*. This is a collective term for several philosophical currents that take man's existential situation as their point of departure. We generally talk of twentieth-century existential philosophy. Several of these existential philosophers, or existentialists, based their ideas not only on Kierkegaard, but on Hegel and Marx as well."

"Uh-huh."

"Another important philosopher who had a great influence on the twentieth century was the German *Friedrich Nietzsche*, who lived from 1844 to 1900. He, too, reacted against Hegel's philosophy and the German 'historicism.' He proposed life itself as a counterweight to the anemic interest in history and what he called the Christian 'slave morality.' He sought to effect a 'revaluation of all values,' so that the life force of the strongest should not be hampered by the weak. According to Nietzsche, both Christianity and traditional philosophy had turned away from the real world and pointed toward 'heaven' or 'the world of ideas.' But what had hitherto been considered the 'real' world was in fact a pseudo world. 'Be true to the world,' he said. 'Do not listen to those who offer you supernatural expectations.' "

"So . . . ?"

"A man who was influenced by both Kierkegaard and Nietzsche was the German existential philosopher *Martin Heidegger*. But we are going to concentrate on the French existentialist *Jean-Paul Sartre*, who lived from 1905 to 1980. He was the leading light among the existentialists—at least, to the broader public. His existentialism became especially popular in the forties, just after the war. Later on he allied himself with the Marxist movement in France, but he never became a member of any party."

"Is that why we are meeting in a French café?"

"It was not quite accidental, I confess. Sartre himself spent a lot of time in cafés. He met his life-long companion *Simone de Beauvoir* in a café. She was also an existential philosopher."

"A woman philosopher?"

"That's right."

"What a relief that humanity is finally becoming civilized."

"Nevertheless, many new problems have arisen in our own time."

"You were going to talk about existentialism."

"Sartre said that 'existentialism is humanism.' By that he meant that the existentialists start from nothing but humanity itself. I might add that the humanism he was referring to took a far bleaker view of the human situation than the humanism we met in the Renaissance."

"Why was that?"

"Both Kierkegaard and some of this century's existential philosophers were Christian. But Sartre's allegiance was to what we might call an atheistic existentialism. His philosophy can be seen as a merciless analysis of the human situation when 'God is dead.' The expression 'God is dead' came from Nietzsche."

"Go on."

"The key word in Sartre's philosophy, as in Kierkegaard's, is 'existence.' But existence did not mean the same as being alive. Plants and animals are also alive, they exist, but they do not have to think about what it implies. Man is the only living creature that is conscious of its own existence. Sartre said that a material thing is simply 'in itself,' but mankind is 'for itself.' The being of man is therefore not the same as the being of things."

"I can't disagree with that."

"Sartre said that man's existence takes priority over whatever he might otherwise be. The fact that I exist takes priority over *what* I am. 'Existence takes priority over essence.' "

"That was a very complicated statement."

"By essence we mean that which something consists of—the nature, or being, of something. But according to Sartre, man has no such innate 'nature.' Man must therefore create himself. He must create his own nature or 'essence,' because it is not fixed in advance."

"I think I see what you mean."

"Throughout the entire history of philosophy, philosophers have sought to discover what man is—or what human nature is. But Sartre believed that man has no such eternal 'nature' to fall back on. It is therefore useless to search for the meaning of life in general. We are condemned to improvise. We are like actors dragged onto the stage without having learned our lines, with no script and no prompter to whisper stage directions to us. We must decide for ourselves how to live."

"That's true, actually. If one could just look in the Bible—or in a philosophy book—to find out how to live, it would be very practical."

"You've got the point. When people realize they are alive and will one day die—and there is no meaning to cling to—they experience angst, said Sartre. You may recall that angst, a sense of dread, was also characteristic of Kierkegaard's description of a person in an existential situation."

"Yes."

"Sartre says that man feels *alien* in a world without meaning. When he describes man's 'alienation,' he is echoing the central ideas of Hegel and Marx. Man's feeling of alienation in the world creates a sense of despair, boredom, nausea, and absurdity."

"It is quite normal to feel depressed, or to feel that everything is just too boring."

"Yes, indeed. Sartre was describing the twentieth-century city dweller. You remember that the Renaissance humanists had drawn attention, almost triumphantly, to man's freedom and independence? Sartre experienced man's freedom as a curse. 'Man is condemned to be free,' he said. 'Condemned because he has not created himself—and is nevertheless free. Because having once been hurled into the world, he is responsible for everything he does.'"

"But we haven't asked to be created as free individuals."

"That was precisely Sartre's point. Nevertheless we *are*

free individuals, and this freedom condemns us to make choices throughout our lives. There are no eternal values or norms we can adhere to, which makes our *choices* even more significant. Because we are totally *responsible* for everything we do. Sartre emphasized that man must never disclaim the responsibility for his actions. Nor can we avoid the responsibility of making our own choices on the grounds that we 'must' go to work, or we 'must' live up to certain middle-class expectations regarding how we should live. Those who thus slip into the anonymous masses will never be other than members of the impersonal flock, having fled from themselves into self-deception. On the other hand our freedom obliges us to make something of ourselves, to live 'authentically' or 'truly.' "

"Yes, I see."

"This is not least the case as regards our ethical choices. We can never lay the blame on 'human nature,' or 'human frailty' or anything like that. Now and then it happens that grown men behave like pigs and then blame it on 'the old Adam.' But there is no 'old Adam.' He is merely a figure we clutch at to avoid taking responsibility for our own actions."

"There ought to be a limit to what man can be blamed for."

"Although Sartre claimed there was no innate meaning to life, he did not mean that nothing mattered. He was not what we call a *nihilist.*"

"What is that?"

"That is a person who thinks nothing means anything and everything is permissible. Sartre believed that life *must* have meaning. It is an imperative. But it is we ourselves who must create this meaning in our own lives. To exist is to create your own life."

"Could you elaborate on that?"

"Sartre tried to prove that consciousness in itself is nothing until it has perceived something. Because consciousness is always conscious of something. And this 'something' is provided just as much by ourselves as by our surroundings. We are partly instrumental in deciding what we perceive by selecting what is significant for us."

"Could you give me an example?"

"Two people can be present in the same room and yet experience it quite differently. This is because we contribute our own meaning—or our own interests—when we perceive our surroundings. A woman who is pregnant might think she sees other pregnant women everywhere she looks. That is not because there were no pregnant women before, but because now that she is pregnant she sees the world through different eyes. An escaped convict may see policemen everywhere . . ."

"Mm, I see."

"Our own lives influence the way we perceive things in the room. If something is of no interest to me, I don't see it. So now I can perhaps explain why I was late today."

"It was on purpose, right?"

"Tell me first of all what you saw when you came in here."

"The first thing I saw was that you weren't here."

"Isn't it strange that the first thing you noticed was something that was absent?"

"Maybe, but it was you I was supposed to meet."

"Sartre uses just such a café visit to demonstrate the way we 'annihilate' whatever is irrelevant for us."

"You got here late just to demonstrate that?"

"To enable you to understand this central point in Sartre's philosophy, yes. Call it an exercise."

"Get out of here!"

"If you were in love, and were waiting for your loved one to call you, you might 'hear' him not calling you all evening. You arrange to meet him at the train; crowds of people are milling about on the platform and you can't see him anywhere. They are all in the way, they are unimportant to you. You might find them aggravating, unpleasant even. They are taking up far too much room. The only thing you register is that *he* is not there."

"How sad."

"Simone de Beauvoir attempted to apply existentialism to feminism. Sartre had already said that man has no basic 'nature' to fall back on. We create ourselves."

"Really?"

"This is also true of the way we perceive the sexes. Simone de Beauvoir denied the existence of a basic 'female nature' or 'male nature.' For instance, it has been generally claimed that man has a 'transcending,' or achieving, nature. He will therefore seek meaning and direction outside the home. Woman has been said to have the opposite life philosophy. She is 'immanent,' which means she wishes to be where she is. She will therefore nurture her family, care for the environment and more homely things. Nowadays we might say that women are more concerned with 'feminine values' than men."

"Did she really believe that?"

"You weren't listening to me. Simone de Beauvoir in fact *did not* believe in the existence of any such 'female nature' or 'male nature.' On the contrary, she believed that women and men must liberate themselves from such ingrown prejudices or ideals."

"I agree."

"Her main work, published in 1949, was called *The Second Sex*."

"What did she mean by that?"

"She was talking about women. In our culture women are treated as the second sex. Men behave as if they are the subjects, treating women like their objects, thus depriving them of the responsibility for their own life."

"She meant we women are exactly as free and independent as we choose to be?"

"Yes, you could put it like that. Existentialism also had a great influence on literature, from the forties to the present day, especially on drama. Sartre himself wrote plays as well as novels. Other important writers were the Frenchman *Albert Camus*, the Irishman *Samuel Beckett, Eugène Ionesco*, who was from Romania, and *Witold Gombrowicz* from Poland. Their characteristic style, and that of many other modern writers, was what we call *absurdism*. The term is especially used about the 'theater of the absurd.' "

"Ah."

"Do you know what we mean by the 'absurd'?"

"Isn't it something that is meaningless or irrational?"

"Precisely. The theater of the absurd represented a contrast to realistic theater. Its aim was to show the lack of meaning in life in order to get the audience to disagree. The idea was not to cultivate the meaningless. On the contrary. But by showing and exposing the absurd in ordinary everyday situations, the onlookers are forced to seek a truer and more essential life for themselves."

"It sounds interesting."

"The theater of the absurd often portrays situations that are absolutely trivial. It can therefore also be called a kind of 'hyperrealism.' People are portrayed precisely as they are. But if you reproduce on stage exactly what goes on in the bathroom on a perfectly ordinary morning in a perfectly ordinary home, the audience would laugh. Their laughter could be interpreted as a defense mechanism against seeing themselves lampooned on stage."

"Yes, exactly."

"The absurd theater can also have certain surrealistic features. Its characters often find themselves in highly unrealistic and dreamlike situations. When they accept this without surprise, the audience is compelled to react in surprise at the characters' lack of surprise. This was how *Charlie Chaplin* worked in his silent movies. The comic effect in these silent movies was often Chaplin's laconic acceptance of all the absurd things that happen to him. That compelled the audience to look into themselves for something more genuine and true."

"It's certainly surprising to see what people put up with without protesting."

"At times it can be right to feel: This is something I must get *away* from—even though I don't have any idea where to go."

"If the house catches fire you just have to get out, even if you don't have any other place to live."

"That's true. Would you like another cup of tea? Or a Coke maybe?"

"Okay. But I still think you were silly to be late."

"I can live with that."

Alberto came back with a cup of espresso and a Coke. Meanwhile Sophie had begun to like the café ambience. She was also beginning to think that the conversations at the other tables might not be as trivial as she had supposed them to be.

Alberto banged the Coke bottle down on the table with a thud. Several people at the other tables looked up.

"And that brings us to the end of the road," he said.

"You mean the history of philosophy stops with Sartre and existentialism?"

"No, that would be an exaggeration. Existentialist philosophy has had radical significance for many people all over the world. As we saw, its roots reach far back in history through Kierkegaard and way back to Socrates. The twentieth century has also witnessed a blossoming and a renewal of the other philosophical currents we have discussed."

"Like what?"

"Well, one such current is *Neo-Thomism*, that is to say ideas which belong to the tradition of Thomas Aquinas. Another is the so-called *analytical philosophy* or *logical empiricism*, with roots reaching back to Hume and British empiricism, and even to the logic of Aristotle. Apart from these, the twentieth century has naturally also been influenced by what we might call *Neo-Marxism* in a myriad of various trends. We have already talked about *Neo-Darwinism* and the significance of *psychoanalysis*."

"Yes."

"We should just mention a final current, *materialism*, which also has historical roots. A lot of current science can be traced back to the efforts of the pre-Socratics. For example, the search for the indivisible 'elemental particle' of which all matter is composed. No one has yet been able to give a satisfactory explanation of what 'matter' is. Modern sciences such as nuclear physics and biochemistry are so fascinated by the problem that for many people it constitutes a vital part of their life's philosophy."

"The new and the old all jumbled together . . ."

"Yes. Because the very questions we started our course with are still unanswered. Sartre made an important observation when he said that existential questions cannot be answered once and for all. A philosophical question is by definition something that each generation, each individual even, must ask over and over again."

"A bleak thought."

"I'm not sure I agree. Surely it is by asking such questions that we know we are alive. And moreover, it has always been the case that while people were seeking answers to the ultimate questions, they have discovered clear and final solutions to many other problems. Science, research, and technology are all by-products of our philosophical reflection. Was it not our wonder about life that finally brought men to the moon?"

"Yes, that's true."

"When *Neil Armstrong* set foot on the moon, he said 'One small step for man, one giant leap for mankind.' With these words he summed up how it felt to be the first man to set foot on the moon, drawing with him all the people who had lived before him. It was not his merit alone, obviously.

"In our own time we also have completely new problems to face. The most serious are those of the environment. A central philosophical direction in the twentieth century is therefore *ecophilosophy* or *ecosophy*, as one of its founders the Norwegian philosopher *Arne Naess* has called it. Many ecophilosophers in the western world have warned that western civilization as a whole is on a fundamentally wrong track, racing toward a head-on collision with the limits of what our planet can tolerate. They have tried to take soundings that go deeper than the concrete effects of pollution and environmental destruction. There is something basically wrong with western thought, they claim."

"I think they are right."

"For example, ecophilosophy has questioned the very idea of evolution in its assumption that man is 'at the top'—as if we are masters of nature. This way of thinking could prove to be fatal for the whole living planet."

"It makes me mad when I think about it."

"In criticizing this assumption, many ecophilosophers have looked to the thinking and ideas in other cultures such as those of India. They have also studied the thoughts and customs of so-called primitive peoples—or 'native-peoples' such as the Native Americans—in order to rediscover what we have lost.

"In scientific circles in recent years it has been said that our whole mode of scientific thought is facing a 'paradigm shift.' That is to say, a fundamental shift in the way scientists think. This has already borne fruit in several fields. We have witnessed numerous examples of so-called 'alternative movements' advocating holism and a new lifestyle."

"Great."

"However, when there are many people involved, one must always distinguish between good and bad. Some proclaim that we are entering a new age. But everything new is not necessarily good, and not all the old should be thrown out. That is one of the reasons why I have given you this course in philosophy. Now you have the historical background, you can orient yourself in life."

"Thank you."

"I think you will find that much of what marches under the New Age banner is humbug. Even the so-called New Religion, New Occultism, and modern superstitions of all kinds have influenced the western world in recent decades. It has become an industry. Alternative offers on the philosophical market have mushroomed in the wake of the dwindling support for Christianity."

"What sort of offers?"

"The list is so long I wouldn't dare to begin. And anyway it's not easy to describe one's own age. But why don't we take a stroll through town? There's something I'd like you to see."

"I haven't got much time. I hope you haven't forgotten the garden party tomorrow?"

"Of course not. That's when something wonderful is going to happen. We just have to round off Hilde's philosophy course first. The major hasn't thought beyond that, you see. So he loses some of his mastery over us."

Once again he lifted the Coke bottle, which was now empty, and banged it down on the table.

They walked out into the street where people were hurrying by like energetic moles in a molehill. Sophie wondered what Alberto wanted to show her.

They walked past a big store that sold everything in communication technology, from televisions, VCRs, and satellite dishes to mobile phones, computers, and fax machines.

Alberto pointed to the window display and said:

"There you have the twentieth century, Sophie. In the Renaissance the world began to explode, so to speak. Beginning with the great voyages of discovery, Europeans started to travel all over the world. Today it's the opposite. We could call it an explosion in reverse."

"In what sense?"

"In the sense that the world is becoming drawn together into one great communications network. Not so long ago philosophers had to travel for days by horse and carriage in order to investigate the world around them and meet other philosophers. Today we can sit anywhere at all on this planet and access the whole of human experience on a computer screen."

"It's a fantastic thought. And a little scary."

"The question is whether history is coming to an end— or whether on the contrary we are on the threshold of a completely new age. We are no longer simply citizens of a city—or of a particular country. We live in a planetary civilization."

"That's true."

"Technological developments, especially in the field of communications, have possibly been more dramatic in the last thirty to forty years than in the whole of history put together. And still we have probably only witnessed the beginning . . ."

"Was this what you wanted me to see?"

"No, it's on the other side of the church over there."

As they were turning to leave, a picture of some UN soldiers flashed onto a TV screen.

"Look!" said Sophie.

The camera zoomed in on one of the UN soldiers. He had a black beard almost identical to Alberto's. Suddenly he held up a piece of card on which was written: "Back soon, Hilde!" He waved and was gone.

"Charlatan!" exclaimed Alberto.

"Was that the major?"

"I'm not even going to answer that."

They walked across the park in front of the church and

came out onto another main street. Alberto seemed slightly irritable. They stopped in front of LIBRIS, the biggest bookstore in town.

"Let's go in," said Alberto.

Inside the store he pointed to the longest wall. It had three sections: NEW AGE, ALTERNATIVE LIFESTYLES, and MYSTICISM.

The books had intriguing titles such as *Life after Death?*, *The Secrets of Spiritism*, *Tarot*, *The UFO Phenomenon*, *Healing*, *The Return of the Gods*, *You Have Been Here Before*, and *What Is Astrology?* There were hundreds of books. Under the shelves even more books were stacked up.

"This is also the twentieth century, Sophie. This is the temple of our age."

"You don't believe in any of this stuff?"

"Much of it is humbug. But it sells as well as pornography. A lot of it is a kind of pornography. Young people can come here and purchase the ideas that fascinate them most. But the difference between real philosophy and these books is more or less the same as the difference between real love and pornography."

"Aren't you being rather crass?"

"Let's go and sit in the park."

They marched out of the store and found a vacant bench in front of the church. Pigeons were strutting around under the trees, the odd overeager sparrow hopping about amongst them.

"It's called ESP or parapsychology," said Alberto. "Or it's called telepathy, clairvoyance, and psychokinetics. It's called spiritism, astrology, and ufology."

"But quite honestly, do you really think it's all humbug?"

"Obviously it would not be very appropriate for a real philosopher to say they are all equally bad. But I don't mind saying that all these subjects together possibly chart a fairly detailed map of a landscape that does not exist. And there are many 'figments of the imagination' here that Hume would have committed to the flames. Many of those books do not contain so much as one iota of genuine experience."

"Why are there such incredible numbers of books on such subjects?"

"Publishing such books is a big commercial enterprise. It's what most people want."

"Why, do you think?"

"They obviously desire something mystical, something different to break the dreary monotony of everyday life. But it is like carrying coals to Newcastle."

"How do you mean?"

"Here we are, wandering around in a wonderful adventure. A work of creation is emerging in front of our very eyes. In broad daylight, Sophie! Isn't it marvelous!"

"I guess so."

"Why should we enter the fortune-teller's tent or the backyards of academe in search of something exciting or transcendental?"

"Are you saying that the people who write these books are just phonies and liars?"

"No, that's not what I'm saying. But here, too, we are talking about a Darwinian system."

"You'll have to explain that."

"Think of all the different things that can happen in a single day. You can even take a day in your own life. Think of all the things you see and experience."

"Yes?"

"Now and then you experience a strange coincidence. You might go into a store and buy something for 28 crowns. Later on that day Joanna comes along and gives you the 28 crowns she owes you. You both decide to go to the movies—and you get seat number 28."

"Yes, that would be a mysterious coincidence."

"It would be a coincidence, anyway. The point is, people *collect* coincidences like these. They collect strange—or inexplicable—experiences. When such experiences—taken from the lives of billions of people—are assembled into books, it begins to look like genuine data. And the amount of it increases all the time. But once again we are looking at a lottery in which only the winning numbers are visible."

"But there are clairvoyants and mediums, aren't there, who are constantly experiencing things like that?"

"Indeed there are, and if we exclude the phonies, we find another explanation for these so-called mysterious experiences."

"And that is?"

"You remember we talked about Freud's theory of the unconscious . . ."

"Of course."

"Freud showed that we can often serve as 'mediums' for our own unconscious. We might suddenly find ourselves thinking or doing something without really knowing why. The reason is that we have a whole lot of experiences, thoughts, and memories inside us that we are not aware of."

"So?"

"People sometimes talk or walk in their sleep. We could call this a sort of 'mental automatism.' Also under hypnosis, people can say and do things 'not of their own volition.' And remember the surrealists trying to produce so-called automatic writing. They were just trying to serve as mediums for their own unconscious."

"I remember."

"From time to time during this century there have been what are called 'spiritualist revivals,' the idea being that a medium could get into contact with a deceased person. Either by speaking in the voice of the deceased, or by using automatic writing, the medium would receive a message from someone who had lived five or fifty or many hundreds of years ago. This has been taken as evidence either that there is life after death or that we live many lives."

"Yes, I know."

"I'm not saying that all mediums have been fakes. Some have clearly been in good faith. They really have been mediums, but they have only been mediums for their own unconscious. There have been several cases of mediums being closely studied while in a trance, and revealing knowledge and abilities that neither they nor others understand how they can have acquired. In one case, a woman who had no knowledge of Hebrew passed on messages in that language. So she must have either lived before or been in contact with a deceased spirit."

"Which do you think?"

"It turned out that she had had a Jewish nanny when she was little."

"Ah."

"Does that disappoint you? It just shows what an incredible capacity some people have to store experience in their unconscious."

"I see what you mean."

"A lot of curious everyday happenings can be explained by Freud's theory of the unconscious. I might suddenly get a call from a friend I haven't heard from for many years just as I had begun to look for his telephone number."

"It gives me goose bumps."

"But the explanation could be that we both heard the same old song on the radio, a song we heard the last time we were together. The point is, we are not aware of the underlying connection."

"So it's either humbug, or the winning number effect, or else it's the unconscious. Right?"

"Well, in any case, it's healthier to approach such books with a decent portion of skepticism. Not least if one is a philosopher. There is an association in England for skeptics. Many years ago they offered a large reward to the first person who could provide even the slightest proof of something supernatural. It didn't need to be a great miracle, a tiny example of telepathy would do. So far, nobody has come forward."

"Hmm."

"On the other hand, there is a lot we humans don't understand. Maybe we don't understand the laws of nature either. During the last century there were a lot of people who thought that phenomena such as magnetism and electricity were a kind of magic. I'll bet my own great-grandmother would have been wide-eyed with amazement if I told her about TV or computers."

"So you don't believe in anything supernatural then."

"We've already talked about that. Even the term 'supernatural' is a curious one. No, I suppose I believe that there is only one nature. But that, on the other hand, is absolutely astonishing."

"But the sort of mysterious things in those books you just showed me?"

"All true philosophers should keep their eyes open. Even if we have never seen a white crow, we should never stop looking for it. And one day, even a skeptic like me could be obliged to accept a phenomenon I did not believe in before. If I did not keep this possibility open I would be dogmatic, and not a true philosopher."

Alberto and Sophie remained seated on the bench without saying anything. The pigeons craned their necks and cooed, now and then being startled by a bicycle or a sudden movement.

"I have to go home and prepare for the party," said Sophie at last.

"But before we part, I'll show you a white crow. It is nearer than we think, you see."

Alberto got up and led the way back into the bookstore. This time they walked past all the books on supernatural phenomena and stopped by a flimsy shelf at the very back of the store. Above the shelf hung a very small card. PHILOSOPHY, it read.

Alberto pointed down at a particular book, and Sophie gasped as she read the title: *Sophie's World.*

"Would you like me to buy it for you?"

"I don't know if I dare."

Shortly afterward, however, she was on her way home with the book in one hand and a little bag of things for the garden party in the other.

The Garden Party

. . . a white crow . . .

Hilde sat on the bed, transfixed. She felt her arms and her hands tremble, as they gripped the heavy ring binder.

It was almost eleven o'clock. She had been reading for over two hours. From time to time she had raised her eyes from the text and laughed aloud, but she had also turned over on her side and gasped. It was a good thing she was alone in the house.

And what she had been through these last two hours! It started with Sophie trying to attract the major's attention on the way home from the cabin in the woods. She had finally climbed a tree and been rescued by Morten Goose, who had arrived like a guardian angel from Lebanon.

Although it was a long, long time ago, Hilde had never forgotten how her father had read *The Wonderful Adventures of Nils* to her. For many years after that, she and her father had had a secret language together that was connected with the book. Now he had dragged the old goose out again.

Then Sophie had her first experience as a lone customer in a café. Hilde had been especially taken with what Alberto said about Sartre and existentialism. He had almost managed to convert her—although he had done that many times before in the ring binder too.

Once, about a year ago, Hilde had bought a book on astrology. Another time she had come home with a set

of tarot cards. Next time it was a book on spiritualism.
Each time, her father had lectured her about "superstition" and her "critical faculty," but he had waited until
now for the final blow. His counterattack was deadly
accurate. Clearly, his daughter would not be allowed to
grow up without a thorough warning against that kind
of thing. To be absolutely sure, he had waved to her
from a TV screen in a radio store. He could have saved
himself the trouble . . .

What she wondered about most of all was Sophie.
Sophie—who are you? Where do you come from? Why
have you come into my life?

Finally Sophie had been given a book about herself.
Was it the same book that Hilde now had in her hands?
This was only a ring binder. But even so—how could
one find a book about oneself in a book about oneself?
What would happen if Sophie began to read that book?

What was going to happen now? What *could* happen
now? There were only a few pages left in her ring
binder.

Sophie met her mother on the bus on her way home from
town. Oh, no! What would her mother say when she saw
the book in Sophie's hand?

Sophie tried to put it in the bag with all the streamers
and balloons she had bought for the party but she didn't
quite make it.

"Hi, Sophie! We caught the same bus! How nice!"

"Hi, Mom!"

"You bought a book?"

"No, not exactly."

"*Sophie's World* . . . how curious."

Sophie knew she didn't have the slightest chance of
lying to her mother.

"I got it from Alberto."

"Yes, I'm sure you did. As I said, I'm looking forward
to meeting this man. May I see?"

"Would you mind very much waiting till we get home,
at least. It is *my* book, Mom."

"Of course it's your book. I just want to take a peek at
the first page, okay? . . . 'Sophie Amundsen was on her

way home from school. She had walked the first part of the way with Joanna. They had been discussing robots . . .'"

"Does it really say that?"

"Yes, it *does*, Sophie. It's written by someone called Albert Knag. He must be a newcomer. What's your Alberto's name, by the way?"

"Knox."

"It'll probably turn out that this extraordinary person has written a whole book about you, Sophie. It's called using a pseudonym."

"It's not him, Mom. Why don't you just give up. You don't understand anything anyway."

"No, I don't suppose I do. The garden party is tomorrow, then everything will be all right again."

"Albert Knag lives in a completely different reality. That's why this book is a white crow."

"You really must stop all this! Wasn't it a white rabbit?"

"You stop it!"

That was as far as they got before they reached their stop at the end of Clover Close. They ran straight into a demonstration.

"My God!" exclaimed Helene Amundsen, "I really thought we would be spared street politics in this neighborhood."

There were no more than about ten or twelve people. Their banners read:

> THE MAJOR IS AT HAND
> YES TO YUMMY MIDSUMMER EATS
> MORE POWER TO THE UN

Sophie almost felt sorry for her mother.

"Never mind," she said.

"But it was a peculiar demonstration, Sophie. Quite absurd, really."

"It was a mere bagatelle."

"The world changes more and more rapidly all the time. Actually, I'm not in the least surprised."

"You should be surprised that you're not surprised, at any rate."

"Not at all. They weren't violent, were they? I just hope they haven't trampled all over our rosebeds. Surely it can't be necessary to demonstrate in a garden. Let's hurry home and see."

"It was a philosophical demonstration, Mom. Real philosophers don't trample on rosebeds."

"I'll tell you what, Sophie. I don't think I believe in real philosophers any longer. Everything is synthetic nowadays."

They spent the afternoon and evening preparing. They continued the next morning, setting and decorating the table. Joanna came over to give them a hand.

"Good grief!" she said, "Mom and Dad are coming too. It's your fault, Sophie!"

Everything was ready half an hour before the guests were due. The trees were festooned with streamers and Japanese lanterns. The garden gate, the trees lining the path, and the front of the house were hung with balloons. Sophie and Joanna had spent most of the afternoon blowing them up.

The table was set with chicken, salad, and different kinds of homemade bread. In the kitchen there were raisin buns and layer cake, Danish pastry and chocolate cake. But from the start the place of honor in the center of the table was reserved for the birthday cake—a pyramid of almond-paste rings. On the top of the cake was the tiny figure of a girl in a confirmation dress. Sophie's mother had assured her that it could just as well represent an unconfirmed fifteen-year-old, but Sophie was certain her mother had only put it there because Sophie had told her she was not sure she wanted to be confirmed. Her mother seemed to think the cake embodied the confirmation itself.

"We haven't spared any expense," she repeated several times in the half hour before the party was due to start.

The guests began to arrive. First came three of the girls from Sophie's class, dressed in summer shirts and light cardigans, long skirts, and the barest suggestion of eye makeup. A bit later, Jeremy and David came strolling in through the gate, with a blend of shyness and boyish arrogance.

"Happy birthday!"

"You're an adult now, too!"

Sophie noticed that Joanna and Jeremy had already begun eyeing each other discreetly. There was something in the air. It was Midsummer Eve.

Everybody had brought birthday presents, and as it was a philosophical garden party, several of the guests had tried to find out what philosophy was. Although not all of them had managed to find philosophical presents, most of them had written something philosophical on their cards. Sophie received a philosophical dictionary as well as a diary with a lock; on the cover was written MY PERSONAL PHILOSOPHICAL THOUGHTS. As the guests arrived they were served apple juice in long-stemmed wine glasses. Sophie's mother did the serving.

"Welcome . . . And what is this young man's name? I don't believe we've met before . . . So glad you could come, Cecilie . . ."

When all the younger guests had arrived and were strolling under the trees with their wine glasses, Joanna's parents drew up at the garden gate in a white Mercedes. The financial adviser was impeccably dressed in an expensively cut gray suit. His wife was wearing a red pants suit with dark red sequins. Sophie was sure she had bought a Barbie doll in a toy store dressed in that suit, and had a tailor make it up in her size. There was another possibility; the financial adviser could have bought the doll and given it to a magician to make into a live woman. But this possibility was unlikely, so Sophie rejected it.

They stepped out of the Mercedes and walked into the garden where younger guests looked at them with surprise. The financial adviser presented a long, narrow package from the Ingebrigtsen family. Sophie tried hard to maintain her composure when it turned out to be—yes, it was!—a Barbie doll. But Joanna made no such effort:

"Are you crazy? Sophie doesn't play with dolls!"

Mrs. Ingebrigtsen came hurrying over, with all her sequins clanking. "But it's only for *decoration*, you know."

"Well, thank you very much indeed." Sophie tried to

smooth things over. "Now I can start a collection."

People began to drift toward the table.

"We're only waiting for Alberto," said Sophie's mother to her in a somewhat brisk tone that was intended to hide her growing apprehension. Rumors of the special guest of honor had already spread among the other guests.

"He has promised to come, so he'll come."

"But we can't seat the guests before he arrives, can we?"

"Of course we can. Let's go ahead."

Helene Amundsen began to seat people around the long table. She made sure that the vacant chair was between her own and Sophie's place. She said a few words about the beautiful weather and the fact that Sophie was now a grownup.

They had been sitting at the table for half an hour when a middle-aged man with a black goatee and a beret came walking up Clover Close and in through the garden gate. He was carrying a bouquet of fifteen red roses.

"Alberto!"

Sophie left the table and ran to greet him. She threw her arms around his neck and took the bouquet from him. He responded to the welcome by rooting around in his jacket pocket and drawing out a couple of Chinese firecrackers which he lit and tossed into the yard. As he approached the table, he lit a sparkler and set it on top of the almond pyramid. Then he went over and stood at the empty place between Sophie and her mother.

"I'm delighted to be here," he said.

The guests were dumbstruck. Mrs. Ingebrigtsen gave her husband a significant look. Sophie's mother was so relieved that the man had finally arrived, however, that she would have forgiven him anything. Sophie herself was struggling to suppress her laughter.

Helene Amundsen tapped on her glass and said:

"Let us also welcome Alberto Knox to this philosophical garden party. He is not my new boyfriend, because although my husband is so often away at sea, I don't have a new boyfriend for the time being. However, this astounding person is Sophie's new philosophy teacher. His prowess extends further than to setting off fireworks.

This man is able, for example, to draw a live rabbit out of a top hat. Or was it a crow, Sophie?''

"Many thanks," said Alberto. He sat down.

"Cheers!" said Sophie, and the guests raised their glasses and drank his health.

They sat for a long time over their chicken and salad. Suddenly Joanna got up, walked determinedly over to Jeremy, and gave him a resounding kiss on the lips. He responded by trying to topple her backward over the table so as to get a better grip as he returned her kiss.

"Well, I've never . . ." exclaimed Mrs. Ingebrigtsen.

"Not on the table, children," was Mrs. Amundsen's only comment.

"Why not?" asked Alberto, turning toward her.

"That was an odd question."

"It's never wrong for a real philosopher to ask questions."

A couple of the other boys who had not been kissed started to throw chicken bones up on the roof. This, too, elicited only a mild comment from Sophie's mother:

"Would you mind not doing that. It's such a nuisance when there are chicken bones in the gutter."

"Sorry," said one of the boys, whereupon they started throwing chicken bones over the garden hedge instead.

"I think it's time to clear the plates away and serve the cake," said Mrs. Amundsen finally. "Sophie and Joanna, will you give me a hand?"

On their way to the kitchen there was only time for a brief discussion.

"What made you kiss him?" Sophie said to Joanna.

"I sat looking at his mouth and couldn't resist it. He is so cute!"

"How did it taste?"

"Not exactly like I'd imagined, but . . ."

"It was the first time, then?"

"But not the last!"

Coffee and cake were soon on the table. Alberto had started giving the boys some of his firecrackers when Sophie's mother tapped on her coffee cup.

"I am not going to make a long speech," she began, "but I only have this one daughter, and it is only this once that exactly one week and a day ago she reached the age of fifteen. As you see, we have spared no expense. There are twenty-four almond rings on the birthday cake, so there's at least one whole ring for each of you. Those who help themselves first can take two rings, because we start from the top and the rings get bigger and bigger as you go. That's the way it is in life too. When Sophie was a little girl, she went tripping around in tiny little rings. But as the years went by, the rings got bigger and bigger. Now they reach right over to the Old Town and back. And what is more, with a father who is at sea so much, she makes calls to all parts of the world. We congratulate you on your fifteenth birthday, Sophie!"

"Delightful!" exclaimed Mrs. Ingebrigtsen.

Sophie was not sure whether she was referring to her mother, the speech, the birthday cake, or Sophie herself.

The guests applauded, and one of the boys threw a firecracker up into the pear tree. Joanna left the table and pulled Jeremy up off his chair. They lay down on the grass and started kissing each other again. After a while they rolled in under the red-currant bushes.

"Nowadays it's the girl who takes the initiative," said Mr. Ingebrigtsen.

Having said that, he got up and went over to the red-currant bushes where he stood observing the phenomenon at close quarters. The rest of the guests followed suit. Only Sophie and Alberto remained sitting at the table. The other guests now stood in a semicircle around Joanna and Jeremy.

"They can't be stopped," said Mrs. Ingebrigtsen, not without a certain pride.

"No, generation follows generation," said her husband.

He looked around, expecting applause for his well-chosen words. When the only response was a few silent nods, he added: "It can't be helped."

Sophie saw from a distance that Jeremy was trying to unbutton Joanna's white shirt, which was already covered with green stains from the grass. She was fumbling with his belt.

"Don't catch cold!" said Mrs. Ingebrigtsen.

Sophie looked despairingly at Alberto.

"It's happening more quickly than I thought," he said. "We have to get away from here as soon as possible. I just have to make a short speech."

Sophie clapped her hands loudly.

"Could everyone please come back and sit down again? Alberto is going to make a speech."

Everyone except Joanna and Jeremy came drifting back to their places at the table.

"Are you really going to make a speech?" asked Helene Amundsen. "How charming!"

"Thank you."

"And you like going for walks, I know. It is so important to stay in shape. And it's so much nicer when you have a dog to keep you company. Hermes, isn't that its name?"

Alberto stood up. "Dear Sophie," he began. "Since this is a philosophical garden party, I will make a philosophical speech."

This was greeted by a burst of applause.

"In this riotous company, a dose of reason might not be out of place. But whatever happens, let us not forget to congratulate Sophie on her fifteenth birthday."

He had hardly finished these sentences when they heard the drone of an approaching sports plane. It flew in low over the garden. Behind it streamed a long tail banner saying: "Happy 15th birthday!"

This led to renewed applause, even louder than before.

"There, you see?" Mrs. Amundsen cried joyfully. "This man can do more than set off fireworks!"

"Thank you. It was a mere bagatelle. During the past few weeks, Sophie and I have carried out a major philosophical investigation. We shall here and now reveal our findings. We shall reveal the innermost secrets of our existence."

The little gathering was now so quiet that the only sounds were the twittering of the birds and a few subdued noises from the red-currant bushes.

"Go on," said Sophie.

"After a thorough philosophical study—which has led from the first Greek philosophers to the present day—we have discovered that we are living our lives in the mind of a major who is at this moment serving as a UN observer in Lebanon. He has also written a book about us for his daughter back in Lillesand. Her name is Hilde Møller Knag, and she was fifteen years old on the same day as Sophie. The book about us lay on her bedside table when she woke up early on the morning of June 15. To be more precise, it was in the form of a ring binder. Even as we speak, she can feel the final pages of the ring binder under her index finger."

A feeling of apprehension had begun to spread around the table.

"Our existence is therefore neither more nor less than a kind of birthday diversion for Hilde Møller Knag. We have all been invented as a framework for the major's philosophical education of his daughter. This means, for example, that the white Mercedes at the gate is not worth a cent. It's just a bagatelle. It's worth no more than the white Mercedes that drives around and around inside the head of a poor UN major, who has just this minute sat down in the shade of a palm tree to avoid getting sunstroke. The days are hot in Lebanon, my friends."

"Garbage!" exclaimed the financial adviser. "This is absolutely pure nonsense."

"You are welcome to your opinion," Alberto continued unabashed, "but the truth is that it is this garden party which is absolutely pure nonsense. The only dose of reason in the whole party is this speech."

At that, the financial adviser got up and said:

"Here we are, trying our best to run a business, and to make sure we have insurance coverage against every kind of risk. Then along comes this know-it-all who tries to destroy it all with his 'philosophical' allegations."

Alberto nodded in agreement.

"There is indeed no insurance to cover this kind of philosophical insight. We are talking of something worse than a natural catastrophe, sir. But as you are probably aware, insurance doesn't cover those either."

"This is not a natural catastrophe."

"No, it is an existential catastrophe. For example, just take a look under the currant bushes and you will see what I mean. You cannot insure yourself against the collapse of your whole life. Neither can you insure yourself against the sun going out."

"Do we have to put up with this?" asked Joanna's father, looking at his wife.

She shook her head, and so did Sophie's mother.

"What a shame," she said, "and after we had spared no expense."

The younger guests continued to look at Alberto. "We want to hear more," said a curly-haired boy with glasses.

"Thank you, but there is not much more to say. When you have realized that you are a dream image in another person's sleepy consciousness, then, in my opinion, it is wisest to be silent. But I can finish by recommending that you take a short course in the history of philosophy. It is important to be critical of the older generation's values. If I have tried to teach Sophie anything, it is precisely that, to think critically. Hegel called it thinking negatively."

The financial adviser was still standing, drumming his fingers on the table.

"This agitator is attempting to break down all the sound values which the school and the church and we ourselves are trying to instill in the younger generation. It is they who have the future before them and who one day will inherit everything we have built up. If this man is not immediately removed from this gathering I intend to call our lawyer. He will know how to deal with this situation."

"It makes little difference whether you deal with this situation or not, since you are nothing but a shadow. Anyway, Sophie and I are about to leave the party, since for us the philosophy course has not been purely theoretical. It has also had its practical side. When the time is ripe we will perform our disappearing act. That is how we are going to sneak our way out of the major's consciousness."

Helene Amundsen took hold of her daughter's arm.

"You are not leaving me, are you, Sophie?"

Sophie put her arms around her mother. She looked up at Alberto.

"Mom is so sad . . ."

"No, that's just ridiculous. Don't forget what you have learned. It's this sort of nonsense we must liberate ourselves from. Your mother is a sweet and kind lady, just as the Little Red Ridinghood who came to my door that day had a basket filled with food for her grandmother. Your mother is no more sad than the plane that just flew over needed fuel for its congratulation maneuvers."

"I think I see what you mean," said Sophie, and turned back to her mother. "That's why I have to do what he says, Mom. One day I had to leave you."

"I'm going to miss you," said her mother, "but if there is a heaven over this one, you'll just have to fly. I promise to take good care of Govinda. Does it eat one or two lettuce leaves a day?"

Alberto put his hand on her shoulder.

"Neither you nor anyone else here will miss us for the simple reason that you do not exist. You are no more than shadows."

"That is the worst insult I've ever heard," Mrs. Inge-brigtsen burst out.

Her husband nodded.

"If nothing else, we can always get him nailed for defamation of character. I'm sure he's a Communist. He wants to strip us of everything we hold dear. The man's a scoundrel."

With that, both Alberto and the financial adviser sat down. The latter's face was crimson with rage. Now Joanna and Jeremy also came and sat at the table. Their clothes were grubby and crumpled. Joanna's golden hair was caked with mud and earth.

"Mom, I'm going to have a baby," she announced.

"All right, but you'll have to wait till you get home."

She had immediate support from her husband. "She'll simply have to contain herself," he said. "And if there is to be a christening tonight, she'll have to arrange it herself."

Alberto looked down at Sophie with a somber expression.

"It's time."

"Can't you at least bring us a little more coffee before you go?" asked her mother.

"Of course, Mom, I'll do it right away."

Sophie took the thermos from the table. She had to make more coffee. While she stood waiting for it to brew, she fed the birds and the goldfish. She also went into the bathroom and put a lettuce leaf out for Govinda. She couldn't see the cat anywhere, but she opened a large can of cat food, emptied it into a bowl and set it out on the step. She felt her tears welling up.

When she returned with the coffee, the garden party looked more like a children's party than a young woman's philosophical celebration. Several soda bottles had been knocked over on the table, there was chocolate cake smeared all over the tablecloth and the dish of raisin buns lay upside down on the lawn. Just as Sophie arrived, one of the boys put a firecracker to the layer cake, which exploded all over the table and the guests. The worst casualty was Mrs. Ingebrigtsen's red pants suit. The curious thing was that both she and everybody else took it with the utmost calm. Joanna picked up a huge piece of chocolate cake, smeared it all over Jeremy's face, and proceeded to lick it off again.

Her mother and Alberto were sitting in the glider a little way away from the others. They waved to Sophie.

"So you finally had your confidential talk," said Sophie.

"And you were perfectly right," said her mother, quite elated now. "Alberto is a very altruistic person. I entrust you to his strong arms."

Sophie sat down between them.

Two of the boys had managed to climb onto the roof. One of the girls went around pricking holes in all the balloons with a hairpin. Then an uninvited guest arrived on a motorcycle with a crate of beer and bottles of aquavit strapped to the carrier. A few helpful souls welcomed him in.

At that, the financial adviser rose from the table. He clapped his hands and said:

"Do you want to play a game?"

He grabbed a bottle of beer, drank it down, and set the empty bottle in the middle of the lawn. Then he went to the table and fetched the last five rings of the birthday cake. He showed the other guests how to throw the rings so they landed over the neck of the bottle.

"The death throes," said Alberto. "We'd better get

away before the major ends it all and Hilde closes the ring binder.''

"You'll have to clear up alone, Mom."

"It doesn't matter, child. This was no life for you. If Alberto can give you a better one, nobody will be happier than I. Didn't you tell me he had a white horse?''

Sophie looked out across the garden. It was unrecognizable. Bottles, chicken bones, buns, and balloons were trampled into the grass.

"This was once my little Garden of Eden," she said.

"And now you're being driven out of it," said Alberto.

One of the boys was sitting in the white Mercedes. He revved the engine and the car smashed through the garden gate, up the gravel path, and down into the garden.

Sophie felt a hard grip on her arm as she was dragged into the den. Then she heard Alberto's voice:

"Now!''

At the same moment the white Mercedes crashed into an apple tree. Unripe fruit showered down onto the hood.

"That's going too far!'' shouted the financial adviser. "I demand substantial compensation!"

His wife gave him her full support.

"It's that damned scoundrel's fault! Where is he?''

"They have vanished into thin air," said Helene Amundsen, not without a touch of pride.

She drew herself up to her full height, walked toward the long table and began to clear up after the philosophical garden party.

"More coffee, anyone?''

Counterpoint

∽

. . . two or more melodies sounding together . . .

Hilde sat up in bed. That was the end of the story of Sophie and Alberto. But what had actually happened?

Why had her father written that last chapter? Was it just to demonstrate his power over Sophie's world?

Deep in thought, she took a shower and got dressed. She ate a quick breakfast and then wandered down the garden and sat in the glider.

She agreed with Alberto that the only sensible thing that had happened at the garden party was his speech. Surely her father didn't think Hilde's world was as chaotic as Sophie's garden party? Or that her world would also dissolve eventually?

Then there was the matter of Sophie and Alberto. What had happened to the secret plan?

Was it up to Hilde herself to continue the story? Or had they really managed to sneak out of it?

And where were they now?

A thought suddenly struck her. If Alberto and Sophie really had managed to sneak out of the story, there wouldn't be anything about it in the ring binder. Everything that was there, unfortunately, was clear to her father.

Could there be anything written between the lines? There was more than a mere suggestion of it. Hilde realized that she would have to read the whole story again one or two more times.

*   *   *

As the white Mercedes drove into the garden, Alberto dragged Sophie with him into the den. Then they ran into the woods in the direction of the major's cabin.

"Quickly!" cried Alberto. "It's got to happen before *he* starts looking for us."

"Are we beyond the major's reach now?"

"We are in the borderland."

They rowed across the water and ran into the cabin. Alberto opened a trapdoor in the floor. He pushed Sophie down into the cellar. Then everything went black.

In the days that followed, Hilde worked on her plan. She sent several letters to Anne Kvamsdal in Copenhagen, and a couple of times she called her. She also enlisted the aid of friends and acquaintances, and recruited almost half of her class at school.

In between, she read *Sophie's World*. It was not a story one could be done with after a single reading. New thoughts about what could have happened to Sophie and Alberto when they left the garden party were constantly occurring to her.

On Saturday, June 23, she awoke with a start around nine o'clock. She knew her father had already left the camp in Lebanon. Now it was just a question of waiting. The last part of his day was planned down to the smallest detail.

Later in the morning she began the preparations for Midsummer Eve with her mother. Hilde could not help thinking of how Sophie and her mother had arranged *their* Midsummer Eve party. But that was something they *had* done. It was over, finished. Or was it? Were they going around right now, decorating everywhere?

Sophie and Alberto seated themselves on a lawn in front of two large buildings with ugly air vents and ventilation canals on the outside. A young couple came walking out of one of the buildings. He was carrying a brown briefcase and she had a red handbag slung over one shoulder. A car drove along a narrow road in the background.

"What happened?" asked Sophie.

"We made it!"

"But where are we?"

"This is Oslo."

"Are you quite sure?"

"Quite sure. One of these buildings is called Chateau Neuf, which means 'the new palace.' People study music there. The other is the Congregation Faculty. It's a school of theology. Further up the hill they study science and up at the top they study literature and philosophy."

"Are we out of Hilde's book and beyond the major's control?"

"Yes, both. He'll never find us here."

"But where were we when we ran through the woods?"

"While the major was busy crashing the financial adviser's car into an apple tree, we seized the chance to hide in the den. We were then at the embryo stage. We were of the old as well as of the new world. But concealing ourselves there was something the major cannot possibly have envisaged."

"Why not?"

"He would never have let us go so easily. As it was, it went like a dream. Of course, there's always the chance that he was in on it himself."

"What do you mean?"

"It was he who started the white Mercedes. He may have exerted himself to the utmost to lose sight of us. He was probably utterly exhausted after everything that had been going on . . ."

By now the young couple were only a few yards away. Sophie felt a bit awkward, sitting on the grass with a man so much older than herself. Besides, she wanted someone to confirm what Alberto had said.

She got up and went over to them.

"Excuse me, would you mind telling me the name of this street?"

But they ignored her completely.

Sophie was so provoked that she asked them again.

"It's customary to answer a person, isn't it?"

The young man was clearly engrossed in explaining something to his companion:

"Contrapuntal form operates on two dimensions, horizontally, or melodically, and vertically, or harmonically.

There will always be two or more melodies sounding together . . ."

"Excuse me for interrupting, but . . ."

"The melodies combine in such a way that they develop as much as possible, independently of how they sound against each other. But they have to be concordant. Actually it's note against note."

How rude! They were neither deaf nor blind. Sophie tried a third time, standing ahead of them on the path blocking their way.

She was simply brushed aside.

"There's a wind coming up," said the woman.

Sophie rushed back to Alberto.

"They can't hear me!" she said desperately—and just as she said it, she recalled her dream about Hilde and the gold crucifix.

"It's the price we have to pay. Although we have sneaked out of a book, we can't expect to have exactly the same status as its author. But we really are here. From now on, we will never be a day older than we were when we left the philosophical garden party."

"Does that mean we'll never have any real contact with the people around us?"

"A true philosopher never says 'never.' What time is it?"

"Eight o'clock."

"The same as when we left Captain's Bend, of course."

"This is the day Hilde's father gets back from Lebanon."

"That's why we must hurry."

"Why—what do you mean?"

"Aren't you anxious to know what happens when the major gets home to Bjerkely?"

"Naturally, but . . ."

"Come on, then!"

They began to walk down toward the city. Several people passed them on the way, but they all walked right on by as if Sophie and Alberto were invisible.

Cars were parked by the curbside all the way along the street. Alberto stopped by a small red convertible with the top down.

"This will do," he said. "We must just make sure it's ours."

"I have no idea what you mean."

"I'd better explain then. We can't just take an ordinary car that belongs to someone here in the city. What do you think would happen when people noticed the car driving along without a driver? And anyway, we probably wouldn't be able to start it."

"Then why the convertible?"

"I think I recognize it from an old movie."

"Look, I'm sorry, but I'm getting tired of all these cryptic remarks."

"It's a make-believe car, Sophie. It's just like us. People here only see a vacant space. That's all we have to confirm before we're on our way."

They stood by the car and waited. After a while, a boy came cycling along on the sidewalk. He turned suddenly and rode right through the red car and onto the road.

"There, you see? It's ours!"

Alberto opened the door to the passenger seat.

"Be my guest!" he said, and Sophie got in.

He got into the driver's seat. The key was in the ignition, he turned it, and the engine started.

They drove southward out of the city, past Lysaker, Sandvika, Drammen, and down toward Lillesand. As they drove they saw more and more Midsummer bonfires, especially after they had passed Drammen.

"It's Midsummer, Sophie. Isn't it wonderful?"

"And there's such a lovely fresh breeze in an open car. Is it true that no one can see us?"

"Only people of our own kind. We might meet some of them. What's the time now?"

"Half past eight."

"We'll have to take a few shortcuts. We can't stay behind this trailer, that's for sure."

They turned off into a large wheatfield. Sophie looked back and saw that they had left a broad trail of flattened stalks.

"Tomorrow they'll say a freak wind blew over the field," said Alberto.

*   *   *

Major Albert Knag had just landed at Kastrup Airport outside Copenhagen. It was half past four on Saturday, June 23. It had already been a long day. This penultimate lap had been by plane from Rome.

He went through passport control in his UN uniform, which he was proud to wear. He represented not only himself and his country. Albert Knag represented an international legal system—a century-old tradition that now embraced the entire planet.

He carried only a flight bag. He had checked the rest of his baggage through from Rome. He just needed to hold up his red passport.

"Nothing to declare."

Major Albert Knag had a nearly three-hour wait in the airport before his plane left for Kristiansand. He would have time to buy a few presents for his family. He had sent the present of his life to Hilde two weeks ago. Marit, his wife, had put it on her bedside table for her to discover when she woke up on her birthday. He had not spoken with Hilde since that late night birthday call.

Albert bought a couple of Norwegian newspapers, found himself a table in the bar, and ordered a cup of coffee. He had hardly had time to skim the headlines when he heard an announcement over the loudspeakers: "This is a personal call for Albert Knag. Albert Knag is requested to contact the SAS information desk."

What now? He felt a chill down his spine. Surely he was not being ordered back to Lebanon? Could something be wrong at home?

He quickly reached the SAS information desk.

"I'm Albert Knag."

"Here is a message for you. It is urgent."

He opened the envelope at once. Inside lay a smaller envelope. It was addressed to Major Albert Knag, c/o SAS Information, Kastrup Airport, Copenhagen.

Albert opened the little envelope nervously. It contained a short note:

Dear Dad, Welcome home from Lebanon. As you can imagine, I can't even wait till you get home. Forgive me for having you paged over the loudspeakers. It was the easiest way.

P.S. Unfortunately a claim for damages has arrived from financial adviser Ingebrigtsen regarding
a stolen and wrecked Mercedes.

P.S. P.S. I may be sitting in the garden when you
get here. But you might also be hearing from me
before that.

P.S. P.S. P.S. I'm rather scared of staying in the
garden too long at a time. It's so easy to sink into the
ground in such places. Love from Hilde, who has
had plenty of time to prepare your homecoming.

Major Albert Knag's first impulse was to smile. But he
did not appreciate being manipulated in this manner. He
had always liked to be in charge of his own life. Now
this little vixen in Lillesand was directing his movements
in Kastrup Airport! How had she managed that?

He put the envelope in his breast pocket and began to
stroll toward the little shopping mall. He was just about
to enter the Danish Food deli when he noticed a small
envelope taped to the store window. It had MAJOR KNAG
written on it with a thick marker pen. Albert took it
down and opened it:

Personal message for Major Albert Knag, c/o Danish Food, Kastrup Airport. Dear Dad, please buy a
large Danish salami, preferably a two-pound one,
and Mom would probably like a cognac sausage.
P. S. Danish caviar is not bad either. Love, Hilde.

Albert turned around. She wasn't here, was she? Had
Marit given her a trip to Copenhagen so she could meet
him here? It was Hilde's handwriting . . .

Suddenly the UN observer began to feel himself observed. It was as if someone was in remote control of
everything he did. He felt like a doll in the hands of a
child.

He went into the shop and bought a two-pound salami, a cognac sausage, and three jars of Danish caviar.
Then he continued down the row of stores. He had made
up his mind to buy a proper present for Hilde. A cal-

culator, maybe? Or a little radio—yes, that was what he would get.

When he got to the store that sold electrical appliances, he saw that there was an envelope taped to the window there too. This one was addressed to "Major Albert Knag, c/o the most interesting store in Kastrup." Inside was the following note:

> Dear Dad, Sophie sends her greetings and thanks for the combined mini-TV and FM radio that she got for her birthday from her very generous father. It was great, but on the other hand it was a mere bagatelle. I must confess, though, that I share Sophie's liking for such bagatelles. P.S. In case you haven't been there yet, there are further instructions at the Danish Food store and the big Tax Free store that sells wines and tobacco. P.S. P.S. I got some money for my birthday, so I can contribute to the mini-TV with 350 crowns. Love, Hilde, who has already stuffed the turkey and made the Waldorf salad.

A mini-TV cost 985 Danish crowns. That could certainly be called a bagatelle in comparison with how Albert Knag felt about being directed hither and thither by his daughter's sneaky tricks. Was she here—or was she not?

From that moment on, he was constantly on guard wherever he went. He felt like a secret agent and a marionette rolled into one. Was he not being deprived of his basic human rights?

He felt obliged to go into the Tax Free store as well. There hung a new envelope with his name on it. The whole airport was becoming a computer game with him as the cursor. He read the message:

> Major Knag, c/o the Tax Free store at Kastrup. All I need from here is a bag of gumdrops and some marzipan bars. Remember it's much more expensive in Norway. As far as I can recall, Mom is very fond of Campari. P.S. You must keep all your

senses alert the whole way home. You wouldn't
want to miss any important messages, would you?
Love from your most teachable daughter, Hilde.

Albert sighed despairingly, but he went into the store
and shopped as instructed. With three plastic carriers and
his flight bag he walked toward Gate 28 to wait for his
flight. If there were any more messages they would have
to stay there.

However, at Gate 28 he caught sight of another white
envelope taped to a pillar: "To Major Knag, c/o GATE
28, Kastrup Airport." This was also in Hilde's handwriting, but the gate number seemed to have been written by someone else. It was not easy to judge since there
was no writing to compare it with, only block letters and
digits. He took it down. This one said only "It won't
be long now."

He sat down on a chair with his back against the wall.
He kept the shopping bags on his knees. Thus the proud
major sat stiffly, eyes straight ahead, like a small child
traveling alone for the first time. If Hilde was here, she
was certainly not going to have the satisfaction of discovering him first.

He glanced anxiously at each passenger that came in.
For a while he felt like an enemy of the state under close
surveillance. When the passengers were finally allowed
to board the plane he breathed a sigh of relief. He was
the last person to board. As he handed over his boarding
pass he tore off another white envelope that had been
taped to the check-in desk.

Sophie and Alberto had passed Brevik, and a little later
the exit to Kragerø.

"You're going awfully fast," said Sophie.

"It's almost nine o'clock. He'll soon be landing at
Kjevik. But we won't be stopped for speeding."

"Suppose we smash into another car?"

"It makes no difference if it's just an ordinary car. But
if it's one of our own . . ."

"Then what?"

"Then we'll have to be very careful. Didn't you notice

that we passed the Bat Mobile.''

''No.''

''It was parked somewhere up in Vestfold.''

''This tourist bus won't be easy to pass. There are dense woods on each side of the road.''

''It makes no difference, Sophie. Can't you get it into your head?''

So saying, he swung the car into the woods and drove straight through the trees.

Sophie breathed a sigh of relief.

''You scared me.''

''We wouldn't feel it if we drove into a brick wall.''

''That only means we're spirits of the air compared to our surroundings.''

''No, now you're putting the cart before the horse. It is the reality around us that's an airy adventure to us.''

''I don't get it.''

''Listen carefully, then. It is a widespread misunderstanding that spirit is a thing that is more 'airy' than vapor. On the contrary. Spirit is more solid than ice.''

''That never occurred to me.''

''And now I'll tell you a story. Once upon a time there was a man who didn't believe in angels. One day, while he was out working in the woods, he was visited by an angel.''

''And?''

''They walked together for a while. Then the man turned to the angel and said, 'All right, now I have to admit that angels exist. But you don't exist in reality, like us.' 'What do you mean by that?' asked the angel. So the man answered, 'When we came to that big rock, I had to go around it, but I noticed that you just glided through it. And when we came to that huge log that lay across the path, I had to climb over it while you walked straight through it.' The angel was very surprised, and said 'Didn't you also notice that we took a path that led through a marsh? We both walked right through the mist. That was because we were more solid than the mist.' ''

''Ah.''

''It's the same with us, Sophie. Spirit can pass through

steel doors. No tanks or bombers can crush anything that is of spirit."

"That's a comfort."

"We'll soon be passing Risør, and it's no more than an hour since we left the major's cabin. I could really use a cup of coffee."

When they got to Fiane, just before Søndeled, they passed a cafeteria on the lefthand side of the road. It was called Cinderella. Alberto swung the car around and parked on the grass in front of it.

Inside, Sophie tried to take a bottle of Coke from the cooler, but she couldn't lift it. It seemed to be stuck. Further down the counter, Alberto was trying to tap coffee into a paper cup he had found in the car. He only had to press a lever, but even by exerting all his strength he could not press it down.

This made him so mad that he turned to the cafeteria guests and asked for help. When no one reacted, he shouted so loudly that Sophie had to cover her ears: "I want some coffee!"

His anger soon evaporated, and he doubled up with laughter. They were about to turn around and leave when an old woman got up from her chair and came toward them.

She was wearing a garish red skirt, an ice-blue cardigan, and a white kerchief round her head. She seemed more sharply defined than anything else in the little cafeteria.

She went up to Alberto and said, "My my, how you do yell, my boy!"

"Excuse me."

"You want some coffee, you said?"

"Yes, but . . ."

"We have a small establishment close by."

They followed the old woman out of the cafeteria and down a path behind it. While they walked, she said, "You are new in these parts?"

"We might as well admit it," answered Alberto.

"That's all right. Welcome to eternity then, children."

"And you?"

"I'm out of one of Grimm's fairy tales. That was nearly

two hundred years ago. And where are you from?"

"We're out of a book on philosophy. I am the philosophy teacher and this is my student, Sophie."

"Hee hee! That's a new one!"

They came through the trees to a small clearing where there were several cozy-looking brown cottages. A large Midsummer bonfire was burning in a yard between the cottages, and around the bonfire danced a crowd of colorful figures. Sophie recognized many of them. There were Snow White and some of the seven dwarfs, Mary Poppins and Sherlock Holmes, Peter Pan and Pippi Longstocking, Little Red Ridinghood and Cinderella. A lot of familiar figures without names had also gathered around the bonfire—there were gnomes and elves, fauns and witches, angels and imps. Sophie also caught sight of a real live troll.

"What a lot of noise!" exclaimed Alberto.

"That's because it's Midsummer," said the old woman. "We haven't had a gathering like this since Valborg's Eve. That was when we were in Germany. I'm only here on a short visit. Was it coffee you wanted?"

"Yes, please."

Not until now did Sophie notice that all the buildings were made out of gingerbread, candy, and sugar icing. Several of the figures were eating directly off the façades. A baker was going around repairing the damage as it occurred. Sophie ventured to take a little bite off one corner. It tasted sweeter and better than anything she had ever tasted before.

Presently the old woman returned with a cup of coffee.

"Thank you very much indeed."

"And what are the visitors going to pay for the coffee?"

"To pay?"

"We usually pay with a story. For coffee, an old wives' tale will suffice."

"We could tell the whole incredible story of humanity," said Alberto, "but unfortunately we are in a hurry. Can we come back and pay some other day?"

"Of course. And why are you in a hurry?"

Alberto explained their errand, and the old woman commented:

"I must say, you certainly are a pair of greenhorns. You'd better hurry up and cut the umbilical cord to your mortal progenitor. We no longer need their world. We belong to the invisible people."

Alberto and Sophie hurried back to the Cinderella cafeteria and the red convertible. Right next to the car a busy mother was helping her little boy to pee.

Racing along and taking shortcuts, they soon arrived in Lillesand.

SK 876 from Copenhagen touched down at Kjevik on schedule at 9:35 p.m. While the plane was taxied out to the runway in Copenhagen, the major had opened the envelope hanging from the check-in desk. The note inside read:

To Major Knag, as he hands over his boarding pass at Kastrup on Midsummer Eve, 1990. Dear Dad, You probably thought I would turn up in Copenhagen. But my control over your movements is more ingenious than that. I can see you wherever you are, Dad. The fact is, I have been to visit a well-known Gypsy family which many, many years ago sold a magic brass mirror to Great-grandmother. I have also gotten myself a crystal ball. At this very moment, I can see that you have just sat down in your seat. May I remind you to fasten your seat belt and keep the back of your seat raised to an upright position until the Fasten Seat Belt sign has been switched off. As soon as the plane is in flight, you can lower the seat back and give yourself a well-earned rest. You will need to be rested when you get home. The weather in Lillesand is perfect, but the temperature is a few degrees lower than in Lebanon. I wish you a pleasant flight. Love, your own witch-daughter, Queen of the Mirror and the Highest Protector of Irony.

Albert could not quite make out whether he was angry or merely tired and resigned. Then he started laughing. He laughed so loudly that his fellow passengers turned to stare at him. Then the plane took off.

He had been given a taste of his own medicine. But with a significant difference, surely. His medicine had first and foremost affected Sophie and Alberto. And they—well, they were only imaginary.

He did what Hilde had suggested. He lowered the back of his seat and nodded off. He was not fully awake again until he had gone through passport control and was standing in the arrival hall at Kjevik Airport. A demonstration was there to greet him.

There were eight or ten young people of about Hilde's age. They were holding signs saying: WELCOME HOME, DAD — HILDE IS WAITING IN THE GARDEN — IRONY LIVES.

The worst thing was that he could not just jump into a taxi. He had to wait for his baggage. And all the while, Hilde's classmates were swarming around him, forcing him to read the signs again and again. Then one of the girls came up and gave him a bunch of roses and he melted. He dug down into one of his shopping bags and gave each demonstrator a marzipan bar. Now there were only two left for Hilde. When he had reclaimed his baggage, a young man stepped forward and explained that he was under the command of the Queen of the Mirror, and that he had orders to drive him to Bjerkely. The other demonstrators dispersed into the crowd.

They drove out onto the E 18. Every bridge and tunnel they passed was draped with banners saying: "Welcome home!", "The turkey is ready," "I can see you, Dad!"

When he was dropped off outside the gate at Bjerkely, Albert Knag heaved a sigh of relief, and thanked the driver with a hundred crown note and three cans of Carlsberg Elephant beer.

His wife was waiting for him outside the house. After a long embrace, he asked: "Where is she?"

"She's sitting on the dock, Albert."

Alberto and Sophie stopped the red convertible on the square in Lillesand outside the Hotel Norge. It was a quarter past ten. They could see a large bonfire out in the archipelago.

"How do we find Bjerkely?" asked Sophie.

"We'll just have to hunt around for it. You remember the painting in the major's cabin."

"We'll have to hurry. I want to get there before he arrives."

They started to drive around the minor roads and then over rocky mounds and slopes. A useful clue was that Bjerkely lay by the water.

Suddenly Sophie shouted, "There it is! We've found it!"

"I do believe you're right, but don't shout so loud."

"Why? There's no one to hear us."

"My dear Sophie—after a whole course in philosophy, I'm very disappointed to find you still jumping to conclusions."

"Yes, but . . ."

"Surely you don't believe this place is entirely devoid of trolls, pixies, wood nymphs, and good fairies?"

"Oh, excuse me."

They drove through the gate and up the gravel path to the house. Alberto parked the car on the lawn beside the glider. A little way down the garden a table was set for three.

"I can see her!" whispered Sophie. "She's sitting down on the dock, just like in my dream."

"Have you noticed how much the garden looks like your own garden in Clover Close?"

"Yes, it does. With the glider and everything. Can I go down to her?"

"Naturally. I'll stay here."

Sophie ran down to the dock. She almost stumbled and fell over Hilde. But she sat down politely beside her.

Hilde sat idly playing with the line that the rowboat was made fast with. In her left hand she held a slip of paper. She was clearly waiting. She glanced at her watch several times.

Sophie thought she was very pretty. She had fair, curly hair and bright green eyes. She was wearing a yellow summer dress. She was not unlike Joanna.

Sophie tried to talk to her even though she knew it was useless.

"Hilde—it's Sophie!"

Hilde gave no sign that she had heard.

Sophie got onto her knees and tried to shout in her ear:

"Can you hear me, Hilde? Or are you both deaf and blind?"

Did she, or didn't she, open her eyes a little wider? Wasn't there a very slight sign that she had heard something—however faintly?

She looked around. Then she turned her head sharply and stared right into Sophie's eyes. She did not focus on her properly; it was as if she was looking right through her.

"Not so loud, Sophie," said Alberto from up in the car. "I don't want the garden filled with mermaids."

Sophie sat still now. It felt good just to be close to Hilde.

Then she heard the deep voice of a man: "Hilde!"

It was the major—in uniform, with a blue beret. He stood at the top of the garden.

Hilde jumped up and ran toward him. They met between the glider and the red convertible. He lifted her up in the air and swung her around and around.

Hilde had been sitting on the dock waiting for her father. Since he had landed at Kastrup, she had thought of him every fifteen minutes, trying to imagine where he was now, and how he was taking it. She had noted all the times down on a slip of paper and kept it with her all day.

What if it made him angry? But surely he couldn't expect that he would write a mysterious book for her—and then everything would remain as before?

She looked at her watch again. Now it was a quarter past ten. He could be arriving any minute.

But what was that? She thought she heard a faint breath of something, exactly as in her dream about Sophie.

She turned around quickly. There was something, she was sure of it. But what?

Maybe it was only the summer night.

For a few seconds she was afraid she was hearing things.

"Hilde!"

Now she turned the other way. It was Dad! He was standing at the top of the garden.

Hilde jumped up and ran toward him. They met by the glider. He lifted her up in the air and swung her around and around.

Hilde was crying, and her father had to hold back his tears as well.

"You've become a grown woman, Hilde!"

"And you've become a real writer."

Hilde wiped away her tears.

"Shall we say we're quits?" she asked.

"We're quits."

They sat down at the table. First of all Hilde had to have an exact description of everything that had happened at Kastrup and on the way home. They kept bursting out laughing.

"Didn't you see the envelope in the cafeteria?"

"I didn't get a chance to sit down and eat anything, you villain. Now I'm ravenous."

"Poor Dad."

"The stuff about the turkey was all bluff, then?"

"It certainly was not! I have prepared everything. Mom's doing the serving."

Then they had to go over the ring binder and the story of Sophie and Alberto from one end to the other and backwards and forwards.

Mom brought out the turkey and the Waldorf salad, the rosé wine and Hilde's homemade bread.

Her father was just saying something about Plato when Hilde suddenly interrupted him: "Shh!"

"What is it?"

"Didn't you hear it? Something squeaking?"

"No."

"I'm sure I heard something. I guess it was just a field mouse."

While her mother went to get another bottle of wine, her father said: "But the philosophy course isn't quite over."

"It isn't?"

"Tonight I'm going to tell you about the universe."

Before they began to eat, he said to his wife, "Hilde

is too big to sit on my knee any more. But you're not!''

With that he caught Marit round the waist and drew her onto his lap. It was quite a while before she got anything to eat.

"To think you'll soon be forty . . .''

When Hilde jumped up and ran toward her father, Sophie felt her tears welling up. She would never be able to reach her . . .

Sophie was deeply envious of Hilde because she had been created a real person of flesh and blood.

When Hilde and the major had sat down at the table, Alberto honked the car horn.

Sophie looked up. Didn't Hilde do exactly the same?

She ran up to Alberto and jumped into the seat next to him.

"We'll sit for a while and watch what happens," he said.

Sophie nodded.

"Have you been crying?"

She nodded again.

"What is it?"

"She's so lucky to be a real person. Now she'll grow up and be a real woman. I'm sure she'll have real children too . . .''

"And grandchildren, Sophie. But there are two sides to everything. That was what I tried to teach you at the beginning of our course."

"How do you mean?"

"She is lucky, I agree. But she who wins the lot of life must also draw the lot of death, since the lot of life is death.''

"But still, isn't it better to have had a life than never to have really lived?"

"We cannot live a life like Hilde—or like the major for that matter. On the other hand, we'll never die. Don't you remember what the old woman said back there in the woods? We are the invisible people. She was two hundred years old, she said. And at their Midsummer party I saw some creatures who were more than three thousand years old . . .''

"Perhaps what I envy most about Hilde is all this . . . her family life."

"But you have a family yourself. And you have a cat, two birds, and a tortoise."

"But we left all that behind, didn't we?"

"By no means. It's only the major who left it behind. He has written the final word of his book, my dear, and he will never find us again."

"Does that mean we can go back?"

"Anytime we want. But we're also going to make new friends in the woods behind Cinderella's cafeteria."

The Knag family began their meal. For a moment Sophie was afraid it would turn out like the philosophical garden party in Clover Close. At one point it looked as though the major intended to lay Marit across the table. But then he drew her on to his knee instead.

The car was parked a good way away from where the family sat eating. Their conversation was only audible now and then. Sophie and Alberto sat gazing down over the garden. They had plenty of time to mull over all the details and the sorry ending of the garden party.

The family did not get up from the table until almost midnight. Hilde and the major strolled toward the glider. They waved to Marit as she walked up to the white-painted house.

"You might as well go to bed, Mom. We have so much to talk about."

The Big Bang

∽

... we too are stardust ...

Hilde settled herself comfortably in the glider beside her father. It was nearly midnight. They sat looking out across the bay. A few stars glimmered palely in the light sky. Gentle waves lapped over the stones under the dock.

Her father broke the silence.

"It's a strange thought that we live on a tiny little planet in the universe."

"Yes ..."

"Earth is only one of many planets orbiting the sun. Yet Earth is the only living planet."

"Perhaps the only one in the entire universe?"

"It's possible. But it's also possible that the universe is teeming with life. The universe is inconceivably huge. The distances are so great that we measure them in light-minutes and light-years."

"What are they, actually?"

"A light-minute is the distance light travels in one minute. And that's a long way, because light travels through space at 300,000 kilometers a second. That means that a light-minute is 60 times 300,000—or 18 million kilometers. A light-year is nearly ten trillion kilometers."

"How far away is the sun?"

"It's a little over eight light-minutes away. The rays of sunlight warming our faces on a hot June day have traveled for eight minutes through the universe before they reach us.''

''Go on . . .''

''Pluto, which is the planet farthest out in our solar system, is about five light-hours away from us. When an astronomer looks at Pluto through his telescope, he is in fact looking five hours back in time. We could also say that the picture of Pluto takes five hours to get here.''

''It's a bit hard to visualize, but I think I understand.''

''That's good, Hilde. But we here on Earth are only just beginning to orient ourselves. Our own sun is one of 400 billion other stars in the galaxy we call the Milky Way. This galaxy resembles a large discus, with our sun situated in one of its several spiral arms. When we look up at the sky on a clear winter's night, we see a broad band of stars. This is because we are looking toward the center of the Milky Way.''

''I suppose that's why the Milky Way is called 'Winter Street' in Swedish.''

''The distance to the star in the Milky Way that is our nearest neighbor is four light-years. Maybe that's it just above the island over there. If you could imagine that at this very moment a stargazer is sitting up there with a powerful telescope pointing at Bjerkely—he would see Bjerkely as it looked four years ago. He might see an eleven-year-old girl swinging her legs in the glider.''

''Incredible.''

''But that's only the nearest star. The whole galaxy— or nebula, as we also call it—is 90,000 light-years wide. That is another way of describing the time it takes for light to travel from one end of the galaxy to the other. When we gaze at a star in the Milky Way which is 50,000 light-years away from our sun, we are looking back 50,000 years in time.''

''The idea is much too big for my little head.''

''The only way we can look out into space, then, is to look back in time. We can never know what the universe is like now. We only know what it was like then. When we look up at a star that is thousands of light-years away, we are really traveling thousands of years back in the history of space.''

"It's completely incomprehensible."

"But everything we see meets the eye in the form of light waves. And these light waves take time to travel through space. We could compare it to thunder. We always hear the thunder after we have seen the lightning. That's because sound waves travel slower than light waves. When I hear a peal of thunder, I'm hearing the sound of something that happened a little while ago. It's the same thing with the stars. When I look at a star that is thousands of light-years away, I'm seeing the 'peal of thunder' from an event that lies thousands of years back in time."

"Yes, I see."

"But so far, we've only been talking about our own galaxy. Astronomers say there are about a hundred billion of such galaxies in the universe, and each of these galaxies consists of about a hundred billion stars. We call the nearest galaxy to the Milky Way the Andromeda nebula. It lies two million light-years from our own galaxy. That means the light from that galaxy takes two million years to reach us. So we're looking two million years back in time when we see the Andromeda nebula high up in the sky. If there was a clever stargazer in this nebula—I can just imagine him pointing his telescope at Earth right now—he wouldn't be able to see us. If he was lucky, he'd see a few flat-faced Neanderthals."

"It's amazing."

"The most distant galaxies we know of today are about ten *billion* light-years away from us. When we receive signals from these galaxies, we are going ten billion years back in the history of the universe. That's about twice as long as our own solar system has existed."

"You're making me dizzy."

"Although it is hard enough to comprehend what it means to look so far back in time, astronomers have discovered something that has even greater significance for our world picture."

"What?"

"Apparently no galaxy in space remains where it is. All the galaxies in the universe are moving away from each other at colossal speeds. The further they are away from us, the quicker they move. That means that the distance between the galaxies is increasing all the time.''

''I'm trying to picture it.''

''If you have a balloon and you paint black spots on it, the spots will move away from each other as you blow up the balloon. That's what's happening with the galaxies in the universe. We say that the universe is expanding.''

''What makes it do that?''

''Most astronomers agree that the expanding universe can only have one explanation: Once upon a time, about 15 billion years ago, all substance in the universe was assembled in a relatively small area. The substance was so dense that gravity made it terrifically hot. Finally it got so hot and so tightly packed that it exploded. We call this explosion the Big Bang.''

''Just the thought of it makes me shudder.''

''The Big Bang caused all the substance in the universe to be expelled in all directions, and as it gradually cooled, it formed stars and galaxies and moons and planets . . .''

''But I thought you said the universe was still expanding?''

''Yes I did, and it's expanding precisely because of this explosion billions of years ago. The universe has no timeless geography. The universe is a happening. The universe is an explosion. Galaxies continue to fly through the universe away from each other at colossal speeds.''

''Will they go on doing that for ever?''

''That's one possibility. But there is another. You may recall that Alberto told Sophie about the two forces that cause the planets to remain in constant orbit round the sun?''

''Weren't they gravity and inertia?''

''Right, and the same thing applies to the galaxies. Because even though the universe continues to expand, the force of gravity is working the other way. And one day, in a couple of billion years, gravity will perhaps cause the heavenly bodies to be packed together again as the force of the huge explosion begins to weaken. Then we would get a reverse explosion, a so-called implosion. But the distances are so great that it will happen like a movie that is run in slow motion. You might compare it with what happens when you release the air from a balloon.''

"Will all the galaxies be drawn together in a tight nucleus again?''

"Yes, you've got it. But what will happen then?''

"There would be another Big Bang and the universe would start expanding again. Because the same natural laws are in operation. And so new stars and galaxies will form.''

"Good thinking. Astronomers think there are two possible scenarios for the future of the universe. Either the universe will go on expanding forever so that the galaxies will draw further and further apart—or the universe will begin to contract again. How heavy and massive the universe is will determine what happens. And this is something astronomers have no way of knowing as yet.''

"But *if* the universe is so heavy that it begins to contract again, perhaps it has expanded and contracted lots of times before.''

"That would be an obvious conclusion. But on this point theory is divided. It may be that the expansion of the universe is something that will only happen this one time. But if it keeps on expanding for all eternity, the question of where it all began becomes even more pressing.''

"Yes, where did it come from, all that stuff that suddenly exploded?''

"For a Christian, it would be obvious to see the Big Bang as the actual moment of creation. The Bible tells us that God said 'Let there be light!' You may possibly also remember that Alberto indicated Christianity's 'linear' view of history. From the point of view of a Christian belief in the creation, it is better to imagine the universe continuing to expand.''

"It is?''

"In the Orient they have a 'cyclic' view of history.

In other words, history repeats itself eternally. In India, for example, there is an ancient theory that the world continually unfolds and folds again, thus alternating between what Indians have called Brahman's Day and Brahman's Night. This idea harmonizes best, of course, with the universe expanding and contracting—in order to expand again—in an eternal cyclic process. I have a mental picture of a great cosmic heart that beats and beats and beats . . ."

"I think both theories are equally inconceivable and equally exciting."

"And they can compare with the great paradox of eternity that Sophie once sat pondering in her garden: either the universe has always been there—or it suddenly came into existence out of nothing . . ."

"Ouch!"

Hilde clapped her hand to her forehead.

"What was that?"

"I think I've just been stung by a gadfly."

"It was probably Socrates trying to sting you into life."

Sophie and Alberto had been sitting in the red convertible listening to the major tell Hilde about the universe.

"Has it struck you that our roles are completely reversed?" asked Alberto after a while.

"In what sense?"

"Before it was they who listened to us, and we couldn't see them. Now we're listening to them and they can't see us."

"And that's not all."

"What are you referring to?"

"When we started, we didn't know about the other reality that Hilde and the major inhabited. Now they don't know about ours."

"Revenge is sweet."

"But the major could intervene in our world."

"Our world was nothing but his interventions."

"I haven't yet relinquished all hope that we may also intervene in their world."

"But you know that's impossible. Remember what happened in the Cinderella? I saw you trying to get out that bottle of Coke."

Sophie was silent. She gazed out over the garden while the major explained about the Big Bang. There was something about that term which started a train of thought in her mind.

She began to rummage around in the car.

"What are you doing?" asked Alberto.

"Nothing."

She opened the glove compartment and found a wrench. She grabbed it and jumped out of the car. She went over to the glider and stood right in front of Hilde and her father. First she tried to catch Hilde's eye but that was quite useless. Finally she raised the wrench above her head and crashed it down on Hilde's forehead.

"Ouch!" said Hilde.

Then Sophie hit the major on his forehead, but he didn't react at all.

"What was that?" he asked.

"I think I've just been stung by a gadfly."

"It was probably Socrates trying to sting you into life."

Sophie lay down on the grass and tried to push the glider. But it remained motionless. Or did she manage to get it to move a millimeter?

"There's a chilly breeze coming up," said Hilde.

"No, there isn't. It's very mild."

"It's not only that. There is something."

"Only the two of us and the cool summer night."

"No, there's something in the air."

"And what might that be?"

"You remember Alberto and his secret plan?"

"How could I forget!"

"They simply disappeared from the garden party. It was as if they had vanished into thin air . . ."

"Yes, but . . ."

". . . into thin air."

"The story had to end somewhere. It was just something I wrote."

"*That* was, yes, but not what happened afterward. Suppose they were here . . ."

"Do you believe that?"

"I can feel it, Dad."

Sophie ran back to the car.

"Impressive," said Alberto grudgingly as she climbed on board clasping the wrench tightly in her hand. "You have unusual talents, Sophie. Just wait and see."

The major put his arm around Hilde.

"Do you hear the mysterious play of the waves?"

"Yes. We must get the boat in the water tomorrow."

"But do you hear the strange whispering of the wind? Look how the aspen leaves are trembling."

"The planet is alive, you know . . ."

"You wrote that there was something between the lines."

"I did?"

"Perhaps there is something between the lines in this garden too."

"Nature is full of enigmas. But we are talking about stars in the sky."

"Soon there will be stars on the water."

"That's right. That's what you used to say about phosphorescence when you were little. And in a sense you were right. Phosphorescence and all other organisms are made of elements that were once blended together in a star."

"Us too?"

"Yes, we too are stardust."

"That was beautifully put."

"When radio telescopes can pick up light from distant galaxies billions of light-years away, they will be charting the universe as it looked in primeval times after the Big Bang. Everything we can see in the sky is a cosmic fossil from thousands and millions of years ago. The only thing an astrologer can do is predict the past."

"Because the stars in the constellations moved away from each other long before their light reached us, right?"

"Even two thousand years ago, the constellations looked considerably different from the way they look today."

"I never knew that."

"If it's a clear night, we can see millions, even billions of years back into the history of the universe. So in a way, we are going home."

"I don't know what you mean."

"You and I also began with the Big Bang, because all substance in the universe is an organic unity. Once in a primeval age all matter was gathered in a clump so enormously massive that a pinhead weighed many billions of tons. This 'primeval atom' exploded because of the enormous gravitation. It was as if something disintegrated. When we look up at the sky, we are trying to find the way back to ourselves."

"What an extraordinary thing to say."

"All the stars and galaxies in the universe are made of the same substance. Parts of it have lumped themselves together, some here, some there. There can be billions of light-years between one galaxy and the next. But they all have the same origin. All stars and all planets belong to the same family."

"Yes, I see."

"But what is this earthly substance? What *was* it that exploded that time billions of years ago? Where did it come from?"

"That is the big question."

"And a question that concerns us all very deeply. For we ourselves are of that substance. We are a spark from the great fire that was ignited many billions of years ago."

"That's a beautiful thought too."

"However, we must not exaggerate the importance of these figures. It is enough just to hold a stone in your hand. The universe would have been equally incomprehensible if it had only consisted of that one stone the size of an orange. The question would be just as impenetrable: where did this stone come from?"

Sophie suddenly stood up in the red convertible and pointed out over the bay.

"I want to try the rowboat," she said.

"It's tied up. And we would never be able to lift the oars."

"Shall we try? After all, it is Midsummer Eve."

"We can go down to the water, at any rate."

They jumped out of the car and ran down the garden.

They tried to loosen the rope that was made fast in a metal ring. But they could not even lift one end.

"It's as good as nailed down," said Alberto.

"We've got plenty of time."

"A true philosopher must never give up. If we could just . . . get it loose . . ."

"There are more stars now," said Hilde.

"Yes, when the summer night is darkest."

"But they sparkle more in winter. Do you remember the night before you left for Lebanon? It was New Year's Day."

"That was when I decided to write a book about philosophy for you. I had been to a large bookstore in Kristiansand and to the library too. But they had nothing suitable for young people."

"It's as if we are sitting at the very tip of the fine hairs in the white rabbit's fur."

"I wonder if there is anyone out there in the night of the light-years?"

"The rowboat has worked itself loose!"

"So it has!"

"I don't understand it. I went down and checked it just before you got here."

"Did you?"

"It reminds me of when Sophie borrowed Alberto's boat. Do you remember how it lay drifting out in the lake?"

"I bet it's her at work again."

"Go ahead and make fun of me. All evening, I've been able to feel someone here."

"One of us will have to swim out to it."

"We'll both go, Dad."

Index

A FAMILY PLACE

CHARLES GAINES

"Remarkable." — Susan Cheever

"Evocative...in the rich tradition of Thoreau's *Walden* and Tracy Kidder's *House*."
— *New York Times*

With their family life in ruins, bestselling author Charles Gaines and his wife, Patricia, decided to build a house themselves on the coast of Nova Scotia, hoping that simplicity and isolation would mend their marriage and bring their children closer. This is Charles Gaines's moving chronicle of his family's search for what is important in life, and the joy and heartbreak they found along the way.

___ 0-425-14878-5/$6.99